OUR HOME MOVIES

PATRICK COSGROVE

To my sons; and to Pam, who has made a second chance possible.

Uncover memories you never knew you had.
Find amazing clips of family and friends
you never knew existed — before it's too late.
— *iMemories.com*

Films are home movies of your past.
— *Director Michael Cimino*

There was no character. There was me.
— *Actor Peter Falk, on Director John Cassavetes's* Husbands

1

fter Marty stole the baby he ran with the child through the Salt Lake City airport like the criminal he'd probably just become. Marty's lungs were engines burning hot over the just-waxed terrazzo floors that were out to ruin him, but no slipping or sliding was going to stop this runner. More dangerous was that with Tub O'Guts comatose in the Snugli and strapped to his chest, the infant's warm weight made Marty want to stop running, give in to his fatigue, to topple over and fall asleep right there in the baby smell. Instead, with his heated momentum he used the tug of gravity to torque himself forward, not down. The marathon had begun.

Already in a dark corner of his Directors Guild of America heart Marty knew that only an Assistant Director could've pulled off this airport escape, that his years spent helping other people make their movies instead of creating his own had at least given him a few pragmatic skills in life. A ticket begged at the last second, a commercial airliner backing up on the tarmac to let them in because of some vague lie about *paparazzi* and a movie celebrity and her secret baby. This was blessedly a bit more than a decade before certain people were trying to blow up certain other people with faith-based initiatives, before Tweets and texts and cell phone videos would've tracked Marty's every celebrity-adjacent move.

Marty had extra wipes to slurp up the stink coming down a fat silly leg onto a foot whose toes were like hairless pink caterpillars. He had outfit changes stuffed into a backpack, everything arranged like props for a production shoot on an airport set. As a *bona fide* Second Assistant Director, Marty had planned their route, he had made the chase scene happen where a mere Director distracted by "Art" or "Cinema" couldn't have figured the logistics — though Marty had just been promoted to be one of those, too. At Salt Lake City International, "Director" was just another piece of himself that he ran from.

Tub O'Guts, what Marty called the baby because the birth parents hadn't named him anything at all, had a little butt-rash developing. Marty slowed to a wobbly walk near the gate as he wondered out loud, "Ointment — did I? — *yes*." Marty sighed against the sleeping infant's ear, thinking, When we get wherever we're going, I don't know what the hell's gonna happen, kid, but — I got you, I claimed you when no one else was decent enough. And they'll have to come in with battering rams and still I'm gonna hold you over my head and say Mine. And your name'll be…. Shit, I don't know that either. But I'll give you one soon, I promise. Who'd you like to be? Sleepy? Dopey? Goofy…?

Marty slid past the computer desk near the concourse gate and waved his boarding pass at a smiling man in a dark blue blazer with a walkie-talkie who snatched the pass and opened the door for Marty to run through. Then Marty was down the stairs, onto the tarmac below, running toward the airplane where a tight-haired flight attendant at the plane's re-opened hatch extended her arms with open hands, but Marty was thinking No, *my* call as he pounded up the rolling staircase through the burnt kerosene smell and the piercing whistle of jet engines.

Instead of handing over Tubs to the attendant, Marty gave her a bottle with formula powder in the bottom and pointed to the baby's ears. He wanted Tubs swallowing during takeoff. She nodded and led them inside. Marty fell into his seat, content to watch the pulsing fuzzball within the Snugli, to feel little breaths go in and out against his face, and told himself not to worry about this moment that he would encase in a steel vault if he could, because there would be plenty of time for worrying later and plenty more to worry about, and because the baby he already loved as Tub O'Guts still slept.

Marty stared through the double-window at a squat yellow tractor pushing another jet away from the concourse, and thought of the enemy they'd just outflanked. Though it might happen with the frequency of a meteorite striking the skull of a snow leopard, later that day the tabloids would get something right: that he, Marty Nyrop, was on the lam with an infant born to one of the biggest stars in Hollywood, a kid who was also the child of one of the leading *avant* artists of the New York theater world. For the degree of credibility involved, they might as well report that Marty carried the space-seed of a Venusian.

Within hours, the *Enquirer* and *Star* were about to report their top story of 1990, that the child was his in the first place, his genetic puddle from spermatozoon to screaming newborn. Not yet. Though as their plane receded from the terminal Marty held him with every intention of becoming the parent. Dad. But the whole truth was more elusive, almost ridiculous if not for all the pained convolutions that had landed this baby in his lap, this child born to actors. The birth father was dead and Marty still questioned himself as to how much that death was his own fault. The mother was never quite of this world, though Marty once supposed that she'd tried to be, and maybe for one brief moment she had even believed she was quite authentic, or had a personal manager think this thought for her and put out the good news in a press kit.

When it hit the magazine racks at grocery store checkouts across the nation, the tabloids' apparently victimless story would then electrify moviegoers and readers for months, until replaced in all corners of public consciousness by the next scandal, and the next, until a worshipful silence would fall over the actress's followers, signaling that they accepted the private pain of a mother who had relinquished her child for the betterment of all involved.

It was beyond ridiculous, then, it was the saddest, happiest situation Marty could have conjured. Tragediculous.

To the thrum of engines pushing them across concrete and tar and asphalt toward a clear runway for takeoff, he was still awash in his moment of choice made just hours ago: when in the presence of an infant so young the baby knew only sensation, only hunger satisfied or not, Marty had been enveloped in a seamless surrender because he'd given himself completely and irrevocably to the cries of another. He'd felt holy with selflessness in a motel suite while an actress adored throughout the world showered and tended to her deepest asset, her skin, as her child cried helplessly until she finally offered him a mollifying bulb of a pinkie finger to suck and not the breast; and when he fell asleep out of exhaustion, she returned once again to the care of her surfaces.

This actress, this mother, was the magic ingredient that Marty had fought for, year after year, while working as an Assistant for others. It was she who had become his own deepest asset, the one he had given his every waking moment toward possessing: a face that would launch a thousand premieres, light up marquees around the planet, while doing his bidding, telling his story, a face obeying his direction as he explained himself to a world-audience through projected shadows. Yet in a moment of attending to the whims of this careless and self-absorbed actress-mother in the latest of too many incidents of the baby's unmet needs, Marty had foreseen the rest of the child's life — a first-time vision of its kind because it was unclouded by concerns over his own fate or the trajectory of a career. And so, at the first opportunity on the site of a distant-location movie production that had just wrapped, he reached into a crib and took and ran. No more actors for the child he had suddenly made his own, and so no more "Director" for himself; and in a way that only a parent would fully understand, no more Marty.

As he tilted back in his seat and was lifted into flight, he wished only that he knew where he and his baby were absconding to. With his rough powerful hands and their punch-scarred knuckles, Marty caressed this soap bubble of a human being, and wondered where he could keep such a fragile life whole until the child had a chance in life that he, and the baby's father, never knew.

2

*A*t the doorway of his son's bedroom an odor of sweat-soaked liners in a pair of skate boots pushes Marty back. It's a silent, vinegary protest, as if the room itself objects to Marty's presence. In the darkness he can make out his son's form slumped across the bed where he's fallen asleep, one cradling arm slid under a pillow beneath his head. C.T.'s been working on a school project — a film, video, multimedia presentation, the term evolves — and the laptop computer still open before C.T.'s face has put itself into sleep mode in a more orderly fashion than the boy has put himself. Marty rotates the laptop and sees that the screensaver has self-activated as a dream, a slideshow of his son captured in suspended, digitized motion: he's vaulting staircases, rolling off low rooftops, grinding rails and ledges by stabbing the plates and wheels of his skates into landing positions called tricks that have arcane degrees of difficulty and inscrutable names like "fish brain" and "porn star."

Marty leans closer to the screen and stares at these floating poses of "aggressive" skating. They're always in street settings, never a pre-fab park or smooth Masonite "vert" course for his lanky, skid-marked kid, and so at seventeen C.T. has already given himself the spine and knee joints of a middle-aged athlete. Marty shifts the computer onto the jumbled desktop next to the bed, then lowers himself into a wooden office chair and stares at the slideshow for another long moment.

He's startled when out of the dark C.T. draws a fingertip along Marty's lower eyelid, smearing the wetness there.

"You okay, Pops?"

He pushes out a quick breath. "Sure. It's just the bleb thing. . . ."

"Eww. Eye juice."

Marty is leaking. It's been two years since an ophthalmologist cut a flap in his left cornea and sclera, then stitched the flesh into the shape of an open blister — a bleb — to drain the glaucomatous pressure that by then had already cost him all sharp focus in his left eye. At odd times, but mostly at night, the aqueous humor of that eye will seep like tears that run sideways along his temple and onto his pillow. Warm and wet, the leak gives only the appearance of weeping, but induces none of the heart- and lung-weakness of an authentic emotion. With one good eye, he sees more as a camera sees, and it's enough. He closes the laptop.

Without the screen's illumination Marty can't (and doesn't need to) see his son's face to know what it looks like now — the easy smile sliding off-center, the rumple of sweaty unwashed curls flattened by sleep, the dimples and clefts and godly bone structure inherited from his biological parents that, altogether, make him pull looks and even squeals from girls at shopping malls when they think he isn't looking. C.T. is beautiful, and skates and throws himself at brick walls as if to prove how little that means to him. This is still my boy, Marty thinks, my C.T. who cried every time he put on his first pair of skates but kept putting them on again and again until the tears were salty streaks through the dirt on his face. Still my baby.

"So how's the project going? Isn't it due pretty soon?"

C.T. runs some unintelligible syllables together as his skater friends do, when by lowering the register of their voices and muttering without articulating individual words they try to become manly, or cool, or something. Marty feels old.

"I'm sorry, I couldn't hear — "

"I said, this assignment's so lame. I mean, fuck this shit."

Marty sighs. "Can we lighten up a little bit? It makes you sound so . . . angry when you do that. I don't think you're an angry guy. Are you?"

C.T. shifts on the bed. "F-word this poop."

Marty smirks a little. "Is it the narrative one? You already got an "A" on the documentary, right?"

"Yeah. I mean, it's . . . so . . . retarded — "

"Hey. . . ."

"Sorry. I hate all this pretend shit. I just wanna get my section done for the skate video. Something like that — you see it, you go 'Hell yeah!' And I got clips for it tonight, I mean, you wouldn't fuckin' believe. Besides, we had to let this other fool in the group direct some shit for the school thing and nothing cuts. You know? It's supposed to be a story and nothing fuckin' matches. Lame."

"I'd offer to help, but this editing software, you know, they keep changing it. . . ."

"Yeah . . . what the hell. It's easy, all timelines and shit. I'll figure it out."

"I'm sure you will. . . . And shit."

Marty smiles at his son, knowing that he can't be seen. With the laptop closed, now that his eyes — his good eye — has adjusted, there might be starlight in the room but not much else. As a teacher at C.T.'s high school, Marty tries to separate his roles at home and at work as much as he can, but he does have a part of his life to offer as help for C.T.'s narrative video assignment. He doesn't know much about the current editing applications, but analog or digital, linear or not, he knows when and why you cut two camera shots together. He knows the occult soul of filmmaking, if not its latest avatar. It's the only class C.T. likes. Marty debates with himself for a moment whether to offer the help, until he hears his son's autonomic breathing take over with a quick drift into sleep.

Would — or even should — this man-child ever come to know why Marty might be an expert of a sort at patching together film stories? C.T. can't know this about Marty, because his story-making skill is something Marty has never shared with the boy, nor has he ever told C.T. the story of the boy's own beginning in life, with or without editing. Not how C.T. got here, the tale of his unnamed birth parents, why Marty once ran with him at an airport and kept running until he thought he'd outrun DNA itself.

Marty had for a time lived among actors and, in the years since has given thanks that his son was not, and is not Them. I had my reasons, he'd thought back then, and still believes as true. Thinking both then and now, Actors — they *are* different from the rest of us. Professional pretenders, and when I worked with them I was getting moved where I didn't want to go. By *their* intent even as I was their damn Director, feeling things where I didn't know if it was me or some alien in my body making me look at my own life in unnerving ways. It was unfair — actors believe it when they lie, and compared to all their emotions-as-weapons, in that fight I was unarmed.

C.T. was never to know about those creatures; this has always been the plan.

Now, in his son's quiet, musty bedroom Marty is overtaken by a day from years ago, during one of his first productions as an Assistant Director when he'd watched an archived screen test preserved from Alfred Hitchcock's *Rebecca*. It's a story in which a man's second wife is haunted by the ghostly memory of his first wife, whose presence is kept alive in the second wife's imagination by the servants' cruel tricks. Induced madness. God, Marty recalls even now in the bedroom darkness, he could understand in two seconds why they cast Joan Fontaine. The other ones they tested, Vivien Leigh and Loretta Young, they were stars, they had obvious skills, they held the screen and made you look at them. But whatever emotions flooded Fontaine, they were right under the skin, sluicing through her veins. The nerves, the paranoia, the fear that she was living with monsters.

After he watched the screen test, Marty had thought, We've all got shit buried inside us like some gigantic compost heap, combusting, giving off steam and smoke. But actors — whatever feelings they need, they're right there in the flesh, they peel them off and hand them to you like it's their own skinned hide they're offering, still bleeding. They make themselves naked to the world, sure, but on a screen forty feet high, forever young and forever seducing you to fall in love with them. To want. *Desire.*

Even with seventeen years elapsed it feels queerly wrong to Marty to have been part of that movie-making process. He had tried to direct them — the biological parents of this boy sleeping here before him — but came only to understand that beneath an actor's skin the higher power of the performer, the needful player, was the possession of a heart simply more available, more ready to rip out of his own being and throw at his audience like a napalm hand-grenade, with the ever-present danger that he might not throw that flaming heart far enough to escape burning himself, as well, into fiery sacrifice.

So besides dismissing the Hollywood origins of his own skill at manipulating images into comprehensible narratives, Marty has withheld entire pieces of C.T.'s life — and of his own — from his son, because what kid wouldn't urgently want to live out his rightful inheritance from glamorous movie stars if he knew where he'd come from, and whose blood ran through him? What child could fail to heed that kind of siren call? Better C.T. should never imagine filmmaking beyond a skate video.

Marty opens the laptop again to see more of what C.T. does in his time away from school and home, away from Marty's efforts at a sheltering touch.

Instead of a skater in flight, one last slide: Lupe, his seventeen year-old son's scarcely older girlfriend, is on a flowery sofa, her small sturdy hands resting atop her swollen abdomen. In the flat glare of the camera's flash she is smiling and very pregnant.

Marty's heart misfires and he rises to his feet, looking to grip something, anything. He freezes and realizes that he needs to calm himself, that this is not the moment to wake and confront his son. Not when his anger and disappointment and fear are whirling together as if in a blender. He can hear his own pulse racing in his ears as he watches C.T. breathe, unaware. He fights to resist bouncing C.T. up and down like a stunt dummy on the mattress, bellowing *what've you done, what've you done? Don't you know? Don't you — No, you don't know —*

C.T. doesn't know what it has meant for a Nyrop to become this — a father — because Marty was always going to save him from any sense of fate, was always going to wrap C.T. in Marty's own bleeding hide if that's what it took, no acting allowed; give him only an empty past, a blameless present, the unfolding future scripted only for college and learning and the freedom to choose a career and a life severed from the narcotic dream of moviemaking, never looking back at what the implications of "fatherhood" in this family have meant. If his own life hasn't been fully lived — an only brother lost, a lover not claimed, a career not fulfilled, emotions not shared on a reflective screen, seventeen years of professional forfeiture for the sake of his son's better life — C.T. has just shredded that sacrifice all to hell.

And yet. . . . The one woman Marty has ever given his heart to once told him that even when it seemed he'd lost his way, he was at least sometimes capable of doing the right thing, for the right reason. If there are deep regrets gathered now from the course of his life, loving this sleeping boy will not be one of them.

For a silent moment in the close, fungal air of his son's bedroom, it's still just the two of them breathing together in the starlight.

Patrick Cosgrove

3

I could kill him, Marty thinks, that'd show him. But then his inner "Teacher" character asserts itself and acknowledges that a murdered kid lying around as ashes atop his fireplace mantel would remember little of the lesson. He hurries out of his empty classroom.

Fourth Period is Marty's prep, the one out of six hours in the high school day when he gets caught up with phone calls, e-mails, grading, lesson planning, and mucking out his darkroom or maintaining the computers that run his photography software. The doors that separate his classroom's hallway from the outdoor lunch quad are propped open and he feels the cool air waft inside as he strides through the students who clog his path, heading toward the main wing of the school building. His leftover habit from his days as an Assistant Director of walking at a near-jog pace puts him out of sync with the slouching shuffle of the adult-shaped children around him. He adores these kids, and on most days it seems they make his life more worthwhile, but they also make him impatient even as they goad him to laugh, and lately so many of them seem not even a little interested in all the things he could teach them.

The hallway is nearly blocked as almost every kid is part of a friend-cluster, each of them catching up on the life-changing events that apparently have transpired since the last passing period fifty-five minutes ago. The bigger the gaggle, the more likely they insist on standing in the middle of the hallway oblivious to others. Texting, their one other voluntary communication, is saved for class time when a teacher's lecture sparks a network of darting, under-the-desk thumbs wirelessly connecting their gossip across campus.

It's Spring in California's Central Valley and the girls are trying to clear everything that doesn't qualify as beachwear from their wardrobe, while the boys give out their fustiness in flannel shirts and heavy jeans of skinny or sagging denim. All of them sway under the weight of backpacks, stepping sideways as much as forward as they seem never to give a damn whether or not they're tardy to their next class. Babble, laughter, shrieking drama. Somehow they usually make it through a doorway before the bell.

Marty squeezes past them, offering "hi" by name to the students who will hold the gaze of a teacher they like. He watches too for acknowledgment, a furtive nod, from students he knows but who won't engage a teacher unless schoolwork forces it. The chatty ones, at ease speaking to adults, are usually the more successful students, but there are also the quiet ones who hear everything, churn private thoughts, and make do on their own. Marty remembers now: Lupe-the-Girlfriend was like that. She was in his classroom three years ago.

Lupe. C.T.. Her belly. *Oh shit, what've you done — ?*

Campus security people are barking out "Let's go, let's go!" to get the kids to pick up the slothful pace and clear the hallways. He reaches the Healthy Start office where Social Work interns from the local Cal State campus help hundreds of kids stay functional even as their personal and home lives unravel for reasons far beyond the reach of the classroom teacher. Or in Marty's case, beyond the reach of a teacher who's also the parent. He's made an appointment to ask a counseling staff member to see if she can get through to his son in a way he's failed to.

The office is a warm cave of yellow walls tucked amidst their school's floor-to-ceiling red and white fighting colors. Seated inside a glassed-in cubicle, the program co-coordinator is a stolid, though kind-faced woman. He refers students to her when they appear to need some kind of intervention; he fills out a form, then she and her interns take over the case and run with whatever public school resources they can muster. Yet he hardly knows her.

Marty sits at a small table jammed into the corner of her space that's lit with shaded lamps instead of institutional fluorescence. He's chagrined once more that on this day he's not the concerned teacher, he's the distraught father.

"Any sign of them yet?"

The coordinator smiles tolerantly. He has to concentrate to remember that her name is Julie. Julie Whatever.

"Not yet. It's pretty unlikely we'll see Lupe this morning. She's an adult. Legally. You know, she was an emancipated minor — got herself out of foster care even before she was eighteen. Almost unheard of."

Marty sure hasn't heard it. Any of it. "And now she's pregnant."

"Mm-hmm. Quite, apparently. So you said, in the message you left."

The tolerant smile again. He can see why kids drift into her office just to hang out, even when they're supposed to be in class. It used to be

12

the nurse's office where they loitered, back when they were budgeted for a nurse.

"What do you hope to get from this meeting, Mr. Nyrop?"

"Please, it's just Marty. . . . My life right now makes me feel like I'm about two, and 'Mr. Nyrop' makes me feel about ninety-two. I'd like to land somewhere in-between."

"Mm-hmm."

She's good. Waiting for his emotions to burble to the top, or end.

"What I'm hoping for . . . is that you can make them understand why it's in their interest — the child's too — to arrange an adoption. I mean, C.T.'s *seventeen.*"

"And he's told you . . . what?"

"That they're gonna keep it. Get married when he turns eighteen, and keep the baby. What are they, orchids? They're gonna live on air? So I need an outside voice here, some kind of authoritative backup —"

"And what about C.T.'s mother?"

"She's . . . out of the picture. Never been *in* the picture." What a word choice. Mom, the Actress. The living movie trailer for *Mother,* a coming attraction that never arrived.

"Deceased? Divorced? There's nothing in his permanent file."

"None of the above. I'd rather not go into it." The tolerant smile has cooled a little.

"I see. What does C.T. know about her, Marty?"

"As little as possible. In fact, nothing at all." Now the smile is gone altogether. "Look, I know what that must sound like. I've raised him. I'm a blood relative — his uncle, if you wanna know — but that's as much as I'd like to go into right now. And for godsakes please don't repeat that to anyone — he doesn't know, and if he did know that I was his uncle it'd open up a whole can of very ugly worms about who his parents really were. I'm asking you to trust that I've got good reasons for feeling the way I do. I've raised C.T. by myself to give him as normal a life as possible, and if you knew more about our family history you'd —"

She's waiting him out, still. He's never felt such oddness to the truth behind what he's just said. And not said.

"So then — C.T.'s adopted, but you can't talk about it. And . . . you want me to advise him to put his own child up for adoption?"

"He's not officially adopted, more 'sort of. . . .' But yeah, that's one way of putting it."

"Mm. His mother's never made contact?"

"*Never.*" Marty is surprised at his own vehemence. "I mean, I've never wanted her to. And I'm damn sure *she* never wanted —"

"And is that what C.T. wants? I'm just trying to see the larger framework here."

"It's not his choice."

Smiles are out of the question by now. Marty holds his tongue rather than offer that this was a mother who got pregnant in the way one might shop for a holiday pet. Somewhere just short of criminal negligence, she had ignored one child to death, miscarried and aborted serially, until she did carry C.T. to term where he became an inconvenience to her life of celebrity. This was not a woman he ever wanted C.T. to know.

"They can get help, Mr. Nyrop. Support. We can put them in touch with agencies. Are you unable to help? Unwilling?"

No, he wants to howl, *I just want my son to have a* life. *A great life.* But Marty isn't going to find an audience here, he's already been demoted again to "Mr. Nyrop." He stares at the school clock. It's all he can think to do. Of course he'll help, but that's hardly the point. *Dreams* are the point. A life where his son can write on his own blank slate, go to college, become anyone and anything without being condemned to repeat family disasters with his own kids, to live his life snapped clean of family ties that might otherwise bind like iron chains. A life that now won't stand a chance if C.T. insists on trying to raise his unborn son. Marty has done everything in his power to protect C.T. from re-living Nyrop dysfunction but he can't save him from being seventeen.

And there's that damn message on his phone machine at home. Her voice again. Her. That human-like creature of Cinema.

The front office Teacher's Assistant steps into the cubicle, a student fulfilling her daily class schedule by running errands. College prep errands in line with state standards, Marty supposes grimly.

"He's not in class, Mrs. Luongo."

"Did you check with Attendance?"

"They said he's been absent all day."

Marty's heart sinks. "I gave him a ride to school this morning."

Julie Whatever — Luongo, that's it — nods and punches out four digits on her desk phone. "Hi, Roshawnna. Have you had C.T. Nyrop in your office this morning? Mm-hmm. In-house? No? Thanks." She shrugs and sighs for Marty's benefit.

"He was here. I brought him. He was here." Marty wants to be somewhere else too.

Julie changes the screen on her computer and dials a local number. It rings for quite a while before she gives up. "That was the last number we had for Lupe. Do you have any more current contacts for her?"

"I didn't know I needed any."

"Twitter? Facebook, for either one of them? There's an older one, Myspace?"

"I don't do Facebook. I mean, c'mon, not with 160 teenagers going through my classroom every day. The hacking, the prying, the pranking —"

"District policy permits it. You just have to be careful. You could learn to control it."

Yes, he supposes he could. One of his few concessions to invasive electronic devices has been to carry a smartphone. He pulls it from his pocket and it looks like it just came out of the box. He touches the screen in what he knows will be a useless effort. C.T.'s number rings, then goes immediately to voicemail. Instead Marty uses text-talk: "where ru." There'll be no reply.

But then suddenly there is one: "w lupe dont worry dont call" and for the first time he's struck by the sense that C.T. will forevermore be living his own and separate life.

4

*M*arty doesn't know what else to do in this twilight hour, so he drives. He's aware that C.T. hangs out with a loose gang of fellow bladers, the in-line aggressive skaters who draw the hostility of skateboarders and get called fruitbooters and much worse. Outliers mocking outliers. C.T.'s never been happy in any group that was designed to be one. Or on a team, or in any organized bunch, for that matter. Skaters instead seem to fall in together just to share tricks and and cigarettes and weed from one another, to bum rides and later to watch videos, to make clips of themselves to post online where they share and learn more tricks.

When his son still needed him to drive to the good rails or ledges, C.T. liked to go to 8th and O Street and that's as good a place as any to start tonight. A father-to-be, Marty thinks, and he's jumping around in tattered jeans with his ass hanging out.

Unless he isn't. Marty doesn't spot C.T. as he circles block after block. For the first time in a while he's struck by how much Sacramento resembles everywhere else but itself. New England, the Midwest, Louisiana — it's all here, re-created in some quarter of the tidy downtown grid. Marty has stopped seeing echoes of his own Midwest origins here, it's just his home now, but without knowing C.T.'s whereabouts it seems he doesn't recognize his chosen city any more.

Marty can't understand why C.T. has done this to him, and to himself. Fathering a kid at his age is inescapable disaster. Marty's guiding theory of parenting is that you tend to focus on giving your kid what you think you didn't get for yourself. Maybe happier families do it some other way, but now he feels punished because he's made damn sure C.T. grew up with the security of one sane parent, something that he knows for a fact too many of his students can't claim. Even if he and C.T. are at least one member short of the American nuclear family, the two of them have managed pretty well, and he's given his son every freedom to be himself, even if that's a fruitbooter. And if C.T. is effectively, if not legally, adopted and that's supposed to give him some kind of indelible psychological scar, then Marty feels sorry for that, but cutting C.T. off from the two parents that birthed him is a blessing his kid will have to appreciate somewhere down the road. Except that now C.T. is on wheels and he's tipped that road downslope, accelerating: have a kid at seventeen with your baby mama and here comes poverty, divorce, uneducated children, hopelessness — a statistical avalanche of Fate made of wet cement. It's maddening that a teacher and coach and former Hollywood Movie Director can't give his own kid sufficient motivation to not screw up.

Marty pulls up at a bank building bordered by a good stair railing, and remembers that it used to have alert security guards shooing the kids away, even calling the cops. Back then he got a kick out of driving the getaway car just before the police prowlers showed up, as C.T. would dive into the backseat and the two criminals would roll open-doored down an alley and off to the next spot where C.T. could rub his cake of wax and grind more ledges and rails. It's an anti-social act, this aggressive skating, them against the world, and he's often thought C.T. does it to leave some kind of mark, literally and otherwise. And after all the failed tryouts and Marty's own impatient coaching in every team sport he pushed his son into, C.T. has found his loner's defiance on wheels where there are no rules. Only scabs and deep bruises. How is this the same kid who thinks he can be a teenage father? Or is having his own kid the whole point, made by the loner, the rule-breaker? Marty has no choice but to find him.

He crawls past a city-sanctioned skate park where just a few years ago they built ramps and half-pipes, but then excluded bladers — 'Skateboarders Only,' the signs said — until a couple of angry letters from Citizen Marty got somebody to change his or her mind and allow inline skaters as well. Now the haters, as other kids call them, just exclude BMXers and their bike pegs that grind up the metal pipe called "coping" on the ramp structures. But tonight, in the mercury-vapor light it's just a few stray skateboarders idling beneath the white bugs that flit through the glow from overhead.

It occurs to Marty that C.T. might've let Bibi know where he is. It's worth the call. Bibi, the now-phantom "what-if" part of Marty's life, was there to help when he brought Tub O'Guts home. She's been the closest thing C.T.'s had to a mother even if it's only meant the occasional visit and phone check-in. Aunt Beebs. Marty never knows how to think of her in his life now, yet she's made herself available whenever he truly needed someone to help him be a single parent, probably putting 20,000 extra miles on her limping Volvo station wagon between Sacramento and

L.A. over the past seventeen years. C.T. loves her, Marty knows that he does. Marty did too, for what good that did him. Or her. She was the only woman he could ever have lived with for very long, but long ago he botched that because directing a movie was more important than directing his own life and casting her in it.

Now he's got to talk his kid down from this leap into oblivion and he can't even find him. He calls Bibi with his stupid smartphone.

Bibi cuts to the chase, and her voice washes his insides tender-clean. "Thought I might hear from you pretty soon."

". . . You're psychic?"

"No, Marty. With everything that's going on."

"Okay. What the hell's going on, then? Was I the only one who didn't know?"

There's a sigh in his ear and it stretches over years, back through missed chance after missed chance to be happy with this woman who has lived mostly (but not always) alone in L.A. ever since he fled the place. He failed to claim her, though she'd once been his to enfold in his arms, caress with his big hands; it was a failure of many steps, but by never returning the simple embrace of giving her first place in his heart and the commitment that love calls for, he had never again found rest in another still spot in the whirlpool of his life. That quiet eddy was the offer she'd once made to him. He chose movies.

For too brief a time he'd had both, Bibi and his place in the Directors Guild. When she was newly arrived in L.A. from Minnesota he first noticed her in a crowd scene he was wrangling with enough hired extras that she could work that day non-union. Marty soon used his relationship with Central Casting to help Bibi get her Screen Extras Guild card, and he could then request her for any of his sets, a small perquisite of being a Second Assistant Director.

It was when he put in a call for a very unfunny comedy that his benefactor status shifted and she was no longer beholden to him. She'd been cast as a member of a landing party of explorers arriving on a nondescript island to be filmed around a muddy lagoon on a studio backlot. Marty had placed his call the day before to Central for dozens of extras to fill in the background as "Natives" and it was his lack of precision in describing them that had probably allowed most of his Natives to be selected from Black members of the Extras Guild. The Director had no problem with this, as apparently to him dark people were dark people; makeup, hair, and wardrobe crew members then set about creating some kind of tribal paradise with strategically placed loincloths, grass skirts, clamshells, and plastic bones that tunneled through piles of wiry black wigs. When the action of the scene, meant to be absurd, nevertheless called for caricatures of scraping and bowing before the White Gods of the landing party like something out of a tropical pickaninnie cartoon, Marty had seen the anger and tears in the eyes of his extras who needed to be there for that day's paycheck.

It was Marty who had organized them, had told his background players to humiliate themselves, and he woodenly set them in motion with a shout of "Background" once camera was rolling. That was his job. But it was Bibi Peterson who stood before their Director after one take and tore her timecard in half and left the set. He numbly watched her go.

Marty then suggested to his bug-eyed Director that the extras just might be feeling the careless racism of the scene, and was fired on the spot. "You fucking don't get comedy," it was explained.

He arrived home that day without memory of how he got there, his fogged mind jammed with Bibi's act: there would be a complaint made to Central Casting, meaning she had voluntarily left "Hollywood." *Nobody does that* he thought again and again, yet here it was. Marty had put in nearly seven years of sixteen-hour days of running and fetching and obeying just to climb aboard and make his way toward the engineer's cab on the locomotive that is a film production. "The biggest electric train set a boy ever had," Orson Welles had said about the studio movie machine, while as a Boy Scout Steven Spielberg had crashed model trains in his first 8mm film, and Walt Disney surrounded his empire with scale tracks. It was the need to be at the controls of the engine that ran deep in the psyche of a Director.

Yet Bibi, if only a passenger in the cattle car, was getting off the train. *Nobody does that.* Nobody who wants to direct, anyway. There had been no way of knowing yet what getting fired along with her had cost him.

But that night with his head in her lap and her fingers combing through his hair he found a kind of wordless sanctuary. He was full of wonder at her — that a "normal" life out of the Industry could be preferred to a filmmaker's compulsions. Normal lives were things Marty could only imagine as tiny, obscure organisms living a vast distance away and seen only through an observatory's telescope if one even cared to look. But the real wonder was that for at least one day she had made him a better person. He'd acted out of empathy instead of expedience and ambition and felt the strange heat of compassion, had sensed the gravity of having an ethical center.

But he couldn't sustain the moment, not long enough to keep Bibi at his side in his relentless need to fill a screen. Within a week he was back to work on a new show with a megastar named Laura Trent-Sampson.

• • •

Bibi's phone voice snaps him to attention. "He's staying at a friend's apartment in Midtown. Lupe, too. They're all right."

"And you know this because. . . ?"

"Because they posted it on their wall."

"I have no idea what you're talking about."

"You should. C.T. tells me they've tried to friend you but you never signed up."

If C.T. and Lupe truly want to be hidden from him right now, they've relied on his social media Luddism.

"I don't get Facebook. I mean, I can't. My kids, the students —" If there's another sigh, he's talked over it.

"They're not hiding. I think Lupe's just afraid you'll try to talk them into things —" Damn straight he will. "She's an adult, Marty. No matter how young. She's got to make her own decision."

"Yeah, well, C.T.'s no adult. And no matter how many crazy-assed things he's come up with, this one obviously tops 'em all. In the first place, I mean, any decision arrived at by your little head instead of your big one —"

"I think they planned this. She told me, it's on purpose."

Now he is beyond speech. Bibi waits him out anyway. She has always known how to do that, to let him twist himself in knots until he needed her to untangle him. He tries to let go of this hot anger, and Bibi's record remains intact: she's steadily if painfully aloof, and at the same time has never abandoned them through almost half of his lifetime, even from over 400 miles away.

"So . . . you know this Midtown address?"

"Lupe'll meet you. She knows you have to talk."

"Not C.T.?"

"No. At the Downtown Plaza. Is tomorrow after school all right? About four? I'll message it —"

"Yeah. Am I supposed to bring the ransom in small, unmarked bills?" Silence. "Okay. Tell her, be on a bench near the Old Sac end of the mall. Right out in the open, she can leave whenever."

"And are you all right?"

"No. No, I'm not. Because my entire life is turning back on me like, I don't know, some kind of acid reflux and —"

"Okay, okay. . . . Call me after. And Marty —"

"Yeah?"

"Don't go there mad. This is about Lupe and C.T., not you. She's either going to do this with him, or she's going to do it alone, but she'll do what she needs to do."

"Me? Pissed? *Never.*"

"And one other thing — Laura called again. I didn't pick up, didn't talk to her but —"

"Yeah, yeah. . . . I got the voice on the machine too."

"What do you think she wants?"

"My blood, my life. Worse." He hangs up.

5

M arty is twenty minutes early but Lupe Villanueva is there before he arrives. She probably had to take light-rail; at least he hopes she did, it seems too far for her to be walking. On a bench she looks tiny, her black hair longer than he remembers it, pulled back from her face with a rubber band around a loose ponytail that goes almost completely down her back. Her dark, fine features and caramel coloring are quite pretty, in a sturdy manner, her limbs short and capable. If he can't stop this sequence of events, or turn it in another direction, he is looking at his future daughter-in-law.

This is not the life I made for C.T.. Not the life I gave up dream and ambition for. But that thought *is* about him. He reminds himself that his second career as a teacher has been a good life, that scores of kids are better off for having spent an hour a day in his classroom for a year. But he also knows that this is a weak pep talk because he's given it to himself over and over again, and still there's the hollow space within him that was reserved for movies that he never made, stories he was going to spread throughout thousands of multiplexes. Hollowness for the too-big feelings not shared with an audience, the hearts not exposed. Being a teacher, father, raising a child — for almost anyone else this would be the real stuff of a full lifetime. He knows. But what is that life amounting to when C.T. goes off and creates another child that he has no chance of raising happily? It feels like the end of the line, of everything.

Marty tries to soften his face, to approach Lupe with a non-threatening smile. Bibi would want that.

They know each other as instructor and student, but he has yet to speak to her in the context of being the girl sleeping with his teenage son. He cuts short a thought about whether he could have her arrested for that. She's quietly watchful, taking in everything, and sees Marty approaching without reaction. As he sidesteps a waddling pair of shoppers, he's trying to glean his visual memory for her pictures created in his photography class. He remembers his kids' images better than he can remember their names, and what comes back to him quickly is a triptych she did for him that he's used off and on as an exemplar for students who have followed. Three photos, square black & white compositions horizontally spaced against a black background frame. In each photograph there is a single bed, tightly made, hospital corners, with the same pair of cheap sneakers placed in the exact center of the tile or thinly carpeted floor beneath the edge of the bed. Three rooms, three beds, one pair of shoes. He suddenly gets it: what he graded an "A" was not the successful exercise in symmetry and rhythmic repetition of geometric shapes swathed in soft-lit texture, not a success in Elements of Art and Principles of Design. This was a foster kid's world. She must have lived in at least three places in the short time he had her in his classroom, a year she started late and left early.

As he gets close enough to speak to her, she's folded in upon herself with a reusable fabric grocery bag on the bench next to her and a small point-and-shoot camera in her hands. She nods to him.

"Hello, Lupe."

She moves the grocery bag. She's saved him a place. The bag is full of something, but not food.

"I miss your class, Mr. Nyrop. It was, like, so much fun."

He gives a short laugh as he sits, instantly disarmed. "Well, you were a good student. A nice eye. And thorough. Took some chances, not just the obvious stuff." He feels as if he's ticking off boxes on a grading rubric, but it's all true. "I remember you left before the year was over. You ever graduate?" Now it sounds like he's judging her fitness for something. He didn't mean it that way. She's got traces of an ESL kid in her second-language grammar but he knows she's quick-minded.

"G.E.D.. It's all good."

"I just meant . . . I hope everything worked out for you. For school. So Bibi tells me C.T.'s with you."

"We're at some friends.'"

"And who are these friends?"

"They got an apartment. It's okay. Not like we're runaways or nothing."

"Okay. . . . So I guess I must've scared you guys off with the Healthy Start appointment."

"We already knew, you know, like — what everybody was gonna say."

Marty nods and stares blankly toward the far end of the mall for a moment. "Look, everyone makes mistakes. You don't have to go through with this. You know what the odds are against you? Against the baby? Just. . . . I'm not talking about an abortion. Okay? I wouldn't ask that of anybody. You're probably Catholic?"

She shrugs. "I made like I believed whatever the house believed. Or sometimes I didn't have no believes. There's houses like that, too. One was Wiccan only they didn't tell nobody. You know, 'Double, double, toil and trouble.'" Her quick smile — it glows.

"You'd be so much better off if you'd just let someone else help you arrange an adoption. Find loving, financially capable parents. It happens all the time, Lupe. It works out. Then you've got the rest of your life in front of you and you can have a family when the time is right. You might even arrange it so you can stay in touch with the baby while he's growing up. She. . . ."

This last point catches in Marty's throat. It's the exact thing — contact with her surrendered child — that he didn't want C.T.'s mother to have. Laura's only grace, the one thing he begrudgingly credits her with, is that she was never interested in knowing her son. But the wall was built against her anyway and Marty patrolled its perimeter to be sure she never breached it because if entertainment and her celebrity — the combined, blinding glow that would outshine anything she would ever have offered as a mother — had cast its light on C.T., he feared his boy could never have resisted. Just being a damn human — how attractive would that have been to the child of a movie star?

With the help of Laura's indifference Marty has made it this far as C.T.'s dad, as Pops. But here on a bench in a Sacramento shopping mall that voice of the actress on his answering machine creeps through his head like a bank of toxic fog that could at any moment envelope these kids, too. As a foster child pushed along her path from one foster home to the next, Lupe might somehow have become a capable and ready mother, as unlikely as that might be with all the piled-on odds stacked against her. But Laura's Hollywood voice will offer magic, a release; C.T. and Lupe will suddenly have characters to play in the ceaseless pageant of fame.

Until now, Laura has never chosen to do so much as call. What does she want? It's not to play at being Grandma. There has never been any reason to hide from her in any consequential way, so if their baby is what Laura is after, if this is some kind of do-over, then Marty aches to shield these kids from what could turn into a ritual human sacrifice — a serving up of their child to Laura's unknown purpose, while they're elevated to some transient stardom even as the infant still shudders and quivers as the latest Tub O'Guts unfurling out of the old one.

Lupe is bright, she has to understand their situation. Or she will, if he gives her enough information. Marty presses forward, wanting to feel altruistic in telling these kids that their child deserves a chance that they can't give it. They need to arrange an adoption before Laura Trent-Sampson the movie star makes some kind of offer of a glittery life with perks on another order of magnitude than anything Marty has to offer them.

"So, later, right? If you and C.T. are really meant to make it together, in a few years. . . ."

"Not if I don't got no papers."

Marty closes his eyes. A crack has opened, if not an abyss: some undocumented mother once had to leave her little girl behind and this is how it's turned out.

"And then our baby wouldn't know his story, neither."

"What do you mean?"

"C.T., it's like. . . . He says you're blood but he still don't know the story."

"You mean like family history? He knows who he is. He sure as hell knows who I am. I've been there for him every minute of his life. I'm a good father, I don't need anybody to tell me that."

She nods. He remembers now her way of looking into you, as if she's focused behind your retinas, penetrating deeper than merely meeting your eyes. It's a look that doesn't let you see back, not in the same way, because it's all one-directional intensity. And while it's frustrating to him in this moment, C.T. will never have to explain why he's so taken with this sturdy girl and her deep almond eyes, irises as black as her pupils. They each watch some of the few stragglers who wander through the nearly abandoned plaza. A third of the stores are empty and the sun that pours through the open-sky courtyards can't brighten the economic gloom here.

"Anyway, C.T. has a biography. He's my kid."

"He don't believe in that. I mean, like, he loves you an' all. You're his Pops for sure. But you could tell him a family, and you don't do it."

He doesn't hesitate to repeat the lie he's been willing to live with: "There's no 'belief' involved. I'm his family. Fact. I guess you could throw in Aunt Bibi. He knows his adoption was a closed case, the birth parents didn't want contact and when they don't want you to know who they are, it's all locked up, you can't get at it. I've never told him who his mother is because I don't know. That's all there is. But maybe you could do it differently, right? There's open adoptions, too."

"So that's it, huh Mr. Nyrop. Just you."

The lie still settles heavily in his gut, and clearly she doesn't believe him. "I'm trying to help him, Lupe, just like I'm trying to help you. It's hard to understand now, but I'm trying to help the child, too. You guys are just in no position to take this on. I mean, where are you even gonna live? How will you eat?"

"We got friends. C.T.'s got videos lined up, some rap stuff. He's really good, y'know? An' he's got a job now. An' I got stuff I can do at home, an' I know how to cook."

Her glad tidings make him want to cry.

A different kind of pedestrian motion catches his eye and he twists around to see a ghostly C.T. floating toward them, rolling on his blades. Against, of course, all posted civic codes. He's unsmiling, his hands jammed in jeans pockets. Marty just hopes mall cops aren't chasing him for waxing down a storefront. The phrase "Baby Daddy" flits through his mind.

C.T.'s appearance makes for ready similes but Marty can't wholly pretend that C.T.'s life — which he's suddenly comparing to foster kid Lupe's — has been like some kind of easy glide, just rollerblading along. In the last few years he's had a small army of school counselors, psychologists, and pediatricians put his son through tests and interviews and observations to try to get at some background melancholy, some Romantic disease of the spirit. Something beyond teenage anomie. Most of the time C.T. and Marty are all right, great even. But C.T.'s occasional spikes of anger, of belligerence, his unwillingness to engage in any thinking about a path through high school into adulthood, his refusal to even consider college, have in concert set off half-assed speculations of depression, ADD, bi-polarism, drug abuse, even one crank-job's guess at Asperger's syndrome without anything to back it up. Marty has witnessed C.T. taking the joy out of his own skating sessions because he's so quick to be wildly frustrated when failing a new trick, obsessively hammering his limbs against rails until he's in tears with pain. Being adopted — it's never been official, legal — of course has something to do with it, but nobody can say exactly what. No one has ever said he wasn't bright or talented. Just adrift. Just sad.

"Hi, Pops."

Marty wants to squeeze him to his heart but C.T. wouldn't tolerate that. He's more likely watching Marty for any sudden movements, for hired thugs to come out of the shadows with nets to drag him home.

Lupe circles her finger at C.T.. "Let's see." He dutifully rotates on his wheels so she can lift his billowing T-shirt from his back. He has what appears to be plastic kitchen wrap taped to his skin like a transparent wound dressing. But it's no wound; it's a fresh, weeping tattoo glistening with ointment on his left shoulder blade.

"Infected?" he asks her.

"Nope. You're cool." She gently peels down the plastic, then C.T. turtles his back for her as she takes a picture. Marty is seeing his first tat-in-progress up close.

C.T. nods and drops his shirt. "Gotta go. Work."

Marty closes his eyes for a moment. "I heard you have some kind of new job?"

The boy nods quickly, kisses Lupe chastely, then lifts his weight atop his skates and half-turns into a backward roll. As he drifts away, he digs into a cargo pants pocket and pulls out a ballcap of some kind and yanks it low on his forehead, staring back all the while. The cap seems to be from a business, green and red, with a logo that suggests a pizza joint. And there goes that godly smile, the dimples and clefts, until he ducks his head and is smoothly pumping away through the other mallgoers.

Lupe shudders for a moment, then bends forward, arms around her belly.

"Lupe, you all right?"

She closes her eyes for a moment. "I'm okay."

"What kind of care are you getting? Are you seeing a doctor?"

"Yeah. There's a clinic." She rummages in her grocery bag and produces a rattling bottle of prenatal vitamins.

"He's seventeen. Y'know, by law he still has to be in school."

"He'll come back. A few more months, he can finish."

Marty holds his breath for a moment, trying to stay open to what they think they're doing. What they're *not* doing is thinking about getting an education, careers, making lives that won't play out in some crappy apartment cutting coupons with a savings account of spare change in a coffee can. But it's not about material well-being, it's about possibilities. Dreams, again.

She sits in silence. A few kid-shouts echo against the store facades. The smell of beef and fries from Johnny Rockets at this end of the mall mixes with smells of taffy and caramel corn from a street cart and coffee from the Starbucks nearby. It all makes Marty's stomach quiver.

"So . . . right now, you two need money?"

"You don't gotta do that, Mr. Nyrop."

She reaches again into her worn bag and pulls out a pad of drawing paper. She folds back the cover and holds her little silver camera over the top sheet. He leans in to see better: the image in the LCD screen that she's just taken of C.T.'s tattoo matches a drawing made within the simple outline of a human torso. It's C.T.'s back, he sees now, and on the paper pad these sketches are framed like panels in a graphic novel within the shape of the body. His son's hide is still a mostly blank page of her brief, hand-drawn story of their lives together.

"Your drawings?" She nods. "Who did the tattoo?"

"Me."

"You're a tat artist?"

"I do lotsa art. Skin art's no different. I get paid."

"Yeah, but do you have a health license for —" and then he stops because she's looking at him like he's completely out of touch.

Marty's gut clenches again, but not from food odors. This scene before him feels like a terrible violation somehow, that his beautiful boy's skin — where it isn't already scarred — is being scrawled on in a way that will last forever, short of a painful burn-off. The panel she's shown him, he can finally tell, is a portrait of the two of them from the waist up in a nude embrace. On the sketch pad she's planned the next tattoos: the second image, to go in the middle on his upper spine, is an action figure — C.T. in flight on his skates — and a small figure of a long-haired girl, crouching below him with a camera. Scene and documentarian. Marty leans closer and sees it's a video camera: a Lupe-tattoo is directing this movie. The third panel intended for C.T.'s right shoulder blade is a livid, red-edged heart with the contour drawing of a baby's head inside. He points to it, to the featureless face, a blank.

"We'll see what she looks like first. Or him."

Marty's heart drops. Tattoos, he's sure, are proof of the adolescent brain's inability to imagine the future, that life might ever be different than it is in the moment, the eternal Now; that the heart and mind might ever grow into something better. He can't think of a single person his age who wouldn't be deeply embarrassed by half of what he or she passionately believed in when they were seventeen years old. Yet this girl before him is going to turn his child's skin into some kind of vellum tapestry with her needles and ink, memorializing until C.T.'s deathbed this blink-of-an-eye emotional supernova they're sharing.

She folds the cover over her artwork. "You just tell him who he is, Mr. Nyrop. If you wanna help us. If you want him around. Sorry, that's just like, what I see an' all. You know?"

He's finally getting a dim glimpse into what she's here to ask of him: to ease his son's heart with a story, not of what Marty has devoted himself to, every day throughout C.T.'s life, but with a story of those damn people who gave C.T. his genes and nothing more, the people Marty has protected him from and would've continued to protect him from as long as Marty drew breath. But Lupe Villanueva, ex-foster kid, is telling him that if he doesn't tell this story of mere biology, then she'll continue to storyboard her own version of her lover's life across his skin and Marty doubts that he'll be in that story.

Yet how does he also make her see that this is a lose/lose proposition? That if he tells this story that she's asking of him, C.T. will be appalled at what he learns of his birth parents, and will read terrible, unconfirmable fantasies into the reasons behind his every problem.

"Look ... Lupe — I never told him about his parents because then he'd have a ready-made — and wrong — excuse for every failure, every unsolved problem, for every stumbling block in his life he couldn't get around. An excuse that said he was doomed with 'what was meant to be' because of who *they* were. And what could've been even worse is that he might've heard their story and thought it was pretty damn wonderful."

The word "dazzling" leaks upward like a tar pit bubble through Marty's chest and he shudders. It's a word from his own childhood, a word from a brother and parents and pain and misdirected compensation. Of survival. His brother the actor had learned early on to be dazzling. . . .

"I just see that you gotta do it an' all, Mr. Nyrop."

And if Marty doesn't do this storytelling, doesn't give C.T. his genealogy, she's letting him know that they'll live their own graphic novel of Romantic tattoos and he'll be a spectator, a reader at a distance.

Has it all been for nothing? To have raised C.T. as motherless, to have told him that her name was unknowable, hidden behind a bureaucratic wall of adoption rules? That in order to hide his mother from C.T., Marty also had to deny the blood the two of them shared and hope every day that being a reliable, ever-present Dad was enough?

But that phone call, that message, that voice. That woman who might now swoop down and carry his son off in her talons to a nest Marty would never find —

Then he can hear Bibi's voice instead, her will: "Lose/lose is about you, Marty. Not them."

Lupe rocks quietly on the bench. This child who is herself without a home will patch holes with whatever tools she can lay hands on, and she sees a hole in his son that Marty has denied until this moment. She's giving Marty a chance to patch a heart, too.

"Okay, Lupe. Here's what we do." He hesitates, trying to frame an idea correctly to a young woman who is standing by, willing and waiting to shoulder a burden on top of life's other burdens that have brought her to this place. Her sturdiness isn't just physical, she's holding out against easy help for the child she carries because, as Marty can see now, holding out is what she's had to do all her life, and now she's doing it for C.T. as well. Marty guesses that in *her* life to come, people will either be there for her, standing firm, or she'll laser a look right through them and they'll vanish.

And he sees that she's stronger than C.T.. She's stronger than himself. "How about this: I tell you, instead. Because, okay, yes. I do know who they were, and I'll tell you all about them, about me, about everything back when we were all working together. And you decide if it'll help him. If he can handle it, if it'll make anything any better. I'll tell you first, because maybe then he won't get so upset, because I know how he overreacts. His temper. And because I already think that coming straight from me it wouldn't make things any better at all when he knows I've lied to him for so long."

Marty doesn't tell her that he'll finally tell the story because his greatest hope is to make both of them fear C.T.'s mother, the woman who abandoned C.T. seventeen years ago because she'd already wrung what publicity value she could out of his birth and had held no interest — and felt no love — in the possibility of raising him. Her actor's performance, her moment of Now, had passed and unlike the bearer of a tattoo she had moved on unmarked. And what's to be said of a birth father who never held him, even once. . . ?

"Deal?"

Another solemn nod from Lupe. She puts the sketchpad back into the grocery bag, then the camera, each precisely in its place. She stands, and as he rises next to her she seems to shrink toward the cement.

"Just how tall are you?" He immediately regrets this.

She waves briefly as she walks away, then pats near the rubber band that holds her ponytail. "Tall enough to reach the top of my head." She stops and looks back at Marty without expression. "Nobody gives you no family, Mr. Nyrop. You gotta go out an' get it."

Marty accepts her assertion. "Tomorrow, then — Here? Same time?"

But without answering she coils up her ponytail into her black hoodie and steps quickly toward a mall exit that will aim her back in the direction of light-rail. His stomach clenches again.

6

*I*t was only a matter of when: Marty has read in the Sacramento *Bee* that the holding of a staged promotional event was leaked to TMZ, a website that claims to specialize in "Celebrity Gossip, Entertainment News, and Celebrity News" as if their distinctions between gossip and news and entertainment had meaning. In charge of this "event" was a gracefully aging actress, once the driver of various movie studios' economic survival or death, who in the latest of her serial self-reinventions has become the host of a "reality" show which means only that it is unscripted by paid writers, however much the shows are entirely planned, and cast, and rehearsed. For the faked spontaneity of the carefully recorded event, the still-luminescent actress found dozens of other working actresses who had themselves been celebrities to varying degree, but are now fading or already faded from view and who have, somewhere early in their sculpted careers, or more likely even before such a thing as a career existed, birthed children whom they gave up for adoption and will never see again — until the once and enduringly famous Laura Trent-Sampson produces a segment about them for her new cable sensation. The actress has tapped into a mother lode — pun thoroughly intended and already in use in online ads and website banners citing celebrity ängst, loss, humiliation, and triumphalism, the conditions that generate the free publicity of gossip. The show is to be called "Hollywood Birth Moms!" The exclamation point in the title seems necessary.

The raw material for the premiere episode of the forthcoming series is to come from the life of Laura Trent-Sampson herself, executive producer and host, who is going to record a segment about her own carefully cultured petri dish, her own experience of tragically losing a baby only to recover that child years later before all is lost. This event will establish her show's template. People who follow such things are already abuzz about who this child could be, postings are going viral, but cloaking his or her identity is part of the marketing strategy, the branding, the building of a viewer base before the show's debut.

No one has to tell Marty who the child is.

When the knock comes at his door, Marty marvels at the actress's surprising decency to show up herself, alone, not sending instead the wannabe investigator-producers, *paparazzi*-class videographers, production assistants, and botoxed microphone holders asking intrusive and inappropriate questions of their victims.

"Hello, Marty. Long time, huh?"

All the intervening years swirl, then evaporate.

"Why are you here? Forget it, I know why you're here. How the fuck dare you?"

"I'm here for my son."

"C.T.. His name's C.T.. Did you even know that?"

"'C.T.' for. . . ?"

"For his name. It's none of your damn business, really. Fuck — what is this?"

"I'm bringing him home. You don't have any legal right to stop me, y'know. You never did."

"So . . . it took you seventeen years to figure that out? You're cleverer than that, Laura. And his home is here, it's always been here. He doesn't even know *your* name, either. Why not keep it that way?"

This actress, this celebrity, once the most compelling sexual presence on screens throughout cinema-world, looks back at Marty with a guilelessness that couldn't possibly be so, not with what Marty already knows about her. Her eyes widen, seem to water just a bit, and all the colors from the blue end of the rainbow play within her irises. It's a hypnotic effect, and he doesn't trust it for a second.

"Our movie did all right, didn't it? Marty? Why didn't you ever come back?"

"You want me to think Hollywood — that you — had your arms wide open for my grand return?"

"You could've directed again, y'know. You could've done a lot of things."

"And done what with the baby? He deserved a life. Any kid does."

She wavers for a moment. "I still have that note you left. When you took him."

"Yeah? And what of it?"

"You were right. I knew you'd be a better parent. It's all good, huh?"

"If you leave now, it's all good, sure."

"So, are you still with Bibi?"

"No. You had your little role to play in that, huh? And what the hell is it with this show? You've got all the money in the world, all the endorsements, all the TV guest shots — what do you still need? Why is it that actors can never stop acting?"

"Right now I just need my son. It'll be good for him, I promise."

"You need to go away. Leave him alone. Leave his baby alone, or I swear I'll. . . . It gives me the goddamn creeps figuring out how you even know about that."

"Staff. It's all about staff, Marty. The business has changed a lot."

"Have *you*? No. Just go."

When she doesn't respond immediately he closes the door in her still-remarkable face. Through the leaded glass distortions in the window he watches her step down from the porch stairs, take in the dimensions of his Craftsman bungalow, and turn to the street with one arm raised. In seconds an SUV equipped with a satellite uplink antenna slides to the curb with a sharp chirp of rubber against cement, followed in kind by two vans with all the people Marty had moments before been grateful that she had not brought. They spring from several vehicle doors at once and obediently gather around the actress who is apparently also the Showrunner. Cameras, sound booms, lights, headsets, tripods. Marty turns the deadbolt knob and shuffles toward the dark rooms at the back of the house.

Patrick Cosgrove

7

*H*e meets Lupe at the same time as yesterday, and maybe it's the mix of smells again, but Marty suddenly thinks it's a great idea for them to go just a few more steps through the mall and up a level to get a shake at Johnny Rockets. As they settle into a booth, he plays for a few moments with the tabletop jukebox offerings of primitive rock'n'roll from his childhood. He's pleased when Lupe is willing to let him buy her a shake. Screw it, it's not all about folic acid, pregnancy ought to have a few guilty pleasures. Maybe a burger and a plate of fries with faces drawn in ketchup by their waitress won't be far behind.

"I'm trying to . . . to come up with a story here, you know? A story that had real people in it even though so much of it was about Hollywood. I guess I'm saying that I'm having trouble putting the two together. Hollywood and 'real.'"

Lupe listens solemnly as she averts her gaze and takes over fanning the Rolodex-like list of jukebox songs behind the glass song-dispenser on their tabletop.

"I can be a little snarky sometimes. . . . But 'Hollywood' and 'real,' it's like they're an oxymoron. Which I always thought meant a pack of eight idiots." Her eyes flit toward him but don't acknowledge his attempt at a laugh. "Anyway, it happened. His mother and father . . . it happened to me, Hollywood and acting and directing, it was all real enough. So you're still sure about this. . . ."

"Yeah, C.T. says 'okay,' y'know, about telling me first."

"I don't know what either of you are gonna make of it. Because I'm gonna give you everything. Everything that I can remember, whether I understood it at the time or not. Things I'm still trying to understand myself. It won't make sense unless you guys know the whole thing."

"Okay."

Right. How, Marty wonders, can this be "okay"? But her eyes are boring into him, she's steady, and her tiny stature gives her a low center of gravity, a weight that implies that she can handle anything he throws at her from across the table.

"Please don't take this the wrong way. But you think you're ready to be a mother, and here you are with your teen Daddy." He stops, because this already feels like the wrong way to begin.

She patiently draws on the shake through her straw. Then she seems to sense why he's having trouble shaping the story. "She called, y'know, Mr. Nyrop. He talked to her. She found us, she knows all about everything. An' he knows about her."

His heart stops for a moment, but her news pushes him forward. "Then I have to make you see how complicated it is. How not to get pixie-led by the attention from some movie star. Not even one who shows up with a camera crew in your face. How not to give in. You can't go there."

Lupe seems to be trying to hold in a laugh. "You mean like, this actress, it's true? *She's* his Mom? You mean Laura Trent-Sampson, for reals?"

"You've heard of her?"

"Oh hell yeah. She used to be like a Kardashian or a whatever, only she really did shit an' stuff. And now she's gonna have that show — *that's* why she called? So the thing's gonna be about C.T.? That's hella cool."

"I guess so."

She's looking at him again with those burn-through-your-retinas black eyes, and he drifts back to the night earlier in the week when he sat next to his sleeping son, perhaps living with C.T. under his roof for the last time. He remembers their flight from Utah aboard a whistling jet when, once aloft out of Salt Lake City and headed for LAX, it had been time for Marty to wake and feed the little guy, to detoxify Tubs's jumpsuit in the empty seat next to them on that fugitive flight. If he's going to keep these kids in his life Marty has to pull the curtain aside now, seventeen years after the escape, let the Performers perform, and show the consequences of living only the actors' moment, the Now: to show-and-tell his teenaged boy through his expectant child-bride how C.T. came to Marty as a milky-skinned infant, how he eventually arrived in that star-lit room just a few nights ago as the skater-boy scarred and still asleep with his breath *schussing* in the dark. Time to tell his and C.T.'s shared story like adding some elaborate caption to a studio production photo just as they once did for publicity press kits. C.T. has already shown that he intends to take on a story-role of "Father" for which there's no rehearsal, so Marty needs the better tale, the one that'll convince C.T. to put an end to his impossible idea of parenthood, convince him to say No to that actress who gave him life but had no interest in mothering him. To say No to her tomorrow, and the next day, and the next. . . .

And a reason for C.T. to hesitate, at least, to slow down and ask himself if he's ready to become a dad even as his own birth father — adult and accomplished and vexed by his own childhood — was not.

Marty focuses on Lupe Villanueva who still watches that spot behind his eyes. In the red- and white-tiled clatter of the restaurant suffused with jukebox doo-wop, he's returning in memory to his Hollywood that was like anyone else's Hollywood: it never really existed, yet will forever be there. Be there for anyone who's ever yearned for meaning to come from a screen of shadows and reflections. *And I, Marty among the millions, made my big-time movie. I directed. And yet —*

As Marty sorts through moments, backing up to find a better starting point, it's like a Director describing his next setup, viewing the past through a frame made with his palms out, thumbs horizontal, fingers splayed upward at right angles. He can sit anywhere and use this movie-frame of memory, see the world again as it was during the last time he was confident that he knew the difference between life and entertainment — a difference he has given himself to enforcing ever since. These kids have to be made to see that difference, even as Laura Trent-Sampson comes knocking and offers everything that is fabulous. In passing the story on, Lupe will be Marty's co-conspirator, their family shaman whether she knows it or not. And so he begins the truth about a lie even as he fears that the telling of it might cause the loss of the only family he has left.

Patrick Cosgrove

8

*I*t all goes back, he tells Lupe, to the morning on the Universal Studios lot when the events — the ones that first made him aware of a need to become father to someone else's child — all began. He can go back there easily because, like an eidetic security camera, he can recall almost any moment in his life, like that morning he was outside the pale blue "elephant doors" of Sound Stage 28, shoulders knotted up, his cervical vertebrae ready to snap like cold porcelain as he tended to his leading actress in the makeup trailer parked on cinder blocks just outside the stage. He hasn't always been adept at understanding what his memory-pictures mean, if anything. But he can recount the order of images like a shot sequence in a film, remember how the lighting of a long-ago moment can still be felt as having weight, and substance, and force.

That morning Laura Trent-Sampson had climbed into the Airstream makeup trailer at 5:06 AM wearing her Ray-Bans, and right on time. Even so, the absurdity of the daily makeup-therapy session to follow forced Marty to wonder why he wanted to work in Hollywood. As a Director, fine. But being merely a Second Assistant was killing him, the running and fetching for everyone else's ambitions. So, like most days, until he'd had enough coffee, he was ready to blow his brains out (or at least he was within the melodrama of remembering) and to take somebody with him. Might as well be Her, he thought. The Star. Then he'd finally make the trades, except that it would come out with a headline about her alone. Something like, "Tragic Re-Make — Death of Gold Digger, '89" with Marty as a disgruntled employee in the fourth paragraph.

It was still dark but he didn't blame her for wearing the shades, she was a star with an image to protect. Laura was as huge as they got, one of the biggest box office attractions in the business, and had appointed herself a hyphenated three-names as if "Laura Trent-Sampson" were from England or Australia instead of South Dakota. He'd worked on shoots where half the crew were stringers for the *Enquirer*, and who knew when some *paparazzo* with a flash attachment would jump out of a dumpster?

Marty rushed in after her for a multitude of professional reasons. First, he had to be nice and start her day right. That was no problem, it was his nature anyway. Then he'd have to coyly scold her — or better yet fake-scold the Wrecking Crew, the hair and makeup guys who were in on the whole charade — about how she was such a bad girl for not jumping right into the chair to have her hair rolled. Wayne Hair and Eddie Makeup let Marty do this to them because they were great people, as were most members of the crafts guilds who worked below the budget line for hourly wages, chronically auditioning for the next job they would need to find before their current production shut down. Wayne and Eddie understood that even creating beauty was timed and paid in six-minute increments, tenths of an hour on the timeclock.

When he stepped through the trailer's aluminum door at 5:07 it was like a cocoon inside — the whole point — perfumed sweetness and warmth and light with Billy Ocean on the stereo and Celebes beans in the coffee maker. A guy could do worse at that hour, he thought. Exene was slumped in a folding director's chair with her electric-blue Eddie Bauer vest buttoned to her neck. She still had her shades on against the fluorescent sunshine that ricocheted off the mirrors. But she'd shown up with clean hair and was letting Wayne comb and roll her already, bless her heart, so Marty promised himself that he'd ask the commissary for some special touch to reward her. Usually the boys on the wrecking crew had a line of chatter for him, but today they were quiet. He went behind her chair.

"Morning, Laura. Can I get you something for breakfast?"

She didn't answer and he didn't want to push her. Whether true or not, he liked to tell himself that, as much as he could, he withheld any emotional investment in being an Assistant Director. Why kill himself when he was not in charge, not the creator? So he wasn't about to rock the boat, to get *involved,* especially when the work was getting done. He didn't even know if she'd heard him because he couldn't make eye contact through the Ray-Bans. Wayne Hair scowled at Marty so he backed off. As he reached for the door Eddie Makeup mimed dipping a tea bag, which was a pretty good idea.

But then Marty heard something like an animal in pain and it could only have come from her. Wayne stopped pulling on a handful of blondeness and bent carefully to her ear.

"What is it, Darlin'?"

"I lost it. I lost it yesterday."

Then came the sob. It was incredible, moving, touching. If not real, then better than anything she'd done so far on the picture, which was turning out to be pretty much a string of situational clichés. He hesitated just inside the door to see if he could do anything to help, but Wayne Hair was carrying the ball.

"Oh god no, not this one too. Awww hell, you poor thing." Wayne looked up to Eddie Makeup as if he were going to join in the crying. Fortunately, Eddie was cool, silent. Then Wayne looked at Marty, and he knew what was coming.

"She can't work today. She's gotta be home in bed. Or the hospital! Call the damn studio. She can't work."

"What?" Marty asked. "I'm sorry — what's going on?"

"She's lost her baby."

"You were pregnant?"

What did he know, she wasn't married, but he knew he was supposed to feel like a Neanderthal, or worse, moralistic, for even considering such a thing, or for wondering whom on earth the father could be.

"Yeah, Bebop. Almost three months."

What a kid. He could tell she was struggling to be chipper because she always called him "Marty Bebop" instead of Nyrop when she wanted something out of him but didn't want to come on like The Star. So she flirted. Like she probably called the Gaffer "Sparky" to get a softer key light. She was trying to proclaim that the show must go on.

"Oh, god — that's terrible. I'm really sorry."

"It . . . it's okay."

This was trouble. Laura was in the range of what Marty categorized as a "trowel-job" because it took almost three-and-a-half hours for an entourage of hair, makeup and wardrobe people and all their shop tools to put her together every morning for that fresh natural look. They couldn't fall behind in this process; the boys needed every unimpeded minute they could muster to start her off properly, or today's workday schedule would fall apart and he would be blamed for having let tens of thousands of studio dollars slip irretrievably down the drain because during this morning's awkward complications he hadn't manipulated an actress's pastiche of a psyche with omniscient care. Doing so was tacitly within a Second Assistant Director's job description.

He'd seen dozens of other trowel-jobs come in at five or six in the morning, each as undistinguished as a tub of leftover yogurt. The difference between them and the un-famous was that under the yogurt they had inherited (or had surgically implanted) a terrific bone structure that took the makeup well, that threw the right shadows. They'd gotten a lucky skull. They'd be relatively attractive people walking down the street on their own, but nobody looks like a movie star at 5 AM.

Except Laura. He had already conceded that she was much more than just a trowel-job, because she had not merely terrific, but transcendent facial planes. So her purpose for wanting her time in the makeup trailer could only be that she needed the three-plus hours to become someone different than who she was. But why be anyone else? With the other actresses, by the time the professionals had puttied in the cracks, painted on the colors white women don't come equipped with, stretched and tied the sags back with hair pulls, sprayed the moptop into place, then fluffed and patted and powdered it all right up to the moment the camera was rolling with fill-lights bounced off strategically placed white cards through some kind of detail-diffusing filter in front of the lens, even Lassie could've competed for the third romantic lead on a network show.

But Laura didn't *need* all the cheats. That, Marty had learned, was part of her glamor. And while everybody said they knew all about Reel Life and Hollywood Illusion, they still believed in movie stars. It was global, and the only interesting question was why everybody needed the illusions in the first place. He often thought that the best thing he'd ever done for Bibi Peterson, his girlfriend, was to bring her on a set right after she'd gotten into the Extras Guild and have her stand next to one of his other trowel-jobs. Bibi's self-esteem had blossomed. In time, he came to understand that probably this was also the moment she first imagined that she didn't need him to survive in Hollywood. His heart sank in remembering that just weeks ago she realized that she didn't even need Hollywood.

Finally Laura took off her shades. Was her glamor only bone structure? Marty quickly recalculated the formula as bone-structure-plus-eyes. She had saucer-irises that were what his crayon set used to call cornflower blue. Those eyes, too, made her a little bit different than everyone else, just as her lucky skull did. They were completely open to him and he felt what America — moviegoers everywhere — must feel when Laura Trent-Sampson got a lingering closeup, until he forced himself to speak just above a whisper.

"I'm so sorry. . . . Can I bring you something? Some hot tea?"

All busyness stopped. She stared at Marty for another long moment, then abruptly laughed. "Gotcha — ! Got all of ya!"

Marty stood motionless, uncertain.

"Gotcha, Marty Bebop. You too, Wayne. Boohoo."

Marty stammered: "Then, uh . . . I mean, did it, did you really. . . ?"

"Yeah, yeah. Life's a bitch, huh? Um. What do they put in those burritos that everybody eats?"

"Anything you want. Eggs, cheese, bacon, tomatoes, sushi —"

"*Suuu* - shi?"

An attempt to lighten up, another part of his job. She went along and gave him a little chuckle that was like a purr out of a mountain cat.

"Have 'em put in all of that stuff. And some hot sauce."

Wayne groaned. "No, no Honey. You don't want to do that to yourself, not without a bottle of Maalox."

She gave Marty a smile that shone right out of the puffy red eyelids and vanilla yogurt. "Lotsa salsa, Bebop. And some hot water, with lemon maybe. Pretty please?"

"Comin' up."

• • •

He thought that would be the end of it. It was all pretty remarkable. When Bibi had gone through a miscarriage the year before without first having told him she was pregnant, she was so blue, and disconsolate, for nearly four months. Of course, after a while Bibi too came up with her own version of "Life's a bitch," and carried on. But their girl Laura was a trouper. He could see another *Enquirer* headline already: "Top Star Has Miscarriage — Eats Burrito Through Tears." They would throw in the bit about the tears even if there weren't any. And since that fabricated, yet spine-twisting sob, there weren't.

9

"**S**o like C.T. — so he wasn't, like in your story, the miscarriage that she. . . . Oh." Lupe laughs at herself briefly.

Marty can't help but smile. "No. He wasn't. What I've told you so far, this was weeks, maybe a month or so, before C.T. was conceived. Of course, back then I had no way of knowing that. I don't think Nostradamus would've seen that one coming. Let's slow down here, let me get the day right. It's been a while, you know?" Although as a story, these events have never left him. "Lupe, you have to know *why* I haven't told him any of this. I think the one scrap of wisdom I've picked up as a parent is that you repeat what you know. What you were brought up with, good or bad, unless you fight it every day to make sure that you break the pattern. You know? If you want it to be better. That you're not just pushing your own stuff further downhill so your kid gets stuck pushing more stuff down his own hill. I made a decision with C.T. a long time ago — that if he didn't know what these people did, how they lived, then he'd never have a chance to be like them. Like I was saying, 'I won't give you a single shred of it, nothing to imagine, so you'll never fill your head with some fantasy of who you think they were.' And who you think *you* are because of them."

"But he wonders anyway. All the time. You make 'em sound sorta like bandits. Narcos."

"They were . . . actors. That's not a joke. I didn't want C.T. to ever imagine life as some kind of a performance. Something you just make up to please everybody else. Actors, they. . . . The way you have to really live, it's not a play, or a game, or a pose."

It's not even a tattoo, he's thinking, but he holds that one back.

Next up in the Nyrop story is C.T.'s father — Marty's only brother Craig — who died while inhabiting the self-invented identity of an actor named "Eric Blanc." For the briefest time, Marty had been Craig's Director, and while they made a movie together — all of them, Laura too — Marty had the chance to talk for hours to his brother on their shared movie set as they waited out the many down-times: for lights to be set and flagged, for hair and makeup to create their magic metamorphoses, for grips to lay track or plywood dance floors until camera was ready to roll film. Because of those hours spent with Craig, Marty can now tell Lupe how he and his brother filled that idle time on distant location with stories of their lives spent together, then apart, poking and prodding one another for a connection that should have been natural, but was not.

Perhaps most important, those were hours when Marty heard what Craig alone remembered about two boyhoods that hadn't always inhabited the same family drama. Movie-set memories, retold now by Marty about Craig Nyrop who had re-named himself Eric Blanc, will be the only reason C.T. might ever know certain bumps and hollows of the family heart.

As Lupe listens, her eyes widen and narrow but she is silent. Fries and ketchup arrive.

10

U nbeknown to Marty as he moved relentlessly from one Assistant Director duty to another, running information from makeup trailer to grip truck to prop truck outside the Phantom Stage, Eric Blanc was at the Main Gate staring at the dozens of people who passed into and out of the Universal City Studios lot with impunity. The security station was a driveway with a tollbooth-like guard house set at right angles to Lankershim Boulevard, and stood in the shadow of the Black Tower office building that hovered like an onyx shoebox on its end. Eric knew that this was the place where Steven Spielberg once sneaked onto the lot when, barely out of school, he had entered unquestioned, waving merrily to the guards day after day as he drove by, wearing a business suit, carrying an empty briefcase — his picture car, wardrobe and prop for the scene — all for the "reality of doing" that actors understand as performance. Spielberg had then visibly busied himself in an unoccupied office so he could afterward wander the sound stages and observe working television and movie sets firsthand. Spielberg had re-invented — written, cast, and produced — himself. Eric knew that stories like this made Universal and all other Hollywood studios sources of near-religious apocrypha, locations of scene-fragments of successful ambition and aggression that endured as paradigms to each new wave of moviemaking aspirants.

But he was stuck at the gate. Eric realized that his thick-headed mistake lay in failing to merely pretend that he knew what he was doing. He had needed only to "indicate" business intentions, to fake the emotion of an activity, and this would've carried Eric, too, through the gate unchecked. He was furious that of all people this understanding should've been instinctive to an actor. He decided to give a bad faith performance then, an inauthentic one, because he didn't care about emotional truth in the moment. He focused on the guard.

"It's Susan Goldfarb. That's the name. She's the casting agent who told me to go to the Stage 28 set. I have to meet the Director for a reading."

The guard frowned at a scattering of handwritten notes next to his phone. "Susan . . . Goldfarb?"

"She didn't leave a pass? I've got the sides —" He fumbled in his coat and shuffled pages of a script for effect, an attempt to fabricate the moment's reality of doing. "Look, if I lose this chance —"

And it was nothing more than a chance. Eric Blanc was here to gamble on his suddenly untrustworthy instincts and had no choice but to win. His New York theater group and its workshops were dying from attrition, exhaustion, from his failure at grantsmanship. The group was all he had, but that had been his own choice; Eric was careful never to call for pity. He was seeking a way back to New York, he grandly told his company before leaving for Los Angeles, back to independence, back to the proscenium. Generation after generation before him had left for Hollywood voluntarily, thinking they really wanted to be there, as if they'd ever heard or read about anyone in Hollywood history who was truly happy to have gone, still happier they had stayed.

At his farewell to all the performers who depended on him, he expressed his hope that setting out for Hollywood ("only because I've been *forced* to go there") would work in his favor. Desire, he told his group with spiritual gravity, is ruin. He didn't want movie stardom. He would instead return to the stage. He had promised.

He decided that he couldn't risk trying to "indicate" his way through this. In his failure to slip through the studio gate Eric felt usably anguished. Yet rather than trust the genuineness of this feeling he cast about for a specific image of anguish, something that could sustain him throughout the external distractions of his upcoming scene with the Burns Security guard. He took a moment to will his own privacy amidst the morning traffic — what had the acting teacher Lee Strasberg called it? public solitude? — until he remembered himself as an exhausted child sliding off a vinyl air mattress into the icy black choppiness of Lake Michigan, unable to touch more than stringy, slimy seaweed with his cramping toes, gasping, choking. This had once happened to him, though he didn't need the sense-memory. With the help of skilled mentors, he'd rejected Strasberg's errant notion of feeding off one's own psychic entrails years ago. But sometimes sense-memory had its purpose, like a screwdriver used as a chisel: the wrong tool but effective. There it is, Eric thought, the rational mind knows what it means to be a boy who's too frightened to learn to swim, then too frightened to ask the Father character to save him. So frightened he would accept anything but the Father's help, even death, and *then* the bastard would be sorry. In the remembering, water filled the boy's throat and made screaming almost impossible. He had found it again, Eric was sure: the "as if," the reliable emotional logic, just for a little momentum into this security gate sketch. . . .

He returned to the booth and spoke to the reticent man with blue-on-blue stripes and appliqué patches everywhere. The sun was too bright. Eric felt — and moreover, knew he could now truly project — anguish.

"Look, I understand 'Eric Blanc' doesn't mean anything to you, but call the A.D. again. Marty Nyrop. He knows me, he'll get the Director to confirm all this. Please — I'm out here all the way from New York, I don't have a car, y'know? And if I miss this chance — you don't know, you don't *know* what this means. They're on Stage 28."

His hands were trembling insensibly, and one side of his face felt spastic. But he clamped down; there still had to be inner conflict, a contained ambivalence, he couldn't go this big yet.

The man in the booth sighed and nodded at two drivers passing by in identical metallic-charcoal BMWs. Eric imagined in clear detail what it would be like to drive onto the lot, though he'd never had a driver's license. Then, impatient with himself, he concentrated once again on a drowning boy kicking at seaweed. And how had that scene ended? Who had been there, as rescuer, as Hero? His little brother Marty. Strong, willful Marty saving his big brother who was then, as if in someone's memory other than his own, a boy named Craig Nyrop, long before there was an actor named "Eric Blanc." Marty had hurt Craig then, pulling him by the throat and hair as if to teach him a lesson: I'll give you this, I'll save you, but stop *needing* me.

Eric shoved the script pages back into his coat and felt the other folded scraps he'd brought. Reviews, interviews, a think-piece in the L.A. *Times* "Arts & Leisure" section about his troupe. After almost fifteen years of silence would Marty, his only brother, acknowledge him now, even admire him? I have *this*, Eric would fight the urge to say, right here in my pocket, and I did *this*. . . . I'm successful. Look at me, Marty — your big brother, *successful.*

"Stage 28? Hey, that's the Laura Trent-Sampson set, isn't it?"

Eric shrugged and indicated an "amazed" face. "It is?"

The Guard picked up the phone and pressed four numbers, then shook his head even before looking back to report that no one on the other end was answering. He pointed into the mouthpiece:

"They're probably on a red light. That means —"

"Yeah, yeah, I know." Eric raised his shaking hands, ready to tug at his hair if he were to need the gesture. "It means 'shut the fuck up.'"

11

Half an hour later the Security Guard stood with his back to Eric Blanc. The Guard was long trained not to offend anyone in a company town, yet he had neither an offer that would make Eric happy, nor a suggestion to encourage him to leave. When Eric furiously spun away the Guard turned too, hoping simply to break their connection until he got through on the lot phone. Then:

"Hey Mr. Blanc, wait a minute — Hello? Hey, get me the Second A.D.. This is Security at the Main Gate."

He motioned Eric over and held the phone through the sliding door as he saluted to still more BMWs and a murky-green Jaguar. Eric took the receiver and waited, until:

"Marty? Listen, *please*. It's your brother. . . ."

On the other end of the line Marty twisted the cord around the fist he had made with his free hand, and held the stage phone in bafflement as he acted out his part of the conversation. Marty could perform too, when it suited him.

"My brother, what — ? *Why*?"

"I've got a deal involving real money, and it's for a production. . . .

"You, a pro-*duc*-tion. . . ?"

"What? Yes, a real pro-*duc*-tion. Shut up a minute. A play first, and who knows, maybe later they'll make it into a movie. We need to talk. I want there to be something in it for you too, you *Auteur* wannabe. All I need is five minutes with Laura Trent-Sampson. She's involved, she's — "

"She's *involved*, what does that mean. . . ? Why don't you get a goddamn pass from *her*, then. . . ?"

"Okay. Put her on the line, I'll *get* a pass from her."

"You want me to put her on the line, for *you*?"

"Sure, you tell her Eric Blanc's on the phone and see what happens. Yeah, go ahead. . . ."

"God, I thought the fairy tales were over. I gotta go, I'm hanging up. . . ."

"Hey, don't do that. Don't hang up! You got any idea what it's like to get through to you in there? C'mon, c'mon, I'm not out here for my health. I'm begging here. . . . What? *Marty* —!"

Eric listened a moment more, then cupped his hand over the phone as he pushed it back to the Guard. He wanted to announce that he had arrived to change his brother's life, but he knew that, through the stage phone, Marty had heard nothing like that.

• • •

Marty shoved the phone back into its wheeled metal box, then picked it up again to check with the commissary on the progress of Laura's breakfast order. He couldn't believe his brother was still annoying the hell out of him. Not after all these years, not after Craig disappeared and became "Eric Blanc" like some kind of sick "Who-am-I-this-time?" charade. He wasn't thrilled at being their father's son either, but at least he had the guts to outlive the shame of being a Nyrop. It wasn't Craig that got left behind by a big brother who ran away.

He stepped through the heavy stage doors into the sunlight to see if he could spot an electric cart on its way with a breakfast order for someone named "Exene." Even on the studio lot Marty never mentioned Laura's name to anyone outside the company, nor would he even use her initials within earshot of a civilian because any outsider would instantly recognize her and want to know more. Call it honor or professional discretion or just some vestige of Midwestern manners, but he didn't want to do that to her, to violate her privacy. Hence, "Exene, the X-Girl," a name he and his Production Assistants used like a code to keep her presence quiet over the radios. At the same time, he wouldn't congratulate himself for this small kindness on her behalf, because he'd learned that even though everyone in Hollywood claimed to have decency in their heart, saying so was just another self-indulgence.

Marty's head was still wobbling from the phone call when he got back to the trailer with "Exene's" delivered breakfast, until he realized that the Styrofoam plate was burning into his palm and hot water was running down his wrist — occupational hazards in the Directors Guild of America, Inc.. He shook off the pain and went through the Airstream door to witness what people who believe in movies should never see.

Makeup artists have the skill of hiding their work, but just then Exene's face was all naked technique. Eddie had taken slabs of foam rubber and cut them into squares, then triangles, then smaller triangles until he had precision-edged applicators for a gob of makeup he'd smeared on the back of his hand. Then it was rub, wipe, rub, smear, blend, wipe. Exene stared at Marty in the wall of mirrors and she looked like a frightened raccoon. Eddie took what could pass for white housepaint and drew lines that radiated from her cornflower eyes with his foam rubber triangle, then made one big dollop over each purple eye bag. Marty knew that in the end it worked, but at this stage it made his groin flutter, like hitting an air pocket aboard an airplane.

He couldn't shake Exene's — Laura's — look in the mirror; the morning was only going to get stranger. She had him fixed with those blue saucers, and it was not politic for a Second A.D. to break off a meaningful look with a star. He didn't know what she wanted, but she didn't seem to know either, so he had to wait just inside the trailer door until she'd figured it out. Two bright blue circles with big black pupils and Eddie blending four kinds of beige into the white. Finally Marty saw it: a big round tear the size of a pearl earring swelling up, then dribbling straight down her extraordinary cheekbone. Fortunately, the mascara was going to come last. Wayne saw it right away too and started squealing at Marty.

"See this? I told you, she can't work! We gotta send her home! Right now! Do it now!"

Wayne was losing it, but unless she started tearing her rollers out, this was Eddie Makeup's problem, not Wayne Hair's. Marty figured Wayne was probably a secret actor and he was living out a hidden desire, *becoming* Exene.

Eddie put up one flat palm. "Whoa, cool it, pardner. That's for the Lady to decide. What do you think, Darlin'? Can you make it?"

She nodded, and she *still* hadn't taken those eyes off Marty. He was spooked and breaking down, falling into something like love with two wet circles.

Wayne turned on him again. "Okay, but you tell our fucking Sun God Director the hell with getting a master. He does all the closeups first. I'm not responsible if he doesn't give Baby her closeups first thing. There's no way we can fix her and make her match at the end of the day."

"I'll tell him, I promise. I'll explain —"

But it was too late. Now the tears were turning her lower face into a satellite shot of a river delta. Wayne shouted some obscenity and Eddie just patted her shoulders. Finally she stopped looking at Marty. She got out of the chair and hugged herself, walking in little circles as they all bobbed to her rhythm on the trailer springs.

"I . . . I went to the h-hospital last night. I was bleeding. And they put me on a table, like I was going to have an ex-exam-m —"

Eddie was in a low chant: "It's all right, Darlin'. It's all right. . . ."

" — and, and this *nurse*, this *bitch* kept talking about 'no other products of conception.' Like they were cleaning, I don't know, a store shelf or something. They're scraping me out and calling my baby 'products of con-*cep*-tion.'"

Wayne threw his hairbrush at the mirror. "God I'm sorry Honey, but I give up. We can't work with this."

"And . . . and then she gets ahold of my chart. And she says, oh *I couldn't believe this*, she says 'it's just as well, considering what happened to the last one.' Who the *hell* does she think she *is*? I'm going to call my *manager* —"

Marty didn't know what to say. But it was looking bad for today's shoot and they only had this sound stage for two days, then it was off to do the happy ending on a bus station set on the other side of the lot. She started again:

"So I told her I didn't know what she was talking about, I just wanted to die or something. And she says — you know, off this chart — she says that the last baby was a 'failure to thrive' like that makes any sense. Like it was my fault the stupid lazy *au pair* didn't pay enough attention to him while I was working my ass off *in the jungle* for Christ's sake with an important Director! And what does 'failure to thrive' mean anyway? It's just one of those medical, uh, *jargon* things where they don't know what they're talking about! Okay? I mean, *right*, you want a doctor, at least go and get me a script doctor instead. Clean up the dialog!"

Then she did it: she turned on Marty and came at him with her arms out. Me, he thought — Marty, the Fabulous Burrito Boy.

"What do you think, Marty Bebop? Am I right?"

They were arm-in-arm with clutching fingers. "Well, uh, you know, it's like what Preston Sturges said. About dialog. Something like, 'Dialog's all the clever things we'd like to have said, but didn't think of at the time.'" Where did he get *that* one? And she bought it, the mood shifted.

"Sure, hey, you're right. I guess I just needed a rewrite with that bitch."

It must have been a private joke because then Eddie, Wayne and Exene all locked their pinkies together and screeched, "*Re*-write! *Re*-write!"

"I woulda torn into her all right." She giggled. "What do you always say, Wayne? 'I woulda tore her a new one!'"

Marty had to hand it to her — Exene did a great Wayne. Better than *Wayne* did Wayne . She went back to the makeup chair, blew her nose in one of Eddie's Kleenexes, and nodded. Apparently, with tears and a single sob, Laura Trent-Sampson's range of despair had covered a slight to her celebrity self-regard and little else. Eddie started the repairs.

They would shoot today. For at least twelve more hours Marty wouldn't have to think about what awaited him at home.

12

That evening Marty watched Bibi move about the bedroom as she packed her clothes and a toilet kit. He was fascinated, horrified, helpless.

"I mean, are you moving, like, down the block? Out of town?"

Marty was trying to figure out the scale of her intent, whether intent even mattered, or if it was like what the Teamsters say every time they move the production company to a new location: no matter how far you go, a move is a move whether it's down the street or across town because you still have to button up the trucks and park them all over again. In any case, it looked pretty certain that no matter where Bibi was going or why, starting at this moment he was living alone once more.

Bibi eyed him without altering her deliberate rhythm. She packed her tampons and diaphragm at the same calm step-by-step pace she'd used to pack her dirty socks. Her whole life was that way, graceful, careful, the intimate and the public equally guided by an inner gyroscope. Marty had feelings that were too big for all the civility they were showing. He wanted to punch a wall, scream profanities, but moreover he wanted to catch and preserve a memory of her near the frosted bathroom window, her wavy blonde hair defined by soft white backlight, her boyishly wide shoulders over the plane of her lean back that pinched to an hourglass waist. If he caught her at the edge of this camera-memory just when her averted gaze passed beyond the frame with her eye-line disconnected from the center of the composition, the visual design would graphically represent tension and loneliness. It would look compelling in black & white, a Garry Winogrand moment — street photography, only here in his bathroom.

Then he remembered the self-conscious dissatisfaction he'd sometimes had with her appearance, the moments he'd dwelled upon her microscopic flaws that were confirmed only in that they'd kept her from being the star Exene was. The subtle imperfection of the line of her nose in profile, detected solely by the camera's magnification, was less significant in life than the physical difference between his brother and himself, assuming Craig still looked more or less as he did five years ago. But Marty had sometimes let her image affect his desire, and not until now, where there were no images involved and hating himself for ever letting her beautiful-but-not-camera-magical image count, did he see what he'd cost himself. Images were unthinking, beyond being affected by logic and reasoning. But wasn't love, too? And if he was losing Bibi because of the images he was chasing, because of the screens yet to be filled, were they only the crushes, the schoolboy stuff of sensation, and instead real love — having Bibi — was the giving of himself, somehow? The two of them choosing one another? He couldn't answer this. Didn't want to. The image-stuff that movies were made of, what he must focus upon, required all of his living energy and focus.

She had given up on Hollywood while on the set of a fake tropical island, and tonight had asked him again to leave the Industry with her. Start over together in some other way, some other place. But now that she was no longer part of his odyssey toward control over a movie screen, for that reason alone he was unable to make a big enough place in his life for her. He was staying.

"Should you really be asking me, Marty, or asking yourself?"

"About. . . ? Bibi . . . c'mon, I'm not the one moving out."

"About whether to live this way. With these people. Where everything is . . . a hustle."

"Why shouldn't I? You keep bringing it up, but I've never seen the point. Yeah, it's a hustle, but so what?"

"Because it's making you angry. Frustrated. Cynical. Because you don't even know why you're in it anymore."

"No, no you don't. *You're* the one. The one who's so overexposed as an extra you can't get hired on your 'A' card. You wanna get cast in speaking roles but how can any self-respecting agent take you seriously? You've walked through every network cocktail scene filmed in the last three years!"

She slapped a folded pair of jeans into an open suitcase. "God, I really want to stay now, so *bad*. . . . Thanks, Jerk."

"And that thing at the lagoon, tearing up your time card — you just can't do that. Besides, I'm not cynical. I've just got enough guts to see this thing through, until —"

"You and your 'guts.' Everything's guts. Yes, you're cynical. It doesn't take any guts to be a cynic."

Still she didn't break her pace. She filled one suitcase, opened another. Only now she wouldn't look at him, even meet his eyes with a flat scan of her own until she paused as if silently rehearsing. "I . . . I've always felt like I owed you. . . . I mean, when I first got out here, when I started doing the Extras work, I was a mess. It could've been dangerous, you know? Where I was looking for things that I had no business looking for. You gave me some time, you made me feel better about *me*. . . ."

He wanted to crush her to himself for at least acknowledging that much — that he'd meant something to her after all. That sunburst in his chest of feelings for her made him think of the night she had taken a call for a crowd scene, playing a refugee in a war film where she and her fellow extras had to struggle through wind-machine waves onto the thin beach at midnight, and do it soaking wet again and again until her skin was purple and her limbs locked up in the harsh winter damp of their Castaic Lake location. It was outside the 30-mile drive-to limit and when she called him at 3 AM inconsolable at the thought of going home on a studio bus, he had gladly given up his own sleep to wrap her in down and wool and bring her home where skin-to-skin beneath every blanket he owned he entwined his arms around hers, pressed his legs through and against her silken limbs, gave off his heat to bring her back to the feel of human flesh and blood until languid caresses and shared breathing made them one skin, one body.

"So living with me, here, this has all been returning a favor?"

Bibi stopped packing and hit a latch on a hard suitcase. "*Jerk*. . . ."

"I'm learning how to slough off the nonsense. I'm focused, Bibi. That's all. You have to be, it's in the job description." Then he wondered if he'd said that before, told her to get out. Even with his near-photographic memory, he really didn't remember. Too many sixteen-hour days, too much chronic fatigue. "How long will it be this time?"

"It's over."

"No. I mean, *please* — I need you here. You know that's what I meant." He endured one of those stage beats. "Pause," the scripts sometimes said, writers parenthetically hoping to tell the actors what to do, how to time their feelings between words. Marty remembered old Charlie Foster Kane telling his young wife Susan that from now on they would do things her way, not his, before slipping and saying "don't do this to me." But as in the great movie, it wasn't just him this was being done to.

"You don't know what you meant, Marty. You never do any more."

"Give me a second chance."

She blew out a long breath and started counting on her fingers. "Yeah, it goes like 'second chance, seventh chance, and fourth, and sixth....'"

"Bibi, please, not in the middle of a shoot. Let me wrap this one and I'll get myself straightened out. I can't even *think* when I'm working as a Second."

"You're an A. D. nine months a year."

"Yeah, but the other three months I'm really smart."

She smiled vaguely and shook her head, still bending, stuffing, picking up, her wonderful athletic frame taking the measure of the space only to soon leave it behind.

"I know what it is, Beebs. You want too much from me, too early. Like a house in Encino and, and . . . *kids*, when I haven't even — I need more time."

Why was he lying like that? He stared at the blank expanse of living room wall that he could see from the bedroom. It was where he was going to hang some of his cartooning and drawings and paintings, if he ever got around to drawing and painting again. Or maybe some photography. How did he get himself into this? Before he had ever set foot in Hollywood, he'd innocently thought being in the Directors Guild of America would give him some immunity, some dispensation from personal mess. But he was not a Director, he was a clerk, a cog in K-Swisses with a headset. That was one of the many reasons why it was called The Industry, why he was one of the machine-part "little people" that comedians included in their Hollywood jokes. Small wonder nobody before Bibi would live with him for long, even if he was a clean and reasonably compassionate guy and made more money than he could reveal without feeling guilty. Nobody sleeps with a cog if they have a choice. Bibi had stayed longer than the others but had also seen the truth a while ago: Life's a bitch, life's bearable. It's doable, so you fall down, get up, and you move on. If she could work through the disappointments, why couldn't he? Were his dreams that much bigger?

"You'll never find another place like yours, not in Santa Monica. I mean, with rent control. . . ."

"I don't know, I don't know. . . . What're *you* gonna do, Marty?"

"Finish the movie."

"And then?"

"I don't know either."

"You *ought* to know. It's like you're giving up everything because *someday* you'll be a big freaking Director. And then pushing people around, doing whatever you want to them, that's the whole point, isn't it?" She stared at a space somewhere near his neck. "You're like that weird creepy joke you always tell. The one that's supposed to be so *meaningful.*"

"What? Which —"

"'Why does a dog lick his balls? Because he can.' You go on this way just because you can."

"So it's 'get a life'?"

"No. No, you've got a life. Everybody's got a life. Some good, some really suck, but everybody has one. Only you want to be in charge of everything and everybody except for that part."

"I have no idea what 'that part' means."

She turned on him, wide-eyed. "It's the part that says you don't have to be at a podium accepting your damn Oscar to be happy. Do you know it, Marty? That part? No, but I guess I don't know it either. I'm going home, wherever that is. . . . And maybe it means you have to decide whether you *want* a home. God, I. . . . I don't know what you'll finally get out of all this. Hollywood. Movies. But I'm looking at someone who used to be a sweet, funny guy, who's turning into a . . . who knows what? Up until now, at least every once in a while I'd see a guy who wanted to do the right things. For the right reasons. And you don't seem to have a clue how rare that is."

And still she sat there on the edge of the bed, giving him that chance, though looking as if she wanted to yell at him just for being a moron. If this were a romantic comedy, the Man, played by himself, would now get another chance, step up to reclaim his lost love. Kill something off within himself that had destroyed romantic mating, and come back renewed, "the same only different" as they say in *The Awful Truth*. In happy endings, nobody blows the second chance. He *was* a moron.

Her continued presence might be an opening, an invitation like a blank greeting card where Marty got to fill in the words. Bibi was hurt, disappointed, yet he found himself building a frail scaffolding of hope that she was still willing to stay and even risk getting hurt again if Marty couldn't find some bigger aim, some personal meaning that he could share with her in this soul-consuming Industry. Her gift was giving him something for nothing time and again — affection, attention, an ear in sympathy if not always empathy — giving herself, then giving more without *needing* to give, a choice made with no certainty of receiving anything back from a driven Assistant Who Would Be Director, and apparently not even caring if he became one or not. For a moment he was able to imagine living with her for a long time with the grace of not having to prove much. But he'd *had* a long enough time with her, and here they were.

"So here's *my* idea, Marty. The one you don't want to hear, where me and you, we just pick ourselves up, go somewhere else for a while. Except somewhere in the real world."

"And do what?"

"*Live*. I don't know — what does everybody else do?" She shook her head. "I guess if you're ever . . . you can track me down. It's up to you."

The moment called for wisdom. He didn't have any. If he'd become a little harder on the surface it was because he had to be. He'd done that, just hours earlier with his Brother-From-Nowhere. *Bang*, the hell with *him* without a moment's hesitation, right. . . ? Here in Hollywood you had to see what would help you, and what would stand in your way. Choose. Climb the ladder. Win.

Maybe he did tell her once that she was the one who ought to get real. Get out of the business. He wasn't absolutely sure because the lack of sleep in his job messed with brain-chemistry or something. But if he did say it, he might've broken her heart, and then what? She had a right to her own dreams.

She snapped one final latch. "Do you want to be a Director, or do you want to direct movies? There's a difference, y'know. . . ."

She was getting up now, pulling her luggage across the carpet. Time to do something, if he —

The soft *plip* of the bolt as she went out the door shot through him like a brick through glass.

13

*L*upe waits for Marty to go on. His teleology of the day — that a shake leads to a burger and fries, then to trust — has so far proved correct and it's been gratifying to see Lupe accept something from him, even if he's only offering Johnny Rockets's finest caloric overload. He orders sodas for both of them.

"So Aunt Beebs has been there, when we needed her. For C.T.. Just not the way I would've hoped for. I mean, she's had her own life, in L.A. ever since the movie. . . ."

"Her an' you ever get married?"

"Uh . . . no. Long story. Different story." But maybe it's not, maybe he has to reveal even more than he intended. Maybe he has to tell both C.T. and Lupe how hard it is to stay with anybody, how hard it is to live up to their expectations even as you try to match the expectations you have of yourself, kids or not. That's the payoff for finally relinquishing this story to them — that they'll understand how having a kid doesn't fix anything, that instead it guarantees that things will only get harder if what you truly want is to live happily ever after with each other. Then there would be the payoff of making them understand that a movie star can't give them "happily ever after" either, no matter what.

"So tell me more about how you two are gonna do this, pay your bills. You'll need rent. Insurance. There'll be doctor's bills, you'll need a car. More school, if you decide you need it."

"Like I said before, I can do stuff, make money. Work at home with the baby."

He forces a smile. Stuff. Compared to what he went through to bring C.T. home, to get him away from his birth parents and take it all on by himself, this plan of theirs isn't exactly a three-act Hero's Journey. He knows he's self-aggrandizing, but when you do the parenting the right way it's as if you offer up your own small death for the new life of another, and how can these two do that when they haven't even lived yet? In his improvised flail of bringing C.T. home from a movie set, he botched whatever goodwill he might still have scrounged up with Bibi. Gave up everything besides the child that he thought mattered at the time. Movies, love, all for the baby.

"You're never ready, but you two are a lot less ready than most. Less than I was. And could you do it alone? Without C.T.? Because that's what the odds are, that you two won't make it together."

Lupe seems unfazed by this consideration. "So when you an' Aunt Beebs split, she didn't love you no more?"

"I think it was more she gave up on me. And later, when I had another chance, I made some mistakes."

"An' she gave up on C.T. too? Just visits and stuff?"

"No, it was never . . . giving up. He was just never her problem. He wasn't part of her life. At least not enough, not at the beginning. I'm just grateful that she's been around sometimes through the years, that he knows her. All the check-ins and cards, and the phone calls whenever C.T. needed someone to just hear him out. Someone besides me, especially when we were knocking heads."

The story he's trying to share, intended in part to show them what they'll be giving up in each other if they bring their baby home, didn't make for a very clear picture back then, or even now. It just ended lonely.

• • •

When they finish their food, it's an easy stroll from the mall to the State Capitol Park where the giant white Capitol itself was built during Abe Lincoln's time. There are trees here almost as old, and the squirrels are huge, on a scale with the looming dome, fed daily on state workers' lunchtime handouts. Lupe seems to draw energy from the clear air, and the movement, even though the weight of her child is starting to give her a swaying gait.

"C.T.'s father is dead. You both know that, right? So with all this Hollywood talk, it's not like some secret king from the hidden fortress is coming back, nobody's gonna claim his throne and make C.T. prince of all the land." He tries to ignore the nagging fear that Laura Trent-Sampson might be trying to do just that. Lupe stares at him that way again; he concedes it's his fault this time. "There *is* family, though. People C.T. doesn't know about, in fact people *I* don't know anything about either, except that I assume they're alive. How's he handling things so far?"

"He's bein' hella cool. I think now he wants to hear it straight from you, though, know what I mean? Like maybe you oughtta tell it to him more yourself now."

Marty hopes "hella cool" means that he's raised a resilient kid who could listen to this Nyrop-saga and not turn it into some kind of personal failure, that he's not one of those sad cases where a child blames himself for death or divorce in the lives of his parents. But Marty knows from his classroom years that being a resilient kid is, first, luck of the draw, a miraculous innateness, though as an educator he's supposed to be able to cultivate it within a kid; there are techniques, they say, if you get ahold of them before high school. Before kindergarten, even. And he's had C.T. from his son's first breath, his first sad cry for air, so his hope might not be misplaced.

"He's okay so far, with who his mother is?"

"Aw, it's kinda weird, you know? Like it's a fairytale or something."

"Mm-hmm. How mad is he? That I've never told him any of this?"

"I don't know, it's like he don't say much about it. And you being blood after all, an' you coulda tol' him a long time ago."

Marty is trying to formulate a tale-spinning strategy on the fly before C.T.'s mother does something beyond tracking them on the phone. He needs to make his decision to hide her from C.T. at least understandable, if not easy to accept. But his second angle of attack will be to deliberately fill his son's head with the errant life of his birth father as well, and make C.T. understand that in his and his brother's lives, long before C.T.'s birth, there were histories, family pain, decisions made that were never to be repeated.

Marty had once re-created himself as a movie Director only to find that it was not by being a Director, but by giving it up, that he had ended a circular anger within the Nyrop family, running with a child until he found a way to make a new family where no inescapable template awaited. While it's probably too much to ask of anyone, let alone an emotional seventeen-year-old, C.T. has to understand that.

They find a bench and immediately attract entitled pigeons. Lupe heaves a sigh, content in the warm sunlight to let Marty continue.

"Okay.... Look, he's gotta learn some more things about his father. Things I don't think he'll like. That's why you're such a help to me right now. I think it'd still be too much to hear all of it from me, like I had an agenda or something. Like I'm trying to make comparisons between his father and me or justify what I did, and I know how easily he gets pissed off."

She nods, not appearing entirely convinced. So he tries to get the backstory right, the part just before C.T.'s father and Marty saw each other for the first time in almost five years, the time Eric the actor came to Hollywood to cast Marty for a role in the theater of Eric's life.

14

E ric eventually had a chance to tell Marty how, after Marty turned him away from the Studio gate, he retreated that evening to the Château Marmont under an unfamiliar, nearly-extinguished Los Angeles sky. At the time, Eric felt like one of his favorite film characters — David Bowie, as "Thomas Newton" in *The Man Who Fell to Earth* — as if he'd left a wife and children behind on his desiccated home planet for a world apparently made of water. Eric was just hoping not to end up like Bowie's Newton, alone and marooned and face-down in gin.

He awoke in his room from an hour's sleep and considered taking a shower but had no energy to stay on his feet. He fell back across the bedspread and studied the ceiling, a traveler in the wrong time zone. He thought of his first visit in nearly a year to his small daughters, Amy and Jenna, at their mother's apartment; how two nights ago, just before he left New York for California he'd read to them an Alison Lurie book about *Fabulous Beasts*. One of the beasts among the unicorns and dragons and basilisks was the Mimick Dog — an animal who, if you hadn't been kind to it, would shame you by imitating you relentlessly. It would see you for exactly who you were, shadowing your every word and gesture until anyone witnessing you and the Mimick Dog together would fall down laughing. Laughing at you, as you were humiliated by this mirror-creature. Eric's daughters were fascinated by such a beast, asking Eric to read the Mimick Dog page three times:

> The Mimick Dog is one of the cleverest of known creatures, and has a wit surpassing that of most humans. It can easily be taught to jump, dance in time to music and play many tricks; and of its own accord will imitate all manner of beasts and men. . . . You are sure to be agreeably entertained as long as you treat it with respect and consideration. Indeed, to do otherwise is risky. . . .

I've never been that, or done that, Eric thought that night. That's a power I've never wanted.

Then he'd done Daffy Duck for his girls, watching them dissolve into blubbery laughter with tongues halfway to their chins, spitting and slobbering at each other as Little Daffys until their mother sighed her disapproval at the doorway and the fun went out of the bedroom like air from a pin-burst balloon. He was ushered out of the apartment by the same wary caseworker who had permitted the exceptional visit. Now he wanted to stop thinking of his girls' faces because the hurt was too much. But their expressions of desperate expectancy — worn like party masks on his rare visits, so that they might receive unremitting entertainment from him — came lapping back in waves. He tried to summon a perverse balm of childhood "sense-memory," of a distracting connection with his own father, another screwdriver-for-a-chisel. His weak attempts at it were disintegrated by the insistent images of his daughters and there were no given circumstances of a scripted scene to carry him aloft into performance. He could only conjure instead the memory of his hands, the fingers and palms of bone and sinew that had betrayed him, betrayed his precious sweet children; if he could only burn the skin from these hands he would, back then or now, and strip out the tendons and ligaments and muscles that had met those little faces with force and shock that wasn't meant for them at all but for vengeance against a long-dead parent, hands that hit at a memory strangling a boy who wanted not just hands but limbs too, simply to feel them around himself, the embrace of a mother, a father. For himself. He hit his daughters because they wanted what he had wanted and some unspeakable darkness within him played out the scene like an encore. . . . And still they recovered, still later had begged for more entertainment.

Instead, he tried to block Amy and Jenna from his tractionless thoughts by dwelling on the twin deaths in today's headlines: of cartoon voice man Mel Blanc, and Sir Laurence Olivier. It was natural, not morbid, to guess who'd be next, what voice, what actor. It gave him renewed focus to think about death scenes, almost always an actor's silliest moment. He hoped that when he drew his own last breath it would be just like a cartoon when either Daffy or Bugs or Yogi Bear is about to escape some revoltin' development: his legs will blur like spinning wheels, there'll be a zippy *bzeewww* bullet sound, he'll have speed lines shooting out behind him in the opaque dust. And all the while there'll be the guy on the slide-whistle going *Fwhee-oo-whee-oo-whee-oo.*

It was working. Eric could no longer see his daughters' faces at all, only Road Runner-like *whooshes*. He picked up the newspaper from the hotel carpet and re-read the headlines for the second time that day. He smiled; it was difficult to feel sad for Sir Larry, Man of a Thousand Noses. Olivier did so much for so long and then, from what Eric could read above the fold, had gone quietly in his sleep surrounded by his loving family. The same day as Mel Blanc. And with Blanc, there went Daffy. And Bugs, and Sylvester, and Pepe LePew. Eric couldn't remember making a specific decision about it, but Mel Blanc was like his own confabulated family, the source of Eric's acquired name.

Eric shifted his head on his pillow and was struck with a creeping despondency that had nothing to do with Olivier. He'd come to find his brother Marty. He'd found him. And nothing worked, nothing about it seemed right, as if the moment they'd last seen one another five years before when Marty learned of Eric's unforgivable act against his own children had happened only moments ago; as if the day they had parted as brothers amidst guilt and betrayal almost fifteen years before had been only yesterday. Eric tossed the newspaper at a chair.

He wondered if his jet-pilot father heard the slide-whistle every time his plane leaped from the runway and its wheels *whumped* into the plane's belly. It must've felt like an escape for Jim Nyrop too, like playing an improvised character: his father, running from what he'd just been, to what he'd be next, avoiding the trap of predictability; an actor playing his character as *being* an actor within the scene. New, re-newed, made up from moment to moment by the reality of doing, by the task of controlling the flying machine regardless of whatever mess he'd just left behind at home. Big scary Jim Nyrop, maybe humming, "Off we go, into the wild blue yonder. . . ." *Fwhee-oooo.*

That's the guy, Eric thought. Whoever he is, the next guy I'll really miss when he goes is the Whistle Man, blowing the score for his own exit. *Fwhee-oo-whee-oo-whee-oo.* He'll be *out* of there, stage left.

Eric punched out a phone number, waited. Then, with his voice cracking absurdly: "Tthhhhhtill lurking about . . . !"

Eric knew Marty would recognize one of their shared "Looney Tunes" moments, where Daffy lets Bugs talk him into checking out a pursuing danger, sticks his head out of their hole, and gets the crap blasted out of him by Elmer Fudd, who is in fact still lurking about with his shotgun. But on the phone Marty only listened silently.

"Hello, then, Marty. Just hear me out. Five seconds. I've got money committed to a production. There's a lot involved but it all falls into place if I can get Laura Trent-Sampson to play the lead."

Marty's delayed laughter was raspy, out of shape. "So what could be easier than that? Yeah, why *wouldn't* she want to do it? Some little experimental rat's-ass piece of New York cabaret shit, right? She's only the biggest freaking star in the world. What's the part? Joan of Arc? Or a singing filing cabinet? Something to show her range, some stretch for the poor Hollywood bimbo?"

Eric had caught Marty in some impenetrable mood. Empty years between their last time spent together wavered like a desert mirage. "It's revival of a classic, I won't bother you with the title. Look, on Sunday I'm meeting a guy named Takashi Itani at Musso & Frank's. He'll have two men from MSC of Japan with him, hoping they can unload money on an American play. A lot of money. A lot of *cautious* money they want to use developing what'll eventually be a film property. They've learned from mistakes like Sony's where they didn't have any product to run in their machines, so this time they're gonna make their own software for their hardware. These guys are fanatics about preparation, taking it step by step. It's all business with them, and they're gonna buy a movie studio soon. I want you to come with me to Musso's and see for yourself. This is real."

"Real" and "Eric" still didn't go together for Marty. He hung up.

After a moment, Eric fingered a scrap of paper scribbled with the phone number of a former workshop student from New York, a successful young actor who now lived in the Venice neighborhood close to the beach. The actor had a room available if Eric needed to make lengthier living arrangements in L.A.. Eric wadded up the number, threw it into the basket and called room service to order a tuna sandwich and a bottle of Beefeater's.

15

O n the lot the next morning it kept coming back to Marty, over and over in strange vividness: that sob, that indelible sound he heard Exene emit in the makeup chair. He fought his tendency to regard most actors, especially the ones he considered celebrity queens, as quasi-humans getting paid far too much money for their winning draw in the genetic lottery. But now he was reevaluating Exene as an actor. She was clearly capable of doing things beyond the bad script they were all stuck with. Maybe she had some expenses that forced her to take the silly part, knowing she'd get paid half the budget, front end.

And that sob. . . . He didn't like that she had used it to toy with him and the Wrecking Crew. But he also surprised himself in realizing that he didn't really care that much that she'd done it. This promise of some unpredictable skill made her into a much more interesting tool for a director with a little creative imagination, if someone would only use it.

His neck was throbbing again, the muscles rigid, as he sipped at his craftservice coffee. He reminded himself that he really was glad to be here; the feature was a project he'd looked forward to largely because it would be a kick to stand on Carl Laemmle's old chicken farm — Laemmle, the founder of Universal — working on the paved-over acreage Laemmle had turned into a movie studio that once kept itself solvent by producing cheap horror films like *Frankenstein, The Mummy, Dracula.* . . . The *Phantom of the Opera* production once occupied this very soundstage and was the site where Lon Chaney stuck toothpicks inside his nostrils and became unforgettable, immortal. On what has been known ever since as the Phantom Stage, Chaney transcended genre, the skill that remains the occasional genius of Hollywood. Marty knew this to be true, he'd studied it in college.

But what no film student could know beforehand was how many things there were to be done each morning to make a movie possible, none of which were more important than managing Exene's promptness to the set. Though there were no strict expectations made of her, no presumptions of professional duty — she was too big, too famous, too iconic, her fame spilling beyond the boundaries of mere "celebrity" — nevertheless the movie machine couldn't proceed without her.

As he waited on her, Marty formed a plan to stay on the set near camera today. He'd get a production assistant or a sycophant out of the Production office to keep the actors' eye-lines clear of careless crew members. He didn't care if giving away one of his duties to a P.A. was a Directors Guild contract violation, he wanted to be where he could learn something for once and not running off to *shush* the grips for the Sound Mixer.

He especially wanted to see what Exene did with today's work because it was the most human moment in the story, the scene where her character is told by her husband that he's gay, he's leaving her, and he has something on her that he'll use to get sole custody of their children and keep all their money, which was mostly hers to begin with. The dialog never mentions the kids directly, so there is a subtext to work with. If Exene could take some of the behavior Marty had seen in the makeup trailer and get it in front of the camera, he would have an entirely new appreciation of her as an artist. It was what he longed to do himself with someone of her renown, to caress her with his camera and break the audience's collective heart.

And that was why they were all here, wasn't it? Bibi's parting comment still stung: of course he knew the difference between directing a movie and being a Director. He ached to put that understanding into action. With a face like Laura Trent-Sampson's on his screen, he would stroke her likeness with pans and dolly movements, frame her, push in on her, until the audience had no awareness of a distance from her, no sense that her world was separate from their own. His director's embrace of her would be his embrace on behalf of the world, his vision their vision, his feelings everyone's feelings.

He needed to sit down with Exene soon. Get her to talk about what she did to get ready for a scene, and tell her how he wanted to know more about actors. More than the considerable amount he was confident that he already knew. She'd wanted something personal from him the morning before, he'd felt it, and this was where he trusted his instincts, why he knew he'd be a good Director: when he focused on the storytelling, on characters' needs, he had real empathy and wasn't just one of those "My 38mm prime lens goes here and track-pivots over there" clones out of USC.

His head filled with yesterday's memory of Exene's stare. He got it finally, what it was with the blue saucers in the mirror: it was a sadness and a longing they were giving him, but moreover, they were a lot like Bibi's eyes, and with Bibi moved out of his condo there must be all kinds of subconscious associations working on him. As soon as he could, then, he would have to tell Exene that it was going to be okay, that he understood how she must feel about losing something, the miscarriage and all. He would apologize for being insensitive, even if she had jerked them around with the "Gotcha."

And he was thinking that, while he already missed Bibi terribly — there was a shaft of emptiness plunging through his gut when his concentration slipped and he thought of her, felt her absence — he would have to move on. Forget the whole celebrity thing, the X-Girl business. Laura was a working actor with marquee value, bankable. It was that simple. If he was going to claw to the top, get out of the Production column and be called Talent and make his own movies, it was time to strap on his war-gear and use this moment with Laura Trent-Sampson. The time to be with her quietly and privately just to have that connection, that talk, was now.

Camera was close. They were pushing the 8 o'clock shooting call and even here on the studio lot Marty's heat-and-smog-I-Hate-L.A.-headache was already in place. They had the setup and he had put the extras on folding chairs at the other end of the stage with their own donuts and coffee, not wanting to disrupt the lighting of the set with a background rehearsal. He had his spot picked out just off-camera to see Exene's performance, as if he needed to be there to give the extras their action cues. All they lacked now was their star.

He had already updated his immediate superior, the First Assistant Director Cal Reardon, trying to give Cal an idea of the lingering effects of yesterday's sad news; not to violate Exene's privacy, but for professional reasons, because any First A.D. would get reamed if he couldn't turn to an irate Director and tell him exactly why they weren't ready to do a shot, while making delays sound like bad luck and cruel Fate — which carry more weight on a working movie set than lost babies.

Marty hovered near the personnel door ready to sheepdog Exene discreetly past any civilians who might be near the sound stage, or even past studio employees who might slow down near her motorhome, hoping to get a look. He was impatient for a double dose of caffeine and ibuprofen to sheathe his fatigue, until he heard — more closely felt — his name crackling through his radio headset. It was the charmless First Assistant Cal:

"Wheel in the meat."

Marty was now to run and tell the lovely and talented Laura Trent-Sampson that camera was ready, that she was to come in immediately if she would be so kind, and rehearse one last time.

He keyed his radio. "Thanks, Cal. You could've given me a warning."

Cal's mutterings were low, tense: "Don't give me any shit about who should've been doing what. And where are my goddamn extras?"

Marty's heart sank. He'd been caught flat-footed, and now protocol was upside down because he'd have to bring in the star ahead of the background players and camera would be waiting on him as he rehearsed the extras during last-second touchups, giving each of his human "Atmosphere" plausible activity.

"Working on it —"

"Marty, you got some issue with getting her blonde ass onstage *now*? Talk to me, kiddo. Bottom line — our bereaved Exene's willing to work, right? Nobody's shutting down, no production-killer here, no God-inflicted *force majeure*, yes? So what the fuck's the problem? You copy that?"

Cal was a big fan of CB jargon but instead of giving him a "10-4" Marty keyed his radio microphone twice, making two quick static pops back into Cal's ear to indicate that he was on the case.

On his way to the makeup trailer he was headed off by Steve the craftservice man, a thin young laborer with a shaggy '70s haircut and cigarette-stained teeth. Steve mimed holding a phone and Marty jogged to the portable stand. Camera was ready, the engine that drove film production and combusted its money was revving, waiting for him alone to perform. He wrenched the receiver to his ear, fearful that he might be detained for more than a few seconds.

"Marty? It's Craig *and don't hang up again.*"

"Who . . . Craig? What — Craig who?"

"Oh, stop it. Would you just listen —"

"Jesus Christ. . . . Again? And why the. . . . Where *are* you?"

"I'm right outside the lot on, uh — I'm on Lankershim. Look, I went through this yesterday, the Burns Security clown won't let me through the gate without a pass. I swear to god, I'm the only person on the planet who's *not* walking right onto the lot today, like I'm wearing some sign that says 'Harass Me, I'm an Idiot.' What's this place you work in, Marty? Junior High? Call over and leave a pass, would you please? Will you do that for me?"

"My *brother* Craig, huh? So that'd make you. . . . Who? 'Craig Nyrop'? God. Let me think. . . . Nope. Don't know a Craig Nyrop. Used to, maybe, before he left me in a cloud of dust in some damn driveway. Before he fucking . . . *hit. . . his. . . kids*, after everything we'd been through. Well, it's been nice, gotta go —"

"Knock it off, would you? Leave any name you want. Come on, it's important. I need to get inside and talk to you."

Time had stopped. "Hey, I know, we could get you hyphenated. We could call you Craig-Eric, ah, DuBois-DeBlanc. I could tell everyone you're like Belgian royalty or whatever. You'd love it, you'd feel the kindness of strangers. . . . *Gotta go* —"

"Marty please, I'm serious."

Marty stared through the double-paned plastic square embedded in the personnel door. The outside light throbbed around the window edges, his irises couldn't keep up with the contrast between inside and outside. He clamped his eyelids to stop the ache. His headset came alive again with an almost inaudible beam of signal presence, a hiss of empty tone that made the hair rise on his neck. It was Cal again:

"Marty, *Marty*. . . . Sing me a song — 'Wheeling in the meat, wheeling in the meat, we will come re-*joi*-cing. . . .' C'mon, *talk* to me Marty."

He decided he didn't need a family reunion just then with his-brother-the-actor. The brother, he thought, who had probably ruined him on having kids forever. He looked at the telephone still in his fist, then jammed the receiver against the clear plastic tube of his headset mouthpiece:

"Gotta go. Really." He hung up.

He skipped outside and circled the long sound stage perimeter to the opposite side where Exene's mobile home was parked. He banged on her door and waited with his uncovered ear inclined toward the bumpy enameled skin of the trailer. He heard no sound, saw no jiggling of the trailer's truck chassis that would give away movement inside. It wouldn't be like her to simply ignore him, so he ran again, this time toward the makeup trailer. He should've known exactly where she was, should've had her "on his radar," as A.D.s described it, that was his job, his damn profession. . . . He pulled back the spring latch of the Airstream cocoon. Eddie and Wayne were putting their tools away into their cleverly hinged puzzle-box kits. Eddie at least made an inquisitive expression.

"Bringing her in?"

"Yeah. Seen her?"

"We're done with her, Pardner. As far as I know, she went back to her trailer."

"Okay fine — " Marty ran back toward the motorhome. The pounding motion kept him locked-in to duty, it kept his brother Craig's unforeseen appearance contained. *Fuck him. After all this time why now?*

He knocked, waited, knocked. He opened the door and found Exene sitting upright behind the compact kitchenette table, improbably sound asleep. He touched her fingers gently, expecting to startle her. When she didn't awaken, he found that he couldn't let go of her hand. His urgency to hurry her onto the set subsided. It was a miracle: she was radiant, flawless even to the human eye let alone the Panaflex cyclops. Wayne and Eddie had really done a job today, and right on time. Forget the extras, he'd been saved again. Turning over her pale monkey paw, he was surprised at the child-like thinness of her fingers, then marveled at the perfection of her nails, the dry warmth of her unmarked, unwrinkled skin. She was right *there*; he had never been this close, it was impossible not to imagine what the flat of her palm would feel like on his own cheek, how her hand would glide down his arm and tuck itself neatly into the small of his back and press him forward right into the rest of her.

He wondered how close to her face he could loom without waking her, if it was worth the risk of appearing a bit mad should she awaken with his tired red eyes watering inches before her own, if she would tell anyone about it, Eddie or Wayne probably, who would then tell everybody else. . . . Exene was polished off, lathed, camera-ready. It was too cruel to think of her now as a trowel-job, she was simply different from life. Perhaps superior to it, but really in another category, an artifact, her manufactured appearance just as much a part of her identity as was the vanilla-yogurt-plus-bone-structure-plus-cornflower-eyes creature who showed up at 5 AM. Without the distraction of the Wrecking Crew, Marty noticed that even her hair smelled sweet, her lips were parted and there was an animal spice on her breath like an odor pure coriander might make on the tip of the tongue. Something warm was within her that wafted out of the mucosal linings and organs of her insides and was not merely cosmetically applied. For the first time, Marty allowed that there was a beautiful living thing beneath the flawless patina. Someone who might care, feel, think, worry, give — give what? He had a purely animal need to be next to her, to slide down onto the seat and sink against her, flow around her, that paralyzed him. Her eyes opened; his heart flexed.

She smiled weakly, as if his presence were quite normal. "Ready, Bebop?"

His smile back was just as weak. "At your pleasure, Your Highness."

Next was to be "Picture," the camera would turn, photons would strike film stock, and with the Director they had on this feature, more unearned melodramatic pretend-emotions would become latent chemical imagery — unless his newfound artist-girl came through.

Soon he would take her hand once again, and somehow let her come to know the greater part of himself that was more than "Marty Bebop, A.D.."

• • •

As Marty came back through the personnel entrance with Exene, First A.D. Cal made a show of jamming shut the inner and outer doors behind them, yelling for effect: "All right! *Boys!* Shut it down. If you have to talk, take a walk. Boys, *boys* — ! We're on a red light! Settle!"

Marty winced. Only assholes ever said "settle" on a movie set, yet the expression had spread unchecked like a virus throughout the Industry from A.D. to A.D.. Then again, Cal was an asshole. And movie crews, like grade-schoolers, never would shut up.

He waved at the Sound Mixer and made the "rolling" gesture, a circular wiggle with his forefinger to prompt the Mixer to toggle a switch next to his Nagra tape recorder. This touched off a guttural buzzer and connected several flashing wigwag lights, the police gumball machines spread about the stage floor. Outside the personnel doors, red "recording" bulbs in wire cages lit up to prevent anyone outside the stage from walking in and spoiling a take. It was all overkill, they wouldn't be making picture for some time until after rehearsals, touchups, camera and lighting adjustments, a hundred other little things. But it was Cal's set for everything but creative decision-making, everything but what mattered. *O*, Marty thought, to move up to First Assistant Asshole.

Steve Craftservice hurried to him again, loping with worried responsibility. He waved back toward his gurgling coffee urns. "Picture next, Marty? I just put on a new pot — do I gotta shut it off?"

"Nah. You know Cal. He's just . . . being Cal."

Steve imitated shrewdness. "Ah-hah. Ahhh, *hah*. . . . Hey, that guy's back on the phone — he says he's your brother and he's on the outside line."

"Oh, shit." He went to another phone mounted on a plywood board between wall studs and stared at it. When he did pick it up, he whispered: "I can't talk now. We're on a red light. I'm *shushing* in here, you know? — Marty the Human Wigwag. I'll call you."

He hung up again, wondering for a moment where he would reach Craig even if he wanted to. Still at the Château? He hadn't been very kind last night, not when he hadn't talked to his brother in years. But he had no desire to speak with him then or now, and had long nursed his feeling of being justified with an acute righteousness. They'd been orphans together, except Craig lied about their plight, cruelly repeating a fantasy that their mother wasn't really dead but had run from them when a freak of mistaken identity allowed it, that she made her magical presence visible to his brother on occasion but not to Marty and for no understandable reason except to hurt him. His brother had a way of making Marty feel abandoned by his own mother over and over again, and then at eighteen Craig ran away to the bright lights or some such illusion and left fifteen-year-old Marty alone, running after Craig down a stony driveway behind the first

Yellow Taxi Marty had ever seen, alone in the swirling dust with the cab spitting gravel at him from its rear tires until it became small in the wavy mirage of hazy trees and Michigan heat and humidity. Without the words to describe the falling, bottomless sensation, Marty knew at that moment that he would never allow himself to have a dependent need for anyone again.

He tried to imagine what Craig must look like out there, probably pacing back and forth atop the scant curb space next to the security booth with its aluminum sliding doors closed to him. Theatrically cursing the traffic that hissed up and down Lankershim. Cursing Scotty or whoever had the Main Gate post today. Cursing California and all things Hollywood, cursing his little gone-Hollywood brother.

But it was the ghost of that eighteen-year-old in the rear window of a receding taxi that Marty could most clearly imagine, not whomever Craig must have become by now, and if he didn't let Craig onto the lot he wouldn't be forced to transform that ghost into the adult who'd been stuck outside the gate, wouldn't have to deal with a bodily apparition who might share memories with him from a boyhood but nothing else to be trusted. Instead of meeting his brother, it would be better for Marty to leech any utility — creativity? — when the time came from memory alone; from the loss of parents found by Michigan State Police as carbonized forms inside the husk of their father's Cessna, from Craig selfishly inflicting fabrications upon Marty just to help himself survive, swearing hysterically that their mother had survived the accident, that she lived to this day. Then more cruelly, that Mom, like a Dickensian spook, perhaps the Ghost of Parenthood Past, visited Craig from time to erratic time, choosing to appear only to the son most like herself and not to her bullheaded, heart-of-iron Marty.

Or, when the day came, Marty could use for creative fuel the bitter recollection of being orphans together after a plane crash, when the thing that could sustain an orphan most — a brother — was taken from Marty by Craig who left him behind as soon as he legally could. Marty's sterile reality after that leave-taking was fighting through each joyless day in the prison of a high school in a new town, then another school in another new town, fed and clothed by indifferent relatives, strangers in vague "cousins-removed" relationships until he could draw on the life insurance and Social

Security money to run, too, finding passion finally in studying — reveling — in what movies could be beyond Bolex fantasies. Marty gathered up his own learning, that in turn led him to the opposite coast from his brother.

Craig had begun as a fifteen-year-old to torture his twelve-year-old brother like this, and kept it up for three more years until he headed for New York to become an actor of all things. Not the career likely to lead to making amends over lying, manipulating, pretending. Not after leaving Marty alone in strange homes, strange towns. Lying, fabricating Craig-the-performer had shamelessly begged for love and approval from their parents, not in words but in pose and song and stagey gesture, had annoyed Marty and enchanted their mother and had driven their pilot father toward sarcastic and abusive rejection. This Craig, who was at least part of the reason their father flew drunk and took their mother down with him, deserved to be left and abandoned himself outside Marty's sanctuary of a movie studio. *Fifteen years, and the bastard thinks showing up on Lankershim is cause for celebration. Fuck him.*

And worse, much worse, was that the one time Marty had come to New York, had tried to at least see in the flesh his only family, brother-to-brother as adults, he learned that Craig Nyrop had become a man capable of slapping his kids around. Only once, but bad enough to cause a restraining order, and for a Nyrop, it was another surrender to fate.

With Exene delivered to the set, Marty called out for the extras, his "Atmosphere" to go to their starting marks, not bothering to round them up as individuals. At least with fifty of them on payroll today he could get thirty or thirty-five without trying, then fake the rest by "Loveboating" them back and forth in the same shot. They were his human coastal fog, as if by naming them Atmosphere they might arrive on the set as Nature does, unaided, a kind of weather he could do something about. Extras did indeed begin to roll in for him, his reward for having been decent to them so far today.

• • •

Then he lost her again. After rehearsals Exene left the stage for one last touchup before picture, but she wasn't in the makeup trailer. Marty ran to her motorhome. She was probably wringing it out, since everybody was allowed to have finite bladder capacity but a Second Assistant. Just as he skidded to a stop the door clunked, the motorhome jiggled. She was coming.

"Marty —?"

He moved forward so she could see him closely. She stepped delicately down from the trailer and stood so near him that he could smell the Binaca puffing from her tiny nostrils.

"Bebop, you know what else that bitch said to me?"

"Uhhh . . . the nurse the other night?"

"Yeah. She was leaning over me, you know, I was helpless on that table. Just . . . so helpless. And she looked so superior, like those nuns always did, you know what I mean?"

He smiled. He did know.

"And she says, 'Lady I don't care how famous you are, beauty's only skin deep.'"

"She . . . really said that?"

"Yeah! Well what do you *think*?"

Well of course, he realized, it was one of the dumbest clichés he'd ever heard in his life even though no one could function in this business without pockets full of catch phrases. But then here came the tears again, cornflower irises sparkling. Real tears or not, it was too late to get cute and sing "Beauty's only skin deep yeah yeah yeah" while he did the Temptation Walk. He couldn't believe he was putting his hand on her waist. *Her.* She was so thin.

"I think . . . I think it's probably pretty much true. People wouldn't keep repeating it if there wasn't something to it. You know. That's how we get stuff like that in the first place." He ground his teeth. *Wrong, Marty. She's scared.*

"Yeah? But what about, I mean, you don't think —"

"Sure, shhhhh, I think there's a little bit to it, but geez, wait a minute Laura. Steady here. Skin deep, but y'know — I think you have very . . . really *very* . . . deep skin, you know what I mean?"

He was embarrassed, ready to turn on anyone who might show up and to ask them, *Yeah? What'd you come up with?*

The camera was waiting at $7,000 dollars an hour and they needed this shot *now*. He didn't know if Exene was going to slap him or fall down laughing. Instead she threw herself at Marty with her fingers clenched in his hair and kissed him full on the mouth for what seemed to him like minutes in front of half of the Universal City Studios lot. Long enough for him to taste her sweet salty teary insides.

16

*A*fter they had a master shot tagged "print" for the Technicolor lab, Marty finally gave in to Craig's persistence at getting him to the stage phone. The guy was calling in with *voices*, as cartoon characters or imaginary people he was making up on the spot.

"So what do you do out here, Marty, what's it really like? Does the Assistant Director actually assist the Director? *Become* a Director?"

Marty laughed at the thought: *assist the Director, my ass*. He was willing to visit Craig in his room for a few minutes that night, so if Craig really wanted the details of an A.D.'s life, he could find out then. He named a time and told Craig to go away.

But the question stung, and on the way to the Château Marmont he wondered what his brother was trying to do to him. Marty was in Production, training only to become a broken-kneed, pot-bellied Unit Production Manager, standing in line to move up someday to sign cast and crew paychecks in some worn out trailer-office. He was no closer to directing his own movie than he was back at school in the TV/Film Department. Maybe further away, because now he had a sizable paycheck, a mortgage on a Bibi-less condo near the beach in Santa Monica, and a red Acura Legend humming and hissing around him as he drove to the Château. At least the car was paid for. Defeat could be so smooth and comfortable. Unless, unless. . . . He still burned from Laura's kiss, yet had no idea what it could mean.

It was sorely tempting to indulge in one of an actor's "What ifs?" What if Craig really had a "go" project, a potential green light — if they even used terms like that in the theater — awaiting only the last hurdle of Laura Trent-Sampson's attachment? But it was absurd to think so. After years of acting with his dilettantes in some New York closet, who did Craig think he was (besides "Eric Blanc," a pathetic name if Marty had ever heard one)? Maybe things were different in the theater. But then again if Craig needed Exene and her star-power, maybe they weren't. His brother spoke of producing a play, maybe having it adapted as a movie. But did he understand movie stakes, that they were huge, almost beyond an individual's comprehension? That even if an independent feature production had been put in the can for a dime, it would still cost millions and millions to advertise and distribute it? Of course, Laura Trent-Sampson's name alone was worth millions and millions. But what would Craig know of the calculus, the bogus math of dirtbag producers who understood only the power of ownership and hiding profit from the deserving? And why fool around by starting with a play? If he was so sure he could get Exene, he should just make a damn movie.

Marty had full confidence in the faultlessness of his reasons to wish Craig off the face of the earth ever since their parents died. Marty had buried the memory of Craig Nyrop well enough, only to hear him return — on the Phantom Stage no less — from the grave, penetrating through a wall phone, haunting Marty from the Universal Studios main gate. It was unfair, a victory over the past being overturned, nullified.

Invisible pals, invisible Mom. . . . Craig's childhood, then his adolescence, were a web of unresolved fantasies without climaxes, stories that he tried to press upon Marty, open-ended replays of early television's sitcom *Topper* and its friendly hauntings by the deceased, but with no final-draft shooting script for the Nyrops. What Marty could've handled instead from his brother was an epic, a made-up tragedy. He and Craig could've clung to each other back then as orphaned brothers while they were passed from relative to relative, telling their story back and forth like voice and chorus, using their father's Bolex camera (the one they'd used before for more pointless reasons). *That* was the movie they should've made together, playing out their own story until it became heroic, elevating the narrative's meaning to a transcendence won by parentless children of destiny. But then Craig ran.

Toward the end of their last vestige of family, when they'd still play-acted the Craig and Marty Show, they had talked about movies with teen-aged, magical leaps of thought about how so-called New Wave movies like *Bonnie & Clyde* and *The Graduate* were going to change Hollywood forever. Smart critics said so, it was in the papers, and the brothers would surf the crest of that wave to fame. But Craig, still stuck in fantasy and even now a cipher after fifteen years away, had instead become someone named Eric Blanc. So if the Nyrop family had any story left to tell, Marty was going to make damn well sure that he was the storyteller, and that beyond the public's need for Hollywood illusion, discovering "family" out of impossible circumstances would be the core of his *oeuvre*, his *Auteur's* embedded theme as some bright graduate student could pontificate in the next century. Of course, first he needed to direct something, anything. But maybe, he suddenly hoped, directing the Nyrop Story, or something close to it, would be what Bibi had meant by doing the right thing for the right reason, if he could only make that happen. Others could learn: his story would model recovery and triumph, a happy ending out of an unhappy family.

But before events went any further Craig had to be told clearly, firmly that he was not welcome here. Not on the set, not in L.A., not in Marty's life. He would soon be done with him. Again.

He avoided the freeways on his way to the Château since even surface streets in L.A. were clogged from 5 AM until midnight. No normal person would live here willingly. He squeezed the steering wheel at his seventh consecutive red light and scolded himself into considering that he might still forgive Craig's becoming someone else. As silly as "Eric Blanc" sounded, he could see where Craig-now-Eric's acquired identity must've felt right, sort of an emulation of their childhood hero Mel Blanc, the voice of Looney Tunes. He could see where Craig Nyrop becoming Eric Blanc — all of a sudden to be vaguely foreign, white, empty, and funny by association with Mel merely by re-naming himself — probably struck his brother as a colossal joke when he took off for his performing arts school. He could imagine Craig doing Mel doing the pre-Warner Brothers Woody Woodpecker: "Hi, I'm Eric Fill-In-The-Blanc. *Huh-huh-huh-AAA-ha!*" But the joke hadn't come in time to avoid the godawful humiliation and screams of "faggot!" from their father when Craig won a lead role in his first try at a high school play. The punch, the blood, the drunken challenge to be a man, to grow a pair, had all come before Craig's escape three years after the fiery crash, to wear makeup and costumes and pretend things in front of strangers. . . .

Finally he hit a green light, relaxed a little, then got through another one and turned onto Sunset with a circular wave of the steering wheel. He had to deal with Craig as efficiently as possible tonight, and fortunately that was one of a Second Assistant's real skills. Physical survival as an A.D. meant nudging the reluctant to do what was necessary to get them off the clock. Plus, if he dispatched Craig quickly enough he might get a little recovery sleep after working merely twelve hours from four-thirty to four-thirty today, prompting three different jokers at the wrap to ask, "Hey, working half-days?"

He found a parking spot on a side street away from the valets. On the other side of the brick pool-decking he came to one of the bungalows and knocked. He didn't know what to expect; after all the times he'd phoned out-of-town actors staying at the Château, he'd never seen the inside of the place. It'd been five years since that one visit to New York. Maybe by now Craig was fat, or whittled to the bone by AIDS, you never knew. The door opened, Marty stared. It was Craig just as he'd remembered him: several years of what — experience? not really age — were finely etched into his face. . . .

and then those fifteen empty years and even a few more before that vanish until Marty bounces a tennis ball off the wall above a backyard patio and he tries to remember why he ever enjoyed running after a real baseball, timing its hopping rhythm in the infield and seeing it into his big hands, swinging with all the torque he could give thirty-four inches of lathe-smooth ash with an Al Kaline signature burned into the barrel to hit that baseball over people's heads. Ever since his parents died he's had no team, no desire for one, and he's bewildered that it has turned out to mean something after all to play for someone else and not just for himself and now there is no one else. The shingle-sided dwelling he and his brother Craig are housed in belongs to people somehow related to them, but exactly how this is the case has not been part of a conversation as yet. Bouncing the tennis ball will eat up some time and help the slow crawl toward the weekend when Marty can roam nearby woods and creeksides without anyone telling him to be anywhere or do anything at someone else's appointed time.

His brother startles him by shoving open a sliding aluminum door and standing in Marty's way as the tennis ball dribbles off the edge of the patio.

"I got it this time — you're gonna see, I got it —"

Craig is holding a flat yellow Kodak box with a black bottom. He pries it open and there is a metal reel inside, solid to allow the Kodachrome to be loaded in daylight without exposing the 16mm film stock within. Marty waits passively as Craig pulls out several feet of developed film and sees only colorful streaks of light-struck leader; his hands grip tighter, move faster when he pulls out foot after foot of photographic blobs, meaningless shapes captured in frame after frame.

"You stupid idiot. You threaded it wrong."

Craig drops the box and reel to the ground. He's stricken, his fingers clutch at something untraceable. "I swear, Marty — I saw her."

Marty sees only that the truth machine, the Bolex camera that could redeem his brother and that could patch the ongoing, angry rupture of brotherhood, has been misused as a tool and by Craig's intent, and for that he has to turn and run across the yard and onto the oiled dirt road before he smashes his big brother's red and teary face with a fist. When he returns under moonlight and no one seems to have been aware of his flight, he finds the Bolex camera his brother doesn't understand and brings it back outside and breaks it into pieces on the cement patio.

• • •

Marty stared at his brother, then grunted and shoved Craig to the floor. "That's for showing up in my life again, motherfucker. I didn't know whether to hit you or fall down laughing. . . ."

Craig was breathing slowly, deeply, while flat on his back between the doorway and the bed. "So you assaulted me. I understand that's called 'Meeting Cute.'"

"And you can eat shit. And die. There — I've told you to your face, now leave me alone."

"Hello, I'm fine, the girls send their love to Uncle Marty. Never met him, but what the —"

"That's not my fault, you're the one who —"

" — It's *entirely* your fault. And how are you?"

"Save it. What's the big deal, you have to come all the way out here? Why now, why me?"

Craig rose slowly from the floor, working his shoulders loose. He sat on the bed and gestured Marty toward a chair. Marty stood in place, disappointed. There was nothing particularly special about a Château room. And the creation of "Eric Blanc" had no special presence either, no reality. Craig sighed and watched him, probably trying to read the scant output of Marty's clenched features, then rubbed wanly at the back of his head. When he finally spoke again it startled Marty, he'd already forgotten why either of them was here.

"So blunt. . . . As always. But you just betrayed your interest, pal. You already gave your exit line, and you're still here."

"You're a liar and no better than a murderer, and even worse with your own kids, and you know it."

"I'm not going to dignify that. You want to get into it again, now?"

"I don't have to —"

" — About how wonderful Dad-the-Alcoholic flew his plane juiced? Not once, a hundred times? With passengers? He *screwed up*, Marty. That's what happened. He's lucky, we're *all* lucky that they think it was only Mom he took with him and not 150 commuters out of Cleveland. You gonna let that paralyze you for the rest of your life?"

"'*That . . . they . . . think* —'? You're still — It's because you made him crazy. And Mom crazy. You turned us all crazy, you'd do anything for attention, you *made* them alcoholics."

"Aw, god. . . . No. Get it. . . . Children . . . are not capable. If you ever get around to having kids — or a little therapy — you'll understand that. *You're* the one with the convenient memory, Marty. You can blame me to your own grave, but —"

"And still the *lies*, the lies about Mom being alive. . . . '*That they think it was only* —' Just drop it, huh?"

"Sure."

"And another thing —"

"So we're not dropping it? You really do need professional help, Marty."

"Like you don't — ?"

"*Acting's* my therapy. If I could've taken you with me, I would. I was eighteen, Marty, what the hell did you expect me to do? Maybe that's what this is really all about, huh? This time I *can* take you along, make up for everything you think I ever did to you."

"An 'actor' is gonna take me along — A fuck of a lotta good acting did for you as a father, huh?"

Craig appeared to be fighting conflicting impulses, trying to find a quiet place within himself. "You need to learn what an actor does. Learn how to respond to your partner no matter what the script says you're supposed to feel. That's how you get real. The lens can see it, you should get that. And you look good, Marty. California becomes you."

Marty lied: "Yeah? You look five years older than you did five years ago. So what are you doing here *really*?"

"'Really'? I told you — all I have to do is explain the part to her and she'll want to do it. Isn't this how things work in Hollywood?

'Hey, look at me — I'm networking! Attaching an Element!' Marty . . . all I want you to do tomorrow is say, 'Laura, this is my brother. He'd like to speak with you professionally for two minutes.' That's all."

"Talk to her yourself. You're such hot shit, whattya need me for?"

"You know I can't get to her, no thanks to you hanging up on me. And I want you involved. It's what we used to talk about when we were kids. We could finally do something together. Make a real play, tell a story. Not crap like this you're doing here."

"What do you know about it?"

"What do I *have* to know about it? Here, my agent called around, I got some sides from your script —" Craig-as-Eric went through the pages quickly, reading bad dialog aloud for effect. Marty already knew what his point was. "This is total garbage. I'm in a place now where I could arrange things for you. Like being the Director. On *stage*."

"So I come to New York and live in a garret. For what, bread and water? Or do I pay you for the privilege?"

"Seven years here and you're still an Assistant Director. I don't even know what an Assistant Director is. I know what a filmmaker is. You used up seven years to be someone's Assistant? *Second* Assistant? This is a chance to move up. A career move."

"Like Elvis dropping dead off the toilet —"

Craig shrugged. "You'd have nothing to lose."

"Except my paycheck. Is your Producer going to pay me eight-hundred a week over scale?"

"I'm talking about a creative opportunity Marty, I can't believe. . . . What's *happened* to you out here?"

"Eight-hundred a week over scale."

"What the. . . ? Important actors do stage work for *nothing*. If the cast is all no quote — that's a movie expression, right? — why can't you do it too? For profit points down the line? I could get that for you, maybe later when it gets filmed. And you haven't even asked me what the play's about — or don't you care about that sort of thing anymore?"

"First of all — you don't know how any of this really works, do you? First, there's no such thing as 'net profit' in this business. They hide all of it, charge it all off. You're handing out back-end points on the gross? I'd like to hear from your money people on that one."

"Fine, come with me. Meet 'em. What do you want, Marty? A faster car, a bigger condo, some rented ass?"

"Oh god, knock it off. Is that some kind of crack about Bibi? Because if it is —"

"She the one who answers your phone? *You* sure as hell don't."

"She's moved out, she's nothing." His heart pounded, a flush moved through his face. How could he say such a thing about Bibi? That empty shaft through his gut again, boom — straight down to the floor. "What's it to you, what I want?"

"I'm sorry I asked. *Jesus.* I guess I don't have to worry about any nieces or nephews, then." Eric laughed, and in a way it felt all right for them to be together. At least the annoyance felt familiar, the way it always had as kids. "And you're still treating me like some kind of ax murderer. Look, nobody's sorrier or more heartbroken than I am about my kids"

"You've been lying about Mom and Dad, about yourself, ever since it happened. What's gonna change?"

"That was so long. . . ."

"You brought it up."

"No, you — Because I'm the only one who ever dealt with it. I was the only one who got *through* to them. You pinched your little butt so tight you squeaked when you walked out, *always* walking out. On them. On me."

"*I* walked out on *you* — ?"

"We both had our ways. Who cares anymore? We're *brothers*, Marty. We're all that's left."

Marty lurched out of his chair. They had just tried to catch each other in a net of guilt, a prelude to deeper thrusts of some sort they had yet to configure. Marty wandered the room, aimlessly playing with hotel props. Better to remain a moving target. No, it was better to get out of here because too many useless things were flooding back. He tried to leave. Craig blocked his way, so he lifted the front of his shirt six inches, with Craig in it, then dropped him on his heels so his head bumped the door behind, but he kept Craig in his grip.

"Stay out of my life. I was doing just fine."

"You're scared, aren't you Marty? Scared of me, of what I can do. Because I can make something. Out of nothing. That's what I could do when we were kids, and I can still do it. Laura, you ask her, she'll want to be part of that. I know you — for you it's always, 'Do it my way or go fuck yourself.' But are you any closer to having everything your own way? Are you creating any moments out here, anything that'll last? Huh? Jimmy Stewart, the 'pieces of time' we used to talk about? You've been out here for years and you're not even close. You don't assist the Director, then what do you do all day? When are you gonna make *your* movie, Marty? With what?"

"Not with you."

"You think you don't need me, or what I'm offering here. You're wrong. Tell me about today. You tell me what scene was so important you had to hang up and leave me standing outside the gate like some vagrant. You tell me what piece of precious Art you shaped with your own hands today."

"It's not my job to shape any precious fucking Art with my hands."

"Then why are you here?"

He didn't know at the moment. His aching joints, his ragged temper wouldn't explain it to him. This shoot, like any other, consumed his energy, his time, there was no way to think about anything else. He had two weeks to go with Laura Trent-Sampson, he was part of something fifteen or twenty million people might see, but for what? Already you could tell how the entire thing would play out. No one on the set was searching, discovering.

Finally he released Craig's shirt. His anger refocused quickly. Frustration with the here-and-now and past disappointments all fused. This bastard staring at him was right, he wasn't anywhere near getting his own shot at directing after working on shows with budgets piled by now into the hundreds of millions. Shows he wouldn't bother crossing the mall to see. And every disintegrating hunk of cartilage from his waist down told him every morning that he was already too old to have actresses call him "Bebop." He had to make something happen, with no idea when or how.

Craig seemed to have heard his thoughts, another of his annoying skills from childhood. "Given a chance — okay, what would you have done today if it was your own movie? C'mon, don't you at least wonder? Or do you get brain-dead just being out here in the sun? Like, surf's up, Dude?"

Marty sat on the bed for a moment as the day's shoot rewound and played back through his head. It was the day Exene had a chance to at least make one of Eric's "moments" that mattered. But of course it didn't happen that way. With a fat shooting budget and the biggest star anyone could hope for — she had a built-in audience and hauled it around like a Clydesdale pulling a beer wagon — they were wasting their assets to film a melodrama that no one could possibly believe in or care about, mounting it like a TV movie of the week. After all of Marty's dancing around her personal problems, after all the explanations and cautions about her lost products of conception and her fragile trowel-job, they had gone ahead and shot a useless master, a wide shot showing the whole scene in one piece from beginning to end just as it's taught in Cinematography 101. To them, that was production value, that was getting their money on the screen. Or — who knew? — keeping their money *off* the screen, because the lizardly producer Paul Amato knew he had Laura Trent-Sampson to guarantee his profit and why waste one moment, spend one dime extra on thematic shot design?

Here, Marty thought, was where a problem could've been an opportunity. Another of their Industry clichés. But no, his creative genius Director brought her in the restaurant door, walked her across the dining area and sat her down, making her Groucho a bit as she slid into her seat to keep her in the shot — a maneuver that was worth twelve blown takes by itself. Then he did all of her dialog in an over-the-shoulder two-shot, her with her husband. Cut, talking head single. Cut to husband "Hank," reverse-angle two-shot. Cut, reverse talking head single. Boink, boink, boink and not one single camera movement, the style choice that gives the audience their point-of-view, puts the viewers in the scene.

And what chance did any of that have to come soon to a theater near you? Here he was, a Second Assistant Director, he didn't even want to move up to First. He'd had his days in for two years, but who wanted the responsibility of organizing other people's idiocy, who wanted ulcers and no credit, no control, no voice that said *see this* and not *that*.

"What would I have done with Exene today? Okay, I'll tell you. What would *anyone* competent do...? It's like — like, take Scorsese —"

"The other Marty?"

He sputtered, then smiled. "Yeah, the other me. I would've hung the camera from the ceiling, done the whole thing in one. I'd get in the whole restaurant real quick from up there, then *move*. I'd descend, and track, pivot around with her. Make you sick with motion so you'd feel Exene's sickness, what her character felt. It's form-and-content, thematic metaphor, objective correlative —"

"How academic."

"It works, it's why they teach you that shit freshman year. Go for it, you'd find the scene. Then you drink her in, give her a chance to show the emotion and if you can't get it from her, you *give* her the emotion. You do it over and over until you break her down and get that sob again."

"What sob? And who the hell is 'Exene'?"

"Shut up a minute — You close-push and hold the camera right there in her face, for an hour if you have to. That's what America wants to see. Laura Trent-Sampson all in pieces, filling up the screen. She could do it, and she'd thank you for it after she saw the dailies."

He knew this. He, and a Wrecking Crew had stood witness: she could do it.

"That's tellin' 'em, Marty."

"Aw, fuck off."

"But you know what I'm hearing? No, it's what I *don't* hear. All I'm getting from you is 'the camera.' I don't even know the scene, but I don't have to. It was probably some kind of argument, right? Where's the love in her character? Or the love in whoever she's arguing with? What were they fighting for? You just want to take two helpless puppies by the neck and ram their skulls into the camera lens until something breaks. And that ain't directing, pal."

"What do you know about it?"

"I know what makes for bad acting. Easy negative choices. One-dimensional choices, no conflicted feelings. Every family scene ever written, I guarantee most actors'll just pick the negative motivations that make for the conflict. My daughter's a slut, so I hate her. My mother's too protective, so I hate her. Just the obvious.

Nobody stops and says to themselves, 'Where's the love?' Because that's where the real conflict is, it's inside every heart. People do *bad* things because of love, too, Marty. Maybe they're wrong, but the love's in there somewhere and you'll never understand anything until you look for it. That's directing. That's what you help actors with. You give them something to fight for."

"Yeah, well, I guess I know about actors —"

"I doubt it. I can see what you still think of me. But what I'm saying is truth, it's not a stage trick. It's how life works. Even with Dad, it would've been true."

"We're back there again? Oh, oh, I get it. So you're telling me it's because of 'love' the son of a bitch was almost never there? And when he *was* there he was plastered? And when he was drunk he was hitting us or hitting Mom or fucking anything with tits because he *loved* us so much?"

"Maybe. Maybe he had his reasons. He had an old man, too. I don't know. It's too late, we'll never know what all his reasons were, but at least I tried —"

"You didn't try, you made up a bunch of shit and then you ran away. Shut up, shut up, just . . . *god*."

His brother was only using their father again, knowing he could tie Marty in knots just with the mention of him. It was all too easy: Big Jim the United pilot was gone constantly. He would come home to sleep for fifteen hours, then wake up only to wave goodbye and go golfing, boozing, card-playing, whoring, or flying over Michigan lakes and pinetops in his Cessna four-seater until the day his plane went down with their mother aboard. When Craig tried to fill Marty's head with his tales, his arabesques of who their Secret Dad was really with during that last flight, it was as if those steaming flame-licked human shapes left behind in the accordioned cockpit had no finality. Craig's stories shifted, they grew new characters, new endings, new intrigue, until Marty's rage at him for re-telling his confabulations probably drove out Craig's faith in the power of his own storytelling altogether. By eighteen he'd finally stopped making things up for Marty. Perhaps until now. Why would Laura even listen to him?

You don't owe him anything, Marty thought, and he'll never help you and that's the only reason you deal with anybody out here. This is the guy, Marty ol' pal, who drove Dad so nuts with his clinging and pathetic begging for attention that Dad hit him and took off that last time drunk. Stinking blind soused and he flew his plane into the ground flaps down and throttle up. Craig pushed Dad away from both of us, tried to push Dad away from Mom too, with the girlfriends he knew about and all their "dazzle me, Craig" shit. Tried, but he couldn't entirely, and when they found Mom with her fingers burned into Dad's arm the two of them were just one huge roasted pig at a luau. *That's the guy you're dealing with, Marty.* Put a fucking Motown cap on it: "Love me? Love me? Do you love me now that I can dance?" *That* Craig Nyrop.

"So. . . . Are we gonna put on a show, Marty? Are you gonna leave a pass for me tomorrow?"

"God, you piss me off."

"Just leave my name. I'll show you what I can do for both of us."

Marty smiled tightly. "If you can do this, if you get Laura Trent-Sampson to say yes — I'll sweep out the theater and sell tickets and grill the hot dogs for free and say thank you for the opportunity. On my bleeding knees. Lying asshole."

● ● ●

On the drive home in the thinned-out traffic, the Acura Legend massaged Marty and helped him wait out the adrenaline rush of seeing his brother. A few channels of cool ocean air slid down the hillsides into the Valley and through his side windows. He felt lighter, purged. Before he got drawn into any more craziness, though, he had to think: why do this? Why help Craig in any way? Maybe Bibi had been right about another thing, but for the wrong reasons. Maybe it really was time for him to get out of here while he could still *get* pissed, still had his energy.

He didn't have to stay out forever. When he was reloaded with ideas and had some kind of property under his own control he'd come back to "The Industry." They called it that even before the screen could talk. It had *always* been Show and — a pause — Business; yin and yang; dreams and factories, all the rest of the paradoxes. But the would-be tigers and wolves who came out here to

Hollywood never saw this oxymoron of art and industry in time, or forgot about it once they'd seen it and let themselves lose their purpose. They were sucked in, spit out, until nobody could tell the tigers and wolves apart while they fed off one another's livers because they'd become all vicious Business and no Show.

Marty understood how the high-concept geniuses back at the studios made their money. Einsteins of the logline. The Edisons of movie marketing. They had the answers when they asked themselves "Why do this?" because they had some sorcerer's intuition, they understood Want and Need and Desire and could see the answers projected, made palpable in a one-sheet movie poster. To them, everyone else's wants were available like wounds to be bandaged and healed with the distraction of pictures in motion. Sort through the Wants, check the price of Desire, make the film, collect on the gross. But the directors, the actors — they were supposed to answer the question too, turning it onto themselves

So once more, with feeling, he thought: Marty — what do *you* want? And Bibi's face floated before him, he could hear her again telling him that there was a difference between directing and being a Director. He felt he knew the answer to her question about what he was trying to do, as exact as it could be without words. It was just taking so long to get there, it was such a protracted crawl, and he assured himself, *I'm* one of the guys who'll make it, because I can hold both things in my head at once, the money and the art. And shut up about it while I'm crawling my way to creative control. I can do this, I can direct. But how to get there. . . ?

So yes, he'd get out for a while after this shoot was over. A tactical retreat. Forget Craig, he'd get his face rubbed in it tomorrow on a real set when Exene asked, "Eric *who*?" For Marty, it would all come together when the powers weren't looking, when just once someone forgot to be scared and forgot they were always supposed to say *No no no* to movie ideas because god help them if they said Yes and became *responsible*. . . . One way or another, he would get out of this A.D. trap, make his deal, and come back as Marty Nyrop, Director. He'd have something they wanted, and needed, and with that he would direct what people saw, his vision would become theirs. And finally, that would be enough.

17

T he next morning the grips needed to get a camera crane outside as the shooting company was preparing a midday move to the next stage, only a half-day behind schedule after all of the previous days' complications. As Steve Craftservice opened the suspended door slabs at the far end of the *Phantom* Stage, Marty watched the dolly grip and his hammer crew push the mantis-like machinery against the brilliant sky that flowed into their unsealed cave. The low winter sun caught the chrome handles near the crane's counter-weight at the rear of the metal seesaw, where plates of solid lead were fed into an open box until the arm's back end exactly balanced the front load of Panaflex and camera crew. Chapman cranes were elegant machines, silent and rotatable levers; Marty was always drawn to them, imagining with every touch of his hand how he would someday use one of these fluidly rising and pivoting steel transporters, each of their graduated sizes named after a Greek God, to capture stories with imagery through his own lens.

Just outside the Stage 28 entrance beyond the grips and their crane, beyond a floor riser where once the main aisle of the *Phantom of the Opera* set passed beneath private side-boxes that still hung there decadently as chipped plaster façades, was his brother Craig — no, *Eric Blanc* Marty almost said aloud, why should he care what Craig called himself anymore? Eric was hunched over, gaunt, spectral, inappropriate in his black East coast trench coat yet oddly dashing, a flapping bat of a silhouette in the nearly blinding backlight. It was an entrance, and Marty briefly considered applauding.

Eric strolled down the aisle with his Daffy voice engaged: "Well, fancy meeting *you* here, Laughing Boy. You're dethhhpicable, Marty old pal."

Marty's "Bugs" was out of practice: "Yeah. Ain't I a stinker."

"And here I am. . . ." Eric laughed, wagging his face from side to side in mock disbelief at finding himself in this place. Before Marty could move Eric out of the working crew's way, Exene glided into the harsh glow cast by a stage worklight, a bare and swollen globe mounted atop a wheeled tripod. She bowed passively at the waist and let Wayne Hair brush her out, fluffing her downward so she could toss it all back through the air when she stood upright. Exene's hair caught the light, the yellow of her mane a falling spray, a glittering sea foam at sunrise. Marty was paralyzed again, helpless within her radiance, suddenly and resentfully aware that the mere sight of her acted on him like massive gravity. He was being pulled into a lower orbit around her each day, losing altitude and power, slowing and feeling greater frictional heat with each sideways glance at her, each remembered inhalation of her insides. Even with her head upside-down she caught him staring at her, and only then did he realize that his throat had constricted. She flipped the hair back.

"Bebop?"

Eric raised his eyebrows appreciatively at Marty. Then with a pose, a slouch, Eric stared back at Exene, rolling his eyes upward as his head drooped forward, penetrating her. Eric knew how to pull her look, to command it, to measure its depth. Marty warned him back with a frown as he went to Exene, alone. He drew near her and smelled the hot fragrant air coming from Wayne's hair dryer, the evaporations of her.

"My god, Bebop — isn't that Eric Blanc?"

"Yeah, *now* he is, I guess. How'd you know?"

She flared at him, arching her brow and nostrils into an intensity he had seen only once before, two years ago when she played a black widow of a character who consumed her delirious mates. "Eric *Blanc*, Marty.. *The* Eric Blanc. They say he's a genius on the stage. What's he doing here?"

"Ah. Well. . . . To tell you the truth, he wants to meet you."

"Really? He really does? Oh god. Would you have him come to my trailer, in about, uh . . . five minutes?"

At that moment he would rather have splattered his brother with a round from a .357 Magnum than take him into Exene's private trailer-world. He nodded dumb agreement and went back to Eric. "You've been granted an audience. Or maybe she thinks it's the other way around. She was impressed, god knows why."

"It's the New York mystique. We're all Stanislavski, or something. You know, Ac-a-*ting*! Can I get some coffee?"

Marty pointed out the craftservice cart and told Eric that he would walk him out to her motorhome when the right time came. Marty was nonplused as he watched Eric slowly move away, portraying an injured dancer. He searched for some understanding of how this jerk could extract such attention from a creature as exquisite as Exene. To Marty, he looked like his asshole brother, pretending.

A wardrobe assistant, Arlene, interrupted. "So Marty, who's your evil twin?"

He looked through the costumer, then at her, trying to place her. "What?"

"Who is that guy? He looks just like you."

"You're kidding. You. . . ." He was spinning, stuck. He'd forgotten her name. "You. . . . You think so? *No.* Don't ever speak to me again if you really think that." She smiled patiently until he relented. "Okay, he's a new lover I met in a bar. No? All right, he's my brother. His stage name's Eric Blanc. You impressed?"

She shrugged and smiled again to show off a deliberately ditzy ignorance, a happy, empty chipmunk grin they often shared to acknowledge a moment's festering insanity within their trade. He was relieved that at least he wasn't alone in being unimpressed with Craig's acquired name.

Yet the costumer's reminder of his physical resemblance to Craig had startled him — a pretty wobbly morning so far. These brothers had spent no time together since they were teenagers, and had only come to closely resemble one another as adults. Although on every shoot someone — usually an older script supervisor or a female hair type — would remark to Marty that he was on the wrong side of the camera, that he was better looking than the men in the cast, still his own appearance never meant much before. There was no apparent trade value for his features except to calculate fatigue in a makeup mirror. He felt deflated, though, at the possibility that "Eric Blanc" easily commanded respect from movers and players, people like Laura Trent-Sampson with the power to get movies made; a "yes" from her would make a studio management team do a corporate backflip. The subtle external differences between his brother and himself, when an actor's exterior was so critical, implied that there was in his brother's face something ineffable, a chance inheritance which might turn out to be what — out here — was called Talent, the quality Marty feared might've been covertly, randomly bestowed only upon a few of the chosen. Worse, then, it might be that "Talent" — an actor's or director's creative ability, visible or not — might not be available to the unlucky, no matter what level of reasoning or aggression was engaged. Either he already had this Talent or he didn't, and by now he should know which, and he might never cross over from the Production column into Talent as a Director for indiscernible reasons more recondite than the scant shades of difference between two brothers' faces.

His lost Bibi had faced something ineluctable in her own life — that she could not fully be herself and still succeed in this business — and had changed plans. Was it time to wise up? He had a new resentment of Craig, for his brother's undeserved good fortune.

But first he had to remember the costumer's name. He quickly spun through her children's names and ages, the occupation and drinking habits and sexual perversions of her ex-husband, her favorite lunch, all the personal trifles shared across the endless hours of ennui on the set that cause film crews to feel they're *ad hoc* family to one another.

Her name came back. "Anyway, Arlene — I'm better looking. Especially in profile, I look much more like James Dean than he does."

"You're my role-model, Marty."

• • •

Craig — Eric — returned with a cup of coffee. "So these extras, Marty — you direct them yourself?" Eric retained the knack of hitting nerves with pretend-innocent remarks, like sugar on a rotten tooth.

"Yeah, I direct 'em sometimes. Y'know, things like 'walk over there.' The classical stuff."

"In New York the extras are hired on their SAG cards. They're all real actors. You should take advantage, talk to them, learn how to work with them."

"I've learned how to say 'Walk over there.'"

He squinted at Eric. Even if it had ended badly, as orphaned brothers they'd been forced to share a lot as they were shuttled through a series of strange homes together, involved with each other more than most siblings are when responsible parents are in the home. Now "Eric" was an actor. Marty had worked with actors for years now, had seen every side of them, and wanted nothing more than to direct them, so it should all come together, a synergy, professional understanding and personal history feeding one another in this unplanned reunion with his brother. Instead Marty realized that he knew only the messiness of actors' personal lives, their childishness, their emotional stains. Nothing, really, about them as performing artists. And he really knew nothing useful at all about his brother, why his brother had become one of them. He remembered only growing up with an obsequious fabricator, a liar, a dissembler — not an artist. At the first opportunity Craig had fled from any lingering connection from childhood they might've retained, yet here they both were in Hollywood, each ambitious to tell a story.

"Do you give them a 'moment before'? Some do-able task, the reality of doing?"

"I give 'em 'Walk over there.' On location I give 'em 'Don't look at the camera.'"

"You're missing out. Actors and Directors need each other."

"Is that another bullshit revelation that's supposed to make me glad to see you?"

Eric smiled briefly and watched the crew's activity. He seemed to easily accept Marty's hostility. Perhaps he'd expected little more from his brother. "What else do you do, Marty?"

"All the things nobody else'll dirty his hands with. For big bucks."

"I know, eight-hundred over."

They could find no easy common ground, nor energy to look for any. Eric shrugged and appeared content to watch his first Hollywood movie set.

Marty looked toward the far end of the Phantom Stage. His next duty would be to round up his Atmosphere again, to rehearse them. He was indeed sometimes allowed to give them an activity — "background action" — if Cal wasn't into pushing them around like toy soldiers himself. In this way he needed his "Atmos.", their designation on the Call Sheet, because they were his only chance to affect the screen, to leave a mark. But now Eric's powers over Exene made things strangely out of kilter. Marty had lost track of his purpose, the one thing you cannot do in this business. Like the recurring dream that came to him at least once a month, he suddenly feared that he wouldn't be able to find any of his Atmos., or direct them, that he'd never seen this script, that he could no longer do his job. Incompetent, exposed. . . .

As he waited on Cal's word to bring the extras onto the set, he felt a disorienting affinity with them. Like Bibi — "like me" stabbed in a straight line through his lungs — none of them would ever become Talent, they too were on the wrong career track. He tried to reassure himself that extras *had* to be more lost inside the shapeless boundaries of their lives than he, Marty Nyrop, DGA Assistant Director, possibly could be. He rejected the aberrant identity Craig/Eric had imposed on him and tried merely not to fear or resent the extras, to calm down.

He'd seen a cartoon once, maybe in the *Lampoon*, that showed a girl named Charlotte living through the "Four Ages of a Hollywood Career." First panel, the cartoonist drew the Young Innocent as she once was; Second, her Brief Success; Third, her Downfall; and Fourth, her Retreat to a Nunnery. The captions beneath each character read in order, "Charlotte, Starlet, Harlot, Charlotte." Worth a small grin at the time. But the truth behind the joke reminded Marty that the moment to use Exene was *now*. Youth and beauty and glamor and celebrity together had an expiration date like a dairy product, and it came to him, the thing he had to do, the reason he was in this Industry: he could give Laura a chance to be part of something a hell of a lot better than this thing they were all slogging through, because while his brother had found Marty simply to use him to get at Laura Trent-Sampson, in order to salvage something in his own professional life, there was no reason it couldn't work the other way around. Marty grabbed at Eric and held his arm too tightly.

"Craig, Eric, Baby, Sweetheart." Marty squeezed harder to make sure it hurt. He watched Eric's smirk fade, the color drain from his face. "I'll let you see Laura Trent-Sampson for one reason only. You want to promise her your own play for somewhere down the road, that's your fucking business. But first — I let you see her now *only* because you're gonna ask her to do a movie with you. I've got a script at home that any studio in Hollywood'll let me direct if it has Laura Trent-Sampson in it. Fuck your play. You think she wants to act with the great Eric Blanc, first you get her for *my* movie. You use her to get me attached."

"If it's your script, why don't *you* ask her?"

"Because I'm not a player. I'm 'Bebop.' She'd never take me seriously, or none of her handlers would let her. You think she'll be so damned impressed with you, go on, get her to listen. Tell her you're in the movie too, the male lead, fine, whatever you want."

"I can't get her to do that —"

"Why not? You're *Eric Blanc*. You agree to try. Agree that you'll ask her, and don't lie to me."

"Ask her about what? I don't know what your script is. Marty, that's not why I'm —"

"That's the only way you get close to her. Otherwise I don't know you. I get Security to throw your ass off the lot right now. Lie to me, blow it off, and I'll fucking kill you. My movie, or nothing."

His stare quieted Eric. Eric finally nodded. Marty released his arm, not realizing until now he'd held it so tightly that the tendons in his own forearm were cramping, popping like piano wires coming through the skin.

When sufficient time passed for Wayne and Eddie to make Exene flawless once again, he walked his brother to her trailer, knocked, and gestured *the* Eric Blanc inside. He banged the door behind him and began putting the rest of the cast and the largest groups of lingering extras on his radar. Maybe it's like knowing where to find the actors, he thought: maybe Destiny shows up on your radar too.

He breathed deeply and waited. When Cal wanted them, Marty would now enjoy calling out for his "Atmos.." He would show his brother Craig-now-Eric what to do with extras, what the reality of doing was. And, more simply, he would be true to his word and murder Craig if he didn't make Marty's sudden and clear creative opportunity happen.

18

hen Marty gets to the Emergency Room, Lupe's caramel coloring has given way to dun. She lies on a gurney that's shoved against a wall outside an exam room while various ranks of nurses in color-coded scrubs and medical residents in white coats walk with brisk deliberation from room to room, from supply cabinet to computer station, leaving Lupe apparently untended while she's tethered to an IV drip stand that rolls with her makeshift bed. C.T. has found a doctor's low, rotating stool in one of the examination rooms and has hijacked it to sit with her, motionless, holding her hand while bent forward with eyes closed and resting his forehead on her thigh. Lupe stares at the ceiling.

Marty watches this tableau without letting them know that he has arrived. C.T. texted him that Lupe was showing signs of premature labor and Marty guesses that by now she and the baby have been rescued, stabilized without losing the child, her contractions calmed with potent drugs. He doesn't know yet what either of them thinks about the situation. Are they relieved? Or anywhere close to feeling Marty's own shame that he's disappointed knowing Lupe — that all of them together — have been spared the loss of a child none of them is ready for?

The story of Hollywood and actors and lost family that he's been telling Lupe and C.T. is meant to persuade them to give up this almost-arrived kid for adoption, to help them understand that being parents is beyond their grasp. C.T. especially needs to know the emotional contraption of a birth father he was born to, and Marty must make damn well sure that C.T. understands Craig Nyrop as a father before trying to become one.

But where Marty has left off in the telling, so far, he's only made this a story about himself, about the Industry, about what C.T.'s father was like as an actor and a brother, when instead it has to be a history that'll make C.T. and Lupe want to live just for each other — to move on with their skates and tattoos and their videos and declarations of "forever" or whatever someone their age can imagine as a lifetime — pledged to one another without hauling a mewling child between them. Yet, as Marty watches these two, C.T.'s head reverently bowed at her still and rounded form, their own unfolding story is, in the moment, potentially more watchable than any story Marty ever hoped to direct. Doomed young characters do not stretch plausibility; in fact, they invite a tragic narrative arc. His chest hurts.

While she's been listening to Marty's backstory during the past few days, Lupe has been incredulous that he once had a brother he had no desire to know further. Marty's realization is growing, that her reaction is filtered through the lens of a foster kid who can't imagine anyone throwing away blood family on purpose. But she and C.T. don't know the all of it yet. Having extended family doesn't make everything better any more than having a child does. It doesn't save you, there is no given grace to it.

Marty is trying to protect them both, these sad sleepy kids in repose with their hospital gurney. The next thing to tell them is how C.T. came to exist, because the circumstances matter, and he's wondering whether he should go there, that he should tell C.T. that he thinks there's even a chance that Marty witnessed C.T.'s conception. The scene sounds funny, gross, and maybe what Marty saw that day on the Universal lot wasn't the precise moment of sperm cell and egg colliding; it probably wasn't even physiologically possible, with Laura's miscarriage coming just days before. But with Hollywood stars, who knows? Maybe whatever gives them lucky skulls also gives them superpowers of ovulation. But however the getting of C.T. happened, it happened in a damn hurry.

Lupe has already told him that C.T. is looking for something more from her pregnancy than just parenthood. He wants his own story exposed, he wants his own fit there, his own family continuity, and together he and Lupe might play out the coming of a grandchild to get it. Since C.T. can't begin to know yet what being a father means, let him meet his biology, then. Let C.T. take Lupe home to rest, wherever that is for the time being, and when they're ready let the story continue, let them hear about the day that Marty and Craig sealed their fates together.

• • •

Three days after her labor scare, Marty chooses the Downtown Mall again to continue telling Lupe his story of actors and movies. Lupe seems to enjoy the movement, the smells, the protection from Valley heat as much as Marty does. He has to pick through his words to her a little more carefully, as the story will no longer sustain an "R" rating and even though she is fully adult from a legal standpoint — and pregnant — he hasn't yet broken through his teacher-student mode of exchange with her; it seems she will always be his student, and she will always call him Mr. Nyrop. As they walk through the mall, he remembers too that in re-telling his brother's story he has already let that one awful detail slip in: that Craig Nyrop who became Eric Blanc still couldn't escape their father's mortal sin, and by hurting his own children, lost them.

Patrick Cosgrove

19

T hey were close. The First Assistant Cameraman uncoiled his measuring tape from the Panaflex's film plane out to the Stand-in's nose, then grease-penciled his focus marks onto the lens barrel. The D.P. — Director of Photography — had stopped pointing to the heavy lights C-clamped onto the pipe grid around the catwalks above and was comparing key-to-fill-light footcandle ratios with his Sekonic light meter as he painted levels of contrast with his lamps.

First Assistant Cal and the Director were figuring out how many of Exene's one-shots they really needed for coverage before she melted into her daily makeup puddle. Once they'd decided, Marty would again push himself near camera even though yesterday's one scene that contained trace humanity hadn't really worked. Exene was good, but not that good as a performer, at least not with this script; the hold she had on a starstruck globe had only a little to do with an acquired skill. Her talent lay elsewhere — with Marty as her Director, in his newly sparked vision.

The maroon Mole-Richardson lamps soaked up the powerful river of direct current spun out by the lot's generators. Fresnel lenses on the lamps blew an incandescent bubble of focused and shaped illumination into the corner of the sound stage. Supported by the black-on-black floor of cables and rubber mats, the glowing light-bubble became like a fish tank of solidified color, a three-quarter scaled version of a bus station submerged beneath the dark unlit void of soundstage air above the lights. Marty was entranced by the aquarium-like effect, watching grips move flags and C-stands and electricians fetch scab-red "tweenies" and "inkies" and 10K lamps like so many earnest guppies. He tried to stir himself, pacing to avoid getting caught unready again.

Cal put on his show of running a tight set: he jumped up and down on a foot pedal at the Sound Mixer's cart and threw switches at random, finally setting off the buzzer and red-flashing wigwags. He screamed for quiet and again yelled "Boys, boys!" Variously annoyed crew members shouted at the Mixer to turn off the red light so people could still use the stage doors. The Mixer was trying to resist walking off the set. Marty's headset crackled:

"Picture next. *Meat, meat, meat —*"

Marty keyed his radio: "We're ready?"

"Yeah, we're ready and we're waiting on you, pal. It's our set, c'mon."

"First I've heard about it. Goddamn it Cal, you did it to me again. How about a little warning some time for touchups, like I've been asking?"

Cal chanted "Bring her in, bring her in" through Marty's headset until Marty shouted "*Fuck you Cal!*" loudly enough to be heard across the Phantom stage. Amidst the crew's sporadic applause and a conspicuous silence from his First, he trotted offstage to retrieve Exene.

Even with breath coming short and his radio slapping against his thigh, he couldn't outrun his thoughts this time. Flushed with adrenaline, he fantasized doing great physical harm to Cal, the jerk. First Eric, now Cal frying his ass. He accelerated to a full run.

He knocked loudly on the motorhome door twice, wondering if his brother's — and now his own — silly scheming had put Exene back to sleep. If there's a god, he thought, she's not passed out on her face. As he waited, the faux-militaristic nature of his job came back to him like insistent surf, more discomfiting by the moment. What had he just done? His profane disrespect toward Cal was a breach of code: the First Assistant was to be obeyed by the Second, and the Directors Guild took notions of rank and insubordination seriously. Still, he longed to use his fist to push Cal's beaky nose back through his forehead, to watch Cal's wire-rim glasses shatter into safety-glass snowflakes that would fall and lodge in his scraggly red beard. Marty wanted to stand over Cal with a director's finder held tight to his eye, framing Cal's body as it fell writhing next to the camera dolly in the focused glare of the lamps, twitching up and down like an electrocuted snake. He would softly urge Cal to stop flopping like that and "settle." It would be a happy set.

He waited a half-minute more, then knocked again and pulled the door open and jumped onto the metal step. He stared stupidly at something he didn't at first understand, until he recognized it for what had to be a hallucination. But then no, it was only a visionary point-of-view of Exene that he had never beheld, and would never willingly behold again. He was less than three feet away and at eye-level with the bare underside of her thighs, just below the curve of her slack unweighted calves, looking up at the bottoms of her shoeless feet — at her flawless surfaces pulsing, waving in unison at him, all upside down on the motorhome bench seat. One thin ankle was still entangled in a noose of pantyhose, her toes were clenching at the moist, dank trailer air. Between her upended thighs — this space that had become a desecrated altar and was until now unimaginable as palpable flesh — was the vaguely familiar backside of his brother Craig Nyrop (*No, Eric Blanc*—). Two light whorls of rough hair circled beneath each Nyrop buttock, a reddened sack of whiskery pebbled skin swung up and down. An agitated stalk of flesh descended into, then rose from the yielding rim of Exene's rent, puffy cleft. Eric's butt swung in and out, Exene's ankles hinged up and down; then all stopped. Marty made his own trembling foot go backward off the trailer step until he was completely outside again. He shut the door tightly.

It was an unwanted clarity: that he'd fallen between places, between people's secrets and their visible surfaces, grasping neither realm, because he — who should've known better, *did* know better — had imagined that a movie star in person, an actress within his infantile dream of privacy and possession, would be a different thing than a movie star projected upon a theater screen. He'd let himself consider notions of need and tenderness based on magnificently deep skin. Actors were different than he was, he'd always known that, but he should've known just how different, in kind and quality. Role and player weren't different from one another after all, the screen simply used the layer most available to it. Marty had no instincts left to himself intact, nothing he could any longer trust.

Arlene from wardrobe came to him holding Exene's costume jewelry for the scene.

"Marty, are you all right? You look terrible."

He wanted to cry, but couldn't. He laughed, then his voice broke into a high cackle. "Asshole —"

"Excuse me? Marty. . . ?"

He laughed again until finally he did cry. At least thought he had cried. He could see himself doing it, as if watching Marty the A.D. through the Panaflex eyepiece. He grew convinced he was doing both, the laughing and the crying, at once. "Asshole. My brother. My brother's asshole." He had to choose which activity to concentrate on, whether to get the laughing or the crying right, or whether he should just try to juggle the two until he fell down, thinking, Hit or fall down laughing. Hit or fall down —

He sat against one of the motorhome's slick Armor All-ed tires and felt a low vibrating rhythm through the wheel's chrome lug nuts. He realized fleetingly that it was only Bibi he loved, and wondered if love — not Talent — was in truth the most covertly, randomly bestowed gift, if he had ignored whatever "love" was for too long. Arlene still looked at him as if he hadn't explained anything to her. But of course he had: "Asshole." It was the topic of the day. First Eric, then Cal, now Eric again. *Asshole asshole, my brother, my brother's asshole.* He looked up and pushed a palm dryly across his cheeks — he hadn't been crying after all — and tried to speak to Arlene:

"My brother. . . ." He stopped when Cal said something over the radio. He twisted the volume knob off.

Moments later Cal was on the way, almost sprinting. In his squat against the trailer tire, Marty had let all his joints seize. As he got to his feet and stared vacantly back toward Cal he felt ancient, he'd become a ruined statue. Cal was screaming something into his own mouthpiece and pointing repeatedly to the radio flapping away on the belt at his hip. He was panting when he grabbed Marty by the shirt.

"Where is she?"

"Let it go, Cal. For chrissakes."

"Where is she, Marty? You wanna come explain to my Director why he's waiting? Why his fucking budget's down the drain while you jerk off by the motorhome? Huh? Maybe you'd like to call my Producer and tell him why you can't even answer the goddamn radio when I call you?"

"Stop it, Cal. Act like a human being, like you know anything about it —"

Cal tried to throw Marty backwards by the grip on his shirt but Marty was too solid. "You little — You conniving little son of a bitch —"

"What — ? Conniving, about what?"

"About making me look bad! You want my job, don't you?"

"Cal, you can stick your job up your ass sideways." Cal's eyes were beginning to bulge at the edges of their sockets.

"Bull-*shit*. You've got your days in to be a First, and you know it. Sweet little Marty, innocent little goddamn mutinous Marty's got everyone on his side. Hell, he's too *nice* to be an A.D., how can he stand that fucking prick Cal? I heard it in there, Marty. 'Fuck you, Cal,' and the crew *applauding* —"

"I said, I don't want your job."

"You want it. You can smell the money. You'll even pimp to get it."

"What the hell's that supposed to mean?"

"The whole company knows what's going on in there Marty. You think this is the first time?"

"In where?"

"Get that cunt out of the motorhome and onto my set, or I'll have *your* job in a butt can. I'll have you tossed out of the Guild, so goddamn help me."

Marty could feel a peaceful dreaminess softening his face. "Hey, Cal?"

Cal had already spun away, but he squeaked to a stop in his spotless white aerobics shoes and turned back; he thrust his hatchet face into the marshmallow of Marty's beatific smile. Marty watched his own closed hand rising, its path extending toward Cal's slowly opening mouth. What must have been happening almost instantaneously exploded for him in smeary streaks over long, silent seconds. For the first time he accepted the special effects convention that slow-motion represented faster than normal time perception. Marty was Flash, then he was the Six-Million Dollar A.D.. He watched his knuckles smoothly split the open mouth's pink flesh, saw red snot whipping upward to drape over a wire-rimmed lens, saw Cal's head snap and wave backward, then forward, as a broken yellow-white tooth with a red spot at its center tumbled upward against deep and faultless blue L.A. sky.

Then in the distance Marty saw the Director rounding the corner of the stage, his hands buried in his woolly cardigan sweater pockets, his gait somber and his eyes lowered upon Cal's unmoving form crumpled at Marty's feet. The Director was coming, so he resumed his professional duties.

He opened the motor home door and announced, "We're ready for picture, Exene." He inhaled odors of exchanged bodily fluids and piney air freshener stick-ups and hair spray, then clanged the door shut again.

He smiled down at Cal. "He's my Director, too. Asshole."

20

*M*arty knew he had nowhere to go. His A.D. role in the Industry, his springboard from where he would leap skyward, arcing, to alight in the Director's seat of control atop a Chapman crane, was now no more than a pirate's gangplank. He wandered up the asphalt hill next to what used to be a dressing bungalow for the contract stars. Perhaps this one — one of them around here, anyway — had been Lucille Ball's.

Behind him, the film's Producer Paul Amato was a madman, crazy with joy. Amato was within seconds of amputating the part of someone else that was most like the necrotic vestige of creative ambition that still rotted within Amato's own being. He was highly successful as a budget man, had mastered the techniques of career advancement in Hollywood that called for the use of power for its own sake. Firing people came with a special glee — a dog licking its balls because it can, in a culture where power trumped money.

He drove a studio golf cart slowly behind Marty, apoplectic with eagerness. He could barely steer it along the same bungalow path that Marty walked; Amato's knees banged together arrhythmically, his bearded, ringleted head lolling on his doughy shoulders. His tiny eyes were glassy pinpoints, his smile a pulsing oval stretching in and out.

"H-h-h-h-hey Marty! I love it I love it, goddamn! Huh? The smell of career death, you little shit! What's that I see in the sky? Vultures? *Huh?*"

Marty stared ahead, walked. He took a right turn back toward the center of the lot. Amato banged a rubber tire off a soundstage wall and smacked squarely into the lift gate of a camera truck. He backed up, couldn't figure out forward, until with a screech he sped up to Marty's heels again.

"Shut up, Paul."

"Huh? 'Shut *up*, Paul?' Listen to him. He's dangling from the rope around his neck, pissing straight up and he says *Shut Up Paul.*"

Amato cackled. Marty kept making right turns around the same stage.

"I know your type, you little rat bait! You're too good for us *schlockmeisters*. You're holding out 'til you can fuck Art with that pathetic little college-boy cock of yours. Sniffing your turned-up nose at the rest of us *entertainers*. I know this. I know this because you *tell* everybody! You *exude* it."

"Then don't shut up. Say it, Paul. Go ahead."

"What — ?"

"Show us how smart you are. Say it."

"Say what?"

"'You'll never work —' C'mon, *timing*, say it with me: 'You'll never work in this town —'"

"Fuck you!"

" — again.'"

"And you won't! Hah! Career death! What a smell!" Amato cackled again and sped away on his golf cart.

Beyond the bungalows, Marty gripped a railing near the film concession stand built to look like a giant 35mm camera. A tram from the Studio Tour pulled up chock-full of tourists beneath its happy striped awnings. The electronically amplified Tour Guide expounded upon how movies are made. Marty listened to himself hailing the tourists with a loud, "Hi, hi!" as he gave a smile and a wave, then was surprised to hear himself explain to the uneasy tram-faces that he, Marty Nyrop, was what an authentic Assistant Director looked like. He was aware that he was doing something forbidden, interfering with what had become the Studio's primary reason for existence: a penetrating and utterly faithful peek behind the motion picture screen at the guts of Real Hollywood that only a Tour Guide and her propane-driven tram could provide. He wanted to meld invisibly into Universal Studio history, its Laemmle chicken-ranch lore, to channel Desi Arnaz, to release his love of Lucy, to shout "You got some 'splainin' to do!" with a passable Cuban accent.

The schoolgirl Guide was frozen, horrified by what this intrusion might do to the beats of her memorized speech. Marty realized that he must look dangerous to her. He was sorry, he hadn't meant to do that. He unstrapped his radio belt and only then noticed the bloody dripping knuckles of his right hand. He gave a small boy in the front seat of the tram his $3,500 Motorola police radio and his Plantronics accessory headset, showed the boy where none other than the Laura Trent-Sampson shooting company was secretly communicating today on channel 2, then walked toward the studio lot's parking structure at the edge of the concrete Los Angeles River. He waved goodbye silently and a little wildly to everyone on the lot he passed, goodbye to windowless gray barns with sky blue elephant doors, goodbye to the Phantom Stage, waving goodbye, he suspected, to Marty Nyrop. He looked back and saw jacketed Burns Security guards running toward Exene's motor home.

He needed to lie low, to hide out somewhere in case real cops got involved, and headed toward the center of the lot where the sawmill was. There in a numb shuffle amidst the carpenters and their machines he tried to appear busy and felt the magnitude of what he'd just done creeping toward him like a poisonous red tide. In the course of twenty-four hours he had, against all family history and his clear better judgment, allowed his brother to walk onto the lot, back into Marty's life; he had pushed his brother into a corner, coerced him to agree to pursue Marty's ambitions, not his own that he'd traveled 3,000 miles to test; then, upon allowing his brother to tamper with the object of ambition for both of them, had witnessed his brother fucking their dreams away in a motorhome; and from this, Marty had punched out his boss.

What distance had he come in this business, only to have it end here? In Marty's eidetic memory the images of his time in L.A. rolled like a movie trailer. In his first week in the Directors Guild Training Program he had been placed here at Universal as one of the annual crop of bright young hopes for the Industry, an outsider invited inside because he was smart enough to pass a battery of outmoded Army I.Q. tests. But he wasn't yet savvy enough to know that he would be therefore slotted in the Production column of movie-making, not the Talent column, trained up to be forever a cost-efficiency salaryman. He'd been on the wrong career trajectory from the beginning.

That first week as a Trainee he wandered by mistake into this very sawmill instead of his company's shooting stage and didn't immediately realize his error. The cable- and pulley-hung doors that could let even 10-ton diesels in and out, the screaming power saw blades, the burnt-sap smell, the hammering and cracking of planks, and the piney sawdust that whisked up his nostrils were all so similar to the sensory load of the shooting stage that the two sites, the one of fresh-cut lumber and the other of just-completed set construction, were to Marty momentarily equivalent. It was only the presence of windows, the overhead view of sky that had told him he was lost.

Now, seven years after not knowing a sawmill from a working set, and months after becoming the Second Assistant for a production with one of the biggest stars in the world, he was about to be nowhere in the Industry at all. For this, he had let Bibi walk out of his life.

He spent an hour feigning interest in posted blueprints for interior sets to be built on various sound stages, then left the sawmill and hoped that no one in a uniform was posted at his car. As he approached the bottom of a small dip that the asphalt took just before the entrance to the parking structure, a white stretch limo majestically docked itself in reverse, its power steering hoses making low squeals. From within its hidden interior, where opaquely tinted windows kept insiders insulated from outsiders, Eric Blanc emerged to greet Marty with small hand gestures, an elegant mime that told him to get into the limo alongside Eric.

"So Marty — *Quo vadis*, Booby?"

Whither goest I? He had no answer. This Eric Blanc, Marty saw, he's a player, he's here three days and his money-for-a-play people have pulled levers, turned gears, sent a limo to retrieve him, and now Eric calls to me, his brother.

Of course I'll go with him, Marty thought, of course. Who was I, ever, to think I'd be a Director, someone who'd say, "This is my white rectangle, not yours," the one who would make a film set do his bidding, who'd say this prop and not that prop and this color and texture and filter and face will go on *my* screen, you shits.

Who was I?

21

*M*arty doesn't yet know in how much detail or in exactly what manner Lupe is passing on this tale of ancestral mating to C.T., but he still hopes that it was a good call to let her put it in whatever terms that C.T. can handle. There have been plenty of recent days, before C.T. and Lupe went into their bunker mode somewhere in Midtown, when saying "Good morning" to his son seemed like committing a terrible trespass, so he's hoping that it's not too much to ask of Lupe that she find the right words, make the edits, fix the tone because even in the re-telling, his brother has gotten Marty's blood up and down again and he's leery of embroiling C.T. and his boy's still-adolescent emotions into the mix. *Our blood, the three of us, brothers and their son-in-common.* Would C.T. ever forgive him for letting him believe he was adopted by a stranger? Would he understand that if he'd confessed their blood tie he'd have to have told him who his mother was, too, the mother who never loved him? But since Laura showed up, since Hollywood has come to Sacramento, there is no choice. Marty's options have been canceled like a wave peak meeting a trough on an oscilloscope, it's all one flat line now and no choice remains.

The smell of worn-out skates is part of C.T.'s remaining presence in his abandoned bedroom. There's also the left-behind jerry-built editing station he's put together between his laptop and one of Marty's outdated monitors, so that C.T. has a multiple-screen cinema display that gives the seventeen-year-old the capability of digitally assembling a feature film with the technical sophistication that scant years ago would've required a crew of hundreds, not to mention the backing of an acres-wide studio, in turn backed by unnamed banks in New York. Marty double-clicks a video file and watches skating clips slide back and forth on a timeline, with at least two soundtracks waiting below the video track to propel the aggressive skating tricks over rhythms of pirated rap music. The camera work is made up almost entirely of smooth, hand-held follow-shots through a fisheye lens and has been recorded with a birthday gift of an HD camera that has a surprising sharpness. Yet as always, the amateur giveaway is the filmmaker's lack of interest in lighting the shots. Not so many grips and electricians were brought along on this digital revolution.

He's transfixed by C.T.'s videos, feeling the kinesthesia induced by C.T.'s image in liftoff, flight, and landing, and wincing when he, in C.T.'s own phrase, "eats shit" in a bad fall. Marty can feel himself behind the camera, seeing as a lens sees, framing the world as he once did during his own schooldays before he landed in the Production track of the Industry. And while he explores two-dimensional art along with his high school photography students, it's also the way he catches himself experiencing the world now that the neglect of his vision has cost him the sharpness of his left eye. He sees clearly only with the one undamaged retina but lives with that by thinking that he sees what a camera sees: a world that's flatter, less dimensional, but with better-defined graphic relationships among subjects. And he chooses to keep his photography students there in that flat world, leading them into nothing closer to storytelling than an assigned photo essay. Stories make too many connections. He thought he had left them behind. Until now.

Marty has probably inherited his risk for glaucoma from his father — who knew? But C.T., even if biologically a nephew, inherited in turn a natural sense of composition from him, or from some Nyrop at least, and here's the wonder of his boy: he makes films that also have no story, that control no characters; he strings visions of himself together that are only that, only imagery, only the direct statement that says, *see this? On skates I've driven myself to nail this trick, and this trick, and this one. . . .* And by landing on some rails and falling off others and defacing public property by lubricating his way through the world with wax rubbed onto concrete ledges and beneath his skates, this beautiful child full of scabs and dotted from healed stitches is telling the world through the camera *I know who I am and if you fucking bother to look you'll see. And if you don't look or can't see, then fuck you, I don't give a shit.* He's unsocialized, and Marty catches himself cheered by that.

Marty plays with a few more video files and sees that C.T. has a very good feel for editing rhythms. What more does he have ambition to do as a filmmaker? Is YouTube enough? No, how could it be, when Laura Trent-Sampson and her entourage are in town looking to make him famous?

• • •

Once, Marty had wanted nothing more than to go to Hollywood. By college he already knew how movies made him feel, so in his first eager research on the Film Industry he tried to figure out what stuff their magic was made of, how — beyond the art — the business and technology worked too, so he could command their magic. He learned that film historians describe the invention of movies as the exploitation of "vision persistence," of the too-slow adjustment our brain's visual center makes to changes of light and movement from one frame to the next. Academicians pinpoint this persistence of vision — this connection of one still-photographic frame on the retina blending to the image on the next frame — as the physiology that makes movies possible. But neurologists will tell you a somewhat different thing; if a single frame's lingering past image continues to fill the briefest of moments before the next (and present) image arrives on a screen, then each new image will get superimposed atop the one before it. The unmoving still images will then in turn multiply, accumulating each upon the next until time and sequence break down into an incomprehensible, pulsing glow of light that is both the past and present. Chaos. No, Marty came to understand, our retinas in conspiracy with our brain simply lie and reassure us that we are not in fact sitting in the projector's complete and factual darkness between frames during more than half of a movie's two hours. Film vision, instead, has something to do with first suppressing the once-seen picture before the next one arrives, shutting down the past and not allowing it to mix with the present. It's about how frame-by-frame we blank out the image that's gone by, our retinas (but mostly our brain) wiping the slate clean in order to receive a new image that's fresh, in the continuous present. That's only this moment, this fraction of a second, *right now*.

In their own context, actors must intuit these present moments without pasts, and demand to be loved within them. Marty now gets this: that together these moments are the one indispensable reason why Hollywood is what it is: "Love me now," even for one forty-eighth of a second. Since the time of cinema pioneers

Muybridge and the Lumières and Edison and Méliès, "love me in this moment regardless of my past" is in fact the only movie vision that persists.

He turns off C.T.'s computer. Because Laura is now here with her "Hollywood Birth Moms!" crew in tow, Marty has to tell the rest of the story as completely as he can, he has to keep C.T. and Lupe and probably their child too from sliding down that greased pole of Laura's celebrity to wherever she would take them. There is no choice but to keep storytelling.

22

If the police awaken you with an hour-of-the-wolf telephone call to ask if you're the father of a certain child, the world you thought you lived in recedes as quickly as any interrupted dream.

This time the desk sergeant on the line is just as quickly reassuring Marty that C.T. is physically all right, though he's in serious legal trouble. That's the tactful way of leading up to the situation in which his son, a juvenile delinquent, smashed the shit out of some other kid's face and is squatting in jail for a possible charge of assault. It's hardly funny; Marty's second thought (after "my son's going to die in prison") is that Lupe is somewhere pregnant and alone.

The scenario — there's no better word for it, there's a play-acting tinge to this — is ludicrous. He is told over the phone that C.T. and his "crew" were skating through the most commercial street in Midtown with C.T. in the lead, lip-syncing to music played through headphones while he was recorded by a camera operator who was also on skates. They were a nuisance, jostling pedestrians but nothing more, until C.T. bull-rushed some kid in a cluster of homies and bedlam erupted. Someone produced a baseball bat, but apparently C.T. put an end to that plan with his fists. The rest is now criminal investigation, if not history. Marty's kid, new father-to-be. New role model.

He's allowed to see C.T. later in the morning. He sits with him on a modernistic bench in a hard-shelled hallway where every surface reflects glaring fluorescent light but nothing feels clean. C.T. is folded in upon himself, somehow looking abject and surly at once. It's actorish, Marty thinks fleetingly, then scrapes the thought from his mind. The kid is scared. Marty is scared.

"What the hell were you thinking?"

C.T. won't answer, beginning only a slow rocking motion on their shared bench in a common area in this quite-new building that looks like the spawn between a high school and a prison — not a huge style-gap to traverse.

"You need to talk to me. They said your first court date is called a detention hearing. They can keep you here for 48 hours until they decide when the hearing's gonna be. Locked up. Two days. Am I making any impression here? It's Saturday. Your 48 hours won't even start until Monday."

Marty looks at his cell phone to see if there are any messages from his friend Takashi Itani, a lawyer. At least in another life Tak was a lawyer. He's going to drive up from L.A., mostly because Marty doesn't know any other attorneys. And this is special, his coming here — Tak was there at the beginning of everything. Not this stupid bit of juvenile mayhem, but the literal beginning of C.T. because Tak produced the movie that in a complicated way has produced Marty's life, and C.T.'s life, such as their lives are, and it seems good that C.T. has known Tak all of that time.

God help us *somebody*, Marty thinks. *C'mon Tak*. But no messages.

"What've you said to them so far?"

C.T.'s voice is a whisper. "Nothing."

"Good. Tak said not to. They might even be miking us right now, to get something on you."

"Whoa. Paranoia, Pops." He smirks.

"Common sense. Which seems in short supply around here. You were making a video? Of what?"

"A song."

"You were singing a song about hitting people in the face? In Midtown?"

C.T. snorts.

"What, then?"

"Some rap shit. Then this lame-assed bitch thought we were throwing signs and came up on me. He started shoving me in the middle of the sidewalk and I'm on my fucking skates, I'm gonna crack my head open so I made sure he can't do that. That's all."

"By slugging him in the face."

"By putting him down before his bitch-assed friend could get his baseball bat on me. Did they tell you that? I mean *fuck*, what'm I supposed to do?"

"Shhhhh, jeez. . . . Walk away, is what."

C.T. stares at Marty, incredulous. "It's called cred, Pops. Stripes. You're not gonna get it."

"Street cred? Are you. . . . C.T., my god, you're a white kid, the son of a schoolteacher. You live in a nice little paid-for house. You had braces. I've saved money for your college. What fantasy league are you playing in, here?"

"Dude without no front teeth in his head is feelin' it pretty real."

"And you're proud of that."

"It was me or him."

"Great. Because clearly all that mattered was you making your video."

C.T. stares at the waxy floor.

The sudden memories of his own movie-making roil Marty's insides. *The camera goes here, my screen, you shits, this and not that and I'll frame the world, I'll make you see —*

He could never tell anyone what exactly he thought becoming a Director would mean to him personally, though he tried, but then would back off when the megalomania of it creeped up on him. He couldn't justify it convincingly to Bibi as the ambition that kept them from making sense of their feelings for each other, and she'd grown weary of waiting. And after all that, here he is with his kid in trouble for making a movie.

Marty's phone chimes and he's finally got a text message from Tak: "Checked w juv attorn will enter denial of petition pending eval of state case. Do nothing. Wait for me."

As if they have a choice. Then Marty realizes *he* has one, but he's not going anywhere. C.T. slumps again in his Juvie-issued shirt and sloppy khaki pants. A Sacramento County cop who seems all hairy forearms and leather gadget-belt touches C.T. on the shoulder, and they go down the hall together while somewhere distant a girl screams. Marty sees that he's going home after all, alone.

C.T. looks back over his shoulder as he's led away. "You lied to me, Pops. My whole life. . . ."

Marty watches him disappear around a corner with the cop. He's forgotten to ask C.T. if they got their shot on camera, then realizes he was hoping they didn't.

• • •

While Marty waits for C.T.'s release he leads an adolescent's life of text messaging. Tak Itani the lawyer is keeping him up to date during his progress up the 5 from L.A. as Tak reports on any similar advancement he's making over the phone in convincing the probation people not to file a petition that will lead to a juvenile court case.

Marty scores his own triumph of mobile technology by using his online gradebook application for a student's home phone, and gets one of C.T.'s school pals to give him Lupe's cell phone number. Lupe allows him to pick her up at a downtown street corner and will let him bring her and a beaten suitcase home because, Marty guesses, without C.T. she's not so comfortable in some loser guy's Midtown apartment. She's tough, sure, but she's also very big and pregnant and has already had miscarriage scares.

She wants to cook. It's not to be sweet, or kind, or a good guest; it's to show Marty that she's in charge of her own life. They stop at a tiny store that sells what seem to be authentic Mexican food staples in the outer stretches of the Stockton Boulevard corridor below Little Saigon. It's the kind of place he would never have known existed, nestled between an auto shop and a foreclosed tire store. Inside Lupe runs her hands over the plastic sacks of flour and corn meal, the spices that are sold in brittle cellophane packets, the open bins of local vegetables. It's as if she's trying to draw memory from touch in some kind of empathic recipe gathering. She uses Marty without hesitation, dropping what she finds into a red basket with floppy handles that he carries behind her. There are a half-dozen kinds of small green peppers, all of which he would have called jalapeños, but Lupe deftly gathers them with tomatillos and puts each separate batch into its own paper bag. When she has added dried corn and several canned goods to the handbasket, she steps near the door and waits with her eyes cast downward as Marty goes to the cashier.

They ride home in silence, but he's grateful that she's willing to be with him. The messages keep coming from his lawyer friend Tak, who has nearly arrived; he's advising Marty to start gathering any documents he can that will show a juvenile judge or court-appointed referee that C.T. is indeed a good boy. Report cards (not so much help there), certificates of achievement (can punk an asshole carrying a baseball bat, but no written proof), letters of recommendation. . . . He should be able to bring C.T. home Monday morning, according to Tak, though he keeps reminding Marty that he's not a juvenile defense attorney, which is a little unsettling. But Marty doesn't want anyone else involved. He's finding himself deeply, surprisingly protective of Lupe, who shivered when he said he was going back to the detention center to see C.T. throughout the weekend.

"I'm not going near no cops" was the beginning and the conclusion to that conversation.

• • •

In his kitchen she's trying to be self-sufficient, though he's hovering, probably annoying her, but he needs to find things for her and he's not the most organized housekeeper.

"You probably don't got a *metate y mano.*"

"I guess I don't. I don't know what it —"

"Okay. How 'bout a Cuisinart?"

"No, but at least I know what it is."

She stares at a bowl he has given her that she's filled with whole kernels of corn. Tamales? Tortillas? He sharply feels like White Guy at the moment.

"Do you need to grind that up? The corn? I'll go back to the store —"

But she shakes her head adamantly. Instead, in rapid succession she asks him for a half-dozen ingredients — he catches "oregano" and "lard" and either "lime" or "limes" but misses the others.

"I'll go, just write the names down for me."

It's then that he sees her left hand tremble for just a moment. Then a sniff. He doesn't know what hope looks like, but he can clearly see its absence.

"What is it, Lupe? I'll get you whatever you need."

"My mama. . . ."

Oh, no. Not here, not now. "You need, what, her recipe? We'll find one. It'll be like the darkroom. HC-110, Dilution B,

remember?. The Kodak recipe for fine and beautiful negatives. . . .
Hey, if we could do that, then we — C'mon, we'll find a video online,
we'll watch how it's done."

But Lupe bows her head and leans over the sink, pressing her
child-ful belly against it. Then, one stifled cry from her breast and her
small strong fingers are trying to smear tears one-by-one as they slip
down her brown cheeks.

"Lupe, we'll make it like it used to be at home. Try, anyway.
Like you remember it."

She pulls her hands away from her face, rubs them on the
hem of her sweatshirt, and then digs her palms into the bowl of corn
and leaves them there in stillness.

"It don't matter what we watch. It's not the same hands."

A half hour later when Tak arrives, Lupe is walking
somewhere in the neighborhood and is not answering her phone.

23

S ince sharing the motorhome fiasco on the Universal lot with Lupe, Marty isn't sure how much of what next happened to C.T.'s natural parents (and to himself) will be about things C.T. wants to know. It might be TMI, the kids say: too much information. But sooner or later he's going to want to hear a lot; after watching his skate videos, the next thing Marty found on C.T.'s computer was a QuickTime movie file of *User-Friendly*, the romantic comedy his birth parents and Marty made together, so C.T. has now seen his mother and father on the screen and has watched Eric's and Laura's characters falling in and out of love with a happy ending. He's seen the shot of the movie's finish that was made with a stunt double because his father had died on the day it was supposed to be filmed. He'll want to know why he doesn't know these characters as people. Why they never knew him, especially, though of course they couldn't, since one is seventeen years dead and the other simply didn't want to know how to know him, or how to love him, either. And of course, Marty lied and hid it all from C.T. anyway.

Marty clicks the mouse and drags the handle back and forth across the *User-Friendly* timeline and images like speeded-up mannequins get jumbled together into a year's worth of experience across the screen, dancing shadows hippity-hopping through the story. He remembers why he couldn't use his own name when his one chance to direct finally arrived, how during what might've been C.T.'s conception Marty sat against a tire on Laura's motorhome and didn't know whether to go back inside and slug C.T.'s father, or fall down laughing. So Marty had gotten to his feet and hit Cal the Asshole instead. He wonders now if he's now so superior, so less compromised than his son — who just last night went skating on a rap-video baseball bat rampage and is now locked up for the weekend in Juvie — only because Marty didn't get arrested on the Universal lot so long ago. Goddamn genes.

Marty watches a few more scenes from *User-Friendly* for the first time since it was released, seeing the faces and the camera work that captured them. He remembers every cut, every dolly move, every composition of that world within a frame that he chose. It's from a time so remote from what his life has gradually become that it doesn't seem right that the film is in color and not timeless shades of silver.

•••

When Marty was only a few years older than C.T. is now, he set out on a path that he'd thought was a straight line to becoming a Director of movies. Starting a little sooner, his brother Craig had journeyed through another world alien to Marty, on his way to becoming an actor. What should've been an obvious, even happy Hollywood synergy of sorts in the reunion between the Actor Brother and the Director Brother hadn't turned out that way. They'd finally had a chance to find each other, though, he and Craig-as-Eric, and that chance, that movie they'd made, was only possible because of a man who became Marty's Producer and friend before he became his lawyer. So even though Takashi Itani doesn't yet know it, beyond giving legal advice, Tak's going to take on some storytelling duties. Not that he owes Marty anything other than friendship, but with C.T. in Juvie, Marty's solo parenting isn't working out so well lately and he needs help.

Tak earned his first movie credit as Executive Producer of *User-Friendly*. Like baseball stats, Tak's credits are online to be looked up, but Marty can't be found anywhere as a Director even though their film was a major release. His students ask him annually about his A.D. credits on IMDb.com, and he tries to dismiss his years as a Second Assistant Director as some kind of anomaly. But when his kids persist and want to know how he could've worked in Hollywood and ended up as a high school teacher in Sacramento, he says only that he left the business to raise his son. With that, they know as much as C.T. used to know about Marty's old life, the one before C.T.'s arrival, and Marty is coming to understand that it's been a terrible mistake to not tell his son any more than this. But like any other excuse-making, he always had his reasons; no character ever thinks he's the bad guy.

• • •

Tak has always volunteered that Marty was the making of the Industry professional Tak has become. Over the years they've shared the big and small particulars of their lives as well as they could at a distance. How, for instance, each time Tak drives out of his L.A. neighborhood he tries to make it a point to appreciate his abundant material life, as he often forgets to do. Living in gratitude is oddly harder the more things there are to be grateful for. He has the kind of beautiful hillside home above Hollywood that can be seen in quarterly magazines, with lots of windows so the occupant can, smog permitting, sit indoors and look out at his landscaping against a limitless ocean horizon as he contemplates suing his neighbors for *their* landscaping. Or contemplate being sued by the Mt. Olympus Property Owners Association because he painted his door an unapproved color. The neighborhood is quite nice, while overpriced, and of course that silly Olympian entrance gate has got to go someday, though CC & Rs probably forbid such changes. But he's soon moving from the neighborhood. He'll stay in the business — since he became a Producer that first time for Marty, he's never been out of work — but he no longer wants to live in L.A.. It's never really been home. A year ago Marty wished Tak luck in working outside of L.A. and said he thought Tak just might pull it off:

"You're about the only person I've ever met in the Industry who knows the difference between making movies and remaking himself. No wonder the place isn't for you."

• • •

Marty calls his friend from C.T.'s room and tells Tak about the trouble C.T. is in, and Tak agrees that if talking to Marty's son in the young man's awkward situation can do any good at all, Tak is willing to try. Marty murmurs his gratitude.

"He's been making these skate videos for quite a while now. Go figure — a Nyrop gets in trouble for making movies. Who saw that coming, right?"

"So, you think maybe C.T. could be distracted from this dead-ender thing — I mean, sorry, but it sounds kind of self-destructive. Maybe by some kind of apprenticeship down here? One of the guilds?"

"C'mon, Tak — you were there." Marty is relying on Tak's understanding that Hollywood is the last thing Marty wants for his son; not surprising, since it was Tak who once drove Marty and his abducted baby to the Utah airport. "And now it's not only jail and pregnancy, but it's ten times harder than it has to be, because Laura's shown up like some film can rolling out of a storage vault, and she wants to get him wrapped up in a production of hers. Through all that, C.T.'s gotta get the whole fatherhood situation, how it's just impossible. If you could help him with that, make him see what Eric was like. . . ."

"But he's seen what *you're* like, Marty. Isn't that enough?"

"Fuck . . . no."

Since Tak's counter offer to Laura's move on C.T. with an entry-level movie job isn't an option, Tak accepts the storyteller role, to at least fill in some of the last year of Eric Blanc's life for C.T.'s benefit and give him a memory of the Nyrop family from someone who's not a Nyrop. The story should have been shared some time ago, but Marty would never let that happen.

Within an hour, Tak leaves Mt. Olympus, hits the access ramp to the 5 North, and heads for Sacramento.

•••

Tak arrives at Marty's neat bungalow after sunset. Solid and modest, the restored Craftsman might have been ordered as a kit from Sears & Roebuck a hundred years ago and shipped by rail with complete assembly instructions for the handyman. Once inside Tak quickly explains C.T.'s legal situation within the limits of his competence on the matter, and reconfirms his optimism that they can bring C.T. home and get to work on clearing this unfortunate incident from his record immediately. Marty is subdued, but compliant, and is clearly even more grateful to Tak than when he called him in L.A..

Throughout the weekend, into early Monday morning, Lupe is a nearly silent presence, polite but aloof, with a cat-like grace in her weighted movement. There is something regal and Mayan that pulls the center line of her face slightly forward, but also a gloom in her that she mostly masks as they all travel in Tak's absurdly expensive car from Marty's tree-sheltered neighborhood to the more suburban feel around the Juvenile Hall. Better to arrive looking successful, Marty supposes. In case anybody cares.

"He's been watching the movie, Tak. I don't know how he got it. Hacked it somewhere. . . ."

"*User-Friendly*? Yeah, I guess he's never seen it, eh?"

"Hell no. Absolutely not."

Tak lets his silence register his disapproval. They've already argued over Marty's decision to hide the history of C.T.'s birth parents through the years. In their last exchange Marty heatedly reminded Tak, "It's my call, *I'm* the parent."

When Tak responded, "Well then, congratulations — you finally got your name above the title," it was an unkind comment from a kind friend, time for Tak to back off, and he quickly did. Now they both understand that the identity horse is out of the barn.

As Marty has hoped, the Juvenile Hall procedures are *pro forma* and C.T. is released to them with a hearing date scheduled for next week. While they walk together back to the car where Lupe has chosen to remain, C.T. ignores them with total focus on his recovered cell phone, addressing each friend he talks to as "Foo" and wanting to know "Wachoo doin?"

Marty catches Tak's eye to signal that they're listening to the same things and Marty tries to contain himself, until he can't.

"C.T. — what's up with this "Wachoo" stuff? So what's wrong whichoo, Foo? I'm pretty sure English still uses the 'th' sound. Oh, sorry, I forgot you're a *gang*-stah now. Stripes. Cred."

C.T. glares at Marty, then hesitates when they arrive at the car and they both see Lupe in the back. C.T. gets into the front passenger seat without speaking to her. It's going to be a quiet ride home.

Just as Tak turns his wheels toward the driveway a lumbering boxcar of a truck cuts into their path. It looks as if it's armor-plated like a Brinks security vehicle and has two ridiculously large mouse-ears mounted on its roof — more satellite uplinks. From behind the truck the same swarm of camera and sound crew and various levels of production assistants that had assaulted Marty's front door all reappear in search of more raw material for "Hollywood Birth Moms!" It's as if they'd been stored in a Jack-in-the-box for just this moment. Young and energetic and incapable of self-consciousness or shame, they set up an instant field operation of multiple camera positions, each aimed at Tak's car as if to blast it to smithereens with cosmic technology.

Marty sinks into the seat next to Lupe but C.T. springs from the front passenger side, calls out a name, and goes immediately to the young woman holding the nearest microphone. Marty is suddenly aware that C.T. already knows these people, this is a practiced routine.

"C.T., what just happened in there? What can you tell us?"

Marty misses what his son has to say as he pushes on the heavy car door and struggles to get out of the deeply padded seat. His glance back reveals Lupe rolling on her side, pulling her long hair over her face. Marty goes after the nearest microphone.

"What the fuck are you morons doing here?"

The young woman with the mic is the Field Producer, doing Laura Trent-Sampson's dirty work. She ignores Marty and closes in on C.T. even as Marty tries to push in front of a camera to block it.

"Can you tell us what happens here in Juvie? Why you're here? What kind of trouble are you in?"

Marty is fighting his visceral urge to break something, or someone. Tak overtakes him and in quick legal language reminds the Field Producer that C.T. is a minor and has an expectation of privacy even in public space.

The Field Producer eyes Tak with the charm of an eel. "I've got his release, signed and witnessed. By his mother."

Marty pulls C.T. by the arm. "What've you done?"

The Field Producer turns to one of her crew holding a shotgun microphone. "Get that? Tag it for Segment Three — and get it to an editing bay *now*."

Tak waves at Marty to get him physically away from this bunch, but Marty won't move. "You call this fucking 'reality'?"

The Field Producer levels her gaze at him. "A message from Laura: this 'reality' has already happened. We're just working backward from the ending we've already got."

The giant mouse-ears on the roof of the truck are swiveling, aligning themselves to bounce Marty and his small family through space and back to Los Angeles.

Patrick Cosgrove

24

*A*fter a quiet time spent writing memos to himself, Tak watches a few scenes with the three others in C.T.'s room. The intensity of the shooting process, even so long ago, makes it seem as if no time has elapsed at all, as if Marty and Tak saw these shots in dailies only yesterday. But the context for watching these actors has been transformed: C.T. now watches these gossamer apparitions as parents who were never there for him, never held him, never said "I love you." Watching Movie-Mom and Movie-Dad in full makeup with a sprightly score on the soundtrack to jazz things up a little must be head-spinning. However the stories of making the film might salve a lifelong sense of loss, C.T.'s previous imagining of his natural parents — whatever it was — is probably getting pretty abused.

C.T. taps the space bar on his keyboard and pauses the film. He's frowning at the screen, but it's hard to read his intent.

"Why the fuck doesn't he know it was her the *second* time, too?"

It's a story question about the plot point, common to romantic comedies, of mistaken identity that *User-Friendly* hinges upon. Marty and Tak glance at one another, and Marty handles it:

"Sometimes we only see what we *want* to see in other people. Not what's really there. His character 'Albert' needs her for emotional reasons, so he accepts the second version of her as someone new. Different. It allows him to have her back, and that way he doesn't have to face up to how badly he behaved with her the first time. A lot of it's just convention — romantic comedy and all, you know, genre. Plus she's got the new haircut, new clothes, the new accent. . . ."

"Yeah but . . . she's right fuckin' there. No one else is gonna be that . . . pretty. Not fuckin' *twice*."

"Well. . . . Sometimes when you want something that bad, you stop listening to who *you* really are, too."

In silence C.T. watches a paused two-shot of his parents until he bows his head.

"So . . . what was it like between the two of 'em? I mean, like in person, was any of it for real?"

"God, I wish I could answer that, C.T.. I really do. I just don't know. They shared something, for sure. But it was hard to understand, even if you were there."

"Fuckin' bullshit. . . ."

They all hear Lupe take in a sharp breath and turn together to look at her, curled up with her knees under her belly, braced in the corner of the bed against the wall. She tries to press her face into her swollen abdomen, curving her spine forward. C.T. stands quickly with his hands ready for something but he doesn't know what to do with them. Marty leans over her:

"Lupe — ? You okay? What do you need?"

She keeps her face covered and waves them all away. She rocks herself, her fingers laced together around her shins. The room is quiet except for the low rhythmic groan of the mattress. Marty motions everyone out of the room.

They go to the kitchen, not as a plan but because it's likely that Lupe will eventually want something from here. C.T. sits and puts his head on the tabletop like a student passing out in Marty's classroom.

Marty rubs C.T.'s back for a moment, then sits next to him. "It's not too late, you know. They're wrong about this, those idiots from the TV show. The ending's not written yet. Your life's not set in stone, you two can still arrange an adoption."

C.T. snaps to attention. "Fuck that. Fuck you. You did it, and we wouldn't have to go lie about it — "

"I did it when I was fifteen years older than you. I had my degree. I had a job."

"That you walked away from."

"I knew I could teach — "

"And you threw away being a fuckin' Hollywood Director to teach high school — ? That's *bull*shit."

"I came home every night. From school, I came home every night."

"Why? To *what*?"

"To you."

C.T. pushes back from the table with a loud scrape of the chair legs on the tile floor. He leaves the house through the side door.

"I'm sorry you had to see that, Tak."

Tak shrugs. "That, compared to what? Anyway, I'll talk to him again in a while. Maybe I can fill in some more holes. Both of your life's dreams were right there. I mean, you did work together. You and his father made a movie. Have you told him how it got started? Maybe he'll want to hear more about that, what it took to bring you and your brother together."

Marty nods, though he doesn't seem to think it will change anything.

And when C.T. comes home an hour later, Tak tells him some of these things about the making of movies. About how *User-Friendly* came to be, however improbably. C.T. has known Tak all his life but never before as anything other than a polite, occasional visitor who once worked with his Dad. He's now warily watching through a new lens, seeing a Hollywood Producer who once knew his mother and father. While padding to and from the kitchen Marty keeps an ear out for any detail that he might emphasize in his effort to sour C.T. on fatherhood, on his having anything to do with his mother no matter what the pull of celebrity seems to be. In this way, Marty travels back with Tak through the years, listening, comparing memories, letting C.T. get perhaps a more objective view of these actors.

In the beginning C.T. listens with his eyes averted, the way adolescents try to show how emotionally opaque they are while they leak their too-big feelings through every pore. He is coming to know the parents he never met.

• • •

Tak remembers first the waiting, the staring at the brick-red tiles near a restaurant entrance. He was uncomfortable at meeting his first actor. Eric Blanc wasn't a movie star, he wasn't on soap operas or prime time television. But even a casual reader of the L.A. *Times* "Calendar" section might've been aware of Blanc's notoriety as leader of his own theater group. The reviewers said he managed to keep his troupe in production through sheer ingeniousness, primarily with off-off-Broadway works approaching off-Broadway. Eric Blanc performed in what were usually, and meaninglessly (to a tax attorney) called *avant-garde* pieces. He noticed that critics seldom had the vocabulary to describe what it was Blanc actually did. The Open Theater, The Living Theater, these were antecedents but belonged to others equally noteworthy and none of the descriptions Tak found in his research for that first night's meeting ever quite explained Eric Blanc. The best summation of him was by a woman named Leffer who spoke of an obsession "with a theater yet to be born." Blanc was looking to gut plays of the literary, to gut the theater of stories, to reduce the stage experience to only what no other art form could supply: the physical presence of the actor, the aliveness of performer and audience sharing the same air. The unconventionality of Blanc's artistry made Tak even less sure of himself than did the slippery language problem with Tak's Japanese clients. Eric Blanc was a creative force, surely, but an actor-writer-director-producer who tried to do away with most of his own job titles as a matter of principle. What business sanity was there in that?

In his re-telling, Tak remembers too: on this, the Sunday when his walk among actors started, it had been a brown day, the kind of day a Los Angeles native would sometimes notice but not think much about, but the kind a non-native like himself would *always* notice no matter how long he'd lived here, no matter where else he'd come from, because back home there were no days quite like it. The setting for his adventure was within L.A.'s concave basin, a bowl that holds the machine heat and the human dampness within its edges that curl upward into the Santa Monica Mountains until the air becomes manifest, a thin chemical broth. But straight above, the obverse dome of sky is still deeply blue and that's the part the non-Californian can never tire of: this endless paradisiacal blue blossoming out from the inextinguishable yellow sun. Pink dawn comes after pink dawn, all dawns promising many things even if by mid-morning the air will invariably have become acrid at the curled-up meeting place of sky and mountains. Even then, an immigrant from Utah can't help but to look straight up, past the brown to the blue.

He finds simpler words for the memory he shares with C.T., but won't patronize; he wants the boy to know how enticing, how seductive Los Angeles sunlight can be. It can make you want things. Try to be things.

"Hollywood" — Los Angeles, of course — is where non-Californians deliberately come to take part in something that is pageant and temple at once. Every intersection, office building, theater, or restaurant resonates with the electromagnetism of past lives once famously enacted along these very streets and boulevards, their vibrations strummed out again and again every morning, every evening somewhere in the world by the resuscitating, immortalizing power of ever-new technology playing movies from the past. It's a city of art and entertainment relics, a destination assigned by the pilgrim beforehand to mean more than any real place honestly can, giving everything about L.A. a spiritual heft. Tak was conscious of that, but still. . . .

Marty, Tak, and Eric shared that first evening at the Musso & Frank Grill, the perfect setting for fellow pilgrims to discuss a deal. "Oldest in Hollywood, Since 1919" the sign above the entrance said. Somewhere hidden in the back, behind all the dark paneling and crown molding was the writers' room where men like Faulkner and Fitzgerald and West — names of a celluloid cosmology — once gathered as if in a luxurious refugee camp to eat and smoke and drink. Doubtlessly they shared stories about rapacious, granite-headed moguls who had taken away their gifts, who had stolen their words arranged with care and cadence, ripping them from Underwood typewriters to be ravished like maidens in the scaly hands of Greed and Ignorance. But they, the writers, came knowingly, deliberately as non-natives do; and they were no better or worse after their stay in Hollywood for having come, only wealthier, only abler to continue what they had done better someplace else. Their literary greatness, if they'd truly possessed it, preceded Hollywood and was uncontaminated by what the writers themselves saw as the impurity of their own movie work, and nothing they did here matched that previous greatness. Instead, their screen work had only a high level of workman-like quality within a peculiarly collaborative craft, the skill that assembly-line natives understood and could already supply to their Industry themselves. Perhaps the refugees' shared sense of dislocation was merely this: that before these writers had ever got here they were already a transformed Somebody, and therefore they'd violated a mythic sequence. As famed authors their journey of transcendence, of re-birth, had already happened. So eventually they went back home, east of Hollywood, returning to eat, smoke, drink some more and die.

"Never would be a sequence problem for me," Tak tells C.T.. I sure wasn't already a somebody." C.T. stares without indicating whether or not he understands Tak's meaning.

Tak remembers that as he watched his clients from MSC of Japan approach Musso & Frank's from their car parked two blocks away, he was ashamed to find himself wishing that they had captured the feel of California-casual dress a little more accurately. Instead they looked the way Japanese businessmen of the late-1980s often did during free time abroad, their identical blue suit jackets buttoned over tie-less, white knit shirts with inexpensive, obscurely-patterned slacks and brown loafers, and each with a leather bag slung from a shoulder. These executives had recently taken over Tak's private business completely, since MSC's overseas corporate needs — small as they were compared to Mitsubishi, Sony, and the like — had swollen to become virtually all of his tax law practice. Yet to him, Kurumada-*san* and Yamamoto-*san* both looked like kids — diffident, watchfully absorbent but with no apparent self-reflection.

Tak was already uncomfortable around them because of his weak grasp of *Nihon-go*, the Japanese language. He normally used it only with his parents, and since his mother and father still lived near Salt Lake City after being displaced during World War II, through the Camp Minidoka internment camp, even that usage was rare, a yearly fumbling more out of a mix of cultural pride and guilt than pragmatism. He knew when his parents eventually died their last thoughts would be in English, as his own would be. But still he and his Japanese clients understood one another clearly enough. Business had its own communicative power. He was thankful they at least had left their new Sony Mavica still-video cameras in their car trunk and had insisted only on trying out the cement hand- and footprints at the Chinese Theater before coming here to Musso's.

MSC was determined to buy into Hollywood, to be a creator of product for the video hardware they already manufactured. Their initial investment would be somewhere short of buying their own studio outright, as the much bigger Sony was threatening to do with

Columbia, or as Matsushita had recently considered doing with either Paramount or Universal. Tak's clients were meeting here tonight because Eric Blanc had, at the last minute before their return to Osaka, asked the MSC executives to finance a feature film for him in addition to his proposal for the backing of a play. Surprisingly, MSC was apparently considering doing so even though their original intention was only offering to finance the much less expensive theater production.

Tak, when consulted by MSC as their *ad hoc* American representative, had conceded that it made sense to at least consider Blanc's movie script. Tak was a tax attorney by training, a financial adviser only by happenstance when clients considered initiating new business ventures such as this, but he'd been reading the trades; MSC could afford few of the already-celebrated stars in a movie production start-up venture, and to deal directly with an actor like Blanc meant avoiding the profit-gobbling of a successful independent producer or established studio. Tak had learned enough to know that involvement in any financial participation with others already successful in the business would cause any MSC profit to be sliced and finely diced into untraceable grains of production expenses, real or not. MSC would never see a dime.

Eric gave MSC another option. Though no one else in Hollywood had yet enticed Blanc, he had a legitimacy that many working producers found enticing — a name associated with "artistic" quality and whatever that implied, without the price of a track record. But this also meant that there were no guarantees, no built-in box office appeal. MSC had wanted a safer initial route, to spend less money developing a play that would create its own following and make audience awareness much less expensive should they eventually adapt it for film. But now their connection Eric Blanc wanted to dive directly into the Hollywood industry as the price he placed on safety later on. Would artistic notoriety translate into profit? No one could know. Moviegoers and theatergoers were not necessarily the same beast. And wasn't the logic of safety to do the safe thing *first?*

So Tak had just yesterday advised MSC, one of Japan's smaller but rising international corporations, not to go with Blanc's romantic comedy screenplay called *User-Friendly* as the first step on the perilous financial trek that is independent movie-making. He was relieved that they'd taken his inexpert but logical recommendation: tonight they would say No.

The offer to back Eric's play, however, was still on the table. Blanc had mentioned a well-known actress's interest in the script, but pointedly did not name her. Though it might prove interesting, it was a topic probably best left in limbo for the time being. Meeting Eric Blanc this evening, then, would be only a business formality, a courtesy of acknowledging Blanc's theatrical stature. Still, none of Tak's experience in regulatory law and tax percentages and venture capital strategies seem to be of any use in meeting an actor, even socially. An "ingenious" one at that. Don't actors, he wondered, pretend for a living?

• • •

Kurumada and Yamamoto, the two Japanese businessmen, stood dutifully still with their hands folded at their belts. The euphoric paradisiacal blue had darkened, and belonged only to the midday L.A. sky, but Tak gestured up Hollywood Boulevard toward the obviousness of another California sunset. He hoped that they, too, might notice how the West Coast light deepens the pastels of both nature and stucco, how it compresses them into the same saturated colors as were in the now-quickened words of storefront neon and in the Vogue and Ritz marquees beneath the dying sky. Yamamoto and Kurumada gave a knowing "ah" at the sight and remained half-turned from Tak. Someday he wanted to unmask this "magic hour," as they called it here in the Film Industry, to determine exactly what it was about the thickening ambience, the powerful strangeness of the transient light mixing between orange sunset and black night that imposed an unsettling feeling on him.

Part of his unease was that magic hour shifted, even fooled, any sense of season — no matter what the calendar said, once beyond midday it was always Christmastime in L.A.. The sheer excess of multi-colored lights against a landscape of gargantuan terrarium plants constantly reminded him of something from his past he vaguely longed for but would not be returning to. Especially when driving through dusk, he was left disappointed that on a second, more careful look, this magic hour of colorfully banded sky over glimmering neon and blinking light bulbs was clearly not the thing he only sensed at first — not the season, not the cheery holiday — but was instead a burlesque, a mocking echo of childhood.

Maybe this had something to do with the name Tinseltown. Back home there were still a few unembarrassed uses for tinsel, but if he hung strands of it on his L. A. Christmas tree the stuff was simply outshone, out-tinseled by the place itself just outside his door. In L.A. the foil reindeer, the vacuum-molded candles, and the Noël cutouts strung above the streetlights weeks before Thanksgiving were redundant because it was already, and always, subtropical Christmas. What better fantasy could anyone want? What other yearnings could be satisfied here? Plenty, he was sure, but exactly which ones? Sometimes when he was on the Ventura Freeway at night during a Santa Ana, the ground-up bits of palm fronds lifted and driven by the hot winds looked like snow in the glare of his headlights.

Tak and his clients hesitated outside of Musso & Frank's until they bowed quickly to one another and went into the restaurant to meet their actor.

25

*I*t doesn't help that Laura has inserted herself out of nowhere and for stunningly selfish purposes. C.T. can't seem to get beyond the discovery that he really does have a living mother, and who can blame him? So far he's been listening to Tak attentively. It's uncharacteristic and however he's internalizing any of these events, in whatever way, he doesn't communicate it.

The next time he can get C.T.'s attention, Marty picks up where Tak left off at Musso & Frank's on the night that got their deal started, the night he and Eric pitched the movie idea that made them all what they've become.

• • •

Eric and Marty were already seated at a booth halfway to the hidden writers' room in the back. Eric had ordered the cannelloni dinner only because the "Legendary Chicken Pot Pie" wasn't available tonight. The pasta was the cheapest thing on the menu, a tourist special prepared ahead of time. Rather than feel rude for starting without Takashi Itani and his Osaka clients, Eric tried out several rationales on his disapproving brother: that the jet lag headache he hadn't been able to shake in the unseasonable L.A. smog would be eased by food, especially heavy carbohydrates; or that Itani would probably be late because traffic makes everybody late in this town (and Tak was, now, by seven minutes, though still within punctuality by California standards); and that you only got in life what you appeared not to want, a bit of quasi-Zen that Eric thought would play well with the Japanese sensibility. Eric admitted being leery of this last notion, that he was playing a game of culture where he didn't know most of the rules.

More importantly he knew, as any conventional actor or playwright since the birth of Greek stagecraft would know, that a story might have a beginning, middle and end, but audience engagement must be impelled by jump-starting *in medias res*, in the middle. He told Marty that within his preparatory imaginings he would already be well into a performance of their "Pitch" scene when Itani arrived.

Marty turned the script coverage of *User-Friendly* face down and held his warming glass of beer with both hands. "So who am I tonight? I mean, what exactly did you tell them?"

"Nothing yet. They haven't said they're interested. So if you want, you can be 'Marty Blanc.'"

"That really sounds authentic. Mahtee Blahhnc, Eurotwit."

"My, we're in a sour mood. You said it yourself, you don't want your Guild to find you on this one. If they haven't kicked you out already. Pick a hero. We're from Detroit. So — cars. Buick. Chevy. Ford. You always liked Westerns. *John* Ford. . . . There it is. Be the next Ford. Motown Smokey Ford."

"Yeah. Or why not Marty Ford Coppola? Talk about 'other Martys.' Just don't blow this. After what you pulled with Laura. . . . I never trusted you before. I sure as hell don't trust you now. The difference this time is that I'll fucking kill you if this movie doesn't get made because this is my last chance *ever* and I won't let you screw up my life again."

"You're the one doing it again. . . . Look, I don't care what you think of me. I mean, yes and no. But I had to do what I did —"

"Are we talking the hairy orangutan sex scene, screwing up the whole family, the running away, the lying stories, the name change, what you fucking did to your kids, *what* —?"

"Yeah, we're talking a lot of things. *Everything.* You find your own reasons for what you have to do. Neither of us has led a nice, normal life. But we might have talent, and thank god for that."

"How would you know what I have?"

"It's imagination, Marty. That's all that talent is, imagination. If you have to make a movie, find your own reasons. The story, the conflict, the motivation. The need. Imagine it."

"Whatever. Another thing — You cross me one more time, you tell me just one more lie, you try to make me feel one thing I'm not feeling. . . . I've got no job, no girlfriend, no kids, and no future without this movie. You screw this deal up tonight, this one last thing I have . . . like I said I'll fucking kill you."

"Yeah, but it'll be enough, won't it? To get your own movie? Besides, Mr. Ford, you're awful pretty when you get mad."

"Kill you with my own hands."

"Fine. So who're you gonna be?"

"That's your game, not mine. '*Eric.*'"

There, he'd now deliberately used that name aloud. No more Craig Nyrop. Or Marty Nyrop either. He picked up the story coverage again, the screenplay summary written by a studio intern who had read and vetted the script so an executive wouldn't have to take the time to read it personally. He entertained a brief fantasy of the look that would be on his college classmate's face when he called her and told her that her script had been optioned.

Marty re-read the coverage:

```
Independent Story Analysts, Inc.

Coverage #138449
Screenplay: 118 pages
Submitted to: Takashi Itani, MSC Pictures
Submitted by: Eric Blanc, Actor — 12/18/89
Story Analyst: Steven Gabler


            "USER-FRIENDLY"

        An Original Screenplay by
           Melissa Martinez

TYPE: Romantic Comedy/Farce

LOCALE & TIME: Rural West & New York City,
Present

THEME: Through conventions of the boy
meets/then loses/then finds girl genre, love
triumphs after mix-ups and forgiveness.

SYNOPSIS: ALBERT BYRNE makes a technological
breakthrough that allows personal robots to
become a practical commercial reality. These
machines — slaves, helpers, friends — will
change our lives and reap a fortune.

ABM (read: IBM) doesn't want another multi-
billion-dollar Apple Computer scenario to
```

unfold, as it did in the '80s for personal computers. ABM must co-opt Albert Byrne, or destroy him as a competitor. In romantic comedy tradition, their weapon is a human heat-seeking missile — their own strong-headed, strong-willed and ambitious ABM executive GINGER STERLING, with razor intellect and major league pheromones.

Ginger tries to sucker Albert into the ABM fold with business logic, then cash, then ego perks, but Albert is uninterested. He wants to turn his machine over to hackers in the public domain. He's naïve, and sees his robot as a servant of humankind more than as potential profit. This baffles Ginger, but she finally realizes that she is down to feminine wiles as her last resort. She targets Albert for romance.

What she doesn't anticipate is falling in love with him.

By the time her prize — taking Albert's work from him — is nearly in hand, Ginger's heart has gone through a complete turnabout. She plans to explain herself, to confess the bad motivations that have unexpectedly produced true love. But she is too late. Albert finds out about her first and learns how she planned to deceive him. He spurns her and it's painful for them both. His inability to forgive her shows how far he has to grow up emotionally, how much his obsession with programming human behavior and feelings into his personal robots has left his own humanity sadly underdeveloped.

But: through mistaken identity, they have the chance to do it all over again as two "new" people. They each start a new life, pretending new names, new identities. They find each other again. And in a second romance, revenge and forgiveness hang in the balance until love resolves all.

COMMENTS:

Note #1: To be generous to this film's premise, mistaken identity is a legitimate feature of the screwball/farce. There's always the danger of being outright silly, but if it's done right there's no total suspension of disbelief required to make this work.

It has a chance because the "Ginger" character does, after all, come to Albert the first time as someone not entirely herself. And when he sees her the second time she's already made a broad attempt to start over 1) emotionally and 2) in her behavior. Of course the Director would have the obvious hair and wardrobe tricks to play with as well. (Note: it's at least as believable as all the ghosts in someone else's body we've been seeing lately. Sorry, different genre, but still. . . .)

From the hero Albert's POV, he sees what he wants to see. He's repressed, and the second time around he's got emotional and psychological reasons to _not_ want this re-made person to be Ginger. He's just as attracted to her the second time, but he behaved badly the first time and can't have her back. A subconscious denial of her "real" identity is what gives him a second chance — it's her, and yet _not_ her, a role-within-a-role, very actorish. It'll be treading a fine line to get it on the screen the right way.

Note #2: This story structure owes a lot to Preston Sturges's THE LADY EVE with Henry Fonda and Barbara Stanwyck. Maybe too much not to be called a re-make. (Have Legal check the rights.) It will require Sturges's farcical energy. Of course everyone who went to film school says they want to do a Sturges comedy, and still nobody but Sturges has ever pulled it off. Bob Zemeckis, for example, might be capable of maintaining the likeability of characters within a contemporary farce. Maybe Rob Reiner or Ron Howard.

```
The characters' initial selfishness or their
implausibility in this synopsis form will
disappear with enough laughs — this needs a gag
rewrite — and enough energy to keep the
audience distracted, until all the hidden
"real" facets of Albert's and Ginger's
repressed psychology are sorted through. This
will be a stretch for anybody involved and is
full of risk and will probably require very
popular stars to make it play. Meryl Streep
doing the Barbara Stanwyck character(s) would
be worth seeing.

PRODUCTION VALUES: Medium

RECOMMENDATION: Yes _____ No _____ Maybe __X__

WRITER RECOMMENDED: Yes (Pending gag overhaul —
see above)
```

Marty folded his hands around his beer glass and swirled the dregs above the coverage pages. He already had a firm idea of what "forgiveness" would look like on the screen. Movies were full of its images, the greatest fantasy of all.

• • •

Tak and his MSC salarymen waded through a sea of mostly pink tourist skin, through the din of bussed plates and glasses, through squeals from flatware scraping at sauces and a babble undampened by the slack and exposed bodies half-dressed even in January with garish Midwestern summerwear. Eric materialized in the aisle before them, already striking a pose that he must've known Kurumada and Yamamoto would recognize — that of a character from Eric's series of TV commercials that had created a sensation in Japan. Eric had told Marty about an American clothing designer who introduced a men's cologne there and wanted it to arrive with ready-made history, a patina of instant Americana. Eric was filmed as several black-and-white Hollywood reincarnations, almost motionless within silvery set design as he eyed the camera lens. First he was Gary

Cooper from the '30s, then Montgomery Clift from the '40s, finally James Dean from the '50s. Marty could easily imagine how each pose would capture the essence of that actor because Eric could absorb and emit the internal contradiction that to this day keeps these legends alive on the screen: an unstable compound of antithetical traits that makes each star compelling, engaging, more elusive than a type, even when doing nothing more than projecting his presence. It was another factor that had given the men from MSC of Japan pause over the movie project — the Japanese loved Eric Blanc on the screen, even before America knew who he was.

Now, standing loose-jointed in the restaurant aisle, his legs and torso twisting away at different angles as if privately feeling a cold wind against his neck, Eric was James Dean: essential, defiant youth, angry yet in pain, moving forward to threaten; on the verge of reaching out for help, yet breaking away too with his nerves gone raw, exposed. It was an arresting, actorish push-pull, topped off by Dean's duck's-ass haircut that Marty only now noticed Eric had co-opted. The three businessmen couldn't help but to stop and absorb the image, as if the psychology of the moment put Eric/Dean on a shallow plane of focus through a telephoto lens while the rest of the crowded room dropped away, defocused in circles of confusion like the optics of lens perception.

Eric suddenly dropped his hands against his thighs and lowered himself prayerfully in a bow. Tak stared, then watched his associates bow in return with quick glances to make sure that on their second bob they matched the depth of Eric's low angle. Eric straightened, smiled brightly, and held out his hand.

"Eric Blanc."

Tak shook it. "As James Dean, right? 'Jim Stark,' I bet. *Rebel Without a Cause.*"

"Sure, you could say that."

"Takashi Itani. I saw your commercials, just terrific."

"Well, at least those thirty-second movies brought us together. One of life's little compromises, right?"

Tak raised his hands. "No — I liked them. Really. I like a lot of commercials. Their efficiency with a message, eh?"

"And this is my brother, Marty. . . ."

He rose from his seat and shook Tak's hand. "Martin Ford."

Eric smiled with half his face. "Marty's a Director, and he's been in Production too. Knows the business top to bottom. He's the one we'll trust with all the nuts and bolts on the set."

Tak smiled back uneasily and nodded at this minor complication of having another person to disappoint. He introduced Mr. Yamamoto and Mr. Kurumada, describing their positions in the MSC of Japan corporate hierarchy. The businessmen looked to one another as if to assess the appropriate positioning, then took the bench across from Eric and Marty. Tak slid into the banquette on the brothers' side, facing his own clients, the better to translate. He used *Nihon-go,* the Japanese language, hesitantly and seemed to quickly judge that the men were following most of what Eric said anyway and were simply reluctant to reveal their own command of English. Eric pointed to his plate.

"I'm very sorry — *Gomennasai,* is it? — please make your friends understand this, I'm sorry that I started eating without you. Since I got on the plane after we closed the last show, I've hardly eaten a thing. And the air out here — I didn't want to faint on you."

Tak assured Eric that it was certainly all right, that Eric needn't worry about protocol; that in Hollywood the Japanese were willing and eager to emulate *us.* From Tak's look, though, he must have guessed that Eric's choice was to not worry about protocol at all. Eric was dressed in a badly wrinkled white dress shirt with chinos and no socks, a studied dishevelment that went with the haircut. So far he probably hadn't turned out to be what Tak expected in an actor. Instead, Eric was someone who wasn't trying very hard to please and didn't seem to care terribly much if he did or not. What could Tak have expected — charm?

Eric downed a huge mouthful before he spoke. "Tak, you've gone over the script? With the company?"

"Yes, I have. A real eye-opener on how these things look. Very clever, very entertaining."

"And very visual, physical. Something that'd cut across cultures. Financially safe, too. I've got a Production background too from the theater. Lived for years off grants. And we've got Marty guiding us from the beginning —"

Marty found his voice. "For instance, I can show you some ideas about where we could use MSC product placement. Props, computers, some of the robotic hardware. You can charge it off to promotion. This movie'll earn back its negative cost in Japan alone."

"Well, yes. The tech aspect, it's all there —"

Marty shook his head, cautionary. "But not the point of the story. It's the character relationship. You'd pitch it to a studio as a romance. That's the concept. Love among robotics engineers. The awkwardness of things that don't fit, but work out in the end anyway."

"Oh sure. Yes." Tak briefly glanced from brother to brother and chose Eric. "I mean, I'm no critic, Mr. Blanc —"

"No, no, no. Just . . . 'Eric.' Look, I don't expect you to be a story analyst, we've already had that done. None of us are dealing through traditional channels, our meeting here proves it. This is an honest script —"

Tak nodded quickly, stiffly, and ran his hand over the cover of his own copy of the screenplay. "Yes. . . ." He hesitated, considering whether he needed to translate further. "Ah . . . I was laughing out loud a couple of times, right? Maybe that happens all the time?"

Marty shook his head. "Almost never, believe me. That's good. A good sign."

"It's a strange thing to read — you don't always catch on to who's doing what. All the abbreviations, the acronyms —"

Eric smiled. "Actors only care about 'CU' — Closeup. Or 'ECU' — Extreme closeup."

Tak laughed and translated Eric's joke — badly, he guessed, with apologies — for his clients. Tak seemed to be appreciating that Eric could turn it on and off, he had presence. The salarymen smiled politely and nodded as Marty continued:

"Yeah, the format. It takes practice. But this is a really good entry into the business. A very low-risk investment. You're not leaping somewhere in the dark, wondering if the special effects or the soundtrack sales are going to carry it. It's got high-concept spin for a romantic comedy, so it's not entirely cast-driven."

"I'm not sure I know what. . . . Yes, I liked it. But —"

Eric touched Tak's forearm before he could respond further. "But we're pushing. You want to say something about it and we're making it hard."

"No, it's not that. It's that . . . my clients have decided to say no. I'm very sorry."

Eric pushed the air out of his chest and looked up the aisle toward the restaurant entrance. Marty glanced at a spot above his brother's head before he muttered, "Tell them. . . ."

Tak leaned forward submissively. "Eric, they feel terrible that you've come all this way. They've already asked me to apologize in a dozen different ways, they want me to extend —"

"*Tell* them, Eric. God . . . damnit."

Eric held up a hand, fingers stretched wide to keep Marty at bay. "No, no, I said — like I said on the phone — I said I had other business. Out here."

"They'll cover all your expenses, for as long as you're here, and your theater salary for a week."

Eric's expression hardened. "It's my theater, I'm not *on* salary. . . ." He sighed. "I'm sorry. No, really, I mean . . . you really talked them through it? They know what the script's all about?"

"I had it completely translated by two different sources for comparison. They've been very thorough."

Eric avoided direct eye contact with Tak. Marty stared across the table at the two businessmen who were nearly identical to one another, not physically but in attitude; they moved in tandem as if yoked together in the same field for life. The one on the left wore glasses, the one on the right had some gray in his hair. Marty watched them meet Eric's eyes sympathetically, yet give him nothing else as they simultaneously shifted their gazes, unsmiling, back to Tak, waiting for the proper cue. It impressed Marty that they could each don so effective a mask in such effortless synchronization. He thought it would be a useful tool to have, but it might take a lifetime of living behind private, interior walls and the right partner to perfect it.

Marty turned his coverage of *User-Friendly* face-up again as if it held an answer. He tapped the cover with his fingertips to get Tak's focus. "Look, I know you'd need a big name to pull this off — what they call the marquee value. And I'm aware that one commercial campaign in Japan doesn't create bankability for Eric. But you guys *are* the bank. That's the whole deal here, isn't it?"

"In a sense. . . . We agreed that you've got something. That *User-Friendly* is a solid property. Is that the word?"

"For the script? A property, yeah."

"And they do expect to see it produced —"

"By someone else? You expect us to take it somewhere else?" Marty made a barking laugh. "We've been put in turnaround by a studio that doesn't even *exist* yet."

"Mr. Blanc — I'm sorry, Eric — this isn't my area of expertise. I can only advise on certain legal and financial matters —"

Marty lowered his voice, to be sure that he wasn't yelling across the table. "Let's get to the point. Eric's had a very interesting casting idea. Eric — ?"

"Just some general ideas."

"Eric — !"

Tak smiled weakly. "Ah. . . . Anyway, there was some concern . . . to tell you the truth, the decision was made before you left New York."

Eric nodded quickly. "I understand."

Marty's look at Eric was clear: *Why, you bastard, are you giving up so quickly, so easily?*

But Eric's capitulation allowed Tak to relax a bit. "I wonder, did you ever read the William Goldman book about the Industry? Where he says, 'Nobody Knows Anything'? To Goldman, it was a rule — nobody in charge has a clue about what makes a good movie. Until after they've seen it, and they point at it and say, 'Oh, there's one.' Fascinating. It must be a very hard way to do business."

Eric nodded again, reluctantly. He looked at Marty, the brother who didn't seem to know any longer why he'd come along. Eric cleared his throat. "I'm familiar with it. With the quote, not the whole book."

Tak smiled, warming up, Marty guessed, because he could speak from knowledge about something from his research into this exotic trade. "Goldman says all anybody seems to understand is movie stars. That if you have one in your movie, then it must be worthwhile. So you jump in, almost blind for a . . . a situation of celebrity. When I read that, it confirmed a lot of things I've picked up on. Maybe it's just an outsider's intuition. But that reasoning goes against everything the Japanese corporation has learned to do. They think long and hard as a group before they act. Then they act quickly. And right now they don't think they've given —"

Marty interrupted: "Yeah yeah, we read all about Japan in *Newsweek*. Look, Mr. Itani, it's a great theory for . . . for CDs, or cars, for things that've already been invented. But every movie, every play, they're *new*. Untested. Or they wouldn't be the creative, the uh . . . the artistic . . . I mean, Jesus, you can't just make a movie and then take it home and try it *out* for a while. . . ." He suddenly lost faith in the sound of his own pitch, and wondered again why Eric wouldn't speak up. Wouldn't offer Laura Trent-Sampson on a platter.

Tak had translated with a chugging urgency, stuck for words, phrases; after a moment he had gained tacit permission to go on with Eric.

"Yes. So it's going to take time. I think they're worried they've offended — Bringing you out here for *your* celebrity, right? You have to understand the concern — the commercials you did over there have been just . . . gigantic. A phenomenal thing, eh? We're all very sorry about this."

Eric shook his head. "Nah. Tell them it's not a problem, nobody's used anybody." Eric sighed. "What the hell, I'm honored."

Marty leaned his forearms on the table, slightly tilting it toward his gut. "Excuse me, but out here you can take 'honor' and shove it up — Can you tell me exactly why, Takashi? Why don't you want to make this movie?"

"It's no one thing."

"It *is* one thing. You're looking at him, aren't you?"

"I don't —"

"I'm not bankable. And Eric's not bankable either. That's two things."

"That's a part of it. Yes."

"With this script, I don't have to be. Okay, *somebody* does, but not me."

Tak nodded once. "But another factor is that no matter how good a romantic comedy like this one is, an audience — it appears to me anyway — they want to see that star. A superstar, a Redford, or a Streep, like the coverage says —"

Marty dropped a hand heavily onto Tak's forearm. "Or Laura Trent-Sampson?"

"For an example? Why not? Laura Trent-Sampson romanced on the screen. That would be . . . fun."

Marty glared at Eric. "Would you just go ahead? Tell them? What're you waiting for?"

Tak watched their baleful stalemate, then tried to continue what he'd started. "And there's usually a proven director involved, someone on the level of James Brooks, Richard Donner. Or it's like, say, if Sydney Pollack or Steven Spielberg decided to do a romantic comedy —"

"Funny you should say that, because Spielberg would want to do this one."

"He would, but he's a little busy, eh?"

Marty knotted and unknotted his fingers. "— Yeah, okay, so of course we don't have Spielberg. We have me. But directors like Spielberg who grew up on movies, they've never been shy about remaking the old ones they loved. This year, he's doing *Always*, based on *A Guy Named Joe*. Like it says in the coverage, *User-Friendly*'s a lot like *The Lady Eve*, with Barbara Stanwyck. I mean it could be pitched that way: High-tech Stanwyck."

"Barbara Stanwyck? I haven't seen her work."

"The Industry has. From the Golden Age, they *worship* it. If you could get today's —"

"— but Spielberg isn't involved. Look, I'm afraid we're getting way off the track here. . . ."

Marty knew Tak could sense weak waves of panic emanating from his chest like Morse Code from a crystal radio set. His brother Eric was re-set in his hurt/defiant James Dean pose. Tak would also see that Eric understood Marty's fear: the movie was not going to happen. Odd, Tak must've thought: did this actor care, or not?

Marty couldn't answer the question himself. He spurned Eric's glance of helplessness. "*Eric* —"

Tak grasped for anything that would bend this discussion in another direction. "And there's nothing attached. Beside yourself, Eric, I'm sorry — If we can go back to the original plan, then? With the stage play? Eric, I understand you have some very good news for us. . . ."

"Yes, well . . . I don't know. I mean, I'm not sure."

"Regarding an actress for your play? Can we name her yet? Maybe if we knew. . . ."

"No, but she's . . . interested. In the play. Maybe we can talk about this later. . . ."

Marty's face reddened, his diaphragm pushed up a throttled gargle. He couldn't look at his brother, and stared vacantly while calculating the odds of getting away with murder in front of witnesses. Across the table the businessmen were nodding slightly, corks bobbing in different phases of an ocean wave. Mr. Yamamoto, the one with glasses, cleared his throat and spoke precisely, slowly:

"If you please. We have . . . gift."

Eric looked to Tak, but Tak was silent until he quickly nodded to Mr. Yamamoto. The businessman reached into his shoulder bag and took out a beautifully wrapped package, a square and shallow box with a gold ribbon around the simulated-lacquer wrapping paper.

Eric looked awkward, unprepared. He smiled sheepishly at Tak. "What should I say?"

"*Doumo* . . . *Doumo arigato gozaimasu.*"

Eric nodded formally and repeated the phrase of thanks. Mr. Yamamoto smiled and nodded back. "*Dou, itashimashite.* It is nothing, not enough, please."

Tak showed a bubbling relief that Eric's disappointment and the job of saying "no" were over. "Go ahead Eric, open it —"

As soon as Tak said this, the salarymen's expressions flattened, their eyes went out across the room. Tak had said the wrong thing and embarrassed his clients; their exiting gesture had been thwarted. Eric was unfolding the ribbon, already deftly unwrapping the box. He sucked in his breath when he pulled out a burnished mask of the *Noh* theater. It was what the classical Japanese actor wore onstage, probably hundreds of years old, worn by generations of masters and shiny with the skin oil of a thousand cheeks and hands. It was an abstract, painted rendering of a timeless face.

Eric had tears. "I know this, I know the value. . . . I'm speechless. Tak? How do you say that you don't know what to say?"

But Tak was staring at the tabletop, until: "I think . . . Eric, I think if either Mr. Yamamoto or Mr. Kurumada has a daughter. . . ?"

Eric was blessedly quick on the uptake, and now he had a bit of business that helped him wall off the fury that he must have felt coming off Marty like heat. "Oh — yes, yes." He spun out of the banquette and retrieved a clean linen napkin from an unused place setting, then pulled out a ballpoint pen. Tak looked again at Mr. Yamamoto.

"Yamamoto-*san*?"

Mr. Yamamoto finally smiled. "I have a daughter. She is . . . teen age."

Eric grinned and smoothed the napkin next to his own plate. "I have two of them myself. Younger, though." He clicked the pen and hesitated. "What's her name?"

"Midori."

Tak spelled "Midori-*chan*" for Eric. Eric signed sweepingly across the entire cloth. Mr. Yamamoto dipped his head forward. "*Doumo arigato gozaimasu.* Thank you."

Eric leaned back. "*Doo, itashimashite.*"

Marty shifted in his seat to get their attention. "Kurumada-*san*, if I may?" Marty hesitated to see if Tak would intercede, but Kurumada was focused on Marty alone. "Mr. Kurumada, the Japanese people love robots, am I right?"

He seemed intrigued. "Yes."

"I've seen priests bless them. They have ceremonies on the assembly lines. They're given names —"

"Yes."

"Have you seen an animatronics exhibit? About ten, fifteen years ago, they had a robotic Marilyn Monroe. She played guitar and sang 'The River of No Return.' Then she gave a little wink, a little bump."

The two businessmen chatted, then chuckled lowly, until this time it was Mr. Yamamoto who focused on Marty. "Yes, we have seen."

"If you'll excuse me for a moment, let me leave you with this: think robots, think Marilyn Monroe. Prepare to make a leap. Think Laura Trent-Sampson."

Eric stared at Marty as his brother rose and went to the men's room. Eric followed.

• • •

Marty was trying not to scream.

"What did you say to her? What did you promise her, you fuck? What about my *movie*?"

When he grabbed Eric's wrinkled white shirt there was no point in Eric resisting; even as boys they both knew that the big-hands little brother was always quicker, tougher, stronger.

Finally Eric looked up, not to face Marty, but to find him in the mirror. "Nothing she didn't want. Very badly. I don't think any one of you ever made her feel worthwhile, Marty. Not for one single minute."

"I guess we should've screwed her on the set more often, huh? 'Hey! Everybody in the motorhome for cluster fucks!' Coulda shot her self-esteem sky-high."

"You should've taken her seriously, that's all."

"I'm *taking* her seriously! That's what doing this movie's all about! You let me come here tonight thinking Laura was a done deal!"

"I tried. You saw. She wants to work with *me*, not you. That's all I had, I couldn't sell her on you too. And I gave it an honest shot tonight. Besides, I think you should come with us to New York, Marty. Learn."

"She'd *have* you! In the movie, she'd work with *you*."

"It's not . . . the *stage*. The art, the discipline, the tradition. I don't care what you think of it, she wants to stand on the boards in front of an audience, breathe the dust, learn the craft. She wants to work with me on the stage."

"You promised, you pompous shit. That's why I let you see her, you *promised* me —"

"That wasn't fair, it wasn't a fair thing to ask for —"

"The hell it wasn't. I did it because . . . because —" He threw Eric against the sink counter. "I'll tell you how this business works. You know why a dog licks his balls?"

Eric couldn't help smiling even as he grabbed at his bruised hip. "No, Marty. Why does a dog lick his balls?"

"Because he *can*. And that's all you need to understand about Hollywood. You have leverage, you *use* it. No, I bet you get it already. You're still a crazy shit, aren't you? When you went in there, in the motorhome, did you at least warn her? Did you say 'Pardon me Exene, but before I whip out my dick, I'm *crazy*'?"

"Her name is Laura. Actually, she went in there and fished it out for me —"

Marty took a deep breath. "She's really gonna do your play? C'mon, it's impossible!"

"Yes."

"They won't *let* her, she's a fucking conglomerate! She's got agents, managers, packagers, a publicist — you think they'll let her go off and do that? I mean, I can't believe — She could do any movie she wanted, work with *anybody* —"

"It's the stage, Marty. It's the presence of the actor. You're afraid of it, but she's not."

"Where does it stop, 'Eric'? You lie to me, to Exene, to them. What's *real* to you anymore? Didn't I warn you not to cross me? Huh?" Marty threw one arm through the air, an empty punch.

"Come back with me to New York. Let's do it together. Where else are you going to go? Where am *I* going now, without you?"

"You forgot already? Back to New York, asshole!"

"Please. . . ."

"No. You tell them she's going to do my movie first. You *promised*."

"You could direct this play, Marty. If I get Laura involved, you could direct it. I can promise that much. I can't explain it, but I need you for this. And I think you need it, too."

"Sure, I know stage directing. If the playwright says there's a bird growing out of somebody's nose, then yeah, there's a bird. I'd be there watching you two, following you around like some little ring girl at your wedding —"

"You don't want it? Because you couldn't have your camera? Work with real actors. With me. You think directing's hiding behind some lens. Learn what performance *means*. I promise, you'll —"

"Yeah, and Mom and Dad'll sell rum zombies in the lobby, right?"

"Please."

"No, you go out there and tell them you're getting her for the movie first, or they don't have a deal. Do that or I'll kill you, I'll take that face of yours and smear it all —"

Eric rocked back and forth on his heels, smiling at Marty, then stepped to the sink. He wanted his emotions, his moment back, and he cut Marty out, sealed him off from his own inner vision. He could always do this, even before there was an Eric Blanc, even as the child named Craig Nyrop.

"Do it, 'Eric.' Go back out there, and do whatever it is that you psycho actors do. And do it *now*."

Eric wavered, as if powerless. It was impossible for Marty to tell what Eric really wanted. Nothing about this added up. Laura had been deeply impressed by whatever "Eric Blanc" meant. Eric didn't need to go through Marty at all, he could've waltzed into her agent's office and probably screwed the agent too, and all the secretaries in a five-way besides. Marty had threatened to kill him now a dozen times this week, so that threat was wearing pretty thin. What was it then. . . ? Marty sensed an edge, his only leverage. He pushed his face into Eric's.

"You do this . . . or I will never help. I will never direct you in anything. Whatever reason you had for coming out here — I will never agree to see you again. Ever. Do it, or from this moment on, the two survivors of this fucked up family are dead to each other. Dead."

"Marty, I need her to keep my theater going. But if you make it a choice, I'll go back with Laura. Without you. Go ahead, break my heart, but I didn't need your permission to deal with her before. And I sure as hell don't now. I was only trying to get you involved. So you make up your own mind."

All Marty had left was an even weaker hand. "All . . . all right. I'll come back with you. The stage, I'll try it. But one thing: you've gotta make this movie deal for me first. The movie, *then* the play, then I'll come. That's it. Movie first. Period."

Eric smiled even as he shook his head. He went into a toilet stall and pressed the heels of his palms against his eyelids. He breathed deeply, then hummed in a monotone, loosening the vocal instrument. He leaned into the side of the stall and did angled pushups against it. He went back to the sink and ran the cold water, then put his wet fingers through his hair and re-combed it into a dark blonde ducktail.

He stood before the mirror as if sensing his physical shell but willing himself not to look at it. Instead he must've imagined his own stony, chiseled leanness that could be mean and hard without much effort, and the soft fullness of his mouth that could make the hardness dissolve into flowery youth with the slightest smile. He could go from marble sculpture to doll instantly, mercurially. He squeezed his eyes shut and shifted his weight to one leg, squinting hard at some inward hurt. Marty watched as he transformed the musculature, tried to expose the nerves, to show both hope and fear, ready to spend what Marty would understand only later as the actor's currency of scarcely contained opposites.

Eric ran the hot water, then plunged both hands under it until he could no longer stand the scalding jet without screaming.

He found Marty again in the mirror with a look that might have said: Watch this, *Auteur*.

• • •

Eric slid back into the banquette first, next to Tak. He hunched forward with his still-burning hands splayed on either side of his dinner plate. He kept his eyes down, feeling for the rhythm, the connection. A waiter passed menus to the two businessmen. When they held their menus without trying to read them, watching only Eric, he must have known he had their focus. Eric was prepared: his eyes were shiny and one of his reddened hands trembled before he leaned across the table. There was both a need, and a radiant happiness, they all seemed to feel it when he spoke.

"Gentlemen. . . . Tak — What I didn't tell you on the phone. . . . I didn't mean to play games here. Laura Trent-Sampson is the actress I was talking about. Laura's also committed to do this film. She wants to do *User-Friendly*. First. She wants Marty to direct. The film, then the play. She's your attachment."

Eric was so clearly filled with triumph and relief at his own glad news that the others immediately accepted the felt truth. Mr. Yamamoto and Mr. Kurumada exchanged congratulatory smiles with Eric. Marty felt nothing.

Tak was the only one who looked unhappy. "What do you mean, Eric? 'Committed'? There's no paperwork, nothing's been signed with MSC that I'm aware of."

Eric allowed himself, almost imperceptibly, to leer. "There was something like a handshake between us, if you catch my drift."

Marty nodded solemnly. "We can time the whole thing off her availability. Figure about eight months from now. Time enough for prep."

"Why didn't you say so before? You said there were no attachments."

"Eric and I wanted to know what you thought about *User-Friendly* as a script, Tak, beyond having a star attached. Having a big name's not the best reason to make a film even if it's the most common one. We didn't want to approach you with just a star vehicle. You and me — neither of us came out here to be one of *them,* did we. Remember what you said — the Goldman thing? You were right: 'Nobody Knows Anything.' Let's avoid that. You admit you like the script. Let's all agree, then —from the start *we* are going ahead for the right reason, because it's a story worth telling."

"I don't know. With her involved, of course that would change things, but — This is all very . . . very strange, very sudden —"

Marty relaxed, slid downward on the bench a bit. "Let's enjoy this, Mr. Itani. Tak. Why else do it? Sure, before it's over you get too much money, your name in lights, a house in the hills, fabulous babes around your pool. You have to pay *terrible* dues. But let's have a little fun, too." Tak smiled, finally. Marty was encouraged. "First, here's the deal — we hire someone on the picture with an empty title, just to hang around the set. Someone who'll have access to things. He's an observer, someone who's gonna find out who's pulling their weight and who's not. We call him an Associate Producer, he'll have plenty of company. Then, what happens when the film's out of control? *Every* film's out of control, sooner or later. The money's gone. The crew's missed a paycheck, they're in mutiny. The bosses — MSC now, it's their contractual right — they bring in some guy called the Executive in Charge of Production, some crusty, snarling Fuck-You-I'm-From-New-York-I've-Seen-It-All type, and this guy cuts the losses left and right. Bodies are flying, Associate Producers' heads are mounted on spikes —"

Eric jumped in, playing breathless: "*O* the carnage, Mother of God, *O* the humanity —"

The businessmen enjoyed Eric's brief, campy radio performance as Marty took back the rhythm: "You cite artistic differences. The director is quietly shipped to Camarillo State

Hospital in a straitjacket. The last, the *only* Associate Producer left standing, the quiet man, the one honest and honorable paragon of numbers that don't lie — he, my friends, is in fact the one who has *become* that Executive in Charge of Production. He holds up the stone tablets of his revised budget estimate. Leads the company out of the desert to completion of principal photography. The picture wraps in triumph. That man, the corporate insider from MSC of Japan — now considered a force in the Film Industry himself —" Mr. Yamamoto and Mr. Kurumada were leaning forward, smiling, nodding. "— That man, now Hollywood Producer, savior of Laura Trent-Sampson's megacareer, is you, Takashi Itani. You."

Tak scowled at the tabletop, then raised his eyebrows at his clients, a gesture of helplessness under the ridiculous circumstances. But Marty had intrigued them with his sparkly Hollywood scenario more than his logic. Tak clearly didn't know why. He was now the outsider, superfluous as a translator. He tried to slow everyone down:

"It's worth considering. Eric, you're in town for a few days?"

Eric and Marty ignored him. Mr. Kurumada was reaching across the table to shake Eric's hand, then Marty's. "Mr. Blanc, we will finance."

Mr. Kurumada had thought short and hard, and acted quickly.

26

A fter their Musso & Frank dinner meeting Takashi Itani, Tax Attorney who might now become Producer, drove Yamamoto and Kurumada back to their hotel near the airport. He went with them into the lobby instead of dropping them off, the least complicated way to say goodbye. At their request, he asked a bellman to take a picture of the three of them. The trio stood pressed together, smiling straight ahead but with their arms tight against their sides. The camera whirred and in this dawn of digital recording, Tak thought how unnatural it was to have his snapshot recorded electronically, his image becoming video yes/no bits on a floppy disk. On celluloid film there is a thing physically present that looks like you, even in a negative, the layers of silver compounds and dye that correspond exactly to the two of your three dimensions that the lens can receive and pass on. The still-video camera had nothing like his person on its disk, although it seemed quite acceptable that later it could be plugged directly into any TV set to reproduce his image there. He smiled at the thought of adjusting a tint knob to give himself more of a California burnish.

His thoughts of video wizardry were a reminder: every forecast of the Industry's future predicted that the new High Definition TV technology — sooner or later to be sharp enough for the theater screen — would eventually replace film stock in movies. And, already conscious of thinking like a producer, he surmised that there would be obvious savings in a technology that could be erased and re-recorded. A division of MSC had shared some of the pioneering HDTV work with Sony and Hitachi; it might be too soon, but he would look into any potential applications for *User-Friendly*. That was his job now, he was suddenly a player with a story to tell. He even envisioned having a down payment sooner than expected for the house he had just looked at in the Mt. Olympus neighborhood.

He took the San Diego Freeway north. Magic hour was long expired with only a black void remaining above. Pale orange mercury-vapor streetlights were sprinkled across the flat Valley grid below as he floated down the long grade before the 405 crosses the Ventura Freeway. Something life-changing had occurred at the Musso & Frank Grill, he was sure of that. Then he clutched the wheel and rode out a small swell of stomach pangs at the foolishness of thinking such things. He had no idea of how to make a movie, not even the modest grace of knowing what it was he didn't know. Still, he couldn't stop repeating the newfound mantra of simultaneous wisdom and opportunity: Nobody Knows Anything. If that were so, what else then was called for? Sheer aggression? He cracked a side window to see if the marine air had reached the Valley yet to push out the unlit brownness. It had. He sighed; at night there was little besides the vanishingly small trace of sea smell to remind him that he was an immigrant here.

He cringed at the memory of his gaffe in the restaurant, embarrassed that his own face didn't always make him instinctively Japanese. His self-imagined status as the go-between, as a man of two cultures, had been knocked flat. He had felt silly, incomplete, but then had surprised himself by thinking on his feet, recovering in time, quickly calculating exactly what had been at stake. In Japan, gifts often signified obligation. MSC was laying out cash for Eric's stay out of gratitude — for bringing his reputation and play manuscript, if not for the late addition of a screenplay — and for the promise of bringing to them a working relationship with one of the most commercial actresses in America, who turned out to be someone much bigger than they had dreamed of. But the mask was obviously selected, probably by Mr. Yamamoto, with great thought and care to express their personal regard for Eric in repayment for something Eric had given them — a chance to use Eric's, and others' talent — which they could not repay exactly in kind. The mask was the perfect gift of return obligation, but they'd never intended to have it opened there in front of themselves, and Tak had feared that Eric's emotional reaction might make them regret the entire effort. He had needed to restore the sense of mutual obligation somehow, to create a gift Eric could give back. Together he and Eric gave Yamamoto, Kurumada, and a teenager named Midori one degree of separation from celebrity.

Tak tried to imagine how *User-Friendly* would look, what the flow of light across the reflective screen would be like. In his hurried Industry research he had been continually fascinated at how cameramen would create a visual equivalent to the emotions of movie stories, how they could frame things and control colors, make them cool or warm with filters and lights, how lenses of different focal lengths could form intimacy or separation. He didn't know how *User-Friendly* should be photographed, but when he got the chance he would suggest to someone — who? — that it ought to have landscapes; huge, sprawling, dominant landscapes behind the human characters and their robots. It would be unexpected, ironic somehow in a romantic comedy. Landscapes of storm-faced mountains rising above the plains, with fingers of snow clawing into the blue-gray ridges and peaks. It would be his only creative interference. He knew of such landscapes back home in Utah within easy road access for what they call the rolling stock of movie equipment, the big trucks he had seen everywhere here in town that supplied the surprisingly mobile film crews. He had other ideas too that were strictly business. For instance, perhaps *User-Friendly* should have a non-union crew in a right-to-work state — Utah again? — to hold down costs.

If they followed his suggestions, he would be near enough to his parents that he could polish his spoken Japanese as well, a good thing for a new MSC employee. He would embrace his mother and father when he saw them. But it would be as salaryman Takashi Itani from MSC of Japan, not as their embodiment of Takashi-*kun*, the student indifferent to all subjects but math who had gone away to a second-rate school so far from home and found no one to marry, only to become a lawyer of all things, a position of embarrassment back in Japan where honor obviated most litigation. That he now practiced tax law, a business function, had helped little to change their disappointment in him. And without children he was unfilial. But perhaps they would greet him this time with new respect, and he would make them end forever their unconscious habit of smothering him with disapproval and rude questions even as they tried to love him.

And he would be sure to have drinks with childhood buddies, but this too would be as Tak Itani, Movie Producer, not as goofy little Tik-Tak with Coke-bottle glasses and a permanent cowlick, ridiculous Tak-the-Jap in fake-pearl-buttoned flannel shirts and high-heeled vinyl cowboy boots who later had aced his algebra tests. Powerful, this making of movies.

He got off at Van Nuys and drove north into the Valley. Gas station signs poked into the night sky now as fluorescent circles and globes, their blue and orange magic hour colors bottled tightly inside. He wondered if there was a magic hour back home, if there had always been one. He had also learned from his research why cameramen love this magic hour — something to do with contrast ratios, with soft natural fill-light for the shadows, the way the sky doesn't bleach out and lose its weight. If he should want to further dissect this kind of sky's power over him, the way it disrupted the seasons here in L.A., he would try at the same time to see it now as a cameraman would. Of course, the sunset sky back in Utah would have the Rockies beneath it, not California's unobstructing ocean to the west. It might make a difference. He would look into it.

And in this way the evening at Musso & Frank's became the moment when he imagined himself into a new life; a magic hour not of ambient light this time but of self-reinvention, and as he jotted down a note while stopped at a red light he wondered: Is this how Producers produce?

27

With tensions subsiding about what Marty might do in the face of the baby's arrival — the lack of a decision has become the decision — Lupe and C.T. have judged Marty's bungalow to be better than Juvie or some slacker's apartment. They're in the living room when Lupe sighs, then lowers herself into Marty's worn, leather recliner and grows very still, her eyes closed until her entire body is rocked from somewhere within. Marty watches her without knowing what she needs. Her eyes flutter open again.

"You tol' me Bibi had a miscarriage too. She said 'life's a bitch' an' got better."

"Yeah, in time. It took a while."

"An' you got better too?"

He's stumped. He has never thought about it that way. He had been working a lot back then while he was still an Assistant Director, but because of the miscarriage, parenthood didn't have a chance to make his life and career even more complicated. It was just one pressure among the many that went away, and the next day he went back to his job. The End. Easier to see now that it was another missed chance to be a better person for Bibi.

"I got better. Sure."

"I want her to come. Please."

"Bibi — ?" He hopes Lupe doesn't mean this, but it makes perfect sense. The contradiction locks him up because he's asked so much of Bibi, time and again, and she's always come through, long since they were a couple. She's even the reason he's able to have Lupe and C.T. under his roof tonight, because Bibi's calming advice made it possible for him to talk to Lupe at the mall just a few weeks ago without scaring her away. With Bibi, he's always asking and has had nothing to give back for years.

He knows that it's dangerously too early for Lupe to be enduring premature contractions. And he's ashamed that while not cheering for it, he's allowing the thought to linger that she and the baby might not get through this pregnancy whole. *But Marty you ass — it's not her "getting through," it's a child, your grandchild, my aching god —*

Tak is gone, his legal help and background storytelling for C.T. is played out. Marty has no one else to rely on except C.T.. Without giving Lupe a direct answer about asking for Bibi's help, he goes to C.T.'s room where his son is listlessly watching some online videos.

"I think Lupe's having contractions again. This might be real labor. How long've they been going on?"

The color drains from C.T.'s face, and his at-the-ready street façade melts. Marty wants to cry at this sad absurdity, that his child with a pizza parlor work hat crumpled beside him on the bed is going to bring a baby into this house. A something, a someone, way beyond his birth mother's variously lost products of conception. C.T. hardens his face again.

"What contractions? She hasn't told me nothing."

"Even if they're just Braxton Hicks, they're speeding up. How are you gonna handle this?"

It's an unfair question, but one that C.T. has refused to consider for months. Marty's own "what if" with Bibi and the child they might've had together never played out because her miscarriage struck down any immediate crisis. Her pregnancy revealed nothing to him in its negation, prepared him for nothing more afterward. To Marty, Bibi's embryo was a theoretical presence that left behind a vague and empty feeling that he pushed aside easily enough; there had been no face, no heartbroken cries of hunger, no tiny hands and feet to keep warm. But when the sheer animal urgency of all the parts of a newborn had abruptly come into his life in a movie location motel room, and that child had needed someone to care, someone who would throw everything aside and flee with him to a Utah airport, Marty had wrapped fatherhood around himself like a thin blanket, around a Tub O'Guts who slept in a Snugli on his chest — and there was no going back. It was the first time he'd done something that he couldn't undo, and once on the run fatherhood was no longer a sprint but a state of being, discovered only gradually by crawling forward day-by-day through what's been Marty's life ever since.

So he's done this baby thing, and it's not that he can't pull the material necessities together as fast as he needs to. Instead, his passivity in responsibly planning right now is an attempt to force the baby's reality onto C.T. and Lupe. All three of them are just letting this arrival happen, they're all passive, all helpless. It's insane.

"What do you need to do next?"

"I don't know, Pops. Maybe she'll lose it. Then everybody'll be happy."

Marty drops his head but then they're both spun toward the bedroom doorway by a kind of magnetism, the electric force of Lupe's stare.

"You . . . piece a shit." She falls to her knees, driven down by her trembling body.

C.T. scrambles from the bed, pulls on his unlaced shoes and runs to the kitchen where Marty keeps his car keys. He comes back as quickly, and as Lupe protests with small fists punching his chest, he scoops her up and carries her to the car. Marty follows, and lets his seventeen-year-old take charge of her needs while he takes the keys and drives them to the emergency room.

And as he drives too fast along the neighborhood streets, it strikes him again that maybe they're all going to be spared this catastrophe. *Yeah, an innocent child as a catastrophe. What makes us Nyrops capable of such thoughts, what rot snakes through us?* He once directed an actor in a movie, then raised the actor's kid, who became Marty's kid, who's now having his own. Did he learn *anything*?

In the hours to come, Marty has to remember it all, the rest of the story of babies and parents and movies, of directing, of what he did to tear new holes in his own life even if, at the time, he thought he was just sewing and mending the other rips and tears already there.

As he forces the car toward the hospital with a jagged rhythm of starts and stops, he tells C.T. to call Aunt Beebs.

28

M arty looked in awe at the Utah sky. The lack of haze, clouds, or pollution made it denser than L.A.'s, more toward liquid than air. From his viewpoint on a flat plain he was surrounded by sharp mountain peaks and rocks that stuck up between white streaks of snow still left from last year, all of it taking on the sky's purple quality and reflecting it back. They would be in a race to beat the coming winter, to wrap this location before rain, then mud, then freezing temperatures made Utah a crystallized trap.

He walked across the parking lot toward the motel room that had become the *User-Friendly* film company's Production Office. They would soon completely fill up several small motels within sight of one another here in Two Cedars, Utah with wardrobe, editing tables, catering supplies, and the key crew members who would fly in from L.A.. The company had nearly taken over the Wagon Wheel Motel, whose door stickers proudly advertised it as a Best Western franchise member; on a distant location with a big studio like Universal, the Production people alone would have commandeered three or four suites by now, run a dozen of their own phone lines, filled the building with the inky chemical mustiness of copying machines and the mildew of rented refrigerators, the warm bitterness of evaporating coffee. But Marty's one-room office would do for now. He hadn't yet become as large as his job would demand and he gladly accepted the small scale of their independent production for as long as it could be maintained. Before entering the room he smoothed his hand over the weathered grain of a half-wheel anchored in asphalt, part of the Conestoga and Prairie Schooner motifs that, along with heavy chicken wire, served as a child-protective railing around the motel pool.

Inside, Tak sat with his feet up on a folding table and wrote large letters on a legal pad, then scribbled circles around the words. When Marty dragged a chair to the table Tak gave him a grin and turned the pad over: "Never Assume Because Assume Makes an <u>ASS</u> of <u>U</u> and <u>ME</u>." Marty smiled tolerantly at his effort; someone had penciled that advice onto a sheet of paper and taped a photocopy onto a wall in every Production office he'd ever worked in, right next to a cartoon of a rubbery guy laughing hysterically and asking, "You want it *when*?"

"What's up, Tak-*san*? What should I not assume?"

"That she's signed."

"Who?"

"Laura Trent-Sampson, the only reason for any of us to be here, is unsigned. Tell me about these Hollywood handshakes, Marty."

"Laura? What do you mean?"

"I don't think your brother — that *we* — even have what could be called an In-Principle Agreement with her. That night we met at Musso's. . .? I mean, with Eric's stage background and reputation and all, I. . . . She has absolutely no binding obligation to make this movie. Nothing. No contract, no paper of any kind. I mean, I knew that, I'm one of the Producers, but I got caught up in all the. . . . And now we can't find her. I had to tell MSC, and they're sniffing disaster, they're ready to abandon ship."

Marty's heart rose in his chest. "What're they afraid of? They won't call it off —"

"I know how they operate. What they'll probably do, they'll find something to negotiate, then draw it out until everybody loses interest, MSC saves face, and the thing just quietly dies at a minimal cost. It's all my fault."

Marty slowly stood and backed toward the same doorway he had just come through. Things were falling inside him like heavy weights, then breaking on impact on the stone of his lower gut. "Tak, I've got to . . . I'll . . . I'll be back in a little while."

Outdoors the sudden clarity of chilled air and skylight made Marty inhale quickly, squint, until he fixed his gaze on an approaching limousine. Here in the middle of nowhere, someone hidden behind privacy-tinted windows had hired a silver stretch Lincoln with a V-winged TV antenna mounted on its trunk. The car rolled to a stop between Marty and the film company's scouting van. Like successive unveilings, first the blackened passenger window rolled down, then a pair of improbably large sunglasses were lowered, revealing Laura Trent-Sampson's sculptural cheekbones and pleasing smile — a smile warmer and more vulnerable than Marty had ever before witnessed, without makeup and more extraordinary because of that. This was a conclusion to a small mystery; no one had been able to find her for several months, not even the *People* magazine writers who called Marty's home number a dozen times. She had gone underground, calling only the outsider Tak to check in occasionally, as if Laura knew that any contact with her established life of celebrity would jeopardize her one chance to silence those who didn't take her seriously, the ones who stole from her only her exquisite surface and ignored the rest.

Now she'd found the *User-Friendly* crew quite on her own. Maybe there was no problem, after all. He felt Eric and then Tak arrive like two spirits drifting on either side of him. Tak exhaled gratefully, as Eric touched Marty's shoulder and used a stage whisper:

"God, Marty. She looks great, doesn't she?"

Marty nodded without looking at him. "I just don't know why she's here already. And we've gotta talk — You've had one thing to do these last few months, and I hope you've done it."

The limo door popped open an inch, then its weight made it sag shut, knocking Laura back into her deep seat. The limo driver hauled his own paunch from behind the steering wheel, tugged at his tight suitcoat and vest, and opened the door for her. She grasped the driver's outstretched hand and pulled herself up as she stepped from behind the door. Under a man's white T-shirt her belly was round, tight as a basketball, and just as large.

Marty felt Eric sag against him. "Oh, fuck. Oh, no, no —"

Her smile never waned. It was all for Eric. "Hi, Daddy."

Patrick Cosgrove

29

*L*ater that night Marty stood near the hum of a soft drink vending machine as he imagined himself floating upward toward Eric's door, number 21. He was a camera crossing the loose gravel in the parking lot, now ascending the metal stairs, Steadicam smooth, a one-eyed lens in his fixity and clarity, pushing in to confront the leavings of family.

And to reveal truth: Stormtrooper, he thought. *Guns of Navarone!* That's me, a stormtrooper assaulting the damn motel room. It's gone too far. Bash the door down, bash the bastard's face in. Everybody using everybody else, it's this business, this Industry, and I'm part of it too but now *her* — Eric the son-of-a-bitch, he's done this to me and my one goddamn chance to make a movie, and to her too, the one maybe I don't care about except for the skin, the lips, the eyes but *at minimum* Laura's a "her" and he's done this to her to get what he wants. Unspeakable. Steals, and uses, and what am *I* — to be here, with him, when I opened the goddamn trailer door and helped him *get* her? Like we have to give in to gravity, like making this movie is the irresistible force and we're powerless but now there's a *kid*, something curled in that belly and between the two of *them* it'll get no one capable or responsible or caring or even sane looking out for it, not a single blood relative — no, it's *my* blood. *Shit! . . . Why?*

Then something snapped, broke, and like a theater-stage diorama the motel-world dropped away and a long-ago, lost world faded in, his memory spreading across a reflective rectangle of light:

and I wind the Bolex again, there'll be no rundown in the middle of the scene this time. The airport calls yet again looking for my father who's gone, but she's there — showering, singing in our house. Singing that she's alone. Taking, stealing. I open her door, she'll be in there, the Bolex will record it and Mom will know, the truth will be her hammer

and she's there toweling off the wetness with drops on skin pearling down. Not hiding, surprised but not scared, cool and assessing, glimpsed as blonde even between her legs, and stealing. She says, Marty you're not in school? And I say I've come home sick, or I was but not now, I'm healed. Storm troopers cannot be sick on a mission. She's looking into camera, there'll be verisimilitude, realism, what I'll know even as a twelve-year-old is the Truth when my mother sees this movie of her, of her the one stealing. And I hear that voice: asking me to stop, and saying Please Marty, then asking will you stop if I do this? or this? and she's dancing behind the towel, smiling because what else can she do, at twelve I'm already thick and strong and I can break things and she can't make me stop. Until she circles me and closes the bathroom door and I hear a click though the deaf Bolex can't and from behind the locked door she's asking Can I see your movie when you're done, Marty? Will you promise to show it to me? Your father'll want you to give it to him, you know that, he'll want it and you can give it to him, he'd like to see too. And we can all be in the movie, Marty — Craig loves to dazzle me, did you know that? He's such a clever boy with his voices and the singing, just turn the camera on Craig too and we'll all have a fun movie, would that be all right, Marty? Dazzle me too? Honey?

    And she's coming out now and the Bolex is exhausted, she's stolen its power, it stops turning and later when I ask my big brother what do we tell Mom, when do we show her, I think today because he gets home tomorrow from Seattle or is it Anchorage and Craig says why tell Mom anything, I like Joyce, she makes me laugh and you know what? She says Dazzle me Craig and I do crazy things and she likes it and then Dad likes it too and he laughs at me

    But I: You've been with them? Together? You've been with Dad and her and you didn't tell anyone? and Craig says why make Mom cry? And I think Cry has nothing to do with it, crying's gonna happen anyway, we'll have to tell the truth to end the crying but Craig says No.

    There is no footage, no record, no world in a frame, the film doesn't turn out or never makes it to the lab and there are no re-takes. It's as if she were never there, stealing. When they pull two carbonized hunks from the Cessna, Craig says Her. Not Mom, but her. Her with Dad. And I know Not true — Mom went to the airport with Dad. But Craig: she didn't get on the plane, they had an argument, and I: So Mom just disappeared? Then who'd they find? She was kind of nuts, Marty, Mom was. So years go by, until she comes to see me, Marty! She uses another name and she got out of there because she couldn't live with it — Then I: but there wasn't anything left, he was dead, and the Other would be too if it was really her and not Mom, so then why didn't Mom come back if Dad and the Other were dead? — but No, Mom couldn't handle anything anymore. But Craig people don't snap and crack like glass, and Craig says Yes, yes they do.

    Just left us? I ask again and again but then can't believe it, never do, and when Craig says Yes, abandoned us through the years, then I know Craig will say anything, do anything, to get his way which is more than just that: it's never being anyone, saying or doing anything that might not be liked. And that's cowardice, but power too, the power of the actor, and it's the power I'd forgotten for all these years until Eric Blanc comes to my set and plants seed, family life, into another one, the new one who's just as blonde between the legs.

And I'm here, damned, helping him because I put images before everything. Too much, this is all too fucking much. . . .

• • •

Marty hesitated at the top of the motel stairway, surprised he'd arrived there, and sensed a danger in acting too quickly. He turned and stared back over the asphalt and gravel parking lot, at the rented Ford station wagons with fake wood panels that only film companies ever used, at the odd assortment of large and small recreational vehicles from every corner of North America. RVs had reflective stickers pasted to their windows, with bicycles, barbecue grills, and aluminum lawn chairs lashed to their sides and tops with bunjee cords. Beyond the lot he could see a small stand of spruce, a welcome bit of familiarity from his memory of the Midwest. The blue-gray branches were a solace after Utah's endless vistas of red and purple dirt and the disturbing shapes of whole city skylines along the horizon that turned out to be only wind-tortured sandstone. Stars were already bright in the still-luminous dusk. He was, he concluded with a sigh, becoming a tourist in his own life, geographically at a midpoint between where he was from and the dreamland where he had arrived. He could be headed back in either direction, or never get out of here alive. I'm the Marty-camel, he thought. That's an A.D.. Ship of the desert. Don't feed us, don't water us, we'll bust our hump for you across Hell and back. We're relentless, impervious. But with all my Second Assistant work in logistics, I should know: which straw is it, exactly, from Eric's bale of hay that's breaking the Marty-camel's back?

He wanted to go to his knees from the sudden weakness of not having Bibi in his life to get him through this, to talk him down, hold him, stroke his hair and make it right.

But first he had to choose from the many reasons to kill his brother. The ethics of spewing random kids aside, Eric might have already destroyed Marty's movie. MSC was trying to calculate the true cost of Laura's pregnancy, still dragging its corporate feet over the final go-ahead. For a moment, he felt sorry for Eric. Nothing about Exene's — Laura's — condition was going to be easy for him. Maybe killing him would be euthanasia, a kindness.

He raised the horseshoe doorknocker below the number 21 and let it fall once. Eric opened the door wordlessly, as if he'd been waiting there for Marty all evening with a hand on the doorknob. But then he drifted away and sagged into a wicker chair near the TV. He was pale, drained, somehow appearing both ill and more handsome than usual, a romantic affect Eric could pull off effortlessly. If that were even what he was trying to achieve.

Marty's next impulse had a logical clarity: punching Eric in the face was the sensible thing to do. Instead he forced his hands to his sides. Shoving and punching people was getting to be repetitious and nothing much good had come of it. He threw the nearest lamp to the floor and watched it roll out of its shade, the bulb unbroken on the chocolate brown shag carpet.

Eric seemed genuinely worried. "What? What is it?"

"I'll tell you line-by-line what it is, motherfucker. How devious can one guy get? You come out here to the golden West and make a beeline for the first object that'll get your play made, so you can go on to fame and fortune. Only that object happens to be a human being. You're like a dog licking his balls — you fuck her because you *can*."

"You said that's how it's done. You have leverage, you use it. And you would've done it, too."

"Great, you did it first. Good for you, she's on board now. You've got a Laura Trent-Sampson project in the pipeline — and with you laying some pipe in *her* — because she thinks she needs you. To be something more than a miserable, rich celebrity. So then you lie to the money chumps. 'Sure, I've got her signed,' only you *don't* —
"

"You told me to say that —"

" — you didn't have anything except a play you probably stole from a student —"

"It's a classic, a modern take on a Greek tragedy, for godssakes —"

" — that'd never get made on its own. That's a good enough rationale to steal it —"

"But instead of the play it's all become a movie, hasn't it, Marty? *Your* movie —"

"If it doesn't blow up in my face, *maybe*. We're probably all on a plane home any minute now."

"I . . . I didn't know, Marty. I didn't know anything about the kid before you did."

Marty waited in silence. There were enough accusations in the open now that Eric ought to be riled, defiant, or at least whiny and defensive the way Craig Nyrop from memory would've been. *Love me? Huh? Please? If I do this, will it dazzle?* But his shift to a hangdog expression made Marty stop. Eric seemed already defeated. The child-to-be was an enormous complication by anyone's calculation. And Eric wasn't actually *convicted* of anything, not yet. . . .

Marty sat on the edge of the double bed and looked at the bathroom door, listening to the shower run. It must be Exene in there. After several moments of trying to recall the sight of her, of her belly preceding the rest of her out of the limo, Marty cleared his throat:

"You're still married, right? I mean, you were separated, or something, when I came to New York that one time. So do you have one of those 'understandings'?" He immediately realized this sounded like a weak joke and he hadn't meant it that way. There was simply too much he didn't know about the adult version of his brother.

Eric managed a short laugh. "Still married. *And* separated, more than five years now. And neither of us knows why. We both thought playing a spouse was a nice gig. . . . Marty, I'm in trouble. I've already *got* kids. I love them, I don't need another one, not like this. Not another one that'll cost me the ones I have."

"From what I saw today we're all in big trouble."

"I'll trade you — my problems for yours."

"Is she really gonna have the baby? She's lost other ones —"

"It's gone way beyond that. She could drop it right now on the bathroom floor and the kid would probably do all right. Why do you think she's been out of sight for the last six months? She didn't want anyone talking her into anything. Least of all me. I didn't even know about it Marty, swear to god, I'm not lying — She says she *wants* the baby. So we're way, way beyond. . . ."

"Well, okay, so there'll be a healthy kid. . . . No big tragic human cost, no sacrifice to the God of Cinema. Fine. Does she want the *movie?* We can't photograph her like that. And we can't wait around 'til she's through lugging around that watermelon under her shirt. What the hell are we supposed to do?"

"I don't know, Marty, and right now I don't care. To me that's a Production issue. You have to figure it out. I've got a bigger problem —"

"Does it cost more than our shooting budget?"

Eric turned on Marty sharply. "She wants me to acknowledge it, pal. She wants me to tell the world I'm the father, or she's leaving. You know what that means? It means that everything I've come out here to do becomes this week's piece of tabloid gossip shit. It means doing this movie becomes a joke, a publicity stunt. 'Life-*shtups* of the Rich & Famous.' It means my theater is dead. There'll be nothing for me or you to go back to, I'll never get you . . . to. . . . Shit. It means my wife goes to court again and I never see my kids, except one weekend out of the year. *Supervised.* It means my *life.*"

"Supervised, huh? Well maybe you should've thought about that before you beat on your kids. You sick fuck."

Eric waved him off impatiently. "Not now. . . ."

"Why's she doing it? Naming you, what's it to her?"

"Laura's got this idea . . . it's like for a kid, just having a father you can blame solves every problem and she doesn't have to be a competent mother. She's already got its neuroses planned out and they won't be her fault. And naming me, she gets legitimate. Her and the kid both. That's really what it is. 'Legitimate.'"

"Geez. . . . You came out here to set her up, you try to set *everybody* up and *POW* — outmaneuvered."

"Like hell. I told her I'd take a walk unless she shuts up about it."

Marty lay back on the bed. "Well, golly gee, Eric. Thanks for letting me know. I guess pretty soon we find out who wants this picture worse. Who's crazier. Or whose lawyer has the biggest dick." Marty laughed. "The seemingly unsolvable dilemma, leading to the reversal of expectations. . . ."

"Aristotle? Why now?"

"We're talking classic three-act story structure here, except you decided to start at the end of Act Two, asshole. And the rest of us haven't even gotten our first cue, until now, and she isn't taking direction. Well, fuck — *in medias res*, congratulations."

"So tell me how this classic story ends, Marty. What's the *peripeteia*, the reversal, the twist?"

Both of them knew there was no answer. A machine had been created, the implacable, breathing apparatus of moviemaking far more vast in dollar cost and now in practical human consequences than anything else in their lives had been, or could be. It was running, clanking ahead, bigger than Laura Trent-Sampson, bigger than her and Eric's child. Yet the movie-machine itself had the power to salvage as well as crush. If there were to be a successful climax to the story Eric had begun, if everyone were to emerge happily after sliding like bloody oil through the gears of the production's climax and denouement — if they completed the movie, if the movie were any good, if other people paid to watch it — then each of them could get what he or she wanted, what they needed. Nothing good, though, would happen if the movie didn't happen. And too much would be lost.

"What kind of story do you want me to make up, Eric?"

"Nothing, forget it. Listen: You and me, we're still family —"

"Yeah, well. . . . A blood test —"

"— and if you'll do something, if you'll agree to it, I think I can get Laura to say that you're the father. Like in a press release, and be over and done with it."

"*What* — ?"

"We look alike, what'll the kid know? It'll have the family name —"

"Which one? Nyrop? Blanc? Ford? Trent? Sampson? My *god* — The kid'll come out with its head already spinning."

"It doesn't matter. Just so everybody'll know it's you and not me. You're gonna be at least Uncle Marty, anyway. . . . Then back East what's left of my own happy little family's not totally destroyed. You get a new family if you want it. Or even if you don't want it, you can walk away and you get a hell of a reputation, 'wink wink nudge nudge' and that sort of shit. So she'd get the Nyrop name for the kid and that's all she's after anyway —"

"— Except that right now I'm a Ford and you're a Blanc, until you come up with a new one —"

"We could figure it out, that's what publicity agents are for. She'd be part of the clan, get her connection. Be legit. Especially after she does the play. She'd never ask you to *raise* the kid."

"Then who *would?*"

Eric stared at him for a moment, as if Marty had used an unknown foreign phrase. "You could go places with this, Marty. It solves problems and it won't cost you anything."

Marty laughed, there was nothing else to do. His lungs were tight from the dry Utah air. He paused, then laughed deeper, coughing, until Exene entered the room from the bathroom naked, without guile or mask, with only a towel turban-wrapped in her hair — heraldic, implying wonders to come.

She looked at Marty, receiving his eyes, his up-and-down gaze, awaiting his judgment. Her mouth parted in a smile with her tongue stuck between her teeth in child-like glee. Oh god, he could only think, Oh god. Why is she doing this? What does she want? Does she *need* to make this . . . this offer? Does she need the gaze, to have herself . . . approved? She's *this*, she looks exactly . . . like *this* — Marty's genitals swelled, then contracted, a primal spasm. She was all luminescence, milky in skin, in lamplit outline, in rounded glandular shape. Yet except for her stomach, the womb-stretched protrusion of it, she was unchanged, different neither from his persistent imaginings of her, nor from his one glimpse of her upside-down sexual brilliance in the motorhome. Her breasts were perfectly round, still high upon her rib cage, her aureoles soft pink puffs topped by softer, pinker nipples; her hips were sprinter-angular, her dancer's thighs taut when her muscles rippled softly under the skin as she shifted her bare, unmarked, pearly feet on the brown motel carpet. This was electrifying — frightening because it was so provocative, compelling because it seemed to call for action — yet moreover, confusing, even mean-spirited because no action could possibly be appropriate. Was she proud, standing there? Confessional?

It was nothing like pregnancy as Marty had imagined it. There was no drooping, swollen, moon-filled belly, no weighted, drifting fecundity, no chrysalis of hormone-doped motherliness hovering about a baby until it was time to drop and grow light, no beautifully blood-warmed swelling that nurtured whoever awaited sleepily within. Only Exene's navel seemed to acknowledge change. What used to be a small, vertical dimple he'd once seen in a body-makeup session and had echoed the folds now tantalizingly veiled by her feathery, copper-blonde pubic hair had now become flattened, a darker round spot in the middle of her hard womb.

"What do you think, A.D.? Isn't it wonderful?"

"I . . . I think it's beautiful. The baby and all. . . . I'm very happy for you."

"There, you *see*, Eric?"

"I see everything Marty can see. Get a robe on, will you?"

She smiled brightly and returned to the bathroom. Her backside was equally unchanged, as sculpturally enticing as the front, even more so without even the belly to give away her condition. Marty made himself breathe slower.

"Is she healthy? I mean, every pregnant woman I ever saw, they gain weight, they get big all over, their boobs change — It's like she could have a C-section tomorrow and be doing love scenes the next day, you'd never even know. . . ."

"Maybe that's her plan. How do I know? Talk to her, Marty, would you? She really likes you."

"Likes me, as what? Her obstetrician?"

"When I tell her the idea, you'll do it?"

"Like fuck. No." Marty pulled the door open and the room inhaled behind him. "Well . . . I gotta say, it was some entrance today, huh? Her getting out of that limo."

Eric smiled. "The Japanese say, 'In Western theater, something happens. In the East, someone arrives. . . .'"

Marty nodded, it seemed like the thing to do. He pulled the door shut, making the horseshoe clack against the hollow wood veneer.

Something — disgust? pity? — made him step to the open room window and watch Eric through the screen. Still on the bed, Eric retrieved from a nightstand the *Noh* mask given to him at Musso's and stared into it, then drew it slowly toward his face, reciting as if it were a memorized drill: "Not the person wearing the mask, but the mask itself sees. . . . The mask is not put on the face, but the face is pulled into and clings to the mask. . . ." Eric balanced it on his own tilted-back face, tying the strings behind his head. In the bathroom Laura's hair dryer went on, a comfortable, breathy hum. Eric cocked one hand in a formal pose above his temple and held still. "Cry with the left hand . . . " then raised his right: "Cry with both hands. . . ."

Marty spat on the ground and went back to his room.

Patrick Cosgrove

30

*M*arty and C.T. fill out paperwork in the emergency room again. Or rather, Marty holds back and makes C.T. take as much responsibility as legally possible while Marty deals with the financing of medical care his teacher's health benefits can't be stretched to fit. Marty wants C.T. to feel overwhelmed. He wants him to see being an adult and being a parent for the enormity that it is, especially when no matter what your creative ambition, your livelihood comes from measuring pizza sauce. And what chance does this boy have to be a fit father? How, when he knows now that he came from a man who hit his own children. That poisonous knowledge will seep into his soul and forever be simmering, a pre-excused primal sin. But Marty has escaped this curse — why can't he trust C.T. to be as strong? *Seventeen.*

And they're all in a race to claim C.T.'s future for him now that Laura is dangling her synthetic, curated fame before his eyes; she's giving him a way out by pulling him into "celebrity" where the child in Lupe's belly won't stand a chance at happiness any more than C.T. and Lupe will stand a chance to love one another as they might.

The staff here doesn't seem to think birth is that close. They're probably going to get sent home again, but this child will be here soon. Now is not the time for Marty to go on about the history of Eric's creative genius not bailing him out of the blunt needs of fatherhood, or about how Bio-Dad-the-stage-genius and Bio-Dad-the-human-being were an unstable, anguished mix. But Marty senses he might be down to his last chance to impress upon C.T. that keeping this child is going to be a death-spiral of sorts for C.T's ambitions. too, a downward curve of possibilities for his and Lupe's own chances in life no matter how clever and talented they think themselves to be. Even if Laura is dangling some kind of job in the Industry in front of C.T., he has to know what kind of world that is.

C.T. has drawn little solace from learning that Eric's plan at the very beginning was to name Marty his father, perhaps because Marty didn't want to go along with the idea. I'll be there, Marty thinks, I won't let these kids starve, but I can't live this parent-life for them if they choose it. And what if they each choose the child, but not one another?

31

I n the Utah chill Marty saw the wardrobe coming toward them before he saw the bearded face above it, the clothes that insisted on recalling old studio stills of the '30s and '40s: an argyle sweater vest over a densely patterned Armani shirt, billowing and pleated pants, hand-sewn Italian shoes in several oddly light shades. Paul Amato. Marty glanced at Tak, who looked as if he were ready to vomit. Just the way Marty felt.

The newly-arrived Amato was headed for the same Denny's restaurant where Marty and Tak had just eaten breakfast. Mr. Career Death's tiny head, covered with black ringlets both above and below his wire-rimmed glasses, made his frightened small eyes smaller. The dense beard and prominent nose had already been used for an easy separated-at-birth gag two years before in *Spy* magazine, pictured next to Fidel Castro. He was imposingly big and soft at the same time; the oval nails on his carefully manicured fingers were oddly narrow and gave him tapered, ineffectual hands that looked as if they would sob for him if he wrung them, as if he were a deity of the tantrum. From whatever circumstances of birth, Amato had re-imagined himself as a mogul, performing every day the hero of his own success story. Marty's face went cold in spots, in localized chills. Finally Amato noticed the two of them and smiled a little at one side of his face. His voice was both high-pitched and growly:

"So this is . . . 'Martin Ford,' huh? Are you truly fucking kidding me?"

Amato knew why he wasn't Marty Nyrop now. They endured a silent moment.

Marty folded his arms. "So . . . I guess I'll be seeing you around, Paul."

"Like stink on shit, Marty . . . *Ford.* Ha."

Marty shuffled like a condemned prisoner as he and Tak arrived back at the Production office. It was Marty's terrible bad luck why Amato, of all people in the business, was here but he already understood the reason for it. Amato, hired by MSC for his American studio experience, was available for independent productions because he, like Marty, was a recent outcast from the DGA in his capacity as a Production Manager. Budget scams he had pulled for years finally caught up with him during his very next project after hounding Marty off the Universal lot. Despite that, Amato would still be a favorite of investment bankers and completion bondsmen and their cartels of dentists with too much cash because of his reputation for ruthlessness with budget numbers, no matter who got hurt. To the insecure, Amato was soiled but valuable, like a good drug cop who couldn't always keep the powder out of his own nose. There would be no pretense of honor here among Hollywood exiles.

It was with Tak's suggestion and Amato's surprising concurrence that they had found the location sets in Utah. Amato's agreeability set off Marty's internal alarm system; he already knew that he should avoid Amato as much as possible, but he'd also been warning Tak that as a Producer, Tak himself was too open, too logical, too honest not to need some kind of conscious, deliberate defense against Paul Amato. Telling him that he had an edge missing, and he needed to watch his back constantly, because Tak wasn't bastard enough. Although Tak was a lawyer and quickly sensed Amato's danger too, if he was unhardened and naïve it was probably because tax attorneys weren't the engines of the legal world, just cogs in a machine. Like I was, Marty thought. But Marty Bebop is dead. I'm here to direct.

32

T he front passenger seat was the Director's throne on any location scout. Marty enjoyed even this minor perk, now that he was no longer an obedient Second Assistant who spent his scouting trips carsick on the rear bench of a maxivan. The scouting party — Eric (now Associate Producer himself, as it seemed he could talk the MSC people into anything), Tak, Marty, the Production Manager/Producer Paul Amato, the cameraman Helmut Wolfer — had arrived at the edge of Silver Cliff, Utah which in fact was all edges. There was no center of town, no town really. No silver, either, not for a hundred years. No unions, no wage scales, no grip skills. No one to utter the word "craft" with a straight face. But at least all the sand wasn't purple any more. It'd been like driving across an asteroid getting here so they could revel in their cheapness.

The scouting party sat in silence for a moment. Ahead of them was one of the few buildings within a gas tank's range of their motel that could serve as their main set, a low bunker of stamped aluminum with its sides and roof bolted onto a rusting-through iron frame. It was just the sort of place where the screenplay's hero "Albert Byrne" would isolate himself, the better to concentrate on his robotic invention that would transform the world if only ABM — the *User-Friendly* script's stand-in for IBM — and true love, in the form of "Ginger Sterling," didn't undo him first.

The dust from the bald tires finally swirled away from the orange van and they piled out of the sliding side door. Marty walked ahead of the others to what appeared to be a warehouse office door. It opened at his touch, oddly reminiscent of the door of a sound stage, thick and padded to keep the outside out. Beyond the entrance, inside the unlit and unlocked storage area, there was no stuff of commerce or agriculture, almost nothing to be seen at all, only a faint scent of sweet-into-rotten fruit, a faraway apple rind smell expanding out of the darkness. Perhaps orchards had once been nearby, or more likely the fruit from elsewhere had come here for local distribution. Whatever the cause, it had left its clinging odor behind though it was nearly as long departed as the silver which had given its name to the surrounding collection of shacks. It was ghost fruit, almost as forgotten as the ore gouged and steamed out of the earth until only hard minerals were left to the people who somehow lived here, who still came to the one pump for leaded gas, to the store for Spam and Wonder Bread, to the Post Office to run a finger inside an empty P.O. Box. Takashi Itani had grown up within twenty-five miles of here.

Tak called out: "Hello. . . ?" There was a faint reverberation, a ringing more than an echo.

Marty was restless. "Tak — who are we looking for again?"

"Matsumoto. He's listed as the owner in the county records."

"He expects us, right?"

"Well, no. I couldn't get anyone to answer the phone. But the folks I talked to here say he's always around. To just come by and we'd find him."

Marty exhaled impatiently. Tak could rightly take pride in being a quick study — a good thing because he had a lot to learn — but Marty's look told Tak that a real Location Manager would've nailed this meeting down in advance. Marty cursed to himself; he wanted this scout to go quickly, there was too much else to be done.

Without waiting for Tak or Amato to hire a First A.D., Marty had broken down every page of *User-Friendly* himself, each scene with its material needs minutely penciled on long thin strips of cardboard that were slid into shooting order on a folding picture-frame "Production board." But they couldn't commit to this first version of a schedule until they knew exactly what scenes would be found on location, what had to be altered by construction crews, what would have to be completely fabricated on a rented sound stage back home. They all hoped that this last option would turn out to be no scenes at all, because being moored on a stage made you a target for people in suits, and going independent like this ought to have some privileges of freedom along with the deprivations.

Amato was surprisingly placid and willing to be precisely where he was. Suddenly he laughed, a constrained cackle at some private thought. He then stared at Tak with a frightening, belligerent glare. Marty caught Amato's Fuck-You-I'm-From-New-York look and found himself worrying again that Amato might break Tak — or even Marty himself, in his debut as Director — into pieces out of sheer malevolence.

"Oh." Tak stepped away from Amato and grinned, perhaps at a memory, and turned back to Marty. "This can't be Mad Dog Matsumoto."

Marty pulled on Tak with a grip around his forearm and spoke quietly as a cue to keep out of Amato's earshot. "What do you mean? The owner?"

"Yeah. Even up in Salt Lake we heard about this guy living around Silver Cliff. He was a legend. Kids used to sing about him in grade school. Remember the theme song from 'Casper the Friendly Ghost'? We'd go, 'Matsu-*mo*-to-san, the Cra-zee *Jap*.'"

"So what'd this guy do?"

"It's . . . it's hard to explain. The Japanese parents never tried to. We were supposed to ignore him and then maybe he wouldn't be real and they could pretend not to be embarrassed. Some school buddies told me he was in one of the camps during the War, maybe it got to him. It would've been hard enough there for a . . . normal person."

"And you think this might be the same guy? What was crazy about him?"

"Do you know what a *waki* is? In Japanese theater?" Marty didn't. "There's always one in a *Noh* drama, you know, the old traditional theater. A *waki* is a traveling priest, he wears a mask like the one Yamamoto gave Eric. And robes, beautiful colors, they're really a sight. The *waki* float onstage more than walk. Sliding around in their white socks. Spirits, I guess, they're supposed to be spirits, or go-betweens, from the Spirit World to humans, I think. Anyway, Matsumoto — there he was. At least in the stories I heard, running around in his costumes here in Mormon country. I guess you can imagine it, eh?"

"'Hi-yooo, *samurai* —'"

Tak smiled. "Yeah, a little cultural, uh . . . texture. I wonder if it's really him. After all this time —"

Marty smiled too, then Wolfer the cameraman found an industrial-strength switch box. He shoved hard and the metal contacts broke through their corrosion. Some of the overhead fluorescents buzzed to life and the darkness before them suddenly became a throbbing space instead of an emptiness.

The perimeter of the warehouse was all dusty crates stacked neatly and unmoved for years. The rectangular I-beam frame rose above them in rhythmic lines like a rusty Parthenon. But in the center of the floor was a wondrous thing: polished, hand-rubbed wooden beams were seamlessly fit together, framing a raised square like an oversized table, a mahogany jewel set in the warehouse dust. Pillars at each corner of the square suggested a building so spare and stylized it was an abstract sculpture. So Japanese, it struck Marty; no wonder they make films there the way they do, it's all geometry, it's the way their world is fitted together. A runway at the rear of the square led to the back edge of the "building" and was partitioned at the far end by a curtain that nearly concealed another tiny, room-like enclosure with four walls.

Amato stared at the polished box, alarmed. "What the hell is all this? Huh?"

Eric trotted to the stage and smoothed his hands along the 8 x 8-inch beams that framed the mirror-smooth floor. He looked up into the mitered, fitted joists of a maple grid above the back edge of the square, half a "ceiling" again merely suggested, stylized.

Amato took his own turn bellowing, "Hello. . . ? Hel-*lo*. . . ?" He strolled to the shiny stage in the middle of dusty nothingness and smiled admiringly. "Nice wood. I could get the Art boys to use some of it, maybe cannibalize it for the office set. Sure as hell in the way, huh?"

Tak shook his head. "I don't think he'll be selling. This wood is probably two-, three-hundred years old. You know, I think it's really him, it was true — Mad Dog Matsumoto built this. He won't let us touch it."

Amato made what started out as a smile, then became a rat-like grimace that pulled his bearded cheeks back toward his ears and wrinkled even the top of his forehead. "He'll let us in here and sell us the wood, and if we shit in his hat he'll put it on his head and say 'thanks' before I get through with him."

Marty turned away, resisting Amato's intent. He wanted Tak to shut up, to keep him from harming himself, but Tak pressed on: "I don't think you understand, Mr. Amato. This stage has been maintained for generations, brought over from Japan. It's bound to have a lot of personal meaning, a lot of family history for someone. It's his culture."

Amato's eyelids lowered. He was staring at Tak's chin and shaking his head back and forth as he spoke: "He lets us in here or we pull out. This whole county and the state of Utah, they lose our money. A fucking *lot* of money. Some friendly donations'll go away. I'll make it in everyone else's interest to find health, safety code violations, whatever it takes. They'll bring in the damn bulldozers if he doesn't cooperate. This is the movie's workshop set. Fucking period." Amato hesitated to see if Tak would persist. He didn't. "Hey — *Herr* Wolfer, you fucking Nazi! Can you make this work?"

The Cameraman was making his way slowly around the outer walls of the warehouse, staring upward at crossbeams where lights might hang, pulling open fuse boxes. "I can make pictures anywhere, my friend. But with the money you give me, we will need to use these overhead fluorescents. So I must have an A.C. generator for HMI lights, without question. The house power will not do."

"Sure, *Herr* Wolfer. Shove another knife up my ass, why dontcha? I'll just lose the wardrobe budget. Yeah? We'll do it naked."

Wolfer smiled at Amato, nearly matching Amato's grimace with creases on his own cheeks stretching up to the top of his shaved skull. Marty watched them, a mongoose and cobra, wondering if this was what actors called "indicating." They made him tired.

He still felt a bone-to-bone numbness from bouncing for an hour on the trip here in their clangorous over-used van, and suspected that it would feel like this for months to come. Hollywood union crews were the Cadillacs of moviemaking, swept along by departmentalized mechanisms that an A.D. would order on his Call Sheet to arrive at a precise time and place. Here instead, they'd be half-riding, half-steering a used Econoline of a crew, jumping out to kick it in the tailpipe when it wouldn't go, hanging onto the bumper for dear life when it did charge off toward the rocky horizon with or without Marty's direction.

In low tones Eric and Tak compared their knowledge of *Noh* theater history, not daring to mount the stage and risk leaving a mark on its unblemished surface. After a few minutes Marty wandered away and found the only other attempt at interior decorating, a section of warehouse wall covered from one I-beam to its neighbor by sheetrock. There were photographs thumbtacked to the plasterboard, neatly arranged glossy black & white prints like those in newspaper archives. Most were of carefully posed families of Japanese-Americans living and working in identical wooden shacks under bare light bulbs hung from the ceiling, each wall of each shack made with sheetrock nailed to 2 x 4s. After a moment Tak nudged him to look at an old bit of hardware he'd found on the floor.

"What do you call this kind of nail? That has this little . . . it's like a collar here, below the nail head."

Marty examined the bent nail in his palm. "Doubleheads. Construction gangs and grips use them. Bang 'em in to the collar, and the top head sticks out. When you're done you rip 'em right back out again. Fast to work with if you're making something just to tear it down. Reusable. Film sets are like that — here, then not here."

The wall of photos caught Tak's eye as well. He studied them for a moment. "And I guess internment camps were like that too. Here and gone. I knew I'd seen these nails before. My parents have some pictures like these at home. Did you notice? That stage over there, a lot of it's traditional mortise and tenon work. But everything that's out of sight, like the frame underneath — he's put together with these . . . doubleheads."

Marty shrugged. Then he realized Amato was listening, grabbing.

"Gimme that fucking nail. A little lesson here, Itani, you want to learn the film business? This is how you crew up: you dig a pit somewhere and fill the bottom with Best Boy Grips. You throw in a bucket of bent doubleheads. The first guy who squats with his hammer and starts to straighten 'em out, he's the one you hire. You lift him out, and the rest of 'em you bury alive."

Tak nodded tolerantly. "How will that work here in Utah, Mr. Amato? I know that going non-union was one of my own suggestions. But more and more I'm wondering if professional experience can save you time, and money —"

"You leave that to me. I can get any department head I want from those fucking guilds in Hollywood, as long as I promise 'em I'm not gonna announce it. Then once they're here I tell 'em, Get the job done, ride herd on the local hires, or find your name on the Local 44 shit list. That 'experience' gets passed on in about two minutes when you put the fear of God into an IA guy working non-union."

Marty watched Tak nod again; Tak must've found Amato monstrous, a troll who fed on any human resource he could exploit. Of course. But it was as good an introduction to the Industry as Tak was likely to get, and he was learning about the business, fast. Parts he probably didn't particularly want to know.

Marty was still mesmerized by Matsumoto's photos. For a moment he didn't care about the here and now. Shot after shot displayed intact families — proud, looking into the lens, aware of their situation, letting their own dignity answer it, defeat it. The strength, the love. . . .

He went to Eric, who had pulled his *Noh* mask from his shoulder bag and was demonstrating a contemplative pose for Wolfer, peering into the mask that he held with both hands cupped inches before his own face. Amato glared at them contemptuously, then pulled Wolfer aside in what appeared to be an animated discussion about how to power the building. A few moments later he spun back:

"Hey — Marty *Ford*! You gotta tell me which way you're gonna look, so I can tell the Art boys where to park their asses. We can't build you the universe in here, kid, so you pick the direction you wanna shoot in after we chainsaw this fucking woodpile."

Tak turned away from Eric and his *Noh* mask and strode toward Amato, appearing as if he didn't comprehend the language Amato spoke, which was uncomfortably close to the truth. "No. Paul. That's just the thing — Eric and I were discussing it — we want this stage here. We want the stage right where it is."

Marty was dumbstruck. At least he had the grace to know that asking *"are you crazy?"* in front of Amato wouldn't help anyone.

Tak persisted. "See, Eric and I, we thought that "Albert" would have the same problem, eh? The same problem we have right now — which is, what to do with this strange, beautiful stage from another time and place, from the past, right in the middle of his high-tech workplace. This past, and what does it all mean to the future? See?"

Marty stepped in to shield Tak even as he resisted the urge to scream *"You 'thought'? I'm the goddamn Director!"* "But Tak, there's nothing like that in the script. It'll change every scene we do in here. We don't even know if we can make that thing work, if the ceiling'll fly, whatever — I don't know, maybe if we tear it down and put it back together when we're done, you know, we'd be careful. . . ."

Eric now stood with a hand softly on the back of Marty's neck. "No, no. Don't touch it. I'll explain it to you Marty, back at the motel. Don't worry about it. Just believe me, we need this."

Amato burrowed into Marty: "I've been after you for *weeks* to get storyboards outta you. I got no time or money to go back to the Production Designer and tell him to rework all his ideas around this Oriental teahouse here. You tell me right now which way you're gonna look, or I'll decide for you. . . . Huh? *Herr* Wolfer — !"

The Cameraman walked slowly back to their group with his hands clasped behind him, still glancing toward the ceiling, imagining where his cables and C-clamps and HMI lights would hang.

"Wolfer — it's your camera, your name's on this thing too. You sit down with little Marty Ford here and you tell me what this picture's gonna look like before *I* tell *both* of you how it's gonna look."

"Don't worry, Paulie. We can collect this."

"Huh? I'm asking you if you can *film* it."

"We can . . . as I said, collect the light, the surface, the image, yes."

Amato stepped into Tak's face and spoke in a subdued growl. "I don't care who you're going down on at MSC. This is no time to get fucking creative."

That seemed to Marty as if it should be quite funny.

33

Though Marty knew that it was Tak who had come up with this Utah location idea, he grew increasingly troubled over having come so far to use this warehouse in Silver Cliff. Its isolation could be photographically faked in any of a hundred industrial buildings in or around Burbank or Glendale, unions be damned. After Marty asked about it several times, Paul Amato finally waved him off with a vague explanation of distribution deals with the major studios, how they had to enforce the bogus discipline of keeping up low-budget appearances for a negative pickup deal in which a distributor would buy the completed movie for whatever the finished film negative had cost. It was the Producer's imaginary circumstance: *as if* they didn't also thrill at the financial prospect of having the biggest star in the world about to try real acting for the first time.

But then a trip with Tak to the County Records office explained the reality: that they were here only because Amato had purchased every square foot of real estate surrounding the warehouse. He'd be renting the land to himself in order to park the rolling stock. It was turning out that Marty's only protection against the likes of Amato was that, with a little research, Takashi Itani could quietly grasp the cause and meaning of most things that caught his eye, and Marty realized that here among pirates and thieves Tak was enjoying Cinema more each day.

Marty surprised even himself when he gave in to Eric about the usefulness of the *Noh* stage. After dinner that night Eric let them into his room, shrugged, then shook his head like a dog emerging from a pond to throw off an irritating wetness.

"So, did you and Tak go over it? I really want this *Noh* thing to stay put."

Tak tried to sound helpful. "That's why we're here. Why the —"

Marty waved him quiet. "I've worked it out, it won't add anything to the schedule. Wolfer says he can light it, so Amato can't whine about it costing anything, it'll just always *be* there —" The truth was that character aside, Marty simply liked the exotic strangeness of it, the textural contrast of tech and mahogany, and couldn't think of a compelling reason to pick a fight over it with Eric.

Tak shrugged. "Does the Producer approve the schedule?"

Marty glanced at him, then let it go. "But I still don't get it. Eric, throw me a bone here. What's that weird-ass stage got to do with anything?"

Eric went to the nightstand next to the bed, took his mask from the drawer and untangled the strings.

"It's like this. . . . You know what they figured out in the Japanese theater, about a thousand years ago? It's what I get called *avant-garde* for now. People don't go to the theater to be told a story, Marty. They go just to be there, in the presence of actors. In *Noh* theater, they don't even try very hard to tell a story. They've got a simple one, but what you go see is the performer, the costumes, the poses, the whole . . . spectacle of it. To be in the same room."

"Like that's got anything the hell to do with a romantic movie comedy starring Laura Trent-Sampson —? And have either of you found Matsumoto yet?"

"I'm talking about the through-line to *User-Friendly*. What Laura's been trying to fake ever since she read the script with all that poor baby, inner child crap character analysis that she keeps trying to talk to me about. Okay, here's the spine that goes through every scene: I'm 'Albert Byrne,' right? I make robots, I try to program them to imitate human beings. There's this contrast between the human and the mechanical — how much we take for granted about what's human and 'us' and only 'us' and can't be reproduced. So while I figure out all of that in my shop for machines, there's just this *stage*, and it's got this human presence, this *actor*, and it gives Albert ideas about who we are when he tries to translate behavior to the machine. It's the character *as* actor, the actor as the role model, the actor as the most human of us all —"

"What actor? You're adding a character? If you mean Matsumoto, does that mean I need to plan eyescan shots of 'Albert' noticing him? Not to mention signing the guy to a deal. And before you pretend it away, Laura's poor baby inner child is gonna weigh about seven or eight pounds from what I can see. Are you dealing with that?"

Eric ignored the question. "Anyway, we'll find Matsumoto, all right? Get him to sign some kind of release. Make sure, Tak."

Marty rubbed at his face. "You're crazed. Absolutely, criminally insane. . . . Well, okay-fine. Sure. Why not."

Marty rose and reached for the doorknob, suddenly anxious to see stars twinkling above the rocks and RVs, dizzy for night air. Eric reached for his arm.

"And another thing— Watch out for Wolfer. He's the enemy."

"The cameraman? You agreed when I picked him, he's got a great eye."

"Sure."

"Then what the —"

"Just watch him. All Wolfer knows is camera. Wolfer's the enemy, yours *and* mine. Remember that."

• • •

Later that night in Marty's own room it was Mad Dog Matsumoto's shrine of black & white photos that stayed with him. Where did the strength in those faces come from? Marty felt tainted in contrast, his pirate's adventure now making him uneasy about what he'd become part of when an hour earlier he'd watched Laura and Eric glare and gesture at each other as they went into Denny's, as if the belly protruding between them wasn't there.

He tried to escape into his memory of the warehouse prints. Detailed 4 x 5 view camera work, the deep focus of catalog images: faces and tarpaper and mountains, barbed wire and windblown dirt. Boys in flannel shirts and rolled up jeans, dusty wingtips and oxfords, girls in corduroy jumpers and ribbons of flowered fabric tied into shiny washed hair. Families attending Methodist and Buddhist churches, playing baseball. Trees planted, carrotwood he guessed, carefully dug watering moats to nurture roots. A rock garden of Zen serenity fashioned out of desert scrabble along a creek bed, dead fallen trees serving to guide the eye along nature's abstract forms, stone paths leading inward journeys beneath machine-gun-turreted watchtowers. Urban professionals and their families living in shacks, smiling, determined to survive humiliation, degradation, with fathers' hands firmly on sons' shoulders, with daughters held tight to mothers' breasts. Family above all. Though imprisoned, lives nevertheless lived whole.

34

M arty next had to overcome his fear of a secret knowledge that actors might share. He needed a strategy of rewards and punishments that would make his performers heel on the set, and for that he needed a better feel for what made an actor an actor in the first place. But as he scouted the Utah landscape for visual inspiration, his view had an opaque roundness at the center, like stereoscopic nickels taped on his sunglasses: it was Laura's belly pushing all else to the edges.

His instinct said that Craig-now-Eric didn't do anything unless there was something in it for himself. How else to explain the lies about their parents, the cruel teasing that his big brother had inflicted on him because it kept Craig alone from having to face their family truth? Or, as Eric Blanc, the selfishness of impregnating Laura Trent-Sampson just to extend the run of his New York theater? Laura had something Eric wanted, needed . . . envied? But what could he give her? He was dangling legitimacy in front of her because "legitimate theater" still had that ring to it, that meaning. If that were the bait, what would be the catch, for Eric? Doing this to her didn't seem to be about money after all. And perhaps it wasn't entirely for his little troupe. Apparently four years of performing arts schooling and the last ten years on stage in New York hadn't fulfilled any kind of dream for him; whatever Eric's presence-of-the-actor flimflam was really about, it hadn't yet been enough and didn't feel as if it ever would be.

The shooting of *User-Friendly* would have the traveling circus, we-are-family side of moviemaking that is always heightened on distant location. Eric seemed interested in that, too, but Eric *had* a family, a wife and kids he at least claimed some kind of allegiance to no matter how estranged or legally held apart. He couldn't possibly love, honor, cherish, respect, even *like* Laura Trent-Sampson. Nor could Marty imagine that Eric had been out there in the movie audience these past few years like all the other adolescent yearners, pasting up Laura's image like a mental billboard, a roadside ad for god-knows-what along every masturbational pathway of thought. It couldn't have been that Eric had a fantasy of making her into his lover, mistress, wife, famous-piece-of-ass conquest. This was too aberrational, too unlike what Eric had done with his "legitimate" life in Art even if that life had left him one dream short.

The wanting, the confusion, it all drove Marty crazy even as he was part of it. A movie without any actors at all definitely seemed like the way to go. Or at least movies with actors who shut up and did what they were told and kept their personal problems personal. There must be three or four of them in the Industry. No — animation — that was it. Or computer simulation. *Virtual* actors, he'd heard George Lucas or somebody at Industrial Light & Magic was working on it. . . .

· · ·

"Of courtthhh you know, Marty — tthhisssth . . . meanths War."

Marty cringed. Daffy and Bugs, together again. Another shard of mutual childhood glimpsed in a long-cracked mirror.

He cleared his throat. "Nyehhhh . . . we attack at dawn, Doc."

Eric grinned. Marty tried to relax in the over-bright conference room they'd rented from a local business. The editor and his assistant had arrived on location, and somewhere down the glossy-painted cinderblock hallway their ancient upright Moviola and their new, chip-driven flatbed machines whizzed and clacked away with test footage for wardrobe, makeup, and hair. Their rehearsal room was paneled with thin brown veneer, and two gray desks with rubbery tops were pushed together to make a square in the middle of the lumpy gold carpet. Old metal supply shelves ringed the walls, sagging from unread memos and requisition forms and several broken coffee machines. It was anonymous and cheap, the perfect place to debut as a film director.

Laura had come early. She sat alone behind her Ray-Bans at the square of desks, looking queasy and unwilling to make eye contact. Tak was somewhere in the building, waiting for Amato. There would be no other judges of Marty's first rehearsal with actors.

He cleared his throat again. He was doing that often.

"With just the two of you guys here . . . I've had time to start imagining this thing on the screen. And you know? Last night I rented this town's only video besides *Texas Chainsaw Massacre*, and, I mean *geez* — it gets me how theatrical a film like *Citizen Kane* is. And it's supposed to be the greatest example of *cinematic* storytelling ever. But all the deep focus, you know, the wide-angle moving camera, the front row POVs —"

Eric rubbed at his forehead. "Oh no. Let's get it over with, let's hear you pronounce *'mise-en-scène.'* Go on, *Monsieur Auteur* — 'Meeeze —'"

"Screw you."

"Remember. You're a Director. We're performers. Don't start talking camera, Marty. Not yet, not with us."

"I'm not talking camera. If you'd let me get it out, I'm trying to say I think you'll be real comfortable with the way I'm gonna shoot this. I'll keep you guys on the screen in two-shots, and let whole scenes play out in long takes where —"

"I get it — Because *User-Friendly* is just . . . like . . . *Citizen Kane*! Or, or *Stagecoach, Rules of the Game, Metropolis*!"

"No, asshole."

"Because Mr. Form-and-Content has seen the ontology of figure and ground? He's codified the semiological signifiers within the cinematic paradigm?"

"Fuck you. No. Because *User-Friendly's* a lot like the romantic comedies of the 30s. All I'm saying. They understood when to let actors act. They put the camera on a dance floor. Moved it around and didn't cut the performances to pieces. Some of the best movies and the best theater aren't as different as either of us'd like to make out."

"Great. So before our first rehearsal you've already storyboarded the slickest film school thesis in history. The entire USC film department will flock to the box office. We'll make tens, even dozens of dollars."

Marty quit trying. He suspected this was only one of many unpleasant conversations to come in the months ahead. He and Eric might mean well at every conscious level and still end up angry, over and over, until inevitably Marty would impute pure evil in his brother's intentions and probably slug him again. Eric said he wanted Marty to direct. Why wouldn't he let him do his job?

He went to the one working Mr. Coffee and felt his stomach flutter when he poured a dark thick liquid over stale Coffee-Mate.

"Eric, Honey — ?"

Laura had spoken; Marty was allowed now to look at her intently, even stare. Something was missing today. This was the least dynamic presence she'd ever given out, as if a pair of sunglasses were wearing a Laura Trent-Sampson wig at that end of the desks. And "Honey"? Were they finally getting along?

"I've been thinking a lot about 'Ginger.' I like her, I think I can relate, I understand her a . . . a little."

Marty sat down across from Eric. They both leaned back, allowing her to go on.

"I . . . I worked out a through-line for her, and —"

Eric pounced. "No through-lines yet. I told you, Laura. We haven't even had a reading —"

Marty waved Eric off. "I want to hear what she has to say. Laura? What's the through-line, to you?"

"Well. . . . It's a love story, right? I mean, what's 'love' to her, when she's always . . . taking *advantage* all the time? So I thought, well, taking advantage like that, that's what she had to do 'cause her father the Boss was afraid that's what he'd do to *her*, his own daughter, and so he just left her sort of *out* there, alone. But there's something inside her that says that's not right. Like, if you love someone, you do sort of *surrender*, you know? But that's not right for a parent, you're supposed to *be* there. And then she meets this guy, and for the first time she thinks she really can surrender to somebody else and give up this . . . this control thing of hers. So at first she does what she knows how to do, the manipulation stuff. But it'll be okay because it's to get him to surrender to her too, so like then they're *equals*, right?"

Marty nodded quickly and eyed his brother. "That's exactly what I was trying to tell you. The whole arc of the characters, it's looking for that equal relationship. It's just hard for them because they start in such a bad, dishonest place. Which is why you shoot it in fifty-fifty two-shots, you put the camera on wheels, you frame the characters nose-to-nose or two-faces-East, and you let performance carry the scene. There's your form-and-content. It's gonna work on the screen, and you know it. That's all I was trying to say. Up yours with *mise-en-scène*."

"And if you don't have any idea about what the beats are and where the improvisation comes from and what the shared moment is for the actor, we're all going to have one hell of an expensive student film."

"Who's gonna be improvising —?"

Tak rapped on the open door. They were all startled, no one knew how long he'd been there. Tak stood aside while Paul Amato eased into the room, impassively eyeing the three seated before him as if they were a *tableau vivant* placed for his amusement.

Tak made the introduction to the actors. Marty watched Amato go first to Laura, then Eric, making easy small talk, exuding a kind of energized charm with each.

"Well, don't let me stop progress. Huh? You started the rehearsal yet? Don't mind me —"

Amato had a copy of *User-Friendly* but left it unopened on the desktop as he slouched in his chair and began wagging his knees back and forth. Tak flipped at the page-edges of his own script and seemed to urgently want Amato to leave.

Marty's directing career began: "Well . . . let's give this a read-through then. . . . Uh . . . the opening, I think that's all self-explanatory stuff, mostly action with the robots to establish the technology. Give it some tech credibility. Let's start further in —"

Eric smiled. "No, no — there's a part in the opening here for you, Marty. 'Dweeb,' the Assistant. This is one of his best scenes —"

"Yeah, but — This is a rehearsal for you and Laura."

"C'mon, Marty. Don't be afraid."

"I'm not —"

" — And Mr. Amato here, when we get to it, he'll be 'Wally the Boss,' right? 'Ginger's' father."

Eric's grin, handsome and ingratiating, was a weapon fired at Amato's wild face. It worked. Amato finally smiled with one side of his mouth again. "Yeah, sure, I'll help out —"

Marty sighed, then set up the opening of *User-Friendly* quickly: how the Hero's lab assistant "Dweeb" runs through a warehouse pursued by a robot — all action without any dialog to rehearse — until Dweeb is cornered like a rat by the machine. Marty knew this part would be all moving image and cutting rhythm. In this part, at least, the screen would be his.

●●●

When they returned from a break Eric cornered Laura and she shrank from him until she had nowhere in the room to go.

"Laura, look — I'll give you two things to remember, always, no matter what the scene is. Number One: Don't ever do anything unless something happens to make you do it. Okay? Don't be afraid to be quiet. Silence isn't *nothing*. And Number Two: whatever you're forced to do then — it doesn't depend on you. It depends on your partner. So don't worry about making things up. Don't force anything. You don't have to. You'll have me. React to *me*."

"Eric. . . ." Marty flicked his eyes from his brother to Amato and back again, a quick plea to Eric not to embarrass her.

Eric turned to Amato. "Laura Trent-Sampson is going to shock the world. With this role, she's going to become an actor. Laura — let's try the repetition thing from the other day. Make some kind of simple observation about me, the way I look."

"What? Now? I don't —"

"It's the Sandy Meisner thing I told you about. Come on, observe. Anything. My clothes."

"Not now, I don't —"

Eric shouted: "What's *wrong* with you?"

Her face transformed. The bones themselves hardened. Colors went through her cheeks, up into her eyes. She had presence. "*Nothing's* wrong with me."

Eric froze, then applauded briefly and laughed. "You reacted that time. Was that a reading?"

Her eyes were shiny. "No."

"*No*. It was a moment. No script. An impulse, real and then gone forever. Were you thinking of a character? 'Ginger'?"

"No, there wasn't any —"

"There was just you. Was there some kind of emotion?"

"*Yes* —"

"Good. Don't tell me — Did you respond as 'Ginger'?"

"No, I was just doing what —"

"You were *doing*. Concentrating. The doing *is* the character. The doing was real. It was the *circumstances* that were false. Contrived. But the concentration gave you the reality of doing. Right here, right now. And you showed us a real emotion. There was no difference between you and 'Ginger,' you wanted the same thing. The moment was true."

Eric turned back to Amato. "Shock the world."

Amato stood suddenly. "Tak, we've got a class act here." He made a deliberate point of staring at Marty, then turned back to Tak. "Just don't let this kid fuck it up. Huh? He's a nobody. You and me, Tak — we make this thing work, we get our own MSC deal on the next one. Then we hire the *real* guys. Huh? Yeah?"

Tak's face was blank, until Amato pointed at Laura. "The belly, you got some way around that yet? I don't know how much longer we can dance around it with these guys. They got one foot back in Japan already."

"Marty and I, we're working on it. Not to worry."

Amato stared, then darted out of the room. Laura avoided Eric's eyes. Marty grew slowly aware that something was rising within himself, going up his spine like mercury in a cartoon thermometer. He didn't know what would burst out when it reached the top of his skull. What was it — Eric playing the bully? Amato's naked rudeness, blunt intentions, his *success.* . . ?

Eric suggested they finish their cold reading after another break. Laura nodded and left quickly. Marty thought she'd said to pee, but he wasn't sure; she had the kid squashing her bladder, after all. Eric took Marty's shoulders in his hands.

"Did you see it, Marty? Did you feel it? What we do — that's when an actor's *alive* —"

"I don't like the way you push her around."

"It's not. . . . Okay, listen. I can't do this to her through the whole production."

"No shit."

"But somebody has to. It can't be me, or she won't get past how angry and frustrated I make her. Her character and mine will never *connect*."

"So what're you saying?"

215

"I'm just telling you why it has to be somebody else besides me. Fine, you go line up your camera and leave us alone to perform, because it's obvious you don't get a single thing about actors. Yet. You don't know what we do or why."

"Like hell I don't know. I know *you*."

"At this rate . . . not for quite a while, pal. With acting. . . . Okay, it's not your fault, it takes time. So I've got someone I can bring in to help. I'll get Amato to hire a guy, my old teacher Hy Matlovsky. Okay? But did you feel it, Marty? For a little bit, what the *moment* is? That's why I'm here. With you. I can teach you things, if you'll ever let me."

Their gazes set, hardening. Then Eric smiled and leaned into Marty's face. "Of courtthhhss you know —"

"Tttthhhisssth meanthss War." Marty sat back and mimicked Amato's knee-wagging slouch. "Ain't I a stinker? *Huh*?"

The brothers laughed. Then Eric rose and kissed Marty's forehead and left. Who, Marty wondered, would he get Amato to hire? Some teacher, he said?

• • •

During the next rehearsal a half-hour later it was Marty's intention that Movie Vision would begin: "Albert" and "Ginger" — his brother's and Laura's faces — were each to talk past one another, but not connect, within one of the script's crucial scenes in which missed connection is the point. The scene would be almost entirely these faces blocked for his rectangle, eyes staring at the edges of the frame, characters seeing the Self but not seeing the Other. This rehearsal would be about touching and resisting, pushing and pulling, ways of working through the missed connection, about how to use subtext to say the unsaid. Time for the actors to begin a screen relationship that would conclude only months down the road, then remain fixed forever. He knew he would be on trial soon because the minds and instincts of his actors would no doubt mesh with Eric's mentor's secret knowledge too, and Marty would have to prove that he had his own creative ideas.

216

Tak seemed to sense that he could help Marty, and diverted Paul Amato by inventing a small union *vs.* right-to-work crisis that would keep Amato bleating into the phone throughout the afternoon.

Marty quickly went through his plan to rehearse just one scene, well into the Second Act. Starting in the middle of "story" was something they would all have to get used to because shooting schedules give little consideration to the chronology of narrative. Film and television actors are the last to feel the urgency of ". . . and then?" except where, through practiced discipline, they feel themselves at a specific point along a story's continuum. Marty was beginning to understand that away from live theater this was part of the force behind actors' search for 'moments' and "beats"; when the end of the movie was shot on the third day on location, nothing else would ever be theirs but the here-and-now. Again that one vision that persists: no past allowed, only the present. Love me *now*.

Patrick Cosgrove

35

D ays later when Eric's acting teacher Hy Matlovsky appeared at the door of the rehearsal room the old man was hesitant. Each movement was weighted with caution, as if he'd been sucked out of a New York skyscraper through a pneumatic tube to squirt out a moment later amidst Western mountains. Convex lenses set in heavy black glasses enlarged his eyes and exaggerated their darting movements. He was thin and bearded like a department store Santa Claus caught out of his padded suit.

Tak ushered Hy to a chair. "Mr. Matlovsky —? Have you got the scene? Where 'Ginger' tries to sign over the patent rights to 'Albert Byrne'?"

"I was just now given a script. On the way into the building. I mean, just *now*."

Hy smoothed his bony hands over the script cover, but then left it unopened. Tak hesitated with extra sides of the scene in hand, unable to tell if Hy wanted them or not. Marty guessed that Hy didn't, and that peevishness wasn't far beneath the skin.

"Okay, since this scene takes place in an office — amazingly, not unlike the one we're sitting in — I'd like to move things around a little bit, and get a feel for the blocking. Laura, you'd be sitting across a single desk from the patent guy 'Pomeranz,' and we can imagine where the door would open behind her. Where 'Albert' would walk in. Eric. . . ?"

Marty pushed the second desk a few inches and waited for Eric's help to get it across the lumpy carpet. Eric fell back in his own chair, and waited instead for Hy Matlovsky to signal what the next step should be.

Hy looked at Marty through the convex lenses. Marty imagined a goldfish staring at an approaching can of food flakes. Hy tilted his head back: "Writers write, even if they have only a piece of chalk and the back of a shovel."

Marty blinked several times. "Okay."

"This is not about sets and props and tools. I am not interested in . . . pretending. For now, actors can act from their chairs without toying with the room."

Marty would not choose his first fight here. "Fine, let's do the scene flat, and then work up to it. I'm happy if I just get somewhere beyond a read-through before the camera's turning."

Laura nodded at him, then turned to Eric with a pleading look. Marty wondered what she needed from Eric, what assurance, what guidance. He wondered how much of acting skill he still didn't know.

When they completed their reading Laura waited out the silence as long as she could, then leaned toward Eric.

"I don't know what to feel. You want me to come at this a certain way, and I don't know where to start."

Eric shook his head. "It doesn't matter yet. You can't *make* yourself feel anything. Just don't show up empty."

Marty could tell Laura didn't understand this advice any better than he did. She tucked her chin until Eric made another offer.

"If you need it, that's where the 'as if' comes in. The moment before. You come in — your *only* responsibility — is you come into the scene filled up. Not empty. You say 'This scene, to me it's as if — ' and your imagination does the rest. You give yourself another — some *equivalent* — circumstance. If you imagine the scene itself, then you'll just play your imagination. You'll model the written scene on your mental scene, you follow? You won't respond to what's really happening. Then you're not reacting to me, you're remembering what you just imagined instead of reacting." He thumped his forehead with his finger. "Copying echoes in your head. Right, Hy?"

Matlovsky tapped at the side of his own head to signal that Eric had remembered a lesson properly. Laura was paralyzed.

"All right. Simpler. You pick an 'as if,' something that's *like* the scene. Just to get primed, just to be feeling *something* when you start. Then forget it. All you have to do from there is react to your partner. Remember? What did we talk about? 'Don't do anything — '"

"— until you're forced to. By your partner."

"Atta girl. . . . Okay, something small. Something from your life, where you can say 'Here in this scene, it's *as if* this other imagined thing had happened.'"

Laura had been handed a gift; she nodded happily, then bowed her head. Marty stole a glance at her and felt guilty for invading her privacy. She looked up and he decided that behind the Ray-Bans she'd given him permission to start the next reading.

"Okay, Laura, you've just sat down in the office. 'Pomeranz' the patent clerk turns to you, and —"

Marty stopped. Laura's shoulders were bouncing up and down, she looked like a jumpseat passenger in a roadster. It finally occurred to Marty: she was crying, trying to dam something up, and she couldn't do the scene.

Hy Matlovsky gripped the desk with both hands, then rubbed at his forehead. "Good god, child, what are you doing to yourself? You're doing it, using some affective memory trick, aren't you? You've read some out-of-print book about The Method, and you've come up with some phony Freudian repression theory about childhood! God *damn* the Actors Studio. That's what you've done, isn't it? Tell me — Give me your moment before. What were you imagining?"

"It's . . . it's this scene, Ginger, she's losing him, it's about losing, and the loss — So what I did, I . . . I remembered losing my babies, I couldn't, c-couldn't. . . ."

"You've done this? This happened, you've lost a child?"

"Yes. . . ."

Hy threw his hands into the air and gave out an "Achh!" worthy of Olivier's "Lear." He jabbed his finger at her. "Those tears do not count! And they must not count." As Marty watched, a last defiant teardrop ran down her cheek. There were no others.

Hy seemed angry. Marty was aghast. A memory of "Gotcha" burned a path through his head but this moment didn't seem headed there. She hadn't done The Sob.

"Can we take a break here, Eric? Five minutes, then we can try again —"

He was ignored. Matlovsky's eyes bore into Laura. "You are not a perpetual log in a fireplace, something you can light up each time you need an effect. You will burn out and have nothing left. You'll offer psychosis as performance. Emotions are not reliable! Work, and technique are reliable. Talent, the ability to daydream, to imagine — *that* is reliable. That's all that talent is. It is your job to use your talent, and your only talent is imagination. Not psychoanalysis, not confession, not self-hate and regret and self-pity. You cannot use up your own life like cheap fuel."

"I'm sorry. . . ."

"My dear . . . we all have our demons." Hy scowled at the tabletop, then shifted his tone. "It is your duty to have *fun*. To enjoy this process we call imagination. This process of finding the 'as if,' then connecting with your partner. Do you see?"

"Sorta. . . ."

Hy came to her and patted her distended belly. "You've never been a Queen. Could you play one?"

"What? I —"

"There's a story. Sandy Meisner, the teacher of us all, tells it. . . . Bette Davis did this once. From her own life, was she ever a Queen?"

"No —"

"Of course not. But what must it be like, to be a Queen? Why, it's *as if* —"

Laura caught the intention, and smiled. "It's . . . yeah, it's like . . . I know — like, I just got to Dorothy Chandler for the Academy Awards? And I'm waving to the people there, and the lights and the cameras —"

"Yes! Yes, it's as if you've shown up for the Oscars! You are adored. Loved. Perhaps even feared. Certainly envied. *That* is imagination. That's your moment before. With that, *now* you can enter a scene. Enter it as a Queen, with that Queenly feeling, and be a Queen from that moment forward! Yes. Your *life* is not queenly, no one's is. So you can't chop what you do have into pieces of eight and spend it like so much coinage. But with your imagination —"

"Yeah — "

Hy smiled brightly, and Laura visibly relaxed. Marty remained dumbfounded. This was utter gibberish.

Eric spoke. "Marty, you read 'Pomeranz' the clerk. Give us that to work from."

"Sure —"

Hy stood again unsteadily to go behind Laura and put his hands gently on her shoulders. "Something from the past. Something re-imagined. It becomes new, it becomes what you feel right now. What I'm trying to do . . . what it takes months, if not years and years . . . what I try to do is put you together with yourself. Then, and

222

now. You say the scene is about 'loss.' Imagine . . . it's as if you've lost something that you can't get back, and don't tell me what it is — of course it wouldn't be your virginity —" Hy mimicked a yellow-toothed lewdness for effect and Laura laughed. "— and I don't care, I don't want to know. That's private, and you don't owe it to anybody. Just don't . . . eviscerate yourself."

Laura nodded eagerly, then tucked her chin, doing her homework assignment.

They read. When Marty looked up from his script to find Eric the next time, where his "Pomeranz" sees Eric's "Albert," his brother's eyes swam in their sockets with an electric charge. Marty felt pushed over by the emotional current flowing one way from Eric. What was Eric/Craig's "moment before"? What re-imagined past — a piece of *their* past together? — was he using to become the person who existed only in this moment?

Patrick Cosgrove

36

Birth was coming quickly, full of pangs and sounds and movements. The baby was several weeks early, would probably be underweight. As Marty burst out of Exene's room and ran down the motel sidewalk toward the Production Office he wondered: Another one skinny and afraid like Mom always said about Craig — ?

He skidded into the office doorway. "Tak, get an ambulance or something. Where's the county hospital from here?"

"Too far, if she's as close as you say —"

"What the hell do I know about it?"

"I called for Paramedics —"

"Where's my brother? Tell Eric to get in here, would you? It's his kid —"

Tak peered toward the Wagon Wheel balcony across the parking lot. "He's not in his room. Or not answering. I'll call around, there aren't many places he could be."

"Well there's only one goddamn place he *should* be. I don't *believe* him — " Marty ran off, then abruptly turned back. "Hey, Tak —" Tak leaned out across the office threshold. "The First-Aid guy, Benjie what's-his-name. Is he in town yet?"

"Yes. We brought him in early. For the altitude —"

"Go get him. Now."

"Right —"

"And don't let him give you crap about not being on the clock."

"I'll *put* him on the clock."

Marty nodded, relieved.

"Marty!" It was Exene. He took a deep breath at her door. She was in there, the world's most famous actress curled in a Best Western double bed like a celebrity dog whelping in its nest. Didn't she know this was going to happen? Of course she knew, she could've called. She wanted it this way — alone, primitive, like some kind of "Little Manger on the Prairie."

He rushed into her room. The bed was empty. The sheets were twisted, tortured into a circular pad. There was a yellowish stain on them, and something else reddish-brown and thick. He looked away, then turned and partially saw her in the bathroom on the toilet, thinking, This is a hell of a time for that —

"Marty, help me —"

He didn't want to go any closer. He inched forward enough to see her with her feet on the toilet seat, squatting naked over the bowl.

"Help me get back to the bed — Oh god, oh god. . . ." He went to her with his hands out, ready at least to guide her gently under the covers. She wanted more.

"Carry me, I —" She came off the toilet part way, one foot back on the floor and her arms toward his. He caught her, felt her full weight, smelled her metallic breath, her sweat, her fear. He staggered, bent backward with her cradled in his arms.

"Wouldn't moving around help? Keep you stretched out, or something? Or would it hurt? Should you walk around the room, or — god, Laura, I don't know what to do."

"The bed —"

He set her on the mattress. She rolled over onto her side. Her thighs and loins quivered, she was gasping, trying to force a regular breathing pattern. "It's close, Marty, don't worry. I've done this, the hardest part's . . . over already —"

His eyelids were stuck on wide. "Shouldn't you have . . . waited?"

She found him with a pained squint, then laughed almost to herself until he laughed too.

As he watched, it was as if she were turning inside-out, the new unfolding from within the old. How could Eric do it, he wondered, how could the son of a bitch do this to me? How could he . . . miss this?

Marty wanted to be more of a comfort, more caring. Nothing occurred to him until he growled to himself: "Where the hell's that First-Aid guy?"

"It's okay, Marty. I want *you* here."

Who knew what that meant. Was he here alone with Exene by design? Maybe she was already part of Eric's conspiracy, maybe she'd agreed to his brother's plan to name Marty the designated breeder. And what about this *bonding* shit, anyway? Was this birthing thing going to spit out a kid who would imprint on him like some hatchling duck?

"I don't know what to do, we've gotta have somebody trained in this, something might go wrong —"

She rolled onto her hands and knees, then her back arched, bucking upward into a semicircle with a powerful squeeze of muscle. She was taut, an athlete frozen in performance, her rectum bulging from its rim in the wrong direction and burning purple. Something round, gray and mucous-covered pushed through the red ring of receding birth-canal tissue. It finally got through to him: the head.

"It's coming, I mean I think I see —"

She groaned and shook the length of her body. Her face was tucked between her forearms, her knees drawn toward her chin. It was here, the child was his catch.

"God, I've gotta wash my hands, or, or —" But he already had a face, wet smears of hair, then shoulders in his trembling palms. Another yell, a belly, something long and attached, looped around a red leg. A baby.

There was a commotion at the door. Marty heard his own voice, then a stranger's. He gently drew the sheets above Exene's now-softened belly and put the baby against her breast. He was soaking wet, too. He saw hands move toward his own, taking the rigid hose from his insensible fingers, clipping the bluish-white connection. The baby's eyes were open, blinking, but he seemed stunned, in silent shock. Son of Exene the X-Girl. X-tro the X-boy. Marty heard Laura's voice from far away.

"Is . . . it alive?"

"Yes, yes . . . " he assured her. "He. It's a he." He wanted to shout it, to go tell of this life on a mountain.

• • •

With the early delivery, it was as if the entire city of Osaka were on a rickety perch against the mountainside overlooking the shooting company, with every MSC corporate executive now watching their little production company through a pair of galactically powerful binoculars. In a fever, Marty consulted a day-out-of-days chart listing the workdays of each cast member until he determined that they could do useful work while waiting for Exene to recover by calling in the actor playing "Dweeb," "Albert's" technical assistant, and filming much of his work weeks before they had planned. By eliminating Dweeb from one scene late in the schedule to avoid carrying him on salary, it would cost the company little more than budgeted. Eric thanked Marty for giving him another actor to work with. Marty thanked Tak for keeping the film moving forward, for buying time with MSC. He knew, however, that with Exene's — with Laura's — child sending out ripples of chaos across their situation, he hadn't yet created anything that was guaranteed to be seen in a completed film. Even being thanked felt thankless.

Then, like a continuing square dance of sequential do-sa-dos Laura thanked him for being there, for her. Eric wouldn't hold the baby; Marty did. Eric wouldn't rent a refrigerator and microwave for the pumped breast milk; Tak did. Eric wasn't there to defrost a bottle and warm it in the microwave when Laura ran dry and the baby was still hungry at 2:12 AM; Marty did, then slept sitting up. Marty was unable to say no to Laura as she continued to ask for his attendance, unable to get her to hire any help, and was unable to turn from his nephew the X-Boy. He'd stopped wondering whether Eric was ever going to say "I am the Father" or not.

In Laura's room one evening Marty held a bottle of formula at the baby's mouth while the baby threw his full life-force into squeezing out a diaper load.

"I can't help it, Laura. I wanna lick his head. I mean, I hold him, he drinks, and with all this slurping he doesn't even know I'm here. And all I can think is 'I wanna lick your head.'"

Instead, he kissed the wispy hair atop the baby's skull, and felt even the gentle pressure of his lips push the fontanel down to where the brain pulsed.

The baby in his hands begged for simile: he was like a screaming belly, like a digestive system with eyes, like a vegetable without much of a root system, like a hairy coconut made a holy fool with swaddling clothes. Each time he held his nephew he hovered with his face in the stream of baby's breath while the child stared resolutely at a spot an inch above Marty's forehead, listening to the music of his own intestines until some synapse fired off to make imminent starvation or defecation overwhelm all other consciousness.

What we have here is a Tub O'Guts, Marty thought, a fine Irish name. Since neither Exene nor Eric had bothered to name the child, that worked fine for him. Better than Xtro, which sounded like something out of "The Jetsons" cartoon show.

And dumber than a dog, he kept thinking. Food and a warm place to shit were the whole *megillah* here. It wasn't even really consciousness yet, it was only needs — the need to suck, that one was tops. What Marty held with all the tenderness he could summon in his suddenly too-big hands was a creature of instincts so raw they were frightening, not even human. The thrashing, the gasping — the newborn threw his head at anything that moved or touched him because it might go in his mouth and might silence the belly. Until next time. And his breath, that sweet cheese out of a perfect vacuum machine, with the rooting, the wanting. . . .

"Anybody who doesn't think we're descended from fish should get a look at this spawn here —"

"They're all like that, at first. . . ." Laura's voice trailed off weakly for reasons he could only guess at — the trauma of delivery, the weight of memory, regret, sheer fatigue, maybe all of those.

He had the urge to swallow the newborn, to imbibe him, inhale him, and join skin with him somehow. But there was no appropriate way to melt together, to do what breastfeeding must feel like. Wondering again, Is this it, the bonding, the little chick with this big dumb cluck? He can't *deserve* the way I'm feeling — there can't be anything else so unconditional. This unearned devotion, this schoolboy crush, it's what falling in love with a beautiful face is like. *Oh, it's so much beyond that. How can I feel this way about someone I don't — can't — even know?*

The baby finished his bottle. His swollen blubbery lips, so shiny-wet, went slack in stupefaction. His satiation was an image, like a great wide door held open to Marty for an instant, then closed again. Bliss, and he'd seen it: needs completely satisfied, a glimpse of something spiritual that might explain everything else.

He knew if he could wake him — almost impossible from a comatose sleep, almost like a psychotic withdrawal — then everything Marty wanted to express, to give to this child, would only scare or annoy the tiny guy. The outside was locked out, the unmyelinated nerves looped back on one another to await only another alarm of starvation.

But that was all right. "You know what, Exene. . . ."

"H-hmm. . . ?"

"I just figured it out."

"Mmmmph. . . ?"

She wasn't awake, either. The hell with it, he talked at the wall next to her headboard. "When you're a kid you get greased with testosterone so you'll squirt your genes around. But then . . . that's it. Once you've done that, Nature just drops you, lets you get weak and gray and then rot. But looking at this kid, for the first time I'm thinking, once you've made one of these things, that's the plan. It's a design, and it's probably okay, y'know? It's okay to get old."

Exene snored once, then curled away fetally from her covers. Marty stood near the edge of her bed and gazed at her milky form. She was a little pouchy below her restored navel, and her nipples and breasts finally reflected the stress of swelling and draining, the yanking and pulling, but he calculated she was roughly three hours of Stairmaster workouts from looking exactly as she had before pregnancy. She had already lost interest in further breastfeeding, using only a breastpump on her own schedule and not the baby's. He resisted the urge to stare any longer. Her body — used by producers and directors for years already to tantalize millions on the screen, her flesh irresistible to the eye and to his weakly fluttering genitals even now — maybe it ought to belong only to Laura and her baby even as she refused to feed him with it. He lay Tub O'Guts next to her and covered them both. He would have Tak order some more formula.

One day soon, he thought, this little guy'll open his eyes, these birth-hemorrhaged marbles will focus and he'll look right at me, the fog'll lift, and he'll see and he'll *know*. He'll know I'm just another asshole.

He knelt and kissed Laura's shoulder and licked his nephew across one eyebrow.

37

"**S**o you were there, huh? You made the catch?" C.T.'s question seems to have some small corner of pleasure in its construction, but he's trying very hard to stay aloof, clinical. Their second trip to the hospital with Lupe and their dismissal from the emergency room yet again has so far only bought them enough time for Bibi to have arrived from Los Angeles. Bibi is quiet and watchful in an armchair Marty has dragged into the spare bedroom where Lupe rests, and while there's not much to be done until true labor sets in, Bibi agrees that with her nursing skills it's better for Lupe's sake that Bibi is here. Marty is just afloat in gratitude.

They're not free and clear. Lupe's water has broken; the proper medical phrase has something, he thinks he heard, to do with a premature rupture of membranes, but it's not the hair-on-fire emergency he'd always assumed it to be. The E.R. nurses have told them that all the necessary amniotic fluids are still being produced, so mostly it's just messier as long as there's no sign of infection. Like a professional courtesy, Bibi doesn't want to second-guess the E.R. personnel, and assures Marty that they can be watchful here at home.

Then: maybe it's because her body has been strenuously rehearsing the moment for weeks, maybe because the baby is smallish and Lupe has an accommodating frame, maybe it's sorcery, but tonight Lupe will give birth to a son. Marty doesn't get what's happening until Bibi tries to lift Lupe out of the bed and carry her toward the car but then decides there's no time to go anywhere, so as Bibi is tearing apart his linen closet for sheets and towels, Marty uses a grip on C.T.'s arm that he hasn't given him since he was a misbehaving eight-year-old.

"Get in there!"

"What the fuck — She doesn't want me —

"Get in there and make the catch, *you make it too. You can't miss this* —"

And C.T.'s there as Bibi guides his hands to a wet mashup of hair and mucous that becomes a face and a shoulder and another shoulder and a blue cord. . . . And this new father is silently crying with tears falling from his chin and he doesn't know how to stop looking at his living child.

• • •

Bibi stays in the room throughout the night with Lupe and the baby to see if she can encourage the new mother to let down her first milk, and to make sure the baby gets the colostrum. It feels almost prehistoric, as if they're cautious cave dwellers, but he and Bibi agree to give mother and child a chance to sleep for a while without pokes and prods and monitors for vital signs. C.T. and Marty sit in the silent and dark living room, until hours later Bibi feels her way down the short hallway and finds them.

"We have a problem here, guys."

Marty waits without a clue. C.T. mutters some profanity under his breath.

"Do you know what I mean, C.T.?"

"Yeah, yeah. . . . She don't wanna stay. She says she 'just don't love me anymore.'"

Marty feels like he's never lived here. "What . . . what's going on? What happened?"

"She called me a fuckup. Like she says I'm some loser who's gonna end up in jail like all my loser friends. She thinks I don't care if the baby lives or dies. I mean, what the *fuck*, we had it all goin.' She had the tat thing, I was getting paid for the videos, I got sponsored for skates, we were gonna make it. And 'cause of that one fucked up thing in the street, she thinks it's all gone."

Marty can see it, finally. For all their ill-conceived (yet deliberate) plans and their fanciful dreams together, all C.T. and Lupe really had was certainty. Something no one has any right to. Certainty which has evaporated.

Bibi speaks past C.T. to Marty: "We've been talking off and on. For a while. Too early to tell, maybe it's a little post-partum blues, maybe not, there's a lot of hormonal readjustment that has to go on. Maybe for months. We can get her in to see somebody who'd know. But she strikes me as a tough little girl, with her mind made up about some things. I think she'll leave the first chance she gets. As soon as she's strong enough. Unless you're ready to put her under lock and key, she might even try to find her mother."

"In Mexico?"

"If that's where she is."

"She'll never get back in. How's the baby gonna survive a trip like that?"

C.T. pushes himself off the couch and heads for the door. "She's such a *bitch* —"

Marty shouts after him: "We're talking about your baby here, too, pal —"

The door slams.

Marty can't look at Bibi just now. He has lived nearly twenty years without her, and whatever choices he made that caused that barren stretch of his life to happen, those were the worst decisions in his life: to not put her life before his imaginary movies; to be unfaithful to her goodness, to take advantage of it. And here the two of them are again, treading in a deep pool of even more bad choices.

"Well. Like old times, huh Marty? Surrogate Mom and Pop again. We'll get our new little mama to a doctor in the morning."

"You're sure she's okay here?"

"For a little bit. Vitals are fine. I don't think she's in much pain. Or she hides it well."

He nods, but his mind is roaming in the past, not within tomorrow's doctor schedule. "Remember that night in Castaic? The refugee scene?"

Bibi is quiet for a moment, perhaps re-aligning her thoughts. "I remember losing my ability to blink. You've made me cold again, just saying the name."

He smiles briefly. "I think of it . . . maybe only Thursdays through Wednesdays. . . . Thawing you out. Most beautiful ice cube ever."

She returns his smile sweetly and regards him again without speaking until, "I'm surprised you never found anybody, Marty."

"How 'bout you? Who'd you find?"

Bibi sighs and sits quietly for another moment. "Me."

"Well, that's one, in how many years. . . ?"

"It's been enough. It's really been about my work. My patients."

"Yeah, I always wanted to think that too. The work, finally. To make it all worthwhile."

She nods. They sit with only a few passing car engines smoothing over the silence of the house.

After Bibi goes back to Lupe's bedside, Marty hopes that by morning he'll recall some of what *not* to do about keeping loved ones together. Bibi has said she'll sleep in the chair next to Lupe's bed, but adrenaline keeps Marty awake as he waits through the night to see what will become of this new family.

Until Lupe regains her strength, until she feels the baby is strong enough too and she alone decides if and when and where to run, Marty will keep giving C.T. everything he can that will help him live or not live with Lupe, by making him know what it is to be a Nyrop. He'll continue to feed C.T. all the cautionary tales he can of the Nyrop fathers, even — or especially — now that he's watched his teen-brained kid throw a tantrum even while still in the aura of his child's birth.

And if the magnitude of what C.T. has taken on doesn't make him relinquish this child, if tales of the patterns of generational crackup won't bring him to his senses, then Marty can only hope that C.T. will be determined to thrash the cycle of Nyrop disaster to pieces, be as determined as Marty had thought himself to be while running through an airport with a baby on his chest. And hope too that C.T. and Lupe will still be together so they can try to do this as two parents, as partners in the way he failed to be with Bibi. And maybe even with all the odds against him, his son will be better at it.

Alone in his dark living room Marty feels in an entirely new way that he has to have faith in his son, faith that every day spent raising him for these past seventeen years has added up to something he has yet to give C.T. credit for.

But then again. . . . While they've awaited birth, each of them dwelling solitarily under this one roof, Marty has watched a self-involved boy dealing with his fears by brooding, has watched a wounded kid bleeding out, and he has seen in C.T. a loneliness, and crushed dreams. He has seen thwarted lust, adolescent horniness, and still sees in C.T. urgent need — love, even, for Lupe — and he sees restless hurt and loss and broken friendship and perhaps now with Lupe ready to bolt, he sees the end of tender companionship and gentleness. There have already been tears and now Marty sees — no, suffers — that his own heart too is ripping, shredding, dropping empty and flat to the unkempt floor and he wants his boy in his arms, wants to fix everything, and he cannot live this way.

• • •

They must have been out there for days and nights, stalking.

Marty walks around his block where the heavy canopy of curbside sycamores makes the sidewalks beneath widely-spaced streetlights dim and quiet and shadowy. He gets a shot of adrenaline when he sees C.T. at the next corner in a pool of overhead light, walking slowly back to the house. As Marty lifts one arm to let his son know that he sees him, that he'll wait for him here without intention, a large SUV swings to the curb and stops next to C.T.. Laura Trent-Sampson alights from the passenger door and moves quickly toward his boy who slouches and stares at her. Marty goes numb, then recovers, finds his legs and runs beneath tree-shadows toward his son a block away. Laura and C.T. both see him coming from far enough away that Laura can say something else to C.T. and the boy can think about it while watching Marty run at him on stiff legs. C.T. pulls open a rear passenger door while Laura skips back to the other side and before her door is shut the vehicle is already on the move, coming at Marty. Then it's past him, rolling through the red light at the end of the block and roaring straightaway down the next dark block.

Marty clutches at his hips, panting. He can't feel his legs at all now, or anything inside his ribs. He watches the movie star, who became an actress, who-became-a-creator/producer-showrunner, receding from him; a pair of taillights mark the path of a self-ordained storyteller who has just made some promise to C.T. that got him into her car, and perhaps cast a spell that will transform him soon into a performer. Through some tale of imaginary circumstances that will, in a few weeks, provide C.T. with an authentic behavior, he will appear to millions as if he were living a Life, even as viewers demand that his story have a beginning, middle, and end. Laura will spin C.T.'s head in a Hollywood where truth means freely adapting facts, re-shaping messy events, where C.T. can be elevated to playing the hero of Laura's tragic reality show about a long-ago stolen baby, raised by a man she hardly knew who hid her child from her by changing his name (though it was to his birth name) and moving hundreds of miles away, until like a dogged investigator, so the story will go, she tracked him down and recovered her lost baby. There might even be wizards and dragons along the way.

Marty knows, *Of course* this is what she has in mind. And how can C.T. resist this when the mother of his own child has just leveraged him out of the house, out of fatherhood, by declaring him a loser? Reality TV: what better way for C.T. to claim his place in the lives of Lupe and the baby? He's Hollywood-bound now, for a show that already has the green light from some mogul who knows the needs and wants and desires of the nation, toward a cable show aimed at an audience in the way movies once were; at the millions who will be entertained, touched, who will occasionally wipe away a tear they have shed for characters in a docu-soap that follows an unscripted script for forty-four minutes and launches Laura Trent-Sampson's latest reinvented self into to a hell of a ratings orbit. It will be an amazing tale, its climax even now taking shape as C.T. is being driven back to the no-longer secret Hollywood that Marty hid from him, to accept his celebrity birthright.

• • •

Days pass. Bibi, Marty, Lupe and the baby stake out private space within the bungalow. All are alone. If he'd had the time, Marty would've told C.T. in more carefully considered stages why and how he left the business, but C.T. let Lupe's oscillating moods push him away from her and their baby, push him toward the blood parent who didn't run away from fame and wealth. She's the parent who didn't raise C.T. to be a fruitbooter Juvie graduate, the parent who can give him his due in a universe he had never imagined for anyone, let alone for himself.

And because Marty doesn't even know where C.T. is he can't tell him the why and how of leaving directing behind, of walking out on a profession that most anyone would've thought answered all of life's questions. Marty probably has the law on his side in this reverse abduction because of his years of child-raising, the day-to-day presence he swore he would never forsake, but the idea of contesting Laura's maneuver, the money it would cost, the likelihood that nothing would come of it until well past C.T.'s eighteenth birthday, means that he is impotent.

The watch over Lupe and the baby continues as Marty mulls more episodes of the flight-from-Hollywood true story that C.T. didn't wait to hear, sifting for clues as to how his life should have gone, what he should have done, or said, what he did that was so damn wrong.

38

*M*arty drove back and forth across the Utah wilderness the next two days, supposedly to scout exterior locations. The windshield and rearview mirror were frames for his mind's eye, his brain in effect glued to a camera eyepiece that parted the sulfurous dust around him. Each rectangle was a place to capture color and line and form, but he needed to prepare his script by maintaining a Director's two brains: one of sharp authority and judgment and guidance, the other mind of a photographic dreaminess that had been darting softly in and out of consciousness in place of sleep for weeks.

If he dwelled directly on his ignorance of the acting process, he might quake; but if he gave up the images that were beginning to stream from his restless nights and entwine his waking states, then as they arrived on the set he'd be merely a traffic cop letting Helmut Wolfer record talking heads. He would have to walk a middle path between surrendering to his actors' whims and feigning authority over their creative offerings so he could still impose his will, still capture Laura Trent-Sampson's face within whatever frame romantic comedy required and make the movie his own face, his own image that challenged the world to see. To see *something*. . . .

During another night of sweat-soaked, restless dream-scouting, thinking himself awake among Laura-images, the phone rang. It kept ringing to tell him he'd drifted off. Bibi used to answer the phone in the evening when the condo was her home, too.

"Marty? It's Tak. . . ." His friend seemed far away, small.

He took several long breaths. "Yeah? What's up? Not *me*, for chrissakes —"

"It's Amato."

"What about —"

"What a malignant guy, eh. . . ? I couldn't control him, I'm sorry. He went past me to MSC. To Kurumada and Yamamoto —"

"For what? What's going on?"

"You're off the project, Marty."

The camera-vision popped, bubble-droplets of faces on screens fell earthward. "What? No — Come on."

"He got in there and stirred the pot. I'm ashamed, really, I. . . . I'm sorry, Marty."

"Why? What the hell happened?"

"Amato got the money people all riled, he said they were throwing away millions by having an amateur directing Laura Trent-Sampson. Especially with the schedule pressure, the delay from the baby. I'm sorry I'm even repeating this to you."

"Who do they want instead?"

"I tried, I told them you were ideally suited to do it because of Eric and everything —"

"No, forget it. This . . . it's not about anything you did. Who do they want?"

"I suggested Hy Matlovsky. After they wouldn't listen about keeping you."

"Matlovsky. . . ?"

"Amato got ahold of him, had to talk him into it. The way it came up, first they offered Hy the 'Boss' role, just to get him onscreen, keep him next to the camera —"

"He was already *on* the set. We're paying him as Dialog Coach."

"Well, you'd have to ask Amato about that one. I don't think he wanted to lose Eric, too, at the last minute like this. Anyhow, the way it went, Hy said he was no longer an actor because he couldn't stand the childishness it brought out in him. Can you believe it? Then Amato offered to let him direct, and Hy said no, he could teach actors but he didn't want to be their Daddy. Finally Amato offered him $500,000 front end — I don't know where he got it. And I swear you could see it, for that much money Hy would've been, I don't know, the family box turtle."

Marty lay back on his pillow, trying to retrace a path through moviemaking intentions. No breadcrumbs here to follow home. His career, his only reliable focus, had in a couple of months gone from disaster to opportunity to disaster again, a three-pop fireworks flower bursting, then fading in a night sky. He considered screaming but thinking about doing it killed the impulse.

Instead he wondered whether his brother had done this to him, whether he'd been set up. Hy made a point after the second rehearsal that Laura was festering with bad habits, that he wished he'd gotten hold of her before she'd ever been in a single scene, ever. That he had to teach her to stop *acting* and look instead for specific behavior. Hy had been arranging his own indispensability, making sure Marty knew of it. But Hy Matlovsky never would've been invited on board if Marty weren't already in place. Then again, maybe that was *why* Marty was already in place, holding that place for Hy, and the suspicion about Eric was true. So Eric lied to him again, and he'd made sure Hy Matlovsky got hired. Then it was, "Direct it, Marty, sure, go ahead. Then when you get shown up in front of the Producer, they'll kick your ass out and I'll get *my* guy in there." And then, *then* Eric probably got Amato to agree on Wolfer, this camera guy out of *Dr. Caligari*, some bastard he knew Hy wouldn't like, and it'd be enough so the poor trusting old schmuck would go crazy with frustration and quit.

"I can see it coming, Tak — whoever's left, they're all gonna have to turn to *him* then, aren't they? 'A Film by Eric Blanc.' But there's a weak link, the whole thing blows up if she walks, right? So first he knocks her up. That'll keep her around. And if she births some poor blob of protoplasm that another *au pair* neglects to death, what of it? You've made it, Eric, you're a goddamn *Auteur. Artiste!* You win, Asshole! And nobody gets mad at Eric, he's too beautiful."

Tak was silent on the other end of the phone line. And what of Tak's own suggestion of Hy as the replacement director? No, that was the one conspiracy to not pursue. Marty decided that he had to have a few instincts left functioning, and Tak wouldn't do that to him.

"You still there, Marty?"

"Yeah, yeah. . . ."

"Maybe somewhere down the road we —"

"Right, look — I'll come over in a while, okay?"

Marty hung up. Thwarted ambition. Freud's stuff of daydreams, was it? He could use this, someday. When he did direct a picture, if he got another chance to be in charge, then losing his brother this way for the second time would be a good "moment before." The moment before what, who knew, but then what would the great Hy Matlovsky say about Marty's one aching tremor, the stifled moan that now lifted him off his mattress, his single tear of self-pity for having his life's only plan go skidding off a cliff? Simply that using a real and silently screaming moment for his "as if" was cheap fuel, too big, too close, too personal. *Doesn't count.*

39

arty had no future in this business. Control was a delusion, there were too many forces at work that would keep *User-Friendly* or any movie, for that matter, from really belonging to anybody. The question now — the fun — was how to go out like a comet. Not as a beaten dog, but wrapped in the Flag screaming, "I've not yet begun to fuck you up!" Marty laughed out loud as he marched past the wagon wheel pool railing. With his own scene to perform now, he'd have a story to tell Eric, proving that his brother didn't get all the talent, all the imagination. He went to Amato's room and banged on the door with a metal clipboard, gouging divots in the pine veneer. Amato opened the door, blinking from a nap, scowling silently. Marty smiled very widely with a sudden insight: a story's protagonist is someone willing to take great risks, to lose everything. It's what makes the audience hold its breath.

"So Paul — The hell with me, it's done. But before I leave I'll help you guys out. Give you a little free advice from a former member of the DGA. Why don't you just get out of Silver Cliff? Find your set in a building around here near the motel. *Huh?* Why dontcha, Paulie?"

Amato's voice was all sleepy whine. "What? What're you talking about? Get the fuck outta my room."

"All these hamlets around here, there's gotta be a dozen other warehouses within ten miles of here. And I bet every one of 'em has easier road access for our equipment than this Matsumoto thing. Huh? *Huh?*"

Marty was uncertain if he'd expressed sincerity and innocence even as he mocked one of Amato's verbal tics. He enjoyed being on very thin ice, he wanted to see it crack, to plunge below, to experience real danger unedited. "I mean, September in Utah — you get your 5-tons and your genny stuck out here when these dirt roads turn to mud and ice, it'll be a disaster. And if it snows, god help you. . . . C'mon, you're experienced, you can see that. So why are you there? *Huh?*"

Amato was staring wildly but seemed not to hear him. It suddenly occurred to Marty that perhaps it'd been nothing personal at all, that as soon as he was out of the way he'd crossed out of the Movie Dimension and was no longer visible to Amato. Marty detested grieving for his aborted career with these people, which made this moment the right time to pull down temple walls, to end it all. Go out with his comet tail whooshing across the sky, the hell with movies once and for all, get a life. What would Bibi think of that? And it stabbed his heart that it was suddenly so important to want Bibi's approval. What in god's name had he given her up for? *For this?*

His jaw quivered at the possibilities. If Amato fooled him and miraculously agreed to find their set elsewhere, they'd have solved a Production headache and Marty would've crashed and burned while still a loyal Assistant Director — a small gift to Tak. He floated at the doorway, thinking, Then for five minutes I would've been a real First Assistant Asshole after all. Top o'my world, Ma. And if Amato didn't agree — of course he wouldn't, this was his personal profit they were talking about — "Marty Ford" was out of here, done, gone to the trash heap next to Marty Nyrop. Re-makes like *User-Friendly* are never as good as the original anyway, you lose the vitality. It was all in Paul Amato's hands. *Do it, Paul, put the gun to my head, pull the trigger —*

"Can you tell me? Paul, can you tell me in all honesty why you're even using that place? Like, you even have '*honesty*' in your vocabulary?"

Now Amato's small watery eyes found him. "What is it, you little *putz*? What're you after? Look, I'm sorry about how it turned out, huh?"

It was happening: Marty smiled confidentially. "Yeah, Paul, it's like . . . like if you didn't know better, you'd think somebody was getting a few bucks off the top to put you in that warehouse. Because there aren't any logistical reasons to be out in West Jesus like that. Hell no. Who's getting greased around here, you suppose? You smell a rat? C'mon Paul — let's get us a car right now, it's scoutin' time. Head on out to the wide lonesome plain and find that bastard —" Marty waved toward the horizon. "Come on, you stinking, fat, career-murdering piece of lizard-shit!"

The pallor in Amato's cheeks now blushed maroon. That was all right, Marty was doing himself a favor — being a murder victim was more honorable than committing suicide.

"What're you accusing me of? *What?* Honesty? You want 'honesty'? In this business? You wanna know how it works? All right — All right, come on in here outta the cold, for chrissakes." Marty stepped into the room and looked for a semi-automatic handgun, or machete. "All right, smart guy. You wanna know how many times I've had Prop Masters come into my office? And say they deserve over-scale because they *won't steal,* like that's some kind of goddamn rare virtue? How many Art Directors I've had that live in houses that're wall-to-wall with custom furniture they had built for *my* set with *my* budget? How many actors I've signed who told my costumers they *had* to, just fucking *had* to have a Rolex in their scene because that's what their character would wear? You want to guess how many of those Rolexes show up after we wrap? So don't tell me about skimming off the top, or any goddamn extortion or any other insult, you little prick. If I rent my own goddamn property to the company it's because they need to rent something from somebody, and if it's me, I got no problem with that. I've saved the company time looking somewhere else. I'm stealing *nothing.* Don't get into a pissing match with me. Firing's *nothing.* I'll cut your heart out, you little over-educated punk."

Marty grinned stupidly, a little disappointed he hadn't been shot dead yet, there'd been no gunplay. "Hey, sure, no problem here, either, Paul. Who cares, anyway?"

There was only one thing left to do. He slammed Amato in the nose.

Amato went down with a soft plop, surprisingly pliable in the body, with shapeless weak arms; only his small bearded head looked hard and mean when it stuck out of a floppy, expensive shirt.

Marty sat on him.

"Get off! Get off!"

"Let me tell you what it is, Paul, you wanna know what it really is about this business? You want little Marty's Grand Theory of the Hollywood Film Industry? It's how you studio fucks get where you are. What your techniques are. The in-fighting, the devious alliance-making —"

"Get off!"

"— back-stabbing, tantrum-throwing, claw-your-eyeballs-out political savvy you creeps use to drag yourselves into a spot where you greenlight somebody else's talent. Somebody else's *life.*"

"Get off me! Motherfucker!"

"Oh sure, you're terribly sensitive once you get there. None of that action-packed, Psychotic-Cop-blows-away-the-Murdering-Deviant-in-front-of-the-Naked-Babe high concept movie crap for *you*. Only gentle tales that reveal the soul of the artist you've kept nurtured and hidden away while you Uzi-ed your fucking way to the top of the corporate picture factory."

"Get . . . off!"

"I came out here seven years ago with movies in my head, movies that could've been on the screen by now. But all I've seen in my seven years is fat psychotic fucks like you who do everything they can to rob and cheat and intimidate and manipulate. Like — I don't know — they've gotta make up for some childhood torture and they're gonna make everybody else pay for it their whole adult lives. And Hollywood lets 'em do that if they're relentless, fucking sociopaths and they'll kill anybody to get what they want. They squeeze the life out of everything around themselves because they have no idea how to *live* a goddamned life. Well, I've *had* it —"

Marty stopped. Amato was struggling with his arms, flailing them spastically against the carpet, and giggling. Marty stood up and shoved at Amato's legs with his foot. Amato rolled to his hands and knees, blew bloody snot onto the carpet, then stumbled toward Marty, his weepy long fingers held wide.

"A hug, Paul? You want a fucking *hug*?"

Amato was laughing in his ear. "Marty, you little shit! I love it, you've got a little brass down there after all, *I love it*. You're all right, kid. What a fucking scene. Maybe you'll be a Director someday, *huh*? Not on *my* fucking set, but who knows?"

He was in Amato's grasp. He didn't know whether to hit again, or fall down laughing, and was shocked to realize a sense of serene completion: he'd been an actor, had played someone not entirely himself and not entirely the Other, and in that moment, in that reality of doing, as Hy had taught his actors he too had been invulnerable.

40

When Marty got back to the Production office to say goodbye Tak was still working in his chair behind the folding table.

"So before I go home — anything you wanna go over? Anything about Laura's contract situation? She must've said 'yes' to *somebody*. She's on payroll — what about her salary, where'd that come from?"

"Paul Amato . . . just penciled something in for MSC. Made it look like a firm budget."

"And what's Amato got to say about this now?"

"Paul's leaving."

"He's *what?*"

"Gone. He doesn't know, I'll tell him tonight. C'mon, you can't stand him either."

Marty noticed a throb from his skinned knuckles for the first time. Right next to the scar from Cal Reardon's tooth. "Of course I don't, he's a thug. But he's still the Production Manager. A Producer. Who else is —"

Tak shook his head, then drew circles with a pen. "You ever heard of *keiretsu*, Marty?"

"Kay — *what?*"

"In Japan it's like a business family. Because different businesses work together. Manufacturers, banks, retailers. They're all family. Literally, I mean there's arranged marriages, the whole bit. . . . I spoke to MSC, about how intolerable Amato was. Ethically and as a personality. I know why they hired him, but I said I didn't think they wanted to have their name associated with someone like him the first time out."

"*You* didn't think — ? What's going on here, Tak? They listened to him just fine about dumping *me*."

"I think on that one he played to . . . some fears they may've already had. No offense."

"Fuck that. So MSC fired Amato, or what?"

"They never fire anybody, not on the corporate level. He'll be promoted to some kind of Executive Consultant. He'll be the Doberman pinscher they keep in the closet for emergencies."

"But the completion bond people, the backup insurance, the American money — Amato was *their* guy. The one they trusted. Now they're gonna pull out and leave MSC with their pants down."

"No they're not. MSC showed the bondsmen how it'd be in their best banking interests to stay."

There was a finality with only a hint of impatience in Tak's voice that was enough to tell Marty to stop. It was just Tak sitting there, but apparently someone who had become Takashi Itani, MSC Studios Supervising Producer. Or what was it that he had made up on the spot at Musso's that night? "Executive in Charge of Production." Only later would Marty fully recognize how much had already changed, that there was a calm at Tak's center, a substance to him, a casual seriousness with his eye on a farther horizon than Marty could see that night.

A submerged fear rippled its tail above the surface of his confusion, then re-submerged to leave inky whirlpools in his moving stream of thought — a vision repressed, until now, in which he understood that movies were made not by scheming weasels like Paul Amato (who was at least comprehensible) but by hidden forces, by sober bankers and lawyers who were in truth the gray eminences who said "This movie" or "That movie," guided by the pressures of market forces and stocks and bonds and leveraged takeovers and investment strategies and tax write-offs and interest rates that Marty would never understand in his lifetime. Seven years in Hollywood, for what?

"Do you know how to produce a movie, Marty? How Producers produce?"

"Fuck no. Nobody does."

"Teach me what you do know. I'll pay you out of my own salary. Let's start with the Production board, how you make a schedule and break down a budget. . . ."

Marty wanted to bang his own head against a wall. "No . . . possible . . . way." He started to leave, but turned back. "Tak —? Right before a woman delivers, shouldn't she have like a huge whale belly? I mean don't they just, like, beach themselves on every horizontal surface they find?"

"I guess so. . . . Why?"

"Exene. . . . I don't know. She . . . at the end, she didn't have a belly button. Not until afterward. . . ."

Tak waited for more, until Marty left the office and went to his room to pack his belongings.

Patrick Cosgrove

41

H e heard the soft knock at his door but didn't know what it meant. It could be morning. The middle of the night. Anybody's room. He listened for the baby's cry. Another knock, harder. No, he was in his own room and it was Sunday. He wanted more sleep. . . .

Another knock. He pushed his legs off the bed and was pleased to find that he was still dressed. He turned the deadbolt but left the door closed.

"Marty? It's Tak."

Marty backed up and slumped into a chair "Come on in."

Tak entered but stood hesitantly, his hands at his sides until Marty waved him toward the bed. Tak sat carefully erect on the one corner where the bedspread still clung to the mattress.

"Do you have a minute?"

"No. I was really involved with . . . snoring. Then I was gonna drool." The morning after the worst day of his life, and he was floating, he'd been freed of something. "What is it? You look worried." Tak didn't answer as Marty rubbed gunk out of his eyelashes. "Now if you're gonna be a Producer, you have to practice a better Worry Face. Go like . . . go *unhhh*. . . . Like you're squeezing piss out of your ears."

Tak wouldn't smile. "I have a room between Laura and Hy. The walls are very thin here."

"Yeah?"

"It's what I'm hearing. . . ."

"They're giving out mating calls? 'By a waterfall, I'm calling youuu-hoo-ah-hoo. . . .'"

"At night, I can hear . . . this strange machine noise."

"Uh-huh. If it's a vibrating, buzzing noise, I don't want to hear about it. No matter which side it's coming from."

"No, it's. . . . I know what it is. I've heard it before. My father died a few months ago."

"What — ? Oh no, why didn't you — ? You mean you were working on this — *Shit*, Tak."

"It'd been coming on for quite a while. He was a heavy smoker . . . emphysema. They put him on oxygen at night, for the last year or so. The oxygen machine . . . it goes like *hiss-pock, hiss-pock.* . . ."

"Uh, no, I know what you're hearing. It's Laura's breast pump. She's trying to get ahead, for when we — when *you* — start filming her. It's this little electric vacuum thing, and you put your finger over a hole and it makes that noise, *sssst-hahh, sssst-hahh* like a little toy dairy farm —" He didn't see any point in going into how the machine also let her evade breastfeeding, cut down her time spent with a yet un-adoring baby.

"No, this is different, and I . . . it sounds very strange, I know, but I listened at the wall to be sure, and it's coming from Hy's room."

"Hy's pumping his breasts?"

Tak finally managed a brief smile. "I didn't tell anyone, but the reason I brought in First Aid early wasn't just the altitude. It was really for Hy. I could see he was having trouble breathing here, and at first I thought it was just the thin air and his age. A local doctor told me he might acclimate a little more easily with oxygen in his room, so I brought in Benjie to see what Hy needed. And when I listened to it last night, I remembered what my Dad's equipment sounded like. . . ."

"So you think maybe Hy's got emphysema?"

"No. Probably not. Like I said before, he passed the insurance exam. I don't know, I guess I was wondering if you'd heard anything more about him, about his health. Through Eric maybe?"

"Eric and me, we don't exactly hang out."

"Right. Well. . . . I happen to know Hy has a lot of life insurance —"

"You *happen* to know?" Marty laughed.

"All right, I checked it out."

"You check *everything* out."

"And we paid Hy up front. He's already cashed the check for his entire Director's salary on this. I think the oxygen explains why he agreed to do the film in the first place. I think he knows he might not finish it, and if he does know that, he's already provided whoever he's leaving behind with a nice inheritance."

Marty sat quietly for a moment. "Tak, you want me to go through the rest of the deal memos with you? Before I'm out of here maybe I could catch a few more things, y'know, before you hang yourself on this long rope MSC's giving you."

"I know we're in trouble. The company's already very upset with the start we've made here. Laura's working without a contract. She shows up pregnant and delivers just days before shooting starts. The Director's fired. The replacement Director's on oxygen. It's only a matter of time before the tabloids show up and have a field day with this."

"We — You're on track so far —"

"Yes, so far. Because your work during prep saved us. But the company, I think, they're dreading the attention they know they're going to get. Japanese corporations don't like to do business this way —"

"Welcome to America —"

"The guy playing 'Dweeb' is expensive. He's already on the way here, so any delays start multiplying the costs, and if Laura —"

"Look, if it comes to that, as long as you've never used the Dweeb guy, you can cut him loose and recast the part. He won't even get residuals. Just write down 'Did Not Photograph' on a production report."

"Laura's making it worse by not letting anyone help her."

"Hey, I help her. Well . . . I have been, anyway."

"But now what? I really need you to stay on. For Laura, for the picture. But even if you do, even then we have to go to normal shooting days this week. You'd be working dawn to midnight. And not to demean Laura, but I think hers is a case where it's a child taking care of a child. She needs someone else."

"Have you talked to her?"

"Several times. But she only trusts you, Marty. Could you persuade her, maybe to hire a nurse, a nanny, anything?"

"I . . . I don't know, I don't know about crap like that."

"And that's just a small piece of it. If Hy has a serious breakdown when the stress of shooting starts. . . . Can you stay? As the First Assistant? Please —"

"Don't ask that. *Don't*, Tak. For godsakes, a *First*? I'd rather cut my own fucking throat!"

"It's for me, too."

Eric suddenly came into the room with his eyes darting from Tak to Marty. It was obvious that he already knew this meeting was taking place. "Tak? Have you talked to him? You've gotta stay, Marty."

"Why? I'm not the Director, what's the point anymore? You guys go ahead, do *your* jack-off movie."

Tak started to say something, but Eric ran right over him. "If you leave, if you go, will you still do the play?"

Marty glared at Eric. Unbelievable, him and his Ac-a-*ting* while everything else fell apart. "No movie, no play. Take Laura back there with you, what do I care? You want your theater, she wants you, *I'm* the only one around here that wanted to do the damn movie. And in case you've forgotten already, I'm not the Director."

Tak's voice had an odd distance to it: "I do, Marty. I want to do the movie."

Marty couldn't help but stare at him. Tak was the last guy he figured to make it personal. He realized that if he stayed on as the First Assistant — a task he was afraid Tak might, at any moment, drop to his knees and beg him to do — he would, for the first time, be then truly assisting the Director. Big shit. But what was his choice? And to leave Tub O'Guts, the X-boy in Laura's hands, and now with Tak wanting —

Marty stood and dented the wallboard with his fist. He wanted to run from the thought that he'd become Cal Reardon after all. Thinking, So this is it, I'm here in Utah playing someone I'm not, to do a job I've never done, that I don't even want. Realizing I never knew most of what Cal did, except I was right about the part where he never pointed the camera and now I never will, either. Not even as "Martin Ford." And Bibi should've come with me, bless her, damn her. She's the one who maybe ought to be a Director, not me, because she was relentless when it mattered, she wouldn't leave "us" alone until she was absolutely sure she'd wrung all the juice out of it. And relentlessness is maybe the hole, the brick that's missing in my fortress of will, what's prevented me from being in charge of a movie. And damn that Craig-Excuse-me-Eric too. I'd lost him for fourteen or fifteen years and he shows up for that one afternoon and my life is fucked.

Then Marty understood what all this meant: Bibi.

He tamped down a thought that having a kid's umbilical cord attached to you was a great way to make up with ex-girlfriends. Instead, convincing Bibi to take over the Tubs seemed like a precious and sweet thing to do — for himself, he knew, he knew. . . . But for Tubs too and he could always hold out the hope that in the end it might help Bibi as well in some way. Marty could make sure, in some material way at least. Weeks of salary for Bibi. A small role maybe.

All his life's threads could be either woven into a comforter or twisted into a hangman's slipknot if he were to help Tak and the nameless child survive a movie that now belonged to everyone but himself.

"I'll see what I can do. *Fuck.*"

42

arty stared at the phone in his hand for the moment before it rang on the other end. Nowhere to run now.

A connection. Bibi's voice, a little too suddenly.

"Yes?"

"Hey, don't say 'yes' too fast. It'll only make you mad again."

"Marty — ?"

"Big as life, twice as natural."

An awkward pause. "How'd you find me?"

He knew she wouldn't blubber about missing him, but the detachment in her question seared. Maybe *he* should blubber but he didn't have much experience. Through the fiber optics strung between them, Bibi was the pinpoint of light at his end of their fragile connection. Not too likely she'd see him as the matching light at her end. He was more the spider on this web, about to invite the Bibi-fly to make an uninviting choice.

"I called in a few favors from Central Casting. I was surprised you gave them your new number. You know, with your leaving the business and all."

"I haven't taken any Extra jobs. But I haven't worked in so long I lost my health coverage. Still don't know what to do about that. And I'm thinking of going back to school, maybe. . . . So how's it going, Marty? Is directing the answer to everything?"

"I got fired."

"What — ?"

"Amato. Long story. I'm still here, as the First A.D.. At least I moved up, huh?"

"I'm sorry. Really sorry."

"Ahh, I'm gonna quit anyway. Quit everything."

"When?"

"After this one." He might've been lying, he wasn't sure. Things were changing so fast. "I'm just kind of committed here, you know? Right in the middle of it. Professionalism and all."

Bibi made an assenting murmur on the other end.

"And we've got a problem." Silence. She was waiting him out. "Exene showed up pregnant. With Eric's kid."

"Oh my god."

"And now she's had it, and she won't do anything herself to help, and Eric's useless, and *I've* been helping but I'm running out of options because we start shooting in a couple of days."

"How could she. . . ? Maybe it's the *au pair* thing? She can't trust anyone?"

He thought of Exene's long stares at the baby, watching him curiously as if waiting and waiting for the time when he would be properly grateful for being born.

"Yeah. . . . Maybe. So anyway, I thought. . . ." Time to talk really fast. "I've got no right to ask, but I thought, you know, we could put you on salary and *per diem* and everything, and it'd be something to do while we're all so dedicated to being in transition around here, and hey, with the health insurance. . . . You think — ?"

"Babysit."

"Well, it's more than that. A parent, practically, I mean it's what *I* feel like. He's a cute little thing."

"What's his name?"

"He doesn't have one yet."

"O — kay."

He winced; he needed her, Exene needed her, the baby needed her, but it wasn't a setup to give Bibi anything *she* needed except mercenary workdays. She'd be tugged in circles that led nowhere except having some spare cash when she got back to L.A.. He waited for her to say "No." Then, a better idea:

"I've got it. I'm telling Tak to put you on your SAG card. It's a great weekly minimum, and you'll get your health insurance back. You know, we could say you're a stunt double, not that it matters —" No end to the maneuvering.

She waited him out again, until: "Were you serious about quitting?"

"Well, I've been thinking about the Life-versus-Movie thing a lot. The Big Choice." Wanting but unable to say, With you here I'd have both again.

"It's not that. Not anymore."

"No?"

"You already chose your life, remember? Whether you direct or not, the question's more like, What's the point? Are you going to *be* somebody in your life, *be* somebody in your movie, or just walking proof of something or other?"

"I don't know what that. . . ."

Bibi heaved a sigh into the phone. "Forget it, we'll just end up going in circles again. And if you really quit? Then what?"

"I've been thinking of maybe cartooning again." In truth he had been, just not very recently. Or very much.

"Yeah?"

"*Yeah* — "

"Prove it."

"What? How?"

"Prove you're thinking about cartooning again."

Marty smiled at the floor. He missed her bluntness. He remembered one of his between-pictures projects, drawing and writing a collection of sarcastic parodies of the Industry. If you couldn't run the show you could at least make fun of it while you waited for your next hire.

"Well, the cartoon book I started about the Business, with the panels? Okay, so one of them, there's this caption above a double frame, you know, two drawings on the same page where a header says, 'Not to Be Confused!' And below that on the left panel there's this little old guy, politely tipping his hat, and the title below him says, 'A Gent.' Then on the right side, there's a bunch of scumbag derelict pirates with eyepatches and their swords and knives drawn, and their title says. . . ?"

A beat. Then Bibi gurgling, snickering: "Agents!"

He grinned and his skin wicked up the sound of her laughter. "Go on."

"What do you mean? Like, 'Aw, go on get outta here,' or —"

"Con-*tin*-ue, you dip."

"So there's another frame and this one, in Gothic lettering it says, 'Religious Filmmaking.' And you've got three guys sitting around on a film set, leaning against the camera or in their director's chairs, and they're all wearing hooded robes, rope belts and sandals, like Spanish missionaries, right? And shades, they're all wearing shades. So the first guy goes, 'Good God, what a beautiful shot!' and the next guy goes, 'My Lord, what a brilliant concept!' and the third guys says, 'Sweet Jesus, are we gonna make money off this piece of crap!' Well?"

He could hear a false start, then a couple of muffled bursts. What he always called gut-chuckles, the part maybe he treasured most about her.

"Okay. I liked the first one better, but okay."

"Just 'okay'? All right — another double panel. Header says, 'Formalism *vs.* Realism.' On the left you've got 'Workers Leaving Factory' like in those primitive silents. The Lumières, you know? And in the panel you see a bunch of, like, circus clowns with big shoes and pointy hats with pompoms walking out of work, and underneath a subheader says, 'European, or Wrong Style.' And on the right you see a bunch of cigar-chomping blue collar hardhats coming out of a factory and the header over this one says, 'Okay or American Style.'"

A hum on their fiber-optic web, then gut-chuckles again. A warm bubbling human spa. If she were there he'd be so tender, use his fingertips on her forehead, eyebrows, he'd press his cheek against her ear.

"Kind of student-filmish, or film-studentish, whichever. . . ."

"Yeah, I guess."

He could imagine her sitting with the phone, squeezing it against her neck, her eyes tired but tolerant. Why on earth hadn't he proposed to this woman years ago, given her everything she wanted? But he knew why. She hadn't been a rung on a ladder. A ladder, as it has turned out, lifting him to this desolation in purple Utah.

"So what do you think? About coming, I mean."

"I don't know. I agree, what you said about having no right to ask. You don't."

"I know that, but what it comes down to is, there's this kid, and he's got nobody."

"And after the movie's done, who does he have then?"

"I get that. But here-and-now's so much in my face that 'after' sounds like somewhere in the next century."

"I don't know, Marty. I'll call you back."

"Are you mad at me? You're pissed, I can tell."

"It's . . . really none of your business whether I am or not."

43

T wo days after the phone call, Exene and Tub-O'Guts were asleep and for a while and would not require his vigilance just to meet their basic physical needs. Marty drove himself to Salt Lake City to meet Bibi's flight. The drive would mean getting one or perhaps two hours of sleep that night, but sleep was the only pliability, the only soft place left in his life that could give when he pushed and still spring back, though even during pre-production he was rebounding slower each day. Tomorrow morning his impatience and foul-tempered posture from this sleep-depriving trip would serve him well anyway as a grumpy First Assistant on the first day of full-bore, balls-to-the-wall principal cast shooting. He could vividly appreciate why the Business had cokeheads everywhere.

Location shooting for a filmmaker was a withdrawal from earthly obligations, would-be (and lost) heavenly relationships included. Working around the clock, living in a motel, eating off the caterer or Denny's or in the motel coffee shop — always thinking, *I'm making movies for godsakes.* Of course, thinking that and only that was how he got into this mess.

And suddenly there at the gate was Bibi: disembarking on time just like a professional human being. He embraced her diligently, timidly, guessing at the new protocol for whatever relation she was to him now — fantasizing whether he might become her intermittent lover again, or just her good ol' pal, or merely an employer handing out room, board, and *per diem* for caretaking a soon-to-be famous baby. He'd have to leave the boundaries up to her.

He asked what he always asked at airports. "How was your flight?"

"Well, I'm here, mostly." Bibi smiled and took his hand and squeezed it lightly before letting go. It was a sweet and warm gesture, and he wanted to weep. It couldn't be this simple, this human-touch thing. . . . "Will you get to direct at all, even for a day? Second Unit, maybe?"

"Not unless Hy drops dead. Which he may well do, any minute —"

"Oh no —"

"Just kidding. No, I won't. And being the First isn't any better than I thought it'd be. I'm helping idiots with all their problems instead of hiring idiots to help me with *my* problems —"

"And what kind of idiot am I? First-class, like the ticket?"

"Real funny. Okay. Good to see you, and thanks. . . ."

"And I feel creepy about the SAG business."

"Sorry."

"Because I need to do it."

"It's done all the time."

"By people like Paul Amato."

"Yeah, that's where I got the idea." That perked her right up. "Just kidding, again. . . ."

Marty was sorry that they were driving back to Two Cedars in the dark because it would've been fun to be a tour guide and point at the sandstone skylines and exotically colored dirt. There were even a few wildflowers from a recent unexpected shower. He wondered, absurdly, if he'd be like that too, if after years and years of being windblown across some arid life, someday he'd be a desiccated seed finally getting a chance — whether a brief shower of directing opportunity would allow him to bloom. Maybe that was what Hy was doing, finally germinating even at his age.

Bibi led him to the baggage claim as if she knew the place. He wanted her to at least act a little uncertain. She wore an aromatic black leather jacket he'd never seen before. He wished he'd given it to her.

"I didn't think you'd come. To help me."

"I had to think about it."

"And. . . ?"

"It was the first time you sounded like you cared. Whether I was there or not. Like maybe you even needed me."

He nodded and looked away. Needing someone — or being needed by someone — had always felt like weakness, alien. He hoped at least he'd recognize her bag when it dropped into the carrousel. "I had the dumbest thought while I was waiting for you at the gate. . . ."

"Go ahead."

"You know how TV news guys zip out to the airport after a crash? They push the camera into somebody's face right when they get the word?"

"Film at eleven. . . ."

"Right. Well, did you ever notice — they could show some ninety-year-old gal, she's just found out that her sixty-seven-year-old daughter's died in the crash, and you know what she says?" Bibi watched him as if she knew the answer but wanted Marty to say it. "She says, 'My baby!' I mean, not 'My daughter, my Mary' — she says, 'My Baby.'"

Bibi nodded, satisfied.

She offered to drive and he expected to tell her all about his nephew and Exene, about his brother's flight from fatherhood and his own approximation of it. Instead, after giving Bibi directions he fell asleep even while dimly aware that his head was thumping against the cold passenger-side window.

44

*L*aura was up and active in spurts, a Spandex Actress snapped back almost into her former shape and once again running three or four miles a day even in the altitude. She had completely given up trying to meet the baby's needs even with a breast pump, allowing Bibi to feed him to feed him each time. Other than her workouts, she slept most of the day.

Since the shooting company didn't have Laura to work with quite yet, they concentrated on one-shots of Eric as "Albert Byrne" alone in his workshop, and on closeups of his robots spinning and lighting up, working in "Dweeb" as they could. With nearly every shot being filmed out of sequence, Eric was discovering the film actor's limits when robbed of context by an editor's and a camera lens's needs.

Working at half-speed this way eased them into routine: local crew members out of Salt Lake City who'd done little more film work than an occasional car commercial learned one another's habits as they cycled the equipment through an efficiency shakedown of storage, deployment, operation, and back to storage in their fleet of trucks. Mad Dog Matsumoto finally appeared, sometimes in traditional costume, to tear apart, then re-build his *Noh* stage over and over like an automaton. Hy's most forceful show of directorial influence was to refuse to allow the Sound Mixer's protests over Matsumoto's endless hypnotic banging to hold up a shot. He ignored Helmut Wolfer's cryptic calls for equipment that had nothing to do with eliciting an actor's resources, such as needing one more "inky" as a kicker to highlight Eric's hair. The *Noh* presence floated through shots whether it would ever cut as matching action or not, as the nonsensical presence-of-the-actor ran riot in some secret subtext Eric and Hy had pledged to honor with Tak's blessing. This was like no other movie set Marty had ever seen.

He had no idea whether Matlovsky could direct a film, if he understood where to point the camera, how to block actors within a flat rectangle, how to cover himself with the editors, how to tell a story with space and objects and movement and color and light and shot rhythms as well as dialog, how to use the skin of the world's surfaces and not just "performance." But it didn't matter anymore. Hy Matlovsky and Eric and even Laura could theorize about Ac-a-*ting* all they wanted, and if that kept everyone happier, fine. Marty decided to drop the paranoia; unless he'd been completely right about Eric's plans, the notion of such an elaborate conspiracy to get Hy into this position was too convoluted even for Eric.

He found himself staring at Hy's profile whenever the old man's attention was broken by a technical mishap. The coloring in his face was wrong, and mottled besides. He breathed too quickly in short, sharp intakes followed by soft panting. Marty had read somewhere of the outward signs of heart trouble — creased earlobes, clubbed fingernails — and came to no conclusion whether or not Hy was etched with these warnings. But clearly there was something terribly wrong with his health. Anyone paying attention could see it. And Marty knew that the stress of doing these shots, most of which amounted to mere pre-production inserts, closeups to be cut into large scenes later on, was nothing compared to the full utilization of the movie machine that had yet to be engaged.

During a new setup Marty went back to the warehouse office. It would be a big re-light, so he could leave Ravi, his Second Assistant out of Salt Lake, in charge. He sat down at a salvaged warehouse desk across from Tak.

"So what's the deal on Hy's insurance? I mean, he got it, right? We're covered?"

"They did a treadmill and everything. He passed."

"Yeah, but people step off treadmills and drop dead all the time. Plop."

"He's old. . . . Maybe we just need to respect that." Tak let this note ring falsely, then subside. "Marty, if we call it off —"

"I'm not saying that. But we'd better have a backup ready who can —"

"If we change one more major player in this deal —" Marty sat in deliberate silence, partly because Tak had never called the movie a "deal" before. "I know that you understand. What that will mean. To all of us."

"Maybe it *should* mean that."

Another weighted pause. "Maybe it should."

"Well. . . . Whatever."

"Let me know right away if Hy looks any worse."
"Yeah. Sure. Okay fine, Tak-*san*."

• • •

Aristotle came to visit again: like a good story-ending, Hy Matlovsky's death was both surprising, and yet perfectly predictable. An hour before Hy crumpled at his feet Marty was summoned to Hy's motel room to discuss the need to commit to one of several shooting strategies. Instead, he found Hy still preoccupied, trying to explain Eric to him, supposedly to enable Marty to like his own brother more than he did. He suspected that Eric had arranged this chat. Peace in our time, through mutual understanding. Bullshit.

"First of all, Martin — never give an actor a compliment."

"No? I don't follow —"

"Something inside him won't allow him to believe it. But he'll give you so much gratitude you'll be a slave to his emotions. And he won't leave it there. One compliment isn't enough. Or two. Or twenty. Not a lifetime of them. It's already too late. Never do it."

"Then how are you supposed to —"

"Martin, I would — my god, as if anybody could — tell you exactly what it is to be an actor. The why and wherefore of it. Presumably, I teach the subject. But to articulate it for all of them, what they grope and struggle to explain so badly for themselves. . . ."

"Well, yeah, he's my brother, and I can't tell you the why and wherefore of *him* —"

Hy cleared his throat noisily, with some difficulty. The spots in his mottled complexion all traded places. "There is a one-member audience for this film performance, Martin. I hope Eric will earn your applause. Without compliments. Remember what Meisner said: 'That which hinders your task *is* your task.'"

And as Marty wondered what the hell that meant, while he stared unfocused at a motel painting of fishermen at sea beneath a machine-brushed varnish texture, Hy Matlovsky keeled from the edge of his bed and died.

There was nothing to save. No intervention that would reverse time. Even so Marty called in First Aid Benjie, watched a performance of professional CPR, and found that he wanted to undergo an ordeal, some kind of ritual that would honor Hy Matlovsky, because the end of a human life was now revealed as not-knowing, as chaos, opaque.

Marty wondered whether having such a rite of passage, connecting him to wherever Hy Matlovsky had gone, could give him a way to will a happy ending upon this story of movie-making they shared. Whether it could make Hy Matlovsky heroic. That would be the furthest thing from the disorder of death. But a scripted happy ending to a screenplay was the only ritual Marty knew, and as paramedics arrived to deal with the body no other meaning would reveal itself.

· · ·

Marty and Tak sat in silence for a while, until: "What should we do, Tak?"

"We have to shoot."

"Without a Director? The day he dies we *shoot*?"

"I know what that sounds like. But we can't bring Hy back. Nothing brings back the dead —"

"Yeah, except like you said, Matsumoto the *waki* —"

Tak ignored that and paced the Production office. "Hy's got relatives. New York. Someone's on the way. . . ." Tak was struggling with something. Discomfort, pain? His habitual placidity looked forced. "But if you want to make a movie. . . . The alternative is to declare a *force majeure*, and MSC will do that. It's just one more thing that's gone wrong, Marty, and believe me — they'll take this new excuse and bail. In a heartbeat. At this point I don't think anything would make them happier. The only thing stopping the *force majeure* will be the completion bond people stepping in and saying we have to see it through, to minimize their losses. Like you told me, when you worked on the Natalie Wood *Brainstorm* thing. So if you want to make a movie —"

"I'm not *making* this movie. I'm the A.D.."

"I said: if *you* want to make a movie —"

"What . . . what the hell are you saying?"

"Take over again. Get us started. If we're behind schedule after the first day, we'll all be on the next flight out of Utah anyway. Do it for Eric, or Hy, do it for Laura if *that* helps. Try to get us through one day, until we get her on the screen. Once she's in the movie they'll see it's worth bringing in another Director, whoever they want —"

Tak's face was set but Marty had seen his hand tremble when he brushed the bangs away from his damp eyebrows. He seemed to want Marty to feel the emotions that were lighting up Tak's internal organs like gamma rays, but he couldn't fully release them.

"I don't know if Eric'll go for it, Tak. Hy meant a lot to him —"

"I'll talk to Eric. We have to get Laura on film. Just get us through today, or it's no movie."

"Director, on ten hours' notice. Yeah sure, but — Before I promise to make a fool of myself, I can't even — God, let me think. . . ."

Marty's pulse beat fast, adrenaline oiled him. He glanced down at the folded Call Sheet in his shirt pocket, pulled it out and slapped it flat across Tak's desk until it revealed the scene numbers and descriptions that had entirely left his head. He came to Tak's side and they peered at the scheduled work on the Production board. It was Laura's first day, the scene of "Dweeb's" challenge to "Ginger's" presence in the robotics workshop. Dweeb, "Albert's" sidekick and suspicious protector, ends up spraying the lab with a fire extinguisher. Characters meet, size each other up. Dialog. Physical gag as topper. Three-and-a-half ambitious pages. Marty thought he could do it.

"All right. I'll try."

"No. Try not. Do or not do. There is no try."

Tak punched him on the shoulder and grinned. He'd become suddenly animated, completely out of character in the face of disaster. Finally Marty realized that Tak was quoting "Yoda" from one of the *Star Wars* movies. Bless him for the dorky effort.

Displace ambition, then. Make it a favor, that might help; any moment wasted on self-awareness, another moment of "look at me, I'm a Director," and Marty would be lost.

"If I'm gonna do this for anybody else besides me, Tak-*san*, I'll do it for you."

As he returned to his motel room he wondered if somehow he was doing it for Bibi as well. Even the baby. If so, that would be two, maybe three people whose needs he'd now placed before his own. It was strange and exhilarating to think so.

45

Hours later Yamamoto and Kurumada were in Utah not to stand ready to applaud their first day of shooting, or to call Osaka with breathless accounts of dailies, but rather to pull the plug. Enough, apparently, was enough. Word had gone from one motel room to the next even as Tak hosted the MSC executives in the Production office.

The making of this movie had become some kind of wave pattern from Hell. Eric's movie career was born. Then Eric's movie career dropped dead. Hy's directing career was born. Hy dropped dead. Marty's directing career was born. His directing career dropped dead. Twice. Let's see, Marty mused, the baby is born. . . . It might be wise to call another ambulance.

Their pit and its pendulum of Fate reinforced what he'd always been sure of, that a good movie was the end result in a chain of hundreds of links, any one of which might easily snap and break the whole damn thing. It wasn't a wonder that so many movies were bad. The miracle was that occasionally a few were good, that all the links had held and defied the laws of probability.

He came back to Tak's motel room shortly past midnight. The diesels were scheduled to fire up in four hours if through Tak's persuasion there was to be a first shooting day with full cast and crew. Tak was drained. He moved slowly, spreading sheets from a yellow legal pad across the top of a small wooden folding table next to his bed like a slow-motion card shuffle.

Marty stared out of the room window. "Did I hear it right?"

Tak nodded. "Probably. If you heard the worst —"

"Is there anything we can do?"

"Don't worry. . . ."

It felt wrong to find this funny. Then again, it was absurd. They laughed.

Tak pretended an expression of shrewdness. "I'm going to talk them out of quitting. Put some figures together. They'll see it makes business sense to keep going. Protect the investment they've already made. There's an ancillary market for anything with Laura in it. Overseas."

"Really —? You think you can do that?"

Tak shrugged without pride, only confidence. The movie was in his tax-attorney hands, he was responsible for millions of foreign investment dollars, for careers that might never happen. "Now I have to. There's no choice." Tak stared across the room at a cable news show with the sound off. The TV was high atop a clear maple cabinet Tak had shipped here from L.A.. "It's just. . . . I'm so ashamed."

Marty inhaled, and sat motionless. Tak was affectless, as if announcing a sum from his actuarial math. Without a clue as to Tak's meaning, Marty knew he couldn't have said those same words. If there were something shameful afoot he'd be too ashamed to admit it — shame's logic.

"Any, ah. . . . Anything you want to. . . ?"

"He died almost two months ago."

"God. When you told me that the other day. . . . I mean, no offense, but you're not the easiest guy to get a read on, you know? I'm sorry —"

Marty realized only then how little anyone knew about Tak, his life, his background, what might trouble him or drive him to smash his new career to pieces against a purple mountain in Utah. Or become that mountain himself. Obviously Marty knew Tak's Japanese heritage before they'd met. When he heard Tak's flat "a's" and his Great Plains twang, and Tak's careful, lawyerly articulation, Marty had made a comment to Eric about how he guessed Tak was pretty assimilated, at least second, probably third generation. But Marty had seen enough in his time in Los Angeles to know this: find any immigrant or son of an immigrant in L.A., and he was most likely carrying around a scenario of re-creating himself, regardless of whether he was in a business that had anything to do with movies or TV. While Tak had sat in a bungalow on retainer for Japanese corporations, there had to be a hole, a flaw in the armor of a young outsider who'd probably fought all his life to belong somewhere and had ended up punching out tax tables on his computer and reading the fine print under the "Hollywood" sign.

"Is there something else going on? Anything we need to talk about?"

"I wasn't there when he died. . . ."

He was beginning to understand Tak's position: that Tak was now one of them, on the dark side, working above the line of a Production budget spreadsheet. All other facets of life could then align themselves behind this one hard truth: Tak had not just a desire, but a newfound need to see this film through, or the loss of something important, the breaking of some string into the ancestral past, was for nothing. If movies were 100-link chains that could snap anywhere along their lengths, what were families?

"*Tatemae*."

"Say what?"

"*Tatemae*. It's been a part of me my whole life and I didn't even know it. A Japanese part of me. Until tonight, until Kurumada and Yamamoto were here, and we were doing business —"

"So this *tatemae* is —?"

Tak didn't respond to the question. "I keep wondering if . . . if all this movie involvement pushed my father over the edge. We could've talked it through. Settled it, with more time, even through the emphysema. But when I say that, it's like I don't even hear myself. *Kichigai*, you know? A little crazy."

"I think you're being a bit hard on yourself."

"I'm sure he always meant well. My father. Even when he'd give me this face I used to call The Stare when I was a kid. Turns out it was a weathered old flower grower's version of myself, what I'm starting to see in the mirror every morning, eh? He had something going on in that face. That's *tatemae*."

"Well . . . okay."

"It's like . . . the outside and the inside. The face you give the world and the face you save for yourself. For the Japanese, both faces are always there, but they take turns without the craziness of choosing, or mixing them together. Akira Itani — my father — the old guy knew that."

"I'm not sure I get the —"

"My mother once told me *tatemae*, that's the face you wear as you live up to *giri*, your obligations to the world. But for yourself, you hold on to *honne*. True heart, true feelings. My father could do that. But he and I didn't get around to talking about it, how to show two faces. Time ran out. And then last night, I'm sitting there across from Kurumada in the coffee shop, and I realize I'm wearing my business face. . . ." Marty kept silent. There was nothing to add but hindrance.

Tak leaned backward in his motel room chair. "On the phone, my Dad, he kept asking, 'Are you an actor, are you an actor?' He finally dropped it when I told him over and over, 'No, Dad, I'm a Producer. Just on the business end of things.' But he probably guessed anyway — even as a Producer I was still around actors. Still . . . floating. Like 'The Floating World,' they called it in old Japan."

"And so, now. . . ?"

"I have to go home because the day after tomorrow it'll be the forty-ninth day since he died. That's a day of spirit transition. *Imi-ake*. It's the day that marks the end of mourning. Though I'm told that as a son, I can mourn for a hundred days. Like an option clause, I guess."

"Geez, you guys — I mean, you've got *rules* about how to be sad?"

Tak smiled a little. "Then, all that'll be left behind of Akira Itani — his essence, eh? — will be his name, written in brush and ink on an *ihai*. A little tablet I'll keep in my new ancestor altar."

He went to the cabinet he'd been staring at beneath the TV. "Isn't it cool? It's called a *butsudan*. Solid maple, hand-stained. And it's got these adjustable shelves here. It'll fit right inside the video cabinet in my living room back in L.A. so when I do my big-time Hollywood entertaining I can choose whether or not to let my A-List guests know that I keep Dad under the VCR. I think Marlon Brando will like that when he comes over for drinks." Tak smiled to himself and continued to stare into the empty *butsudan*. "I don't suppose I actually . . . killed him. Not directly."

Marty kept from blurting "How could you even *think* a stupid thing like that — " by remembering the things he'd already accused Eric of doing. He was liking this new side of Takashi Itani, seeing him pushed off-center, opening up, even if Marty couldn't decipher the meaning of it all.

"So Marty, try to keep the company busy, productive, eh. . . ? I'll talk to the MSC guys again in a few minutes and straighten things out. Then I have to go to my mother's, in Salt Lake. Not far. You start on time, and then shoot days Two and Three the way they are on the board. Then I'll be back. Until then it's up to you."

"And you're sure we'll still be here?"

Tak nodded vaguely. "I have to go home and forget him. . . ."

Marty folded his hands together, a pose taken by the last guy on the planet to question weirdness about fathers and sons. He waited again for Tak who still gazed in the direction of the TV, but more at the cabinet beneath.

"When I get there. . . . Right now, my father's the household spirit. As I enter, I'll be obligated to welcome him. I'll have a big smile on my true face. *Honne*." Tak laughed softly again, shook his head. "When I grew up around here, nobody thought we J.A.s had any feelings. Well. . . . We're just a little more organized with them, I guess."

"God, Tak — If I could figure out where all the damn feelings came from, I wouldn't fucking bother to have 'em."

Patrick Cosgrove

46

*A*fter Marty said good-night to Tak he checked on Laura and Bibi and the baby. Within her motel room Laura had quickly accepted Bibi as having specific parameters of function and performance, like a script's given circumstances. He guessed that Laura saw Bibi's wry affability as an extension of himself, and found Bibi to be enough like herself in blonde beauty and youth and presence that Bibi had become a stand-in, an extra finger to stick in the leaky dike holding back parental responsibility.

It was sufficient tonight for Bibi simply to hold Tubs and see that child and mother were tucked in, and allow Laura to fall asleep nine hours before her makeup call. Bibi wished Marty luck for the morning shoot, and as she reached for the door she reassured him that he was free to think of nothing other than storyboard sketches and his shot list for his first day of directing.

He regretted her leaving. "Going back to your room now?"

"Yeah, I want to be back here early. Have the baby on a bottle when Laura leaves."

"Right. Watch out for the yellow foam. In fact, wear a lead apron. That crap shoots right out of the top of the diaper."

The child was asleep. Bibi smiled briefly but seemed preoccupied. "Come with me?"

"What is it?"

They eased out of Laura's room and walked back to Bibi's without speaking. As she let them in with her key: "Something's really wrong here."

"Make a list, if you've got a week —"

"Why hasn't she named the baby?"

"Tubs?"

"Stop calling him that —"

"Well, until Eric. . . . It's some kind of game between the two of them. I think it's her way of getting him to deal with it — she won't name the baby until Eric comes out in public and acknowledges him. Or maybe it's just to get him to pick a name, get involved, be a dad. I don't know. Something."

"He doesn't *admit* he's the father?"

"Oh sure, to her. I mean he knows, everybody knows. . . . He just doesn't want the *Enquirer* to sell newspapers with it."

"So he's just sitting it out."

"Not exactly. You know what he came up with? He said he's waiting for *me* to claim the Tub. Or for Exene to *allow* me to claim him, whatever — Like a diversion, to draw fire away from Eric and his little art theater, I guess, so he doesn't get tainted by the whole mess."

Bibi's eyes were frozen, very blue. He could hear the word *"men"* echoing around somewhere behind them. Men as Helldogs. He bet she was real glad now she'd come here to Utah.

Bibi shook her head. "Isn't drawing the fire what Peter Pan does for Wendy?"

He shrugged for effect. It killed him to watch Bibi turn away and drop her pair of ripped jeans to the floor, then kick them into the closet. He remembered what they were doing when she tore through the knee, and the memory of the act put his circulation through hydraulic gymnastics whenever restoring hard-ons from the hypersensory replay; it was probably going to kill him someday, when his heart blew downward right through his pancreas. He ached for her physically, but he was aware also of making a descent into romantic regret here, something no other girl had been capable of doing to him. He was still more connected to her than anyone else he'd ever been with, this first woman he'd ever had a relationship with who hadn't been intensely vibrating with unanswerable, needful clinging that always made for an eventual neurotic blowup. He was always just as culpable for the bad endings — first in poor choices of partners, then in his selfish unresponsiveness. He now felt suddenly remorseful at the times he had used his position as an Assistant Director to get extras and starlets to go out with him, to bed them, only to discover again and again that these beautiful young women were just as callously ambitious as he was. When they realized that an A.D. could only do so much for them, that their self-promotion through Marty was going nowhere, their anger and despair would rip apart whatever flimsy relationship they had managed.

Here in the room with Bibi, who was now out of his reach, Marty fully realized how awful that pattern had been, that after years when these young women and he had run their ambitions into one another, in a search for the kind of moviemaking triumph each of them needed, he had become unfit as a loving partner for anyone. Until Bibi.

He watched her change into pajamas and went slack from the sight of her. She looked greater than ever, athletic like Doris Day in her prime, he'd always thought, but with more interesting edges, more pain in her eyes or something, the way they tilted downward a little sadly at the corners. So fair-skinned that she often had to avoid the Southern California sun, even as she did the things that made her appear and behave exactly like what the world defines as a Californian. But what else can you do, *ought* you do? From Minnesota, from anywhere, you go out to L.A. with your bone structure and your blondeness and face up to the unforgiving judgment made upon your dreams. To have gotten even that far, you're the one out of the many thousands of others who never arrived in Hollywood, the masses who longed just as much to be there but didn't have the right nose, the right distance between their pupils, the right golden-mean planes to their cheekbones or right set to their teeth to even attempt the pilgrimage. And if you go and the Industry doesn't say "yes" to you, what do you do then? Go back? Some do. Most stay, and enjoy the weather and the greater ease of being active and healthy and raising tall blonde kids who might someday go to USC, and whether they go or not will love the ocean for the rest of their lives. It beat going crazy in the freezing rain an hour's drive from some polluted Midwestern lake.

As he watched Bibi continue her bedtime routine he needed to recruit her, to share in what he was about to do beyond her caretaking of the baby.

"This whole directing thing — it's like . . . like I've just taken a running leap off a cliff, you know? Like it's all or nothing. And that's good. Any other way of getting here, to the point where I worked up some kind of ladder, begging a bunch of know-nothing producers to give me a chance to direct — that would've killed me."

She paused at the bathroom door. "You haven't stopped exaggerating, I see." She retreated to the sink.

"No, it's true. I mean me, in a single bound I'm going from filling out Production Reports to being in charge of a circus, nobody telling me what to do, with my brain still pretty much intact — I think."

"Just because you weren't a First Assistant?"

"And because after that I didn't become a Production Manager. Getting an ulcer over paying the crew time-and-a-half. I still have movies in my head that I need to see, and from bottom to top here I am, sort of . . . falling up."

He didn't add how he was falling up with the great good luck to be soft-landing on the platform of Laura Trent-Sampson's screen-presence.

"Do you believe in the script? Isn't that what it should really be all about?"

"Well, yeah — I guess. It's good enough, it's like. . . . What's your favorite all-time movie?"

"I don't know, why should —"

"Just tell me."

"*The Awful Truth*."

"A romantic comedy. Screwball."

"Yes."

"Okay, here's the thing. *Everybody's* favorite movie is a screwball romance. Everybody older than ten. So's *User-Friendly*. The gimmick in our story is that this . . . this innocent — the guy Eric plays, the scientist like Henry Fonda's character from *The Lady Eve?* — this nerdy inventor learns how to grow up by building and programming a robot. He invents emotion in a machine while he avoids his own feelings. I mean, yeah, that's the long way of saying there's lots I can do with it. Lots to believe in."

Bibi came out of the bathroom to stare at him until she pulled her toothbrush out of her mouth. "What does Eric think about it?"

"He's going along with it so far. He gave me some actor's jive about how he's got the contrast of the machine with the 'real' to work with, getting at some 'inner life' of what it is to be a human being."

"Sounds like you're making the same movie. Do it. What's the problem?"

Problem? He was getting two hours alone in the dark with anyone who needed a dream. But it meant trying to understand an actor brother who might be using the movie to undo something from the past, and an actress who'd confessed a few things to Marty and kissed him just once but it went on until his mind was scorched. They might both be relying on him. Might listen to his knowledge of how to connect them on the screen, say, maybe by running two cameras at once the way Capra connected Jimmy Stewart and Jean Arthur in *Mr. Smith Goes to Washington*. But probably not. Come to think of it, it was unthinkable.

"Sure. No problem. . . ."

"And how does it end this time, Marty?"

"What — You mean the script? Happy."

Bibi knew his bullshit too well. She leaned into the bathroom doorjamb and simply looked at him. She'd stopped brushing her teeth, probably because they both sensed what was really going on, unspoken. Her stare was the great chewing-out scene in all the best romantic comedies, where the pompous self-righteous partner gets pulled off his or her high horse by the other partner who's reached the truth of their relationship first. But here he was in a business saturated with criminals, sociopaths, moral schizophrenics and emotional cripples, *not leaving* because he was just as pathetic and needful as they were. He'd do anything to direct a movie. Because he had to, no matter how it ended.

He didn't know what else to say. Astonishing woman, Bibi, to listen and listen, with a spot of angelic toothpaste gathered at the corner of her mouth, still waiting for him to sort himself out.

• • •

In his own room Marty planned a few shots that would require most of the day to get right. If there was a movie still in production after that, he'd improvise day by day, minute by minute if he had to. That much would please Eric, anyway.

Regardless of what Bibi thought of him it felt good and right to have the baby in her care. That wasn't what made his temples throb. . . . Noodling with pencil sketches inside rectangles, he felt a swelling in his skull, he was a barometer reacting to a sudden high-pressure front. He scanned the shooting schedule. Maybe his discomfort was that soon, out of cost-efficiency, the *User-Friendly* company would shoot a part of the scripted happy ending. But he'd ordered the physical details of countless happy endings on call sheets.

He was in a business of happy endings, they were a ritual, what he'd felt a need for with Hy Matlovsky dead at his feet. Happy endings weren't just escape if they were earned by the hard choices made by the characters. They were the glory in movies, the way out, the transcendence of a human being who eventually has to die. What was it, then, still bothering him?

If Tak succeeded tonight, Yamamoto and Kurumada would shake Marty's hand tomorrow morning and officially congratulate him for being named Director. On the set, once he had the collaboration of Wolfer the cameraman, he would nod and say "we're ready." Ravi, the newly promoted First A.D. rousted out of Salt Lake City, would *shush* the crew and get his band of local production assistants to shout "Quiet please" several times. After Ravi's cue of "Roll, please" the P.A.s would shout "We're rolling," the Sound Mixer would announce "speed," the Second Camera Assistant would say "marker" and let his clapperboard slap shut. Marty would frame Exene, frame his brother, and create this world of light absorbed by the Panaflex. He felt he was responding to the greatest of callings: In the beginning, before the Word, was the Image.

At the threshold of creating his first motion picture, he could tell already that directing a movie would not be the experience he'd anticipated for so many years; he was sure only that he wasn't in complete control of anything. Yet he now owned a reifying power that came from naming faces and actors and objects, from using your visual style to give them *your* name, as your offspring, if you were any good. In hours, he alone would aim his lens, anoint with his Panaflex, put a frame around fabricated activity to give it context, saying feel *this*, see *this*, just my way. It was wizardry, the naming of the universe on Creation Day.

One last thing nagged at him, part of what gave him this headache: sometime during the shoot he would be in the midst of an agony of mistakes and frustration only to hear a crew member hiss *sotto voce*, "It's only a movie —" Yes, Marty would think, a movie. But never *only*. It had become his life. He had to get it right, had to be good enough to force the production to continue, because so long as the camera was still rolling, Bibi would be here, caring for the baby. If she would not still be his Beebs, at least nearby, still in view.

And tomorrow he'd keep a promise to himself to advise Eric between setups that it was time his Tubs got named too.

47

T ak worked his modest miracle. MSC allowed their truck convoy to arrive on location for the 7:00 AM crew call with an 8:30 shooting call.

Marty could feel the eyes watching him as he leaned with one foot on the grooved rubber platform of the camera dolly. His description of a shooting angle would soon send the grips and electricians scurrying to set their lamps and flags, make the camera assistants crawl about the floor with color-coded tape rolls for actors' marks. Crew members glanced at him, curious to see if he was sagging, cracking. He retrieved a radio from the sound cart to call Ravi, who was jogging about the perimeter of the company encampment trying to be both First and Second A.D. at once until experienced local reinforcements rode in. Marty had an impulse to yell "Wheel in the meat!"

"Can I get a rehearsal, Ravi? What stage are you in out there?"

He got Ravi's return hiss in his ear. "Laura's got her hair up, uh. . . . What —? Oh, makeup tells me we can have her if they get her back for an hour."

"Yeah, tell 'em at least that. We'll have a huge light in here — "

"Okay fine, coming in —"

Marty waited next to Helmut Wolfer. Laura entered the warehouse alone in a teal-dyed bathrobe, her hair in rollers and her face a beige monotone of makeup base without lip and eye accents. Eric came in moments later, hesitant, disoriented, and arrived at the camera with his face open, blank. He was shadowed silently by Ravi, who under stress was reverting to a good, vigilant Second A.D. Marty reminded himself that news about Hy's death had stunned his brother only the night before. Marty's gentle dressing room urgings about professionalism in the face of the project's collapse had gotten Eric here in front of the lens, but apparently in no shape to perform. Jerry Goodell, the freckled actor hired as "Dweeb," trotted behind.

Actors had come to find out what Marty wanted. What he wanted was to drop to his knees as a wave of disbelief swept over him, a self-mocking *What do I do. . . ?* The floor beneath him seemed to pitch until he remembered a red horizon line that once went straight across a round instrument window on a cockpit dashboard and he was transported back to his father's plane. His vision leveled and regained equilibrium, the way Big Jim's dials would go flat when he came out of a bank turn or a barrel loop. Marty steadied.

"The way I see it. . . . What I think happens here is I'd like to get the whole thing in one — from Laura, where you break in the door, to where the sentry robots roll up, and Dweeb — I'm sorry, Jerry is it? — then Jerry challenges you. Eric, you see it getting out of hand with the fire extinguisher, and you tell Jerry to back off. Right? You want to walk through it real slow, see how it feels? Then we'll block it."

The actors each nodded without speaking, probably wondering why the hell they were bothering.

The *Noh* stage was empty; no Matsumoto this morning. Helmut Wolfer walked to a midpoint between the workshop office, and the far end where the entrance was.

"I will place the camera here, and we must have dolly tracks at this —" Wolfer gestured to a diagonal pathway "— at this precise angle or I cannot light it."

Heat raced up Marty's neck, into his scalp. "What — wait, wait a minute. Helmut. I think the camera'll take its turn. And react to the characters. There's a lot of activity here, and first I want everybody comfortable."

"The camera must go here."

"The camera'll wait."

"Here. Don't you see? Then I will give you beautiful soft light from the side. From here to the finish, it will look . . . elegant."

Marty quickly absorbed what Wolfer intended; he was right, it would look good but that wasn't the point. "The camera waits."

Wolfer made several sideways steps toward Marty, adjusting to his position. "I see. Perhaps here, then —"

"The camera . . . will *wait*."

Wolfer stared at Marty, then slowly smiled his mongoose smile. "Of course, Martin."

Marty wanted to raise a sword and cheer. He turned to the actors — thinking, *My* actors, what do I do now, *what?* — to find they'd ignored the entire exchange.

He invited Laura to go to the side door where, as "Ginger," she defeats the lock with a credit card and lets herself in. "Let's do it MOR — *mit*-out robots. We'll work on the special effects for the gizmos while we light."

He gave more instructions. People moved.

There were a few logistics to work out before Dweeb confronted Ginger. Both actors followed Noël Coward's advice to the players: they knew their lines and didn't bump into the robots. They plotted their way toward the office and "Albert," their journey marked by T's scribbled in chalk that would become tape marks in final rehearsal.

Eric emerged from the office. Marty reviewed for him what action would've gone on by that time, where the robot effects would work, what would cue "Albert's" appearance on camera.

Everyone backed up several beats and tried a walk-through. Eric fixed Jerry with a baleful stare and held it. Jerry shifted nervously.

"I'm sorry, I — I've done something wrong, you want me to try it another way, Eric?"

Eric spat out a line of dialog, then: "You stupid fuck."

Jerry shifted his feet several times. He tried to smile. Apparently he couldn't tell — was he being challenged to improvise? To have an authentic feeling? He stuck to the scripted dialog: "'I . . . ah, Albert, I caught her breaking in, she's an industrial spy I tell ya — '"

"You stupid *fuck* —"

Jerry absorbed the hostility and repeated half his line again, then stopped trying. The crew was silent. Marty felt lifted, buoyed by the clarity of instinct. He went to Eric and grabbed him with his own genetic luck, not of having a lucky skull, but ropy forearms and thick hands. Eric grabbed back where he could, focused on Marty.

"Eric? You're losing it, aren't you? Eric? *Come on* —" Eric's eyes darted back and forth, trapped between impulses. "You're losing it here! Losing it!"

"I'm not — I'm —"

"Come on, you bastard. The lab. Your invention. Dweeb's right, you're *losing* it —"

"I'm losing it —"

"You can see everything. One instant, you see it all —"

"I'm not *losing* it —"

"Like you've lost everything else — It's her, it's your work, everything you've ever loved, it's a scam and she's taking it away —" Marty embraced his brother and spoke quietly at Eric's ear. "Everybody's taking it away. Your invention. Your money. Your reputation. Everybody leaves you. You make something and it's gone, people take and take.... It's what they took from *us*, brother —"

"— And I want it back, you *fuck*!"

"You want it back —"

"I want it back!"

"You want *what*?"

"I want it back!"

"Come and get it!"

He shook Eric enough to make his brother's vision bobble. Eric was wild, afraid. He fought, he made a gargled moan. Marty let Eric shake him in return, push him down as if he could bounce Marty off the warehouse concrete. Marty sprang up and gripped him again, took Eric's shirt by the collar and threw him to the floor like an umpire calling "out." They were both panting. Marty sat cross-legged on the shop floor and lifted his brother's head onto his lap. There was no other sound on the set.

"Wanna do the scene?"

There was a catch in Eric's breathing. Marty gazed into the shadows beyond the lights, waiting for anything Eric wanted to say.

"Oh, ba — ruther. You're detthhhpicable."

"Nyehhhh . . . ain't I a stinker?" A stinking *Director*, he wanted to whisper.

Finding a moment, a piece of time, he'd helped Eric find his own "moment before," his momentum into the scene, had kept him from showing up empty on a morning when he needed help. Marty and his brother had found a spot to stand on that had never been visited, as actors who were both themselves and their characters too, radiating in a dreamworld that when captured for two hours on a screen could salve what viewers called living.

After several long rehearsals, Marty arrived at the camera position that Helmut Wolfer had seen in seconds. They would indeed bring Laura in, float the camera back with her on a diagonal dolly track, then hinge the shot by panning into the office to reveal Eric. It would take hours to light, but if they printed it by lunch they would have over three script pages completed, on schedule, with time for closer coverage shots. Death would not stop the movie machine.

When they wrapped for the night it would take the day's exposed footage 48 hours to go roundtrip to the L.A. lab and back for review. Marty was confident that when the workprinted film returned, he'd proudly show the shaky investors their first footage with honest-to-god, studio-made feature quality. Kurumada and Yamamoto couldn't understand how much crucial work was already accomplished with robots and effects during the weeks before camera rolled on Laura — nobody knows anything — but now they'd have a movie star to look at, and to the uninitiated that was the real sign of moviemaking, the thing they *would* telephone Osaka about. *User-Friendly* just might get made, and if it wasn't destined to be great, Marty could already tell: at least from day-to-day, as they lounged on the carpet in their motel conference room and gazed through their fatigue at the dailies, it would feel like a movie.

48

*E*ric showed more every day that he could take over a scene by just standing there, the most commanding "nothing" Marty had witnessed firsthand. Would Eric have been Cary or Jimmy or Monty after twenty years of this? In graduate school Marty read photographic theory by Susan Sontag that claimed that it takes time and death for an image to become magic. That things become more beautiful when they're both photographed and vanishing, or vanished. Eric couldn't be trying to do what he had done in his Japan commercials, no human could simultaneously calculate the dangers of haunting the persona of a former star, avoid simple mimicry, and still perform as an icon-for-the-future. But here in Utah he was pulling off what Cary Grant once did, as the critic Stanley Cavell described in a discussion of Howard Hawks's *Monkey Business*: I'm so handsome, so cool, so far beyond earthly fitness and rightness for your gaze that I can slick my hair back, wear goofy glasses, play a hard-science geek and I'm *still* going to pull your look. *And it's funny.* Of course, Cary Grant had decades of standing there being "Cary Grant," so in Eric's case Marty couldn't know yet if audiences were going to get it the first time around. Still, the guy was doing a number with this role.

Marty's energy on the set was fueled by the surprise — hell, the pants-dropping shock — that some of what they were accomplishing was quite good. He'd thought there were some adequate throw-away lines in the script. (Albert: "People could learn from machines, y'know. They might be a lot happier if they could be more ... ah ... more —" Ginger: "Aluminum?") Laura had come up with her own persona, deliberately or not, where out of the puff-headed gorgeousness she had a paradoxical hustler's edge and she was holding the screen with the tension of the mix.

And so it went: day by day dailies passed inspection, Marty trusted the editor to glue a rough assemblage together, scenes had an arc. As a company, they were finally in a cadence, playing in the zone like NBA champions, discovering things on the set. And what did Eric do? He acted up.

The scene where things between the couple crack apart was crucial for the credibility of the whole story. In the script "Albert" and "Ginger" have already fallen in love once, and failed tests of character. Albert fails more than she does, Marty believed, because while she finds the courage to ask for his forgiveness for what she's done to him as a corporate spy, he can't do it, can't forgive her. So in the scene, they've already split and remade themselves to the world with new identities, thinking they can just start all over again like none of this betrayal and breaking of hearts ever happened. But they meet again. Now it's a choice of re-invention *vs.* re-birth; the first would ignore history and deny the past, the second would embrace the past and forgive it and heal it, move on — a true second chance. Will they choose correctly, and recognize the "real" self beneath the comedy of disguise? Well, one of them does. Will they fall in love again? Of course, but how? It was the Shakespearean core of any time-tested romantic comedy of re-marriage. It was a big scene.

Even with dailies and rough cuts looking as well as they did, the company had been walking a tightrope for weeks given MSC's unhappiness over their sloppy start. Tak figured out a way — bless being a negotiating tax attorney — to juggle the schedule and get Helmut to agree to convert a scene's "New York" interior to something they could shoot in their cheap Utah warehouse. Helmut would blast his arcs at midnight through sheets of white paper taped on the set's windows to fake night-for-day and save thousands of dollars.

Eric's "Albert" will not consciously admit his recognition of "Ginger's" true identity. Instead it's Laura's remade character, wiser by half, who recognizes Eric's remade character immediately. This had to work precisely, or it would get silly-bad, not silly-funny. Her character is going to hesitate. Then she's going to realize her power over him: she manipulates his compelling urge, which is to pursue her without first dealing with their past. He makes a choice of reinvention, to just start over as someone new — and avoids the better choice of first fighting for a rebirth through healing and humility and growing up.

It was all going to be in the timing, in the glances, in the posture of two people in the same rectangle with boiling, unconfronted emotion flowing. In the *performances*, Marty had to admit, although he would've been more comfortable if the script spelled things out a little more clearly. But even his grade school Language Arts classes taught him the core of subtext, to show and not tell. And he knew Laura could do it. She was getting what Eric would call the actor's truth — she was at ease by now with living in the moment, she had eyes only for Eric, she reacted only when provoked, when forced to. She was finding that actor's truth of impulses that bypass the brain and come out unexamined. Authentic behavior under imaginary circumstances — the kind of truth a lens sees.

And then Eric did it. On the day he and Marty finally collided Actor to Director, Eric arrived on the set as if I Am That I Am had personally told him to create his Actors' Cinema right there on that sacred spot. The grips had a plywood dance floor laid out in anticipation of a whole series of dolly moves even if the scene had yet to be rehearsed. They tried it: the two principals ducked in and out of each other's sight, now joined, now isolated within the camera frame. It was working in rehearsal and Marty considered not punching in for a single closeup. Exene was compelling; in *The Lady Eve* — and *User-Friendly* was a re-make though no one wanted to admit it and pay for the rights — the original role was Barbara Stanwyck's, and Laura was holding up her end. During lighting time Marty shared stories with the crew about Stanwyck, how he'd known a few guys who worked with her at the end of her career when she would stand in for herself on "Big Valley" sets and tell the Gaffer where to heat up his key light and hurry it up Bub while you're at it. He was thinking that Stanwyck was always so stylized, so smart — but so *real*. Not Method real; she could sing Preston Sturges's slick dialog upside down tied to a flagpole, and you'd believe in it. So call Laura a softer Stanwyck. If not fire and ice at least a sparkler in the snow.

Eric was ready for camera well before it was ready for him. He returned to the set and pulled a canvas-backed director's chair next to Marty's. They regarded one another cautiously until Marty decided that, since there was little reason to expect his brother to ever again be in his life once they wrapped this shoot, a real Director could afford to be magnanimous:

"Tell me some things about Dad. Anything without lying. You were older, you remember more."

"You don't like to hear what I remember."

"The made-up shit? No — I don't mean the fantasies. Just, what was he like? I was so pissed all the time, I hardly remember." That was a small lie of his own. Marty had countless fragmented, stored visions of their father, image-sequences locked in his security-camera-brain, but few contexts for them.

"He was . . . he liked it when I'd tell him stuff. Re-telling, was more like it. He'd never show up for my baseball games, or basketball. . . . But if I'd re-do the whole game for him, you know, announce it afterward and run around and act out all the best plays, he'd sit there with a drink in his hand and laugh. That's what I like to remember. That's how, as far as *he* knew, I had a higher batting average than you ever did."

"Mm. What else?"

"Handsome guy. Muscular, dark hair slicked back, remember? Smelled like Brylcreem half the time. And that laugh . . . drunk or not, right up from the belly."

"Yeah. . . . Keep going. What else?"

" . . . Ahh. He had a little outlaw in him. Maybe a lot. He liked to push buttons and watch people jump. I think being a pilot, especially in his own plane — Mom told me he used to make plane-crash jokes over the intercom until the FAA got so many complaints he almost lost his job. You know, he found that movie we made, with the fire —"

"No — "

"Do you remember?"

"No, I — "

"Where we used his footage, and I did Jimmy Stewart? 'W-w-well, ah, well ah D-D-Donna —'?"

"I think — No. No, I don't."

"Yes you do. And he loved it. I don't think he got it, that I was doing *him* as Jimmy Stewart. With the stammer?" Eric laughed softly.

"Yeah, all right. I remember. First he beat the shit out of us, *then* he laughed."

"He beat the shit out of *you*, not me. Not that time."

Marty nodded, it was true. Their father usually reserved his fists for the things in Marty that were most like himself. Dad, the glamorous kid with silver wings and big strong hands. His brother caught more words than knuckles, more insulting denigration for

292

being needy, and found that "performance" could get him the attention he craved but it might be an attention that turned to contempt when the highball glasses started clinking.

They shared a look as brothers for a long moment. "Why me, Eric?"

"You don't have to call me that."

"I've gotten used to it, don't undo my progress. Why'd you find me again? Did I just happen to be on the set where Exene was working?"

"Laura? No. It was because of you. Because you're family and we're all we have. The only blood left. I wanted to give it another chance."

For a moment Eric looked as if he wanted to take Marty's hand in his own.

"Oh, give me a break. You've got a wife and kids. Well, sort of." They lapsed into another silence. Eric yawned; it threw Marty off, but he accepted that Eric had been through a lot and his fatigue might be real enough.

"So *why?*" He waited for a response, but Eric wouldn't meet his eyes. "What really brought you out here? After all this time? What's wrong with New York these days?"

"Money. C'mon, it's always money."

"So you *shtupped* Laura Trent-Sampson to raise money. Right. I can't believe it. It just never stops."

"I think it was a real sacrifice on my part."

Marty thought this was probably funny, but he didn't want to open himself to a replay of the feelings he'd gone through during his last day on the Universal lot. "The motorhome, I was ready to kill you. I might still kill you for that one. . . ."

Eric nodded, and while looking toward the scuttling grips with their tool belts full of hammers and pouches of doubleheads, he seemed to accept the heat behind Marty's words. Eric would understand his anger, knowing as well as anybody that Laura was a magnificent creature; she enchanted, she caused men and women alike to project that rescue fantasy upon her. Maybe Eric had even guessed at the hours Marty spent contemplating just such an act in the motorhome for himself, yet possessing neither the inclination, nor the opportunity to make it happen.

"Marty, you lie with the best of them. About Laura wanting to do your picture. At the restaurant you lied to them too."

"She was interested in working with you. I did her a favor. . . ."

Eric laughed. "You think I'm out here slumming, don't you?"

"You're the one who says shit like '. . . the *boards*.'"

"Yeah? Well, I've told *everybody* back there how my own brother's an Assistant Director. How you make an honorable living at the heart of this Industry. Or the bowels. Where is it again, Marty, heart or bowels?"

"Kidneys. Assistant Directors are the kidneys that filter everyone else's piss of a movie. Robert Altman came up with that one, only about Directors."

Eric rolled his eyes. "I've seen good — hell, *great* work on the screen. Even without the physical presence of the actor. I mean, the loss of that entire dimension."

Marty wanted to say something scathing about pretensions to Art, but let it go. He was certainly culpable there, too.

"If I thought I could function out here with the same control I've had in my theater, then I'd have flown straight to the heart — excuse me, *kidneys* — of Hollywood a long time ago."

"Yeah, right."

They lapsed into silence again. Marty couldn't loosen a chronic vigilance in his brother's presence, wondering where Eric might be steering him, what Eric's self-protective calculations were. His casting mission to secure Laura Trent-Sampson wouldn't have been some random thrust; Eric would've picked out his Star long before making the trip west. He would know that Laura drew out of the same pool of resources as Marilyn Monroe once did, each of them a damaged woman-child who broadcast a desperate need for love, understanding, and protection, tacitly promising endless unconditional sex in return. Eric would know that it was Marilyn who'd studied The Method with Lee Strasberg, who married up to Arthur Miller, who wanted to rehabilitate herself until she ran out of time, or willpower, and died a sad cliché. Hell, maybe she started the cliché, after tougher-edged Jean Harlow gave her a head start. Laura Trent-Sampson in all her quivering deep-skinned and moist-lipped poutiness would know in a similar way what Eric Blanc had to offer. To her, Eric was inexpensive credibility, the same thing that MSC of

Japan wanted from him. Credibility and legitimacy were Eric's to bestow; he'd earned it on stage.

So what drove Eric out here seemed to be money after all — he could claim a perverse purity in that. Unlike Eric, though, Marty truly wanted to do a romantic comedy, it wasn't *all* mere calculation on his part. If done wisely, this kind of story pulls its Couple through an honest-to-god relationship. They're stories of second chances, of laughing, crying and growing up, of reclaiming a worthiness that once rightfully belonged to any one of us but in the course of life has been lost, or stolen, or carelessly abandoned; the kind of story, Marty was sure, we'll always need. All of us.

But apart from the storytelling, the moviemaking process is everyone using everyone else. Laura now had her child and was waiting out Tubs's legitimacy as well, to add to the celebrity that mother and child would both then radiate. Marty thought of his nephew, that stupid gurgling eating machine, a child he had a sudden hurting ache for.

"So what kind of father are you gonna be, to Laura's kid?"

Eric looked aghast. "Not now, this is not . . . not a thing for right now."

"For when, then? You just going back to New York, like the kid never happened?"

"Someone has to raise him, sure. If it could only be me, I'd do it, but —"

"That's a total crock."

"No, I . . . I won't be any kind. Of parent. She doesn't want that."

"Like it's her decision? You could go to court —"

"No I can't."

"Sure you can, just because you're separated —"

"No, I can't."

"Is it because of what you did? Because you went ahead and did the one fucking thing neither of us should ever be capable of doing —?"

Eric sat glumly, as if trying to gather some thought that wouldn't set Marty off. "There's still a restraining order, I'm not allowed to be around them. I begged on my knees for the one visit I had all last year." Eric stared at his empty palms until he held his face in them, as much as he could around the makeup. "You knew. You already knew. Yes, I . . . hit my kids, Marty. Does another confession help anybody? I hurt them. As bad as it sounds, as bad as you can imagine. Something I *never* imagined —"

Marty shoved himself out of his chair. "You fucking low-life, you scum. You son of a bitch. After every goddamn thing *we* got put through. . . ."

Eric looked away, wouldn't answer.

Marty lost all further speech. Eric took deep breaths as if trying to inhale the artificial daylight of Helmut's lamps, to inflate himself with cheer. "Hey, I. . . . Would . . . look, we've gotta go forward. After this. The play, would you just read the manuscript?"

Marty stared hard into Eric's sudden diffidence. Tubs's face floated in front of him, then evaporated with a scream. "Don't change the goddamn subject. You mean work with you? *Now?* After you remind me of all this? *Not in a million fucking years.*"

Eric cringed, then spoke quickly in a near-whisper. "If this is going as well as you say, we could do other projects, different stories. Our own repertory, there'd be a chemistry there — like Cassavetes working with his family and friends."

Marty throttled his anger long enough to consider an image of director Ingmar Bergman trying to direct John Cassavetes, the Swedish control freak working with the approval-seeking exhibitionist. "I don't want to make your kind of shit. Not with a sick fuck like you. I was pretty sure I never even liked you before, and now I know it. If I ever hear that you've tried to check up on Tubs, if you touch him, even *look* at him —"

There was an urgency in Eric's voice, not whining but quiet fear. "You promised me, Marty. You promised you'd come back, you'd direct. We'd be working together, with nothing else between us, I. . . ."

"Yeah, well, I know stuff, don't I? *Shit* —"

Eric muffled a word, but then sighed, as if he had expected Marty's refusal all along. "It's the only way we'd ever get to know each other, Pal. Not that it matters. Fuck it, I guess. Fuck everything."

Marty kicked his chair over and walked back to camera.

• • •

How was *that* for a "moment before," Marty thought. Great direction of the actor on my part. . . .

So then Eric pulled the set down like Steve Reeves in *Hercules Unchained*. His marks meant nothing as the camera operator followed him across lighting cables and beyond the reach of their lights. Helmut was trying to pull hair out of his bald head. Exene was giving out moments all over the place, none of which would ever make dailies. Marty had to jump in.

"Eric! Cut, cut, *cut* — Eric, *now* what the fuck are you doing?"

"The scene."

"Like hell you are —"

"You don't. . . . It's the . . . the spine. I'm after . . . needs, *desires* —"

Marty asked Ravi to dismiss the crew for a fifteen-minute break. They melted away in search of donuts. "Then stop fluttering around so the camera can catch up with the outer sack of shit that your goddamn desires are *in*. And what are these inner desires of 'Albert Byrne' that we have to hire a turbo camera car to chase him around?"

"They're not Albert Byrne's —"

"Okay. Someone changed movies and didn't tell me —"

"Don't do that. Not again. You're pushing me around like you always pushed me around —"

"Let's keep it in the here-and-now. Eric. And what you're doing to your actress partner here, that's not pushing around? She doesn't know where the hell you're going from one line to the next. Let's have another rehearsal, and stick with the results, huh? In *character* —"

"There is no character —"

"What. . . ?"

"There's me. It's time, Marty. Let's drop the myth-of-character. It's *me* onstage —"

"You're not *on* stage! This is camera work, there's a lens over there that's gotta be focused if the work's gonna make it onto the goddamn film stock."

"It's *me*. I've got the right — the *responsibility* — to be who I am. It . . . it's all the way back to, it's what Stanislavski said —"

" — Did he ever say 'Shut your ass!'? Get on your first mark."

Eric shifted into Marty's path and spoke too closely chest-to-chest. "My character's hiding. Hiding behind a role, and it's killing him. Like actors hide in their roles, and it kills *them*. I'm trying to rip through that, and I'll bring Laura with me. We'll see the real person. In both of us. And that'll be the moment on your screen, it'll be you and me both doing what it takes, what we always wanted to do when we were kids, making something *authentic*, and, and. . . ."

Eric was a micron-thin wine glass next to Marty's vibrating tuning fork with Marty's anger liable to shatter Eric any second. "That'll be one moment in a landslide of unwatchable shit. We're re-making *The Lady Eve* here, not Cassavetes, not *Husbands*, not *Faces*, not *An Actor Under the Influence*! You know what I think? You're messing with my camera so I'll have to do pickup shots — so I'll have to get the scene in *your* closeups."

"— and . . . no, and, there's no 'Ginger,' no 'Albert,' there's just me, just her —"

Marty leaned into his brother until their foreheads were nearly touching. "And you think that'll sell tickets? Uh-unh, pal. You want the Inner Self? I know who's in there. It's Craig Nyrop. And nobody gives a shit. Nobody ever did. Zip him up and keep him the hell outta my movie."

Marty slouched into a folding chair and waited out the crew as they tried to reassemble the lighting for the shot. Whatever they had found that first day of shooting while sitting in a heap on the lab-set floor was gone. Why, Marty wondered, *why* did he come to *me*? For applause? Because back in New York he *got* applause night after night. With his bows on the stage, the dying and the rising. Dying that way every night, finally as that completed Self bullshit he and Hy went on about. And even if the curtain coming down is the end of whoever that Self is, it's *restored* the next night, he gets it back might after night except Monday, with matinees Wednesday and Sunday. So what is it — some kind of hollowness, when the hands stop clapping, is that why it matters that I'm the only blood left unless you count kids, but kids are needy too *and you hurt them you fucker. . . ?*

And where, Marty wondered, did his own cruelty come from?

Eric's whole career had been "I, Craig Nyrop, became Eric Blanc so I could play someone else you might love and then someone else and someone else. . . ." His every performance asked "Do you love me *this* time?" And now "this time" meant coming 3,000 miles to the Phantom Stage that day on the Universal lot so he could play someone else yet again. For Marty.

With Laura it's been 'Beauty's Only Skin Deep, Yeah yeah yeah.' What now? Same as always? "Do you love me? (Do you love me?), Now that I can dance?" Drop the fuck dead. Craig.

Here in Silver Cliff, Utah Marty didn't *want* that someone else from an actor, he didn't want a brother, and while he was at it, he decided it wasn't up to him to go claiming Eric's damn kid as his own, either. Let Laura Trent-Sampson figure it out.

49

MSC pulled the plug the next day.

Yamamoto and Kurumada now had their "working relationship" and first refusal rights to the next three projects of the biggest star in Hollywood. Signed. Laura Trent-Sampson had become their R&D, their long-view investment. She in turn already had her stature enhanced from risking artistic failure. And somewhere between Salt Lake City and L.A., Laura was on the run with her pedigreed baby. Marty refused to dwell upon the point that she was now free to call him Baby Nyrop or Baby Blanc or whatever the hell else she wanted. He could not let himself care about that wispy hair on his soft head, his sweet breath, his humming moans of satisfaction while on the bottle, that powdery smell — could not care about the child, he *would* not. . . .

In the Production office Tak pushed at his collection of yellow legal pads until some of them fell on the office floor. Marty leaned forward in his chair, rubbing at his temples. "You know what it is, Tak? You know why the money boys from Japan went and did what they did? I'm sorry if it fits every stereotype about how we don't understand the Japanese, but making *User-Friendly* was never what they wanted out of this."

"Apparently not."

"They only wanted Laura Trent-Sampson. Of course, we wanted her too, but they got her. Just like all the Why-We-hate-Japan magazine pieces since 1980. Every 'yes' only means 'we'll continue negotiating.' Only they weren't negotiating with me or you or Eric or even with Paul Amato. They were negotiating with *Laura*. While we sit around yanking our own chains, they make their three-picture deal with her, script and director approval, and *pffft* she's gone, outta here."

"How's Eric taking it?"

"I thought I'd killed him with the news. Outmaneuvered, and he knows it." Marty knew his own tantrum on the set with Eric hadn't helped. "But didn't these money guys know how close we were?"

Tak demurred. Marty guessed that Tak was no longer privy to their thoughts now that MSC felt their tax attorney-turned-producer no longer served their needs.

"Here's the deal, Tak: somehow, someday, I *am* gonna make a movie. And if I have to, I'll gladly walk over my brother's dead body and any actress to get it done. So unless you think making a movie's your last act on earth, stay out of this ugly business. And keep reminding yourself — you're too *nice*. You gotta get over that, or stay home. And another thing I'm sure of — when I do get my chance, when at some crack of dawn I'm the one that says 'The camera goes here' on my *own* damn set, I'm gonna make a movie like *Platoon* or *Lawrence of Arabia* where the entire cast is guys."

They returned to their rooms and packed their bags.

• • •

In the morning, when he no longer had a job, Marty was taken by surprise at the number of things there were to say goodbye to. He wanted to savor whatever it was that defined his first and only movie location as a Director. In part it was a simple, instant nostalgia over things like crew guys in flannel shirts, cowboy boots, and baseball hats who dealt lines like his favorite from a construction gang boss: "I'll build you a damn football field, but you gotta give me a hundred yards of information."

He stood with a pained grin at the entrance of the empty Production office, realizing that as much as any one thing, what it really came down to was trucks. If you didn't love trucks, you'd never love any movie set away from a studio lot. They were your kitchen, your office, lumberyard, power plant, toilet, transportation, your warehouse. You even kept them generic-looking because when you ran out of local traffic you pushed them through your shot for background vehicle action. Trucks were the look and sound of movies, and like butchers and pigs and squeals you used every part of the truck but the diesel soot. Best of all they came equipped with drivers who told jokes about themselves ("What's the hardest thing a 'drover' will ever do? Third grade!") and were impressed by no one. Marty had loved watching Mickey the generator driver lean out of his genny cab one day to yell at Exene as she entered her motorhome, "Hey Baby — gonna tap a kidney?" Nobody but one of these burr-heads with the front-porch bellies would've said that to a Star.

He loved the smell of movies 5 AM, of honeywagons, burritos, grease on hot steel. It was a smell of Diesel Art.

Something icy ran through his core when he realized that with the baby gone — bad enough — and no movie to make, there was no longer anything to keep him in Bibi's view, or even her thoughts.

He decided to use one of his Director's perks a final time before Tak could tell him to leave for the airport. He went three doors down the motel walkway to the Transportation office and took the keys for a picture car, "Ginger's" Jeep Cherokee. In the parking area behind the motel he pumped the gas pedal until the engine caught in the altitude. He gave in to the sudden need to spin the Jeep in circles across the lot, spraying the parked movie trucks with dust and stones. He clipped the genny's bumper with the Jeep's and bounced away, screwing up something that made the engine cut off. His back hurt.

Tak came jogging from his motel room. To scold me, Marty thought. He cranked the starter and gunned the engine again and made more noise and more blue-gray smoke, then said goodbye to the Jeep too. He turned off the ignition and watched Tak get bigger in the rear-view mirror.

"I — I've got MSC, the home office. They're on the phone in Kurumada's room right now."

"To do what? Have us arrested for fraud while they're at it?"

"To finish the movie."

Marty didn't like the sensation of his own jaw dropping. Especially not here in the Rockies, where he might become Wile E. Coyote watching a boulder drop on his head yet again.

"Eric and I were up all night, working on this. And this morning. . . . Listen — they've made a huge investment already. They should get some direct return on it, eh?"

"You played that card on the first day of shooting."

Tak went to the passenger side and let himself in the Jeep. "But it's even more to the point now. We've already got commitments to distributors. We're a lot further along."

"I don't buy it. They're beyond the insurance deductible, it's already as bad as it's gonna get for them. False. What else?"

"I told them, twenty years from now they're going to be talking about *User-Friendly* as the turning point in Laura Trent-Sampson's career —"

"Oh bullshit, Tak."

Tak dampened his own excitement abruptly. Marty didn't know anyone else so adept at doing that. He felt bad. Tak was the last guy he wanted to hurt.

Tak stared through the windshield as he spoke: "I think it's true, Marty. Eric said it'll be like *Bus Stop* was for Marilyn. This will be the movie where the celebrity gets accepted as an actress. You've seen it, she's doing things she's never done before."

"Aren't we all. . . ."

"Here's the thing. It makes the contract they just signed with her more valuable from the start."

It was Marty's turn to stare through bugs smeared on the windshield toward the spruce along the horizon. He wanted something glib and cynical enough to shame them both back to their real circumstances. But finally he could see that aspect of it, the promotional angle.

Tak broke the silence: "And the cover's off."

Marty squinted at him, not understanding. "Off what?"

"Laura was spotted carrying the baby through LAX. The publicity's going to explode. If this film gets finished and distributed we wouldn't have to spend a dime on ads. The whole world is going to be gossiping about how poor Laura Trent-Sampson is happy at last with her own baby. And of course, they'll all be wondering who the father is. . . . The tabloid circus alone will cut promotional costs, hugely."

"You'd do that? Use all that personal stuff?" The mention of Tubs made Marty's chest heavy, as if his lungs had been silently crying by themselves.

"It's already happened, that part's not even up to MSC. We can't *not* use it. Not now. In fact it's going to use *us*, whether we like it or not."

"Maybe. . . ."

"What I have to get from you is a shot list. Can you sit down and tell me exactly what we need to finish the movie?"

Marty stepped out of the Jeep, walked away and stared out over the rocks and sand beyond the spruce, then turned back and leaned through the open side window. "I can tell you right now. We could use some shoe leather and drive-ups for transition and establishing shots, unless you want to go New Wave. But all we absolutely freaking *have* to have is the love scene with the new 'Albert,' and 'Ginger' after she's re-made herself as 'Faith.' And the rest of the ending, the drive-away with this Jeep. The ending I could do in a half-day."

"That's enough?"

"I could do more depending on how many shooting days they give me. You know? 'Do you want it great, or do you want it Tuesday?'"

"I think what we ought to do then is make something that's as close to the finished product as we can, and just indicate where Laura's closeups would be —"

"What do you mean 'would be'?"

"Well, we don't have Laura. She hasn't agreed to come back and finish the picture."

Marty sputtered and slapped the steering wheel. "Then what're we jacking ourselves off about?"

"I think — hear me out on this — I think we could make the ending by doubling Laura. With Bibi."

"Are you *insane*?"

Tak cringed a bit. "Okay, then just the drive-ups, the drive away, the over-the-shoulder stuff. We could slug in closeups from other scenes to show where Laura would go in the love scene, and the ending. For later."

"*Why*? Why even bother?"

"We just need to show MSC the closest idea to a complete movie as possible. That way they can see how little there is to do. Then we use the deal they cut to our own advantage, because with their new influence over Laura, they'll get her back for us. But we've got to go right up to the finish line. Everything but her closeups."

Marty didn't know what to think. He needed time. "I wasn't gonna shoot the ending that way. With over-the-shoulder reverses and crap to hide that it's Bibi. That's TV production value."

"Can you, though?"

"Ahhh. Ah, Geez. I guess so —"

"Okay. Kurumada says he thinks they can authorize three more days here in Utah. Will that be enough?"

Marty was bewildered. He'd already imagined "Martin Ford" on a funeral pyre. Now he had to resurrect the smoking corpse. "This is great, right Tak? Tell me this is the greatest news in the world. Tell me how happy I am. . . ."

"Well . . . yes, I think so."

"Right. But I'm not gonna do it." Tak looked crestfallen. "Look — Bibi's close. But the way I want to shoot the ending — not close enough. And we'd still need Laura for a closeup for this scene here, for that scene there, a closeup or two in a *lot* of places. After all the compromises I've had to make I think I deserve that much. So I'm not gonna do anything until you guarantee Laura comes back. With the baby. Show it to me on paper this time. Otherwise I'm just putting my name on something that's gonna be career suicide anyway."

"I'll talk to MSC."

Then Marty gripped the steering wheel with something like an epiphany: "No, wait. Forget about it, Tak. I know how you can do this. Their deal's got nothing to do with it because I know all that you have to say to her. It's like when I worked with Natalie Wood on *Brainstorm*. She wanted us to use a photo-double for a scene in a pool with this godawful stagnant water. Bathing suit, all stinking, freezing. Didn't want to go in, no *way*. So we tell her, Okay fine. We'll use your stand-in. Then we get her costumer to take her aside and say to her, 'You know, Natalie — the stand-in's got a butt *this . . . wide*.'"

Tak laughed. "And for the big scene, for what you want to show —"

"Yeah. For the *phoompa-phoompa* Laura's gonna want it to be her own equipment. She'll be there. But if I'm wrong, if she's not coming for the love scene, I don't do drive-ups, I don't do drive-aways, I don't do squat."

"All right. . . . Good. It's her scene, really. She has all the . . . internal conflict, is it called? If I understand it, Marty, *you* could even double Eric there, yourself."

• • •

Tak tracked down Laura through her manager and softened their request by expressing every sympathy for her reluctance, and asking only for her approval of using Bibi as a body double. Laura balked and couldn't decide. Tak tried to make it sound offhanded when he allowed that the scene would be a thousandfold more authentic and effective if shot with her whole being rather than with silhouettes and voice-looping; still she was not moved. Her calculus was being privately computed with her own factors.

It must've finally become clear to Laura that if there were a chance the movie might be released, with or without her cooperation, and if she were to be taken seriously for the first time, she would want the details right; she then made it equally clear that she would exert control over her own image. Marty's Wide-Butt-Theory had worked, although the focus shifted. Before saying yes to Tak, Laura reached Marty on the phone and demanded a detailed comparative anatomy of Bibi's breast fullness and curvature, aureole shading, pubic hair configuration and coloring (just in case, she hissed in explanation, the camera wandered, a clear mistrust of his taste and intentions), of birthmarks, stretchmarks, and scars. He tried his best without pimping Bibi's privacy, but that effort quickly collapsed. Laura was relentless until, sensing an inadequate match, she agreed to return. And, she was clear, Tub O'Guts was to be in Bibi's care.

Marty had gotten what he wanted, and needed.

For Tak's sake Marty pared back his shooting demands and continued to compromise shot-by-shot until they needed to get Laura back for just the love scene and a few closeups, one last day's work. Marty storyboarded the shots for the happy ending of *User-Friendly* in their proper rhythm, which they would film by using Bibi. He didn't know what to expect from the performances with Bibi standing in for the long shots, but until Laura was standing on their set they wanted to give MSC the best possible version of a rough cut, so that without making a great leap of imagination — something you never trusted Producers to be able to manage — they'd feel that paying for Exene's unfinished closeups and the love scene would be profitable.

• • •

What astonished Marty when he asked Bibi to do it was that she didn't seem to care much about performing one way or the other. He assumed she'd leap at the chance to give herself to the screen, to be recorded with Eric Blanc, to double for Laura Trent-Sampson, to be viewed (even as a slug-in) by investors in the climax of a feature film. One well-placed release of gossip to the trades would've had the industry buzzing: who was it, so carnally close to this celebrity, that she might soon be a star herself? Could she be the next Laura Trent-Sampson?

Bibi replied, "If it'll help you."

"Don't you want to do it?"

"Can I go home then? I have classes I need to sign up for."

"Come on — you want this, don't you?"

"It's not my scene —"

"But you'll see it. A *lot* of people will. People who get things done — Producers. Executives. Casting agents, later on."

"It's not what I want any more."

"It's what anybody wants! Name one person in the world who if they could, would *not* be in a movie."

"Bruce Springsteen."

"Name *two* —"

"You got me. I don't know. It's just not for me. I want to go home."

He nodded, confused. "But you'll stay while she's here, with the baby? Same salary, same everything, I promise —" He was ready to sing "Motherless Child."

Bibi sighed. Whether she meant that as yes, or not, he said "Thanks" and left.

The next morning Bibi was strikingly professional. She went through full makeup, since there was a chance of using almost any shot that wasn't a tight closeup. Marty was prepared for the script supervisor to read Bibi's lines off-camera, or prompt her with the dialog, but Bibi needed no help. She performed with Eric. It worked. Marty was humbled by her and surrendered completely to a state of gratitude, what adult love — if it could be sustained for months, years — might be like. But who the fuck knew *that*.

At the end of the day they needed only the last drive-away. Marty and Wolfer saved it for magic hour and while they waited for the sun to sink behind a butte, Eric practiced with the Jeep. He had to perform as a worse driver than he really was; it wasn't easy to be bad in a controlled, repeatable manner.

Marty stood in the dusty flatness, shouting, while Eric circled. "You ever drive a clutch?"

"New York — nobody drives anything!"

Marty smiled. It wasn't just New York. He remembered his brother at fifteen, trying to back the family car out of the driveway. Their father had no tolerance for mechanical wear to his vehicles, earthbound or airborne. The experiment ended quickly, and even with Jim Nyrop dead, Eric — Craig — graduated from high school without a driver's license. It must've been humiliating. They'd never talked about it during the three years of their wandering orphanhood they'd shared between the plane crash and Craig's own takeoff for New York as soon as he could leave.

As they all waited until the light was right, until Marty shot the happy ending, he had no idea how much of a role that leave-taking had played and would continue to play in his life.

50

*I*n the arid, purple dust Eric and Marty were still more strangers than siblings. As he stared out across the horizon, Marty sensed that Eric was watching him. They both knew they hadn't connected, there had been no reconciliation, and there were few chances left to feel brotherly. Marty still felt a rage he was trying to keep silent over Eric's abuse of his own kids, the threatening reminder of an inevitability, of something awful that was bound to emerge in any Nyrop who tried to be a father. It was why Marty had sensed for some time that he would never become a father himself. The sad anger gave their twilight setting a sense of finality.

To finish the day's work, they needed something to share — an image, or another memory, if not emotions — before anything pragmatic could cross between them, and they could end this failed experiment in reunion with some small grace and be done with each other.

Eric hopped out of the Jeep and surveyed the path he was to take toward the glowing horizon for the drive-away image that would fade out to credits and a swelling music score. A tree, the only one visible within miles, would frame the right side of the shot. A Titan crane had its wheels turned sideways and the machine had crabbed up a gentle incline to attain their camera position. When its levered arm was hoisted into the air by the grips, the camera would rise and perspective would diminish the players and their Jeep into a landscape of textures and throbbing sunset color.

Marty continued to absorb the horizon as Eric slid a folding director's chair next to him and sat. "So after this all you need is what — the love scene?"

"That's the one thing that's all slugged right now. Everything else's got at least part of what's supposed to be there. . . . And I just need a few closeups. Laura's mostly."

Eric nodded. He and Marty watched in silence as the grips and electricians prepared. There was a barrier here that Marty didn't know how to lower against his brother. Eric had said that Marty was all that was left in his life; their shred of family seemed more important to him now that Marty had heard about his kids and how he'd lost them, and how incapable Eric was of being a real father to Tubs. Eric had tried to make Marty believe that ever since Musso's, like two moths flickering around a flame they'd been close to danger but closer too to a kind of breakthrough — even as they'd been at one another's throats, even as they might swat one another into the fire. They'd been kids together and nothing could ever change that, but it felt as if Eric wanted to say there'd be no center to his present life, no centripetal force to keep him from flying outward into incineration if he couldn't repair their connection. All he needed was a little trust from Marty.

But Marty didn't have the will to let Eric open him up; completing the movie story they now shared would have to be enough if Eric needed his actor's completion.

"You remember, Marty, that time I got to Dad with the phone call? You remember?"

Marty stared at Eric, then leaned into his face, squeezing his brother's forearm with his thick hand, asking "What?" not to hear the question again but to tell Eric to let it go, that this was a past he didn't care to revisit. But the boy's — Craig's — idea seemed to permeate Eric again as it had years ago, and in their shared past Marty knew this moment too:

Time is still. Entering their scene, Father is at home. Father and Mother are arguing at dinner. Craig has left the table, frightened and sick to death of whatever it is that makes his parents fight from their dozens of conjugal topics. The phone rings, and Craig answers. It's one of his school friends, but Craig is suddenly taken with an idea, weird even to himself. He tells his friend he has to hang up, but keeps the receiver at his ear.

Marty stared briefly at Eric and sensed that his brother could still feel the silence from the long-ago Nyrop family kitchen just as the boy Craig once felt it, an atmospheric pressure-wrapping that kept him and his parents packaged, insulated from one another.

Mother and Father wait to find out who is on the phone, each hoping to be taken away from the sourness of argument by some face-saving excuse. Or, their sons both realized only much later, each of them waiting for a girlfriend to betray the illusion of marital peace.

Marty was surprised at the memory's tug on himself as well. "What about it? What *about* Dad?" What Marty meant was, What're you going to make up about him *this* time, you lying bag of shit? It was a heavy resistance for Eric to work through.

"You know how I got to him, Marty? With the phone, I stood there thinking, What if . . . what *if* that call'd been from the airport? And they'd just told me that Dad crashed the Cessna and killed my little brother. Didn't kill himself, the hell with him — just my only brother Marty. The one really important thing I had. I was standing there next to the phone, really like — stunned, you know? *Imagining.* The blood, and fire, and with you dead. . . ."

"You idiot. . . . What're you trying to do? What's this got to do with being out here for the scene or with *any*thing? Have you figured out the clutch yet?"

Eric had been building to a moment, lost it, then regained it. "I always had this . . . imagination, Marty."

"No shit."

"You remember? Finally Dad comes down the hallway to see what's going on."

Father finds Craig sobbing without sound, only with hot wet eyes which Eric now felt once again, which had in time become part of Eric's thirty-year-plus reservoir of available tears. *And when Father goes to his knees, asking "What? What is it?" Craig tries to talk, hiccupping, and finally says, "Your plane . . . at the airport . . . they called and your plane . . . they spilled gas, your airplane burned up and, and the w-w-worker, the worker guy was on fire."*

At that moment Craig believes that Father is going to scream. Father grabs Craig's arms, begging on his knees to find out more (never thinking that no responsible person would've told a child any of this over the phone, or that no child would cry at a stranger's death no matter how gruesome) until he runs to his car and smokes the tires backing out of the driveway.

"The funny thing, you know? The funny thing, I — to this day I don't remember him coming back from the airport. . . ."

Eric still claimed that he couldn't remember the punishment — the scene's *denouement.* He knew of it because Marty had described it to him a thousand times, that when their father returned he beat Craig with a belt across his bare ass until Craig bled. But Eric couldn't, or simply didn't, remember the pain, the recovery, what his mother had to say about it. He didn't remember an arc of guilt, shame, penance, absolution. What he remembered was only the scene's climax, the authentic moment. What he'd made his father feel.

Eric's blinders were now secure, he was enveloped in usable emotion. "This is what actors do, Marty. I was living my imagination, the 'as if.' You know? I really felt those tears, as if *you* were dead. I couldn't just lie about some stupid airplane and gasoline spill and gas attendant I didn't even know. I had to imagine what it felt like. And if I was just pretending to be sad he would've smacked me for making things up."

Marty studied Eric's face for a moment. "Caught 'indicating.' Isn't that what you call it?"

"Yeah. Fantasy, that wasn't a treasured thing around the house, right? But if *I* believed in my moment, he could read any damn thing he wanted into the emotions, and become a believer too. See? With my behavior, I made the bastard an actor. How 'bout that, huh? Dad, my partner. We improvised a truth under imaginary circumstances and he didn't even know it. We connected. . . . You remember, Marty? He saw my tears and got upset. I mean, do you ever remember another time when Dad cared whether I cried?"

"I remember what your ass looked like afterwards. So what? Is this supposed to get you ready for the drive-away? You remember it's the happy ending, right?"

Eric briefly held his head with both hands. "Sure. Forget it. . . ."

• • •

Onstage, Eric's cunning was to wear self-imposed blinders, confining his vision so he could respond truthfully to the artificial predicament fashioned by a playwright. Eric could position himself to catch hold of an emotion from even the bare circumstances of a class exercise because he knew and cared only about those few, given circumstances for that brief moment. The Now. This was the freedom, the power, the uncanniness of the actor — the Self and the Other meeting to form something that was both, and neither. "Being put together with yourself," Hy Matlovsky had taught. They were so very few shots away from completing the form this content would take, and while Marty wasn't sure he wanted to help Eric make this connection, this completion, or if he ever had, it seemed unfitting not to try.

Eric went back to the Jeep and sat sideways on the driver's side, oddly doll-like with legs flopped out the door. "So you think . . . you think we've got it? It's going to get done?"

"Yeah, I do."

"We did it, little brother."

"Uh-huh."

"Will it be any good?"

"Only a fool would predict that. Nobody knows anything. Ask me after an audience preview —"

"Oh come on, you arrogant putz, you *know* —"

"All right. Yeah. I think it has a chance. With Laura, there's a fan base. . . ."

Eric nodded and scanned the orange and blue sky again. The lone tree sketched black lines against it. The air was still. Desert insects sang with vibrato. "Pretty soon?"

Marty turned toward the Titan and gazed at Helmut Wolfer who leaned into the Panaflex eyepiece at the top of the crane arm.

"Five, ten minutes."

"I'm gonna work with the Jeep again. The engine just cuts out, I swear it's not my fault — "

Marty shrugged. No point in telling Eric about his own driving the Jeep into the genny bumper. "So get it right. It's your last shot in the movie before the credits. I've got a stunt double dressed if you can't make it real enough."

"Marty, 'real' has nothing to do with it."

"Call it what you want. Just get it fucking right."

Eric climbed into the Jeep and drove off, then tried to turn and shift at the same time. He let in the clutch without giving the engine gas. The entire Jeep seemed to hiccup, then skidded to a halt, its dead engine engaged with the drive train.

Marty walked slowly toward Eric as his brother made the gears gargle and grind. "That's it. Just get out —"

"No, you can't double me —"

"Get out —"

"You've got to see my face here."

"Get out while you *have* a face"

"No!"

Eric might've been near tears, but Marty couldn't be sure, as Eric worked the gearshift furiously, trying to find reverse. Marty wavered; he wanted to bring on the double and get the day over with. But Eric was right, he'd have to keep the camera on Bibi alone then, and one double was too much already — he'd have to back off and take the shot from the next county to get away with it. And the "Albert" wig was a lousy match on the stunt guy, without enough time to switch it out. Plus, who knew what Marty himself had done to the Jeep? If the engine was cutting out, it might be his fault more than Eric's.

"Hit your mark. Drive out there right now and hit the mark, or I go with the double. I can't have you messing up 'take fifty-three' while I lose my light."

Eric laughed as if this were a great joke. He drove a few feet, then figured out reverse more smoothly this time and rolled back next to his brother with his eyes wide and unblinking.

"Hey, Marty — you remember the seaweed?"

"The *what* — ?"

"The thing with the seaweed, at the lake that time —"

Eric's eyes went glazed, lifeless. Marty guessed that maybe he was having one of his sense-memories, perhaps unbidden this time. Maybe it was the stringy, slimy fingers clawing at his legs, feet, toes, that Eric felt. Water pressing on his lungs, no screaming, no help, no rescue this time because Marty wasn't going to be there for him. Iciness enveloping the boy Craig, paralyzing him, pushing and pulling downward. Marty had been there too, had done the rescuing so long ago, but who knew. . . ?

Marty glared at Eric until he felt Bibi's unexpected touch on his shoulders. He'd forgotten she had the baby on the set. She whispered, "Why don't you answer?"

He raised his voice toward Eric. "No. And even if I did remember, I *don't*. Okay? We're burning daylight —"

"You saved me in the seaweed, Marty —"

Eric held an open hand outward, made a brilliant smile for the three of them, as if for their appearance of family, of a Mom, Dad, and child. Marty caught it, was held by it. His brother was so magnetic like this, so sorrowful because something terrible seemed dammed up inside him, and Eric alone knew how to hold it back, immolate himself within whatever it was. Marty wanted to release him despite all the resentment, to smile back through his own suddenly burning eyes, which might be a small forgiveness. But there was no time for such things so he turned away. Magic hour was upon them. He asked his First Assistant to bring in "Dweeb."

Eric drove off again. He stalled the engine. Before Marty could reach him Eric re-started, popped the clutch, and lurched away toward the Jeep's start mark. Marty searched for Helmut Wolfer to ask when his turn to approve the shot would come. Two gigantic Brutes were burning in, their white-hot carbon rods throwing fill light into the face of the increasingly orange sunset. But the double-take of a startled grip made Marty spin around. Eric had driven past his mark to the edge of the slope, circled, and now was accelerating straight at them.

Marty yelled "*Run* —!" and wrapped Bibi and Tubs in his arms and pulled them away, made himself slide like a toboggan across the grit beneath their bodies.

Crew members scattered from the truck bed under the raised arm of the Titan crane. Eric came at it, the Jeep at full throttle, his face blank with terror. Marty saw Eric twisting the wheel to turn away but the front axle hit a half-buried rock, the tires went sideways into a pile of sandbags and the Jeep's front end airplaned. The Jeep made a diver's arc, silent until its descent brought it against the Titan with a hollow clank, then it ricocheted into the arm's counterweight with a wheezy crunch. There were screams and the crane arm was falling, the sky was shot through with globules of a substance like mirrored lava from a bursting volcano.

Marty rolled over to cover Bibi and Tubs as well as he could. He heard shouts and hisses of liquid on hot metal. He forced himself to sit up, and saw that he was within ten feet of Helmut who writhed on the ground with the camera's broken-off eyepiece imbedded in his right eye-socket.

Then Marty was on his feet. For a moment he pushed down on Bibi with both hands, both to steady himself and to keep her and the stunned and silent baby in place. He staggered to where the Titan crane was tipped on its side, cracked through in the rear bed where the fallen hydraulic arm now rested. The casing of the lever's counterweight gaped open. Liquid metal trickled out. Suddenly Bibi had her free arm flung over him, the other arm wrapped around the baby. She was crying, talking, shouting something, *words* —

Marty found Eric. Or rather, he found Eric's final pose. Upon the ground, beneath the spillage of the counterweight's mercury, Eric was glorious: splayed across the red dirt, leaping with arms and legs outstretched, reaching. He was less than alive, but more than a flat image: a *bas relief* coated and embedded into a mercury frieze-frame, a three-dimensional quicksilver god on a screen of dirt.

• • •

Marty asked Tak if something private could be done before more strangers from New York, like those who'd come for Hy, arrived to return Eric to "family." Tak arranged Marty's last view of Craig Nyrop who had died Eric Blanc. Marty wondered: Have I directed this ending, too?

Afterward Tak drove Bibi and Marty and the baby to the crematorium used by the local Japanese community and left them alone in the chapel until it was time to retrieve Eric's cremains. Then Tak led him by the hand, taking care of him, and Marty wanted to cry. He'd have to, sooner or later. The attendant pulled out a long tray from the incinerator. There in supine repose was a figure very much like Eric in shape and form; yet ash, not Eric. The attendant gave the tray handles an abrupt shake and the ash cloud fell in upon itself, now only dust and small bone pieces. Eric, born Craig, had vanished.

51

*M*arty and Lupe are each waiting for C.T. to come home and make plans together with her for their child. Marty hopes he knows what's in C.T.'s heart right now, but even if he's right C.T. has to know it, too, to decide who and what he is, even more so now as Marty has no idea where Laura has taken him except he's no doubt being enticed — "dazzled" bangs around in Marty's head — by a professional performer. And so in his son's abducted absence Marty pushes forward to weave the remaining threads of C.T.'s birth parent history for Lupe, and in this way help the two of them pass time while attending the new baby. Marty feels like Scheherazade spinning out his movie-tale to buy time, but it's not about saving his own neck. It's quite possible that at this moment in a bungalow office at some L.A. studio, Laura is having an associate producer chart a plan for C.T.. Even drawing up a plan for the baby and a concept for Lupe in the season's bible for Laura's new show. Creating loglines of their future. For entertainment above all.

"Shit, Mr. Nyrop. Did he do it on purpose? Like trashin' the Jeep?"

She's cut right to the heart of a question that has haunted Marty since it happened.

"I never wanted to think so. Maybe for just a moment he was careless. I guess we were all pretty . . . careless. But you see what I'm getting at? How those two, with all their money and fame, and already way into whatever their lives were going to turn out to be — they still couldn't handle being Mommy and Daddy. There's a lot of my brother in C.T., y'know? Everything's drama, everything's bigger than life. And I want him to have every chance at getting this father-thing right. Someday."

She lets the implication go by. She watches the baby in her arms as he reverently watches her back, barely blinking.

"But if he didn't mean it, what was he gonna do next? Just leave when the movie got done?"

"We'll never know."

Lupe shakes her head and settles into the armchair in the bedroom with the baby now drifting asleep in her arms. "There's a lotta you in C.T. too, Mr. Nyrop."

Marty's heart skips.

"So like, he's got sisters? And they're like about 25 now?"

"Yeah. Jenna and Amy. And there's more. There was even a Grandma."

She stares at Marty, not comprehending, or perhaps comprehending too much.

52

*M*arty turned to Tak from the flatbed editing bench. "In my opinion. . . ?"

The film played on behind him, clacking away as tape edits and scene slugs played through the sprockets. He gazed at Tak, then spun back on his office chair to stare again at the flowing workprint checkered with exposed film leader. Grease-pen marks skittered across the view screen like a 60s Pop Art collage double-exposed over their film. "In my opinion it's got nothing to do with an opinion. It's a hard fact that we don't have the critical love scene. A major character transition point. A story point too, obviously."

"And we plan to do that in one shooting day."

"Yeah, but what the fuck, Tak. Listen. First of all, *how?* Without Eric? And the thing that *is* my opinion? — this is more important — I also have absolutely no feel — I'm looking at this story now, start-to-finish for the first time instead of reel-by-reel and I've got no feel for 'Albert.' After all this work, I don't understand him. I don't know what makes Albert the character that he is. So, in my opinion — this movie's not worth releasing. Look, Tak, I had hopes as big as anybody's, but. . . . Save the money. All you'd be doing is exploiting the publicity, 'The Legend of the Lost Actor,' and nobody even knows who Eric is yet. This film was supposed to do that for him. And you'd be exploiting the baby. Maybe that's enough to break even, pay back the investors, but it's going through a hell of a lot of grief. Be a hero, just tell MSC to collect the insurance and run."

"Can it be fixed? I don't think MSC would pay for a *lot* of new scenes but —"

"Patched, maybe, but fixed. . . ? The thing is, I don't think they *should.* You ever see *It's a Wonderful Life?*"

"Of course. About —"

"— Yeah. About a hundred times, every Christmas. But you *can* watch it a hundred times because it earns its emotions. If it didn't do that, you wouldn't keep going back to it year after year. 'Sentimental' doesn't have legs, it's just built into the situation, it doesn't get earned by hard choices the characters are forced to make. So you take 'George Bailey,' you see all these early scenes of him as a kid, right? Then later on you *know* George Bailey the man, because you've spent all that time with his childhood, with him getting slapped around and misunderstood, always trying to do what's right. It's why we care, it's why we watch *It's a Wonderful Life* every Christmas. It's what we *don't* have with 'Albert Byrne.'"

"Literally? Albert's childhood?"

"Or something that pretty clearly implies it. Even in *The Lady Eve* you don't see the Henry Fonda character's past, but you know his 'Hoppy' character was raised a rich kid and he's probably never met anybody who liked him for himself. That's why he chases snakes in the jungle, to make a life as different as possible away from the family beer fortune. So in *User-Friendly*, who *is* this guy Albert Byrne, the nerd who's obsessed with building robots? It's got to mean a specific thing to Albert. The robots are *him* somehow. Like, 'love me for the robot within me,' or 'the clever robot I'm pretending to be,' something like that. 'Love my creation, love me.' We need to know, why does he *have* to do that?"

"Could you write a scene, or some kind of —"

"Me? No. I don't know. Tonight? Hell no. . . . I just know it's one of those clichés that still works, like it'd be the story's 'That was then, this is now' scene. Paddy Chayevsky, the playwright — he called it the 'rubber ducky' scene, the childhood-trauma — he didn't like those 'I'm so sad because of my shitty childhood' shortcuts, but once you see the connection you can't separate 'then' from 'now.' It's the same guy past and present, and so it goes off on a whole other level — Anyway, without the love scene, what the hell's the point?"

There was a quiet knocking at the door. Marty slumped over the editing table while Tak answered. When he opened the door, a wide pear-shaped man who filled the doorframe eclipsed a brief flare of daylight. He wore a starched, shiny white institutional jumpsuit covered at the sides of his gut by a greasy orange hunting vest. His beard stuck out from his round face like a scrub brush. The man blinked, an interruption of a chronic squint. Great, Marty thought, a psychotic hospital orderly. Maybe he'll steal the negative and put us out of our misery.

"This where they're making the movie?"

They stared at the man before Tak apparently decided that the piggish squinting and utter lack of guile meant the man was harmless.

"Well, right now that depends. What do you think, Marty? Is it a movie?"

Marty smiled and turned away. "Yeah, it's a movie." He wanted to go back to playing with the footage, to sending it whizzing through little gates and spinning prisms of light, to find every useful rhythm of faces and words that would cause a stranger in an audience anywhere in the world to feel what he had felt when he'd pointed the camera. He was pretty sure that nothing would ever convince him of his being an effective human being more than the moment when a moviegoer would laugh or cry in the right places at a film he'd made. But his one chance to have that moment was dead, collateral damage from the Jeep's short flight into the Titan.

"Hey, you Martin Ford? Like, the Director?"

The man had rotated slightly in the doorway without coming in. Marty wondered if there were any reason why he should or shouldn't be Martin Ford the Director at the moment.

"Why do you ask?"

"Your mom said, that actor that died? He was your brother. That right?"

Marty felt a dull thump in his chest, then adrenaline squeezed his heart and lungs tight. He went cold and hot inside, metallic and wet at once — what being stabbed might be like.

"My *mom?*"

"So like, is that right? You and Eric What's-his-name?"

Marty looked to Tak, who indicated with a nod toward a folding chair that they should let this wide person into the room. Marty nodded back, and Tak guided the man into the seat.

"I'm Tak Itani, the ah . . . Producer. What can I do for you?"

"Well it's kind of complicated."

"*What's* kind of complicated?"

"What I want. See, it's like a trade."

Tak sighed heavily and leaned back in a swiveling office chair, twisting slightly side-to-side. "Mm-hmm. What-for-what?"

"Huh?"

"In the trade. What do you have, and what do you want?"

"Well y'see, that's the thing. The old lady, the actor's mom, see, she has this stuff —"

Marty got to his feet, then let himself slouch against a wall with his fists jammed into his jeans pockets. "Wait a freaking minute here. This 'old lady' — what's her name?"

"Well it ain't — what's that actor guy?"

"Blanc. Eric Blanc."

"It ain't Blanc. On account of she told me actors change their names all the time, and she said her other boy was Marty and Marty was like in charge of this movie, which made me sort of think like yeah, right, but when she showed me some pictures and stuff — I figured, who knows?"

"You saw him? The actor?"

"Yeah, he came on visits every once in a while. Only family I ever seen."

Marty slapped his hands against the wall, then threw himself back into the editor's chair. He zipped through a scene on the loaded reel until he found a well-lit closeup of Eric.

"Him?"

"Yeah, that's the guy. He told me one name, Eric, and she called him something else. Gary or Greg or something —"

Marty glared at him. "You're a regular Ace Detective. So who the hell are you? Where you from?"

The wide man pushed himself to his feet and swung out his hand as one of those jerks who curls his fingers together so all you can do is hold the outside of his paw. Marty winced, then shook the hand briefly.

"Jeff —! Jeff Gilmore."

"From. . . ?"

"Oh, from over at the home. It's like the county place? Salt Lake? Indigents and such."

"And such. Yeah."

Tak gestured for the man to sit once again. "Look, Mr. Gilmore. We don't have a lot of time for —"

"What's her *name*?" Marty had stood almost on top of Gilmore's feet and folded his arms in the man's face. Gilmore was almost as tall as Marty even while seated. "What's the lady's name?"

"Donna."

Marty sniffed to keep from getting dizzy. "Donna what?" What had his brother staged, what was the trick here, what did Eric go and do, how could he still be tormenting Marty from an urn?

"Don't know. She was like this Jane Doe or whatever, you know, what they call —"

"— What they call a corpse. That's in the Coroner's Office, pal. C'mon, c'mon, this is bullshit!"

"No, she talks about her apartment. Like she has a real place and all. She don't know where she left it. They found her wandering around. Maybe Alzheimer's?"

"Not likely. She'd only be in her late 50s. 60. And her son, the actor? How did he find her? Why didn't he take her back to her place? Why didn't he tell you what her name was?"

"Well okay, he didn't exactly, ah, *visit*, I guess. . . ."

Marty growled. He was suddenly hungry. Or had a headache, one or the other, both. Tak leaned forward. "Mr. Gilmore, with all due respect, what the hell is going on here?"

"It's like she saw him on TV, the actor? After the accident you guys had, it was on the news?"

"And she just pointed him out and said, 'That's my boy,' right? Probably while you happened to be paying her a nice visit, out of kindness?"

"Well no. I read the newspaper piece, on account of I did hear her saying to everybody in my van one day, something about this guy? On TV? And in the paper it says where he died making a movie with his brother — here, I got the thing here —"

The man turned his vest pockets inside out and dropped his keys to the floor.

"So you drove over just to see us? To make our acquaintance?"

"To make a trade."

"Oh, right. What do you have, Mr. Gilmore?"

"Be right back —"

Gilmore lumbered through the door, bumping the jamb and floundering out of balance into the parking lot. Tak and Marty stared at one another, then heard a van door make a hollow roar in its track as it slid open, then clopped shut. Gilmore reappeared with a large soiled envelope. Tak stood and gingerly extracted it from Gilmore's hand.

"What is it?"

"Near's I can tell, family stuff."

Tak set the envelope on the folding table. Marty stepped closely and peered down at a faded Kodacolor print partially exposed under the flap.

"The lady had these with some other stuff in a shopping cart when they picked her up."

"Picked her up, for what?"

"I don't know. The usual, you know — something crazy, like some bag lady, probably screaming at someone. No offense. But it's like . . . you know. And I figured, better to give these to someone before she leaves 'em someplace, huh?"

"Sure." Tak waited to see if Marty had anything to say, but he'd gone to his knees, staring down at the snapshots that were now just under his nose. "And what are you trading these for, Mr. Gilmore?"

"You really got Laura Trent-Sampson in this movie? Like it says in the paper?"

"Yes. She's not here, but she'll be in it."

"Could you get an autograph? Like, get her to sign these?" Gilmore pulled out a paper bag from another slot on the inside of the orange vest. It held a dozen or so copies of *Playboy's* "Sex in the Cinema 1986," the loose pages torn from the magazines. Marty recalled something about a lawsuit.

Tak looked at Gilmore's prize, a hidden-camera photo of Laura nude from the waist up, shot clandestinely during a backstage costume change at a publicity photo session. "Sure. I'll ask her."

"Like when?"

"Leave the pages here, and I'll make sure she gets them."

The choice was clearly agonizing for Gilmore. He decided to take two copies back, and leave the rest. "Jeff. Gilmore. G-i-l-m-o-r-e. It's nothing dirty. It's like collectibles."

"Thanks, Mr. Gilmore."

"Can I meet her?"

"Thanks, Mr. Gilmore."

The bushy, wide man backed reluctantly out of the room. When he drove off, Tak stepped to the doorway to read aloud " . . . Salt Lake County. . . Elder Care" on the back of the van.

Marty was still on his knees. "What was it, Tak? Your dad — after he died, you said he'd come back. *Hoto*-something? *Hoto* — ?"

"*Hotoke-sama*. Household Spirit."

Marty nodded. He took the envelope to the window and held up some square prints from a Brownie Starmatic II camera he remembered. Marty, Craig, Mom, Dad. His family was there, images preserved as surely as if in amber.

53

L ate in the afternoon Marty arrived at a Salt Lake City care facility for the medically indigent. He asked the suspicious male receptionist where he might find his mother, Mrs. Nyrop. The man pursed his lips as if to shame Marty for having a mother in such a place, then seemed pleased to announce that there was no person by that name being cared for there.

The receptionist promptly ignored him, leaving Marty to stare at the floor of institutional tile. High-pitched echoes came from several corridors that led from the reception area, each cut off by double doors. He refocused.

"Her first name is Donna. I don't know what last name she's using, but I think she still calls herself Donna something."

"Then perhaps I should look under 'S'? 'Something, comma, Donna'?"

The man smirked at his own wit, then began to re-file an olive folder. Marty reached over the counter and grasped the man's bony shoulder with one rigid hand. "How 'bout I file your fucking skull under 'B' for 'Busted Shithead?'"

The man's eyes bulged, the white showing completely around his irises. He seemed to be trying to put a shaky finger on a button under the counter, but kept missing. Marty had a brief flashback of Burns Security guards running, huffing across a movie lot. He squeezed the man closer.

"It's my *mother*, goddamn it. I didn't even know she was alive, like I owe you a fucking explanation. In fact I *still* don't know. But I'm here to find out. And if I have to pull you inside out until you're swallowing with your asshole, that's what I'll do until you tell me where Donna is. *Now.*"

The receptionist nodded, or at least tried to follow Marty's hand movements as Marty jerked the man's head back and forth as a "yes" to guarantee co-operation.

Marty remembered some lines from a TV show he'd worked on. "And if you try to sic anybody on me while I'm talking *to my mother* . . . I'll be outside, waiting. Someday, somewhere. . . . Waiting. You follow?"

He pumped the guy's chin up and down again to let him know that he had best understand, and agree. Marty released his shoulder and the man scribbled a room number on a Post-It, then shoved it at Marty and pointed at one of the double doors.

"Thank you." He went quickly down the corridor. He knew the receptionist had already called a guard, or an orderly, or maybe Gilmore the bearded clown who had come to their motel, or more probably even a cop. That would be better, it would take longer. Still, he'd only bought himself enough time to find out what he needed to know.

•••

It was true: Donna Nyrop stood before Marty like an anxious visitor in her own room, which he immediately understood to mean that most everything he had accused his brother of during childhood was false. And now Craig was dead and there was no way to apologize.

She was powdery-skinned, her white hair in short flares of many directions. She had on a greenish gold coat that appeared to be made from carpet, worn over men's trousers and fairly new Nike athletic shoes. She clutched a macramé bag with both her blue-veined hands. He looked into her face to see if anyone was looking back. He wasn't sure. Her eyes jiggled behind thick bifocals. Did his mother wear glasses twenty years ago? Her pretty cheekbones were still there, her teeth seemed all right from the affectless smile she gave but the flesh around these harder structures was etched, tired.

"Hi, Mom. I'm Marty. Your son. I know you haven't seen me since I was twelve years old. . . ."

"Hi, Marty!"

There seemed to be no point in gentle chatter. "Mom. . . . Craig's dead, Mom. I guess you heard. . . ?"

"Isn't it awful? I saw it on TV. So I would've come right over. But I can't find my apartment."

"Come over where?"

330

She smiled for him again. He could only wonder what it was supposed to mean. His mother, alive.

"Right over, Marty, you know? So fast your head'd swim."

"Yes, Mom. I know. . . . But *you're* not, I see."

"Not what, Dear?"

"Dead. You're not dead."

"Oh, no. Heavens, no! Praise the Lord."

"Heavens no, no, no. . . . Can I come in? Sit down? What. . . . *God!* Tell me things. Anything. . . ." He suddenly wished he'd brought Tak. Tak always knew so much, maybe he'd researched this too, and was holding back. His mother stared as helplessly as Marty did. "You sit down too, Mom."

She went obediently to a vinyl-covered armchair, still quick in her stride, her larger movements still capable. She sat on the edge of the chair and clutched her bag, folding herself up to await instructions. He noticed her fingers were shaped like thin white bananas. He didn't know if he should hold one of her hands, embrace her, or curse out loud; thinking, Hit or fall down laughing again. No, not this time, I don't think so — He reminded himself that cops were probably on the way.

Questions he never thought he'd be asking ran through his head: where've you been? did you really show up for Craig, the way he always said? why didn't you come and see *me too?* who was in the plane that day with Dad— Joyce after all? I was a little boy, Mom, didn't you love me? *Dazzle me. . . .*

He faced a void. The timeline he thought he occupied had just been erased behind him. *This was a moment, all right, was that what you lived for, Craig? My images, your moments. But where's the story — ?* Marty trusted none of his senses. His life was a lie or, at the very least, completely (even if innocently) wrong, a mistake. There was nothing here to frame, to visualize, to make others see. He needed better blocking on the actors in his life, a more useful angle, a wider master shot.

"What's in the bag?"

His mother sprang forward, a wispy Slinky toy. She plunged into the bottom of her handbag's mustiness and brought up small, worn yellow boxes, all no doubt filled with cardboard-framed slides. He remembered his mother's Argus camera, a Christmas gift from Big Jim. He read the print on one box: "Develop Before AUG

1962." More envelopes and boxes came out, now mixed with comic-book-like religious pamphlets. Nothing that explained Utah, or much else.

Donna Nyrop sat awaiting further instructions.

"What was it, Mom? With you and Dad? What could make it so bad you'd do what you did? You ran away from us. He was dead, and gone, and you ran anyway."

"He was a bad man. Oh, boy. A wicked man. Praise God."

No, a weak man, a selfish one, but it must've been more complicated than that. They must've needed each other somehow, for a while anyway, used each other. "Co-dependency" was a recently trendy phrase. Everyone has their reasons.

"Didn't you feel like, like you had some responsibilities? Mom, we were your kids. . . ."

"Bad. Bad, bad, bad. The Devil was in him, just like in you. The Devil touched him."

"The Devil. Okay." There was little left to connect with in this human shell before him. His vision went blurry. His jaw and chin felt weak.

Donna pushed out of her chair and slapped Marty firmly across the cheek. "Don't you feel that way. He'll see you!"

There was a siren in the distance. With his mother alive in the same room, he'd been orphaned again.

• • •

So Craig wasn't always a liar, or entirely a confabulator. Not always a fantasizer after all. He'd started with the truth in some things and what chimeras he'd invented for Marty, whether to protect his belligerent little brother, entertain him, mislead him, aggrandize his own role — each action within a role to please Big Jim the Director — somewhere this one started in truth. The plane did go down with a girlfriend, most probably the one Marty once saw that looked a lot like Mom. The one he filmed. Joyce. Someone close enough physically (there was the Nyrop taste in thin blondes coming through again) to not warrant scraping through scorched dental arches, especially when witnesses had seen Mom and Dad both at the airport. There was a manifest with "Donna Nyrop" typed on it, so why bother? In a few days there'd be a missing person's report in another town, another state, for a woman with trampy not-so-secret relationships who was probably asking for a bad end, and in a while all would be forgotten.

As for Mom, when the plane left her on the ground and then violently came back to the ground itself, she stepped through a door suddenly opened to another room, and there became someone else. Perhaps she broke apart and was nobody, really, for a while, then somebody not quite her but based on a Self. "Adapted from Donna Nyrop, The Life." Maybe the time before the crackup had only been character research, only experiences to give her an impelling moment before. Mom's As if: "My life is *as if* I'd been someone else once. But now I'm new, alone, and better. Fancy free. Praise God."

And so, after all these years Craig must've brought her out here, set her up in an apartment to be nearby while they worked in the Utah desert, to be more of a son than Marty had ever been, or was allowed to be. Craig had at least been trying, was dutiful, perhaps loving, as Marty never was. There was no way of ever learning how much time had gone by as she wandered through the emptiness of her newly discovered non-identity before Craig somehow found her. But by then Marty's refusal to have anything to do with his brother, except to use him to make a movie, his refusal to believe anything Craig said, had sealed off any chance of knowing Craig's truth.

• • •

Marty hurried Donna out of her room and found an emergency exit door they could sneak through, out of sight from the main entrance even as an alarm clanged and away from the sound of the siren growing nearer. He brought Donna Nyrop back to the Two Cedars Best Western, the only place he could call home. He introduced her to Tak in the editing room, then fell into a panic. He had no plan for her.

"Mom? Do you know about Amy and Jenna? Craig had another kid too, you know. A boy. You want to see your grandson?" She stared at him, around him, through him. "Mom? Do you want to see him? I could call L.A., and make arrangements. Your new grandson. He's still a baby."

She didn't seem to understand and chose to watch out the window. When Marty was sure that his mother would continue to be quiet for a short time, he asked Tak for ten minutes to himself, then stood under the scalding water in his motel shower until he was throbbing red everywhere, lightheaded, pouring his own sweat into the steaming rivulets that seemed to be siphoning his insides down the drain. Finally he felt purged. Or maybe just dizzy, distrusting his own senses.

This was unfair to Tak. Marty knew he had to deal with his new/old life. He'd make sure she was put into a home with proper caretakers, pay whatever it took to have competent people around her, people she couldn't lose or who wouldn't lose her. He would tell them to see that she never wanted for anything. She must've had a pretty terrible time of it.

When Marty returned to the editing room he wasn't surprised to find his mother gone. He quickly absolved Tak of all responsibility because he already knew what it must've been like: Donna Nyrop staring at something only she could see, screaming, demons coming to get her, then her rigid posture when she stood up and wouldn't let Tak reassure her or guide her to a soft chair. Then the moment Tak's back was turned to get help. . . . He knew.

Marty didn't go after whoever Donna Nyrop had become. It was pointless to race to the County road outside the motel by himself and force her inside a car, because he had nowhere to take her. Marty was a Movie Director, for a few more weeks anyway, and Movie Directors had drivers who could find people for them and make sure they were safe. (Or if they were lucky they had responsible Producers like Tak who'd already seen to it that she would be gently placed in a company station wagon by their Driver Captain and escorted back to her County room with a story and apology that would keep the police from investigating a crime that hadn't actually happened.) In a short time Marty would ask her caretakers for a brochure with pictures of whatever nursing facility would most likely make her happy. He would arrange it, probably in L.A., and pay for it, and maybe visit, and send gifts. . . .

Donna Nyrop had left behind the yellow Kodak detritus given to him by Gilmore the orderly — his childhood exchanged for nude photos of Laura Trent-Sampson. Marty wondered if these prints and slides were clues that only now might reveal why years later two brothers from Michigan would try to make a movie in the desert, a sequel of sorts to the ones they made together nearly twenty years before with a Bolex. Eric Blanc the Actor liked to describe a kind of standing outside of himself, watching. Maybe in the watching Craig Nyrop recognized too much of himself in their mother. Maybe he grew too tired in the end, he saw the cracks, he recognized in her the despair that walking the actor's tightrope only put off for a while. It's you onstage, but it's not; it's the character onstage, but it's not. Is/is not — the actor artfully induces the craziness, but then how long can he maintain?

And where can anyone, actor or not, have one moment of completion, that curtain bow, *even once* offstage? Where, and when, and how, does the actor come to rest?

54

Tak asked Marty to join him in the editing room where Tak had been playing with some outtakes on the Moviola. Shots of Eric and Laura, closeups from completely different scenes, were clumsily edited together with bad tape splices. Tak sat like an alert bus driver steering the lumpy movie back and forth with little knobs.

"Give it up, Tak. . . ."

"No. We have to fight for this."

"There's nothing left to fight for. It's over."

"I don't think that's true. This movie. . . . You know, when they bought into the script in the first place, it was because of all the work Eric had done on stage, the commercials, the reputation he'd built —"

Marty rolled over a nearby chair and sat down next to the editing table. "Like hell. *Maybe* it got us a reading and a free dinner at Musso's. But we were nothing to you guys until we lied about Laura."

"Maybe. Anyway . . . that's not how it'll come out. The movie'll have a crossover element. I mean, it's working well enough on the screen that MSC will have a class project to get itself launched. They'll have money and respectability, and that carries weight in —"

"In Lotus Land? Like your guys understand how it works?"

Tak was exasperated. "Look, Marty — They've been 90% of my tax work. I see their business practices close up. And if this movie doesn't go, if you lose a chance to be the Director —"

"— then we'll never be Japan's answer to Warner Brothers, or Fox, or MGM, or Universal, or Paramount. We won't even be Disney. I won't be Orson Welles. No shit."

Tak closed his eyes for a moment. It made Marty want to hit himself. Then it was Bibi in his head again, her voice telling Marty that it was easy to be a cynic, Mr. Guts.

"I'm not making this up. Eric has this . . . there's a presence on the screen. We've all been to dailies, you see it here in the workprint. I'm not going to say it's like this actor or that actor, but it's there, isn't it? Whatever it is, even to an outsider like me, something's working."

Marty breathed shallowly and turned from Tak, away from the anxiousness. How dare either of them think to compare Eric to Movie Stars? The great ones' visages were timeless, if for no other reason than they were all dead and humans would never be recorded that way in black & white again, glowing in the craftsmanship of Hollywood set design, costume design, lighting design, *actor* design, all in liquid, billion-shaded silver. Although Eric had now managed the dead part. The sheen of the studio age, the chemistry of its nitrates, the radiance of crystalline mirror fragments throwing back the projector's beam in coherent ghost-shapes. All dream-ness, yet all alive forever in a forty-foot high electrified pool of metallic light. No matter what they might want for Eric, and for themselves, it was too late for that. In a paraphrase of his college film history text, the parade had gone by.

Marty tried to slow down, to stop being a jerk with Tak. "Look, there's two kinds of actors I've worked with that're worth anything. There's the type who can't play anything but himself, but he's got something so special it's enough, it's all you want. Just to see him again and again *because* he plays himself. That's Jimmy Stewart. Maybe today Harrison Ford. Then there's the guys who're nothing but a mask. Guys who aren't even *there*, it's like they're hermit crabs but they grab onto these incredible shells and become anything else *except* themselves. I never said Eric didn't have talent. But that's him, a mask."

"Maybe what we're doing — if we're any good here — it'll be a Golden Age to another generation, eh?"

Marty blew out a dismissive breath. Tak turned away and played with the Moviola. Marty couldn't tell if Tak was hurt or annoyed or was simply waiting. Could that be true, about Eric? By now Marty had seen all of the Japan commercials that Eric had made. Eric had caught Gary Cooper's painful privacy, wrapped nevertheless around an iron integrity so that Cooper melted away even as he was unquestionably steadfast. There was Montgomery Clift's skittish neuroticism which looked for a hiding place while his damaged, fragile beauty brought him forward as an excoriated offering. Eric's attempt at Jimmy Stewart, the alternative icon for the '40s — Marty and Eric had both loved Stewart so much as kids — was less

338

successful; when asked, Eric had told Marty that in searching for his persona Stewart's innocence, coupled with a clear intelligence, had wrought an unexpected complexity, the thing that kept Stewart both vulnerable and strong on the screen so that we identified with him instantly. With Jimmy we want not to be cynics, to be smart yet unspoiled; two sides of what we all need to believe is our truer self. Eric told Marty he hadn't been able to project all that in the puny context he'd been given and had requested that Clift's persona, more readily apparent on the surface, be used instead. Was any of that relevant to *User-Friendly*? Usable?

Marty tapped the flatbed screen with his fingertips. "So what's the big idea here, Tak?"

"Look, look at this." A few close-ups and slugs whizzed by. "It's like the early Soviet editing experiment I read about. Shots of a stone-faced actor and a bowl of soup were cut together —"

"— and everybody thought he was performing 'hunger.' Or 'grief' when they cut to a coffin, with the same shot of the actor. 'Dialectic montage.' The guy who came up with that was Lev Kuleshov, and they still teach it."

"Right. The meaning of shots, through 'collision,' they said. Okay, I found out-takes of Eric that could mean anything. Depending on their context, 'Albert' might be longing, or lonely, hungry or frightened, depending on what you cut his closeup with." Tak went past what he'd been looking for, then wound back. "In shots like this one here — filmed with this kind of side lighting— Eric's tight shots could be matted into backgrounds lit to match. More important —"

"Match what, Tak?"

"The love scene. Here — if I cut together Eric's face with Laura's, where she's kind of cooing and urging and showing all the skin you can distract the audience with, then you could shadow everything else with their limbs, use silhouettes of lovers against a dim fireside maybe. What I'm saying is, we have enough of Eric's face that a love scene is possible with you as a body-double."

Marty went numb. Then he absorbed Tak's intent: the publicity of Eric Blanc's death might guarantee that *User-Friendly* really would be released, it might find an audience, might be laughed at and loved. It could be finished off, done, becoming Eric's chance to win the hearts of a movie-going nation, and fix his one filmic image forevermore. There could be no further evidence submitted as to whether the talented young actor from the *avant* stage would be the next Brando or DeNiro, or the next Jimmy Stewart. But there could be *User-Friendly* —

And Marty knew he needed just this one more scene. He saw it: this love scene was a family heirloom, within a story that had become Eric's bequest. He must've seen something in this script that made him willing to derail his plans for a play, must've known the fit that *User-Friendly* would make with his own — with *their* own — lives. It was the proper story to leave behind, the one he would use to do the pointing for him, the explaining. Craig-as-Eric tried to return home to Marty through this story, through the forgiveness of the story's other characters, perhaps grieving over his childhood loss of what should've been there all along (but wasn't and never would be) even though that kind of hole never gets filled.

As his character "Albert," he could reconstruct his childhood through instructions to a robot, to become a fulfilled and realized adult, finally embraced by true love.

Marty felt flushed with a sudden understanding: that we're each of us a Craig, that each of us thinks that what we once had inside us was worthy, deserving, though our child-self inevitably drifts backward into the past, out of reach, and becomes a once-upon-a-time that is finally lost, left behind, and the self that goes forward is stunted, dwarfed, made ugly by all of the Others and all of their circumstances, until our life becomes so much less than it — we — could've been.

Who then would resist the actor's vindication that comes with being famous and being looked at? Twin acts that say, Yes, my dreams and fantasies were right, my worthiness is finally and rightfully adored. If I make a good movie, or even a bad one seen by millions, then didn't my promise, my Self, prove worthy of love after all?

It was now up to Marty to make that worthiness happen by filling in for Eric and making screen-love to Exene. A dream, with purpose.

But mere fantasies are traps, static, and not heroic until a price has been paid. Marty was suddenly so tired of fantasy, so tired of the daydreams of success. What had Eric tried to teach him, months ago? Don't use the obvious, the simple good and bad. Find the internal conflict. Ask, "What are you fighting for?" Maybe that's what Eric Blanc tried to do for the two of them, fighting for love until he went and died.

Marty could no longer blame. But he could body double.

55

*M*arty knocked on the door to room 29 and waited. He could hear Tubs crying inside. A distant, treble-pitched sigh rose faintly over the breeze. Maybe the shower. Exene sure did shower a lot.

Worrying about the baby was still a habit. With Tubs under Laura's care back in L.A. — more likely the care of a hired nanny — his half-awake nights in Utah had been like séances with the dead, the sounds of a baby spirit calling out with cold and hunger and fear of the night. He knocked and waited, then let himself into the room with Bibi's extra key. A jungle dampness clung to him. Next to the foam-cushioned lounge chair Exene had an 18-speed mountain bike mounted on rollers, a stationary exercise setup aimed at the balcony window. Probably for the view, he thought, but it had a mildly disturbing effect as if Exene hoped that when she hit a high enough cadence, revved enough RPMs on the locked-down bike, she might suddenly break free and soar over the Rockies. It was a universal dream to self-propel heavenward, good enough for Spielberg's flying bikes in *E.T.*. What was Marilyn's last job before being discovered? Something in a parachute factory. . . .

It was in fact the shower he heard. The baby was alone in the bedroom of the motel's only suite. He went to the side of the crib and watched the helpless, boneless chin fibrillate, all muscular control going into Tub O'Guts's lungs for ever-weakening cries. Marty took one useless hand and kissed it. He almost swooned, but this couldn't be happening, he was here to describe the mechanics of the love scene to Exene, not to have wild impulses to lick his nephew's head and run with him, anywhere, fast. *Oh god Tubs — how many times have you cried yourself to sleep?*

He sniffed at an odd sweetness. The bathroom moisture composited the baby's breath with open ointment tubes and powdery diapers in plastic casings. Suffused through it all was Exene: her sweat from the bicycling, perfumed and deodorized, animal but all spice. Coriander, he flashed to, the smell of her unguarded, sleeping exhalations in the motorhome almost a year ago on the studio lot.

Marty felt a heavy ache for the baby. He wanted to squash Tub O'Guts into his chest and do something like cherish him. He reached down to pick him up.

"No — don't."

He jerked upright, then bounced his eyes like pinballs between bumpers. There was no place to be, or even to look. Exene was out of the shower, nude, glistening with water and lotion as if wearing a film of beaded light.

"Don't spoil him. I don't want him to think he can get his own way just crying all the time. It'll never stop. I mean, it never stops *any*way. You have no idea what these last couple weeks have been like."

Marty stayed quiet for a moment, not wanting to joke that she could probably afford a robe by now. "Sorry, I'll get out of here —"

She grabbed his hand without looking away from the baby. She wouldn't let him go, or meet his eyes. She purred in high soothing sounds that arrested the baby's attention, made him toss his head toward the voice, the smells.

"Are . . . ah, are . . . You okay, Laura? With feeding and everything?"

"Yeah, sure. Why not? There's plenty of formula."

"I don't know. I've heard . . . you know, with stress and all. It can kind of, like dry you up. But I guess if you're not —"

"Stress . . . ?"

"Well . . . work. The changes. Eric and all."

She met Marty's eyes now, but didn't seem to understand his words. He felt his guts twisting and his blood running, falling, rising — blasting toward whichever pathway was open and trying to arrive at his pelvic cradle as heatedly as it could.

Exene gave the baby the little finger of her free hand, the bulb of her pinkie against his palate. He sucked furiously for several moments, then fell into exhausted sleep. Marty wondered how long she'd let him cry, let him hunger.

She turned and stared at Marty, silent and wide-eyed. Finally, "He'll sleep for a while now."

Exene seemed to mean this as an overture, a prologue. To what, he didn't know. He stared into the cornflower-blue eyes, the best way not to stare at the rest of her. "I'm sorry I came in like this, I could hear him. . . . . I'll go —"

Now he ran his eyes in circles around the room, trying to fix upon anything that would block out the wondrousness of Laura Trent-Sampson's nakedness from his mind, from his nerves, from something inside that threatened to leave him behind like a molted snakeskin and flow fast and sure into her funneling receptiveness. Where was the goddamn door?

She pulled him to the edge of her bed and sat so abruptly that she bounced. He tried to stay upright, dipped his shoulder, then sank next to her as he tried to create an explanation for running outside, one that would satisfy her enough to keep her working on the movie. Maybe this was the sharing, where the pain from the death of the father of her only living child would crack through her transparent veil of lotion and light and connect them in innocent sorrow. Go with it, he told himself, let go, open up, you might need this. When you're out on the set and she wants direction, you might need this —

"Marty? Do you still think I . . . remember like you said once, I still have deep skin?"

Oh shit. She'd asked about her skin. Any pretense of ulterior, superior motivations fell like fractured glass out of a window frame. He had to stare now, to judge. She *wanted* him to. Skin *yes*, then eyes, then perfect toenails, oval teeth, nipples with dots of shower water, one erect, one thinking about it. Skin — deep all right, deep as an ocean — flowing over curving bone, and hair dripping its gold, a rivulet trickling to a thin puff of copper shaved narrow so that it might at poolside hide behind the merest thong that would scarcely cover what was *un*covered right here, right now, all of it asking for eyes to caress.

"Geez. . . . God. . . ." He sank his face into his hands and thought that in the next moment he might weep semen inside his jeans. He had to be still, quiet, blind. Her smell, *don't breathe.* . . .

"I mean, am I any good? In the movie?"

"What — ?"

"Do you love her, a little bit? 'Ginger'?"

"Ginger. . . . She's tough, and adorable. Yes. I love her. Everybody will."

She heaved a sigh. Relief? She swung her face into his and kissed him. Long. Sweet and salty like before, and no one watching. No time limit. A kiss attached to the rest of her.

When their lips parted he lowered his chin and stood and leaned off-center toward the door. It was the most heroic thing he had ever done. Exene rose too, held his face with both hands and bounced to her toes to reach his lips again. A kiss, two, her nose rubbing lightly across his clenched eyelid.

A tug on his belt, his zipper melting, one shove with two hands — his hands? hers? — and he was free to fall into her. For the first time since Eric's death he heard his brother's voice, not just the words, but the rolling tonality, Eric's presence. The presence of the actor without the actor. *Actually, she went in there and fished it out for me —*

He and Exene were coupled, clasped into and around one another, tumbling it seemed or was it only his head that was plummeting? Imploding, everything spiraling inward. Her skin was everywhere now, and who would think/dream/hope to escape? He entered her and came in seconds, a visionless redness, reverie and shame at once, a pounding, an evacuation.

He lay blinking in the room light, the air moister still. She was already somewhere else, where? then over him again with a hot washcloth, wiping him down, caretaking. The baby cried. Marty flinched, threw one arm up. He was wearing shoes.

"No, don't — not now —"

"You have to, Laura —"

"No, don't let him make me unhappy. This is mine, I won't let that baby make me unhappy —"

"Ahh, god —"

She was all over him now, he was dazed by her angles. Each point-of-view was a still image from a strobe-lit dance; the underside of her chin, the back of her knee, sacral dimples, everywhere was perfect in line-color-rhythm, an airbrushed pinup gone 3-D, virtual. It was imagery but with heat and tingling electric touch too. She drew her head back from his groin and he was erect again already, as if he were sixteen, dumbstruck until his own inner voice informed him, *She's beating herself up with my dick —*

It was wrong to be here, to do this, somehow it was unfair to both of them, to the baby, even to Bibi though he was no longer sure in what way. He went flaccid as quickly as his arteries could accommodate — impotence as a decision.

"Look, is there . . . is there a bottle in the fridge? I'll heat it up."

There was anger, and a little humiliation in her voice. "*Marty* —" But he was focused on the pathetic wails from the other side of the room. He wanted to snatch the infant up, push his big face into the baby's little one until they breathed the same air like two scuba divers trading one tank, give and take, sharing what little strength as human beings they had. *Didn't she feel this too?* Baby and parent, a *pas de deux* that would make you throw yourself off the roof if you thought it would help anything? Anything at all, *you'd kill, you'd die* for the child? Why doesn't she feel it, it's her kid, why don't we feel the same about it? We're all the same stuff — my god, being a storyteller *depends* on that, all sharing the same secret heart, dreams, hopes, the yadda yadda —

"Marty, don't you want me?"

"Laura, geez, it's wonderful. You're . . . wonderful. Boggling. But not all this, not all at once, okay?"

"I'm saying, in L.A. you could have me like this, day and night, Marty. Lover." She drew out the next word in a whisper: "Director —"

"No, it's. . . . Tubs there, and Eric . . . just now, with him gone." Her hands were gliding up, across his pelvis.

"Come home with me, Marty. You, me, and baby."

He looked at her and saw only the blue saucers, then the abyss within. She wanted to play house. This couldn't be what she needed. He had no idea what to say. He got to the door before he remembered to dart back and wear pants.

"Marty. . . ? Please? I was . . . I'm just . . . just looking for a little love."

"I know. I mean I'm sorry. I'll send Bibi over. She'll help out."

He closed the door quietly so as not to add to whatever rejection she must be going through. Thinking, What the hell's going on? She could have *any*body in there. The Most Famous Star in the World, rejected by catch-of-the-day Marty. Right. My god. My ass. Hit, or fall down spewing DNA with your jism, for chrissakes.

Patrick Cosgrove

56

O nce again he watched Bibi pack. There was no forwarding address this time either. She seemed like the most serene, sane person on the planet while his head still wobbled within the sexual fog of Exene's overwhelming naked perfection. They were all leaving after one more shooting day.

"Marty, what's going to happen to the baby?"

"I don't know. He'll have your basic Hollywood childhood, I guess."

"And what's that?"

"Uh . . . a housekeeper, some nanny raising him. So she can wrap her under-the-table cash in tears and send it back to her own kids in Nicaragua or wherever. He'll speak with a Spanish accent until kindergarten. Have the reddest BMW and score the purest blow at Samohi or Crossroads. The American Dream, huh?"

"What're you going to do about it?"

"What do you mean, why should I do anything — ?" He pulled this one back but not in time to soften Bibi's scowl. "Eric's dead. She can announce the kid's paternity to the world and he can't sue her and make her prove it in court. So what's to stop her from just . . . raising him?"

Bibi pronounced the next word as a harsh whisper: "Decency."

Marty needed to hold her, fall to one knee and clasp Bibi's hand, kiss the softness back into her face.

A knock at the door, as if they were in a Lego motel, everyone running in and out of plastic cubicles. He opened the door and Exene stepped past him like he was an unsavory butler. She held Tub O'Guts in her arms and looked only at Bibi.

"Sweetie. Have you got any, like douche or whatever? It's a little after the fact, but these Nyrops are awful fertile, you know? Any port in a storm. Like, whatever. . . ."

Bibi stared at Exene, then Marty, and he found himself very interested in something through the door at the far end of the parking lot. He realized he'd now officially lost everything he ever cared about that couldn't be found within a Panaflex viewfinder. Hell, that was gone, too. *Love scene, my ass.*

"No, Laura. No, I don't use anything like that."

Exene *knew*. He knew she knew, about his history with Bibi. Fine. She had her knife in. This was nothing but payback. He wanted to push Exene's head into a wall and draw blood.

"Okay fine." Exene smiled brightly and bounced the baby in her arms as she left without once looking at him.

Marty growled. He'd allowed himself such hope when Bibi answered his call for help. And now. . . . He watched her shake her head slowly and go back to packing. He was appalled. Whatever fantasies he'd clung to, this was final. He got it, about irreconcilable differences.

Bibi decided to pack what she was wearing and put on something simpler. Her indifference to his presence felt painful, wrong, as if he didn't rate a desire for privacy. He numbly continued to watch her change into a sweatshirt, and saw for probably the last time the Scandinavian sheen of her, the unlined, unblemished complexion that always made her seamless, slightly angelic, made him a little timid in the face of it. Though an ideal photo double for Exene, Bibi wasn't shaped exactly like her; bigger through the hips — more womanly, he realized, more maternal — and he now despised every judgment he'd ever made that Bibi was something less than Exene's sexual ideal, or that it should even matter, or that he had even noticed. How could he have let that confuse him, let it delay the flat declaration of love Bibi must've wanted from him at some moment in their past? Or was this just the talk of impending loss, only wanting what you clearly could no longer have?

Child-bearing hips, he thought, that's what they call them. Like she's got the continuity, the generations built right into her. She's *from* somewhere — a little red and white house with a beech tree in the yard and a dog named Cookie who barked and played in the Minnesota snow — and now Bibi's going away somewhere, only I don't know where. And she'll have kids with another guy, kids who are *from* somewhere, with a dog named. . . . Marty fleetingly thought of romantic comedies, those stories of second chances. Their central story problem was often the extinction of sexual love, the falling into a brother-sister mutuality that had killed the essence of mating. With Bibi he knew he'd sunk below even a sibling's status.

She spoke with her back to him. "You screwed up."

"Yeah."

"But at least you know you've screwed up. It's about the only thing left. . . ."

He nodded, the shame returning. He looked away, then glanced at her furtively but she wouldn't give him her eyes. She rubbed quickly at her face as she bent over a drawer and when her hand came away wet a sparkle fell to the carpet. It was the first time he had ever made her cry.

"What's going to happen to the baby, Marty?"

"I don't know. It's not my call."

She slammed the drawer shut. He stood, knowing it was time for him to leave but without knowing whether, after the love scene tomorrow and Exene's flight home, he could ever talk to Bibi again.

Patrick Cosgrove

57

*A*llowing grief over his lost Bibi would do him no good. An hour after he got back to his room Marty called Tak with a proper sense of duty and improper cheer.

"Hey, congratulations Mr. Producer. I just wanted to say, before we wrap this thing up, you're the one guy who's held the rest of us together." On the other end Tak stifled a laugh and refused to take credit. "Now I need you to do something else for me. It's important, so don't fail me."

"Marty, can you hold it a second? — I'm on the other line, and — "

Marty listened to the quiet coming over the receiver, to a distant electronic booping of a machine-dialed number from a stranger's phone that was leaking into their line.

Tak came back. "Still there? Listen. The word's already out that we're going to finish the film, that it's got a chance. Somebody's been showing off the dailies back in L.A.. Marty — there's a script that's been greenlighted at Warner's. A co-production with MSC, and this time they handle the distribution. A major, major thing, Marty, and what they want — are you listening? — what they *might* want is you. Dustin Hoffman has director approval, and he wants to talk to you, you're on his list! Marty! Do you know what this *means*?"

He sat silently. This was not the most unbelievable thing that had happened to him today. "Tak . . . I want my name taken off the picture."

"What?"

"Can you just . . . do it? I don't want 'Martin Ford' anywhere in the *User-Friendly* credits, all right?"

"Oh, you want to deal with having it 'Marty Nyrop'? You know, the Guild —"

"No, no. I think in cases like this they call the Director 'Alan Smithee.' Everybody in the business knows what that means. The guy's got an incredible string of flops going —"

"This is no flop, Marty. This might be very big. Bigger than any of us ever imagined and —"

"— No, stop it. I don't doubt that for a minute. . . ." Marty set his teeth against the back of his free wrist until he was sure he could continue. "Help a friend with a professional mercy-killing here, will you?"

"Marty, you've got to come over here to the office first. Besides the one I just told you about —? this morning I've had seven other calls from producers who want to show Martin Ford their next project. There's development money practically lying on the floor. Oops. There, *Oh my* — ! I think I just blew my nose on a thousand-dollar bill."

The machine. It was coming. It was coming for him. Revving its engine, gearing up. Consuming, manufacturing, confabulating. For him. He could engineer the machine that was here, for him. What now of his need to shape, to name, to make others see. . . ?

"No . . . no thanks."

"I can't accept this — Why?"

"Tak, listen. My ex-girlfriend's finally leaving me forever. My only brother's dead. His kid's as good as in prison already. My mom checked in from Planet Zoogon, then transported back. And because of all that I'm a Director. Should I confess how being a Director makes me feel right now?"

"I understand, just don't make any decisions while you feel this way. But Marty — I think you need to get into this office right now."

"Tak. . . . I will not be there tomorrow to shoot the love scene unless you promise to do this. Kill 'Martin Ford' and put him out of his misery."

"Well . . . I think to do it, there are Guild regulations. We're going to be signatories."

"Then get Amato on it, if you have to. They've kept him in his cage on salary for *something*. . . . Will you do it? Promise?"

" . . . Yes. But stop by in a while, eh? You're all right otherwise?"

Marty was suddenly hurtling through the air in a Jeep Cherokee, about to smack a Titan camera crane into atoms. "I'm not going to harm myself. Not everything runs in families."

58

E xene grinned. "Boys! Boys! Settle! Lights. Camera. *Hard-on!*"

She had the crew in hand. They guffawed and shifted uneasily as she beamed at them one-by-one, making deliberate eye contact with the spare essential crew allowed to stay on the closed set. In the glow of her complete nakedness Marty lay atop her, sweating, quivering, covering her scant privacy with his own Nyrop ass. His shot design — a slow pan and dolly combination move along the length of their bodies which would reveal her completely from the side and leave him in shadow and profile and unrecognizable as a double for his brother — called for measurement after measurement by the camera assistant for critical focus-pulling. Exene endured it happily, languidly. Marty was appalled at his own vulnerability and tried to think only of directing the shot, naming the Seen even in this counterfeit version.

But was that possible? The heat of her body rose through his own. Her skin was as taut as it had been before the baby. During the rehearsals the dent between her breasts had been a good hiding place from the lens for his Eric substitution. Now he had a wild impulse to thrust, to enter her in full view of the crew, to prove how he'd done it once already, to tear through her amiable fantasies and say, You wanna fuck with me? This, Here, Now, *Me*? But there could be nothing real about it. His aching arousal against the equally aching suppression of desire and embarrassment were mixing explosively. The blood that seemed poised to gush into his genitals and become animal fact and presence instead swirled back through his head, made it balloonish, light. The blue balls of adolescent teasing were making themselves felt but with the flaccidity of confusion too. He wanted to give up, to ask someone to come get him, find him a home and take him there.

Exene bit his earlobe and hissed: "You bastard."

He pulled back far enough to see into her eyes, ready to dart his look to Helmut, the gaffer, anywhere.

"What? Am I hurting you?"

"Not paying for the nanny. You're all bastards."

"I . . . what? That's MSC, the budget, because, I mean, if we're ever —"

"You're all in on this together. You forced me to come back and you won't pay to take care of me or that baby —"

Marty held himself silent for a moment to keep his whispered response flat. "Bibi was already here. You said she *had* to be, that was your deal. Besides, you . . . you wanted a damn entourage, Laura. It wasn't a nanny, it was a nutritionist, a trainer, a secretary, a publicist — I mean, you would've brought a fucking astrologist if we didn't say no, all for a one-day shoot —"

The impish smile never left her face. "We'll see who's 'fucking' around here, Lover."

He wondered, Is this her moment before? She's decided that angry sex — love with thorns — *that* is the goal of the scene and this coy snarling bit is how she'll get there? So that's all it was, back in her room — preparation, now performance. *I was her 'as if,'* it's right in my face and between her legs. And get ready, someone's gonna say "Rolling."

As he pushed his weight into her, felt her textures and smelled her every cell inside and out, he was elevated to an unthinking plane where Marty Nyrop and his character were no different. They wanted the same thing. Specific behavior, the reality of doing under imaginary circumstances.

When Helmut's replacement, his Camera Operator, announced the proper T-stop to his First Camera Assistant, when the First Assistant Director Ravi shushed the handful of crew and rolled camera and the clapperboard had pinched shut with a soft click an inch below his right buttock, Marty absurdly pronounced "Action" at Exene's face. As the camera leered slowly along their entwined limbs he shifted his right leg, felt her suddenly cool sweat and silkiness; he held her look until the camera had crept across her topography, until he glanced off-camera to the Operator who withdrew his open eye from the viewfinder's eyepiece and nodded to him.

"Cut."

Shooting had ended.

Even with her pinned naked beneath him, still it came to Marty at this oddest of times: That other ache, again. Tubs — what did she call him? Twice now? *"That baby."*

59

Tubs's eyes rolled with Marty as he paced back and forth in
Exene's room. A patient child. . . . It never occurred to him
that if he left right now with Tubs, she would come after
them. He imagined instead the path Exene would use to flee from
the specter of parenthood: it was a clear vision of Laura Trent-
Sampson and the rest of her career, of Laura *as* a career. It had long
been in the public domain that during childhood she'd been a blonde,
young-again Elizabeth Taylor, radioactive with personal catastrophe
even as she became a Fairy Princess, a success at all stages of her
celebrity. She'd been tainted early on, yet made oddly endearing by a
magazine ad in which the wholesome model posing as her mother
then became notorious in pornographic films, particularly because
the model's sex objects weren't always mammals. As a teen, then a
young adult, Exene left institutionalized parents, rumored and failed
marriages, abortions, miscarriages, one dead child, and otherwise
tragically dead friends floating in her wake. Still, all who gazed upon
her face were tantalized; she was perfect yet necessarily flawed at
once like a gem that needs impurities to shine in full color. Anyone
beholding her, even crew members who prided their indifference in
the presence of fame, seemed reduced to the detachment of a
meditation, only hearing themselves repeat: "That's her. . . ." With a
leap of fantasy so seamless with desire as to be unlike imagining, she
became to each straight male viewer the one he'd secretly planned to
be with for the rest of his life. She was the one he would gather in his
arms and carry home.

Her next path was easy to visualize: she would return to L.A.
like the rest of the production cast and crew to face rumor and
eventually further scandal, to achieve a higher form of tragic stardom
in some yet-to-come reality indistinguishable from a role, the
completion of identity that is the proper death for a character. She
would live out the reason Story exists — the answer to Who am I?
She'd played the end of this mid-stage of her career, had used *User-
Friendly* very well; *her* fantasies had proven worthy. Now she would
begin the Late Middle Period in which she'd be fixed in image by a

cosmetic artist — maybe Eddie, why not? — for perhaps a decade, even more. On-camera she would never age, but would never be seen in life without full hair and makeup treatment. Laura would be emulated, beseeched, stalked, longed for, respected — and through it all she would have approval over her persona, in all its variations. Within image after image she'd be perpetually new, never the same yet *always* the same, a brand in the way a Mercedes Benz is always just that.

Laura Trent-Sampson was now free to be adored for endorsing a new scent, a popular charity, a line of jewelry, a disease perhaps, rewarded in advance for all the movies she might someday make but would likely never get around to making. MSC's paper commitment would languish. Whose last laugh would that be? She'd find new life within the old life she once had as a child, within the controlled boundaries of still-photos. One-eyed *Herr* Wolfer might escort her back there through filters on his own interchangeable prime lenses, both of them abdicating careers in motion pictures whose images moved and implied too much and forced Laura to carry time beyond the instant of a shutter's wink. Instead she'd exist in the flat two-dimensional plane where she could be seen but not touched. Stills of her would forevermore be of her alone. (With the rights of a slave, but without the resentment, a writer once said about Marilyn.) Laura would never again have to sustain a scene, even a moment, only a point in time that had no duration. Hers would be an image of solitude but inviolable, serving viewer and viewed equally.

It was genius. No one, Marty understood now, sustained celebrity by accident.

By comparison parenthood remained a cipher. For the first time in his life he felt that his next decision was irrevocable. (Maybe he'd become a good dramatic character after all. Frank Capra used to say it was all about choices, choices, choices. . . .) With sudden relief he then realized he'd already made this decision. It was very clear, as if he'd flown through an electrical storm, then popped open an airplane door to stare at the top of clouds with sun on his face: whatever else happened, he was here in this Best Western motel suite to claim Tub O'Guts. Let the cops, lawyers, agents, FBI, winged monkeys, whoever the hell she might send on his trail, let them all come. He'd stand at the mouth of his cave, roar across the plains, and protect *his* baby forever.

Before the authorities showed, before there were inquiries, before a Professional Adult decided for Laura that this child would be made a ward of anyone or anything else, Marty murmured to himself: *I surrender, surrender. . . .* It was a yielding to the cries that can't and ought not to be controlled, only tended to. A worthy surrender to saying "My baby," to the sudden understanding of why any parent's most fervent prayer is that they be buried before their children die. A will only to be here. Not to make or shape, only to be present for a writhing set of intestines that looked an awful lot like him and would, in sixty-seven years, still be My Baby even without the plane crash.

He Scotch-taped a full-page note for Exene above the baby's crib. He re-read it again and again with one hand spread against the wall for support as the baby slept next to Exene's empty motel bed. He felt like an extra in a silent-era melodrama, perhaps one of D.W. Griffith's helpless Victorian women-children — as if he should throw his arms wide and shake his locks at Heaven for the tragedy before him. He'd tried to be gracious in the note (as if that were called for during a kidnapping), stating that he hadn't done this to hurt her but to give the baby a better chance with someone they both knew would make a better parent. He had, he realized, finally agreed to Eric's plan and named himself Father.

Near the bottom of the page he wrote that the baby resembled him, at least to the extent that Marty resembled Eric, that there was a Nyrop "look." And if a miracle occurred, if someday he could reverse his mistakes and talk Bibi into permanently helping him raise the child (another example of why, he thought, you don't let Directors write their own scenes during production) — then with Bibi's features no one would ever question them as the natural parents. That way, he thought, Exene could play any role she wanted for the child — eccentric aunt, godmother, stranger — if "mother" didn't fit into her autobiography, her filmography. He was, after all, a blood relative to her child so she could turn away without guilt. He would accept whatever story her publicist released as being advantageous to her career.

Without a proper carseat for Tubs inside another *User-Friendly* picture car, Marty kept his speed toward Salt Lake International slightly below 85 miles per hour. Soon it became flight attendants strapping themselves in, the plane taxiing the runway, Tubs sucking his bottle with squirty noises. All was in place except the rest of their lives.

The flight went easily and when they overshot LAX and circled back to their runway, for the first time Marty gazed out the window like a tourist and was caught by the splendor of the California coast where blue meets brown and their collision makes white. A Kuleshov Coast. He could not yet know that in seventeen years Laura Trent-Sampson would choose, finally, to play a role in their lives, but in this moment Marty and Tub O'Guts Nyrop, this entire family of two, were in flight, incomplete, and almost home.

60

T he crowd at the Alhambra Theater in Santa Barbara wasn't lured with Laura Trent-Sampson's celebrity but only by the prospect of seeing what was advertised as an untitled free movie. The preview audience's response cards were uniform: even in its rough form with an unfinished musical score, *User-Friendly* rated an "A."

Marty permitted himself a moment of joy. Moviegoers had laughed. They'd pressed Kleenexes to their weepy eyes and stinging noses. They applauded the few listed credits. They hugged one another in the salty night air as they strolled up State Street in search of food and drink. Yet none of the media assault that had already started — the offscreen Jeep-and-Titan tragedy, the Celebrity's conversion to Art, the rumors of did she and Eric or did they not really do it onscreen, what became of that baby she'd been seen with? — none of it had been a factor tonight. Publicity would now only be an accelerant for this self-earned spark. The story seemed adequate and Eric and Laura were quite good, doing things that rose above the material. "Performance" was the push over the top. Marty suspected *User-Friendly* stood to make many millions as "Alan Smithee's" comeback bid. Were he still a member of the club he would now be reading scripts thrown at him by producers desperate to hire "an actors' director." Tak had already fielded such queries.

What no one at the Alhambra had written about on their response card, but what everyone would tell his or her friends about, was the love scene. The Camera Operator and Marty had conspired to create a Laura Trent-Sampson utterly revealed — briefly, yet unmistakably. Marty used the slow buoyant camera move, the gauzy lighting, the teasing shadows for atmosphere, to manufacture generic suggestiveness and the implicitness that romance requires, but only up until that moment when he moved himself aside from her, thigh from thigh. Then there was no longer any physical mystery to Laura Trent-Sampson; she had fully become her surface, her deep skin, by yielding every square inch of it, even the soft folds that might kill their Production Code rating.

Marty had fought dirty but it was to finish directing *User-Friendly* as his first and last movie. There were no half-successful directors, not in The Cinema. Only the good and the forgotten, and he'd now done what he could to be both. Through the 1990s wonder of the Pause/Still button on VCRs and the more explicit "Director's Cut" when the videotape was released for home viewing, he would give the world a few frames of Laura Trent-Sampson (too brief, it would turn out, in screentime to be censored or badly rated) that could be collected, possessed. Anyone could now have a nightvision snapshot of the goddess. And by giving the world the totality of Exene's skin and hair, the blood-draining, heart-speeding inspiration of flesh made perfect and rawly beautiful, Marty had also given her a raised platform, a new mythos from which to live as a Star: like us, and not like us, more available and less attainable, more familiar and more different. She would now fully live the is/is not of the actor/character.

And with death in place, and all time yet to come, his brother's image had become magic.

• • •

Tak and Marty drove together back down the 101 and stopped at a small seafood place near the pier in Ventura. Marty glanced uneasily at his watch as they went in; babysitters had their limits, and though Laura had given no indication of any interest in her baby, he carried a vivid reverse-childsnatching scenario in his head now wherever he went without Tubs.

Tak was preoccupied as they ordered. They had ridden waves of optimism and pessimism since the day in the editing room when Gilmore, the Utah orderly, showed up; however, Tak now didn't seem to feel the same buoyancy about the film's chances as Marty did.

Marty tried to feel him out, to talk around the moviemaking process until he hit on something. "You know, Tak — not once in the whole course of this adventure did anyone, even once, say 'I want to tell this story.'" He thought of his brother's need to return, to find

Marty as family, but that seemed to live outside the making of the movie. "It was all deals, advantage, leverage, investment. . . ."

"I agree. Yes."

"Okay. Even so, I bet everyone who touched this thing figures it's *their movie*, their personal vision of life on this earth. The writer, Wolfer, the editor, me, you. Eric. Even if, in a way, it's a goddamn mess."

"A workable mess, yes."

"But it's gonna succeed. You wanna know why?"

"What is this — *Rocky*? Sure, Marty. I wanna know why."

"Because what I believe in, what I'd bet my considerable remaining fortune of about twenty-four dollars and eighty cents on —"

"MSC's check's in the mail —"

"— Yeah, right. Because I'd bet that every couple that sits through our story loves each other a little bit more at the end of the movie. They see this guy screw up, try again, screw up again, ask forgiveness, until by god he gets forgiveness by giving it. And everybody goes home squeezing hands just a little bit tighter."

Tak didn't exactly disagree with that, but he lapsed into silence.

"What is it? What'd you see that I missed?"

"It's more what I didn't see. You remember that day in the editing room? I asked you if it was releasable?"

"Yeah, the day my mother. . . ."

"And you said you didn't know 'Albert.' What connects 'then' and 'now,' the missing childhood or whatever else it might take to show why he does what he does —"

"What drives him. Where the character's passion comes from."

"Yes. Well, I've finally seen your point. That hole is there. Still. And I think it makes the film unreleasable, after all."

"Seriously? Unreleasable? Tak, were you awake tonight in that theater? Did you see any of those cards?"

"Well. . . . Maybe not that bad. Just not . . . great. Not what it could've been."

Tak seemed overwhelmed by the sadness of this. Marty understood his point, but he'd been so caught up with seeing his shots on the screen in a sensible order, images going by with the sound of live human laughter at something he'd helped create that he had lost his critical distance. He didn't know what to do about this hole in the story, though. The film didn't even have a Director anymore.

"Anyway, Marty. Can you come by the editing room sometime this week?"

"What for?"

"Not to work, don't worry. There's some . . . personal effects. Eric's wife mailed a number of boxes. They're addressed to you, care of the production company."

"What the hell. . . ?"

Tak shrugged and welcomed his plate of scallops.

61

T wo days later Marty sat at a flatbed Moviola zinging a *User-Friendly* workprint back and forth, mesmerized by the familiarity coupled with the elevated "movieness" of it now that he'd seen a screening of it with an audience. Tak was hunched at his phone in an adjacent office within an improvised MSC studio space on L.A.'s west side. Marty found himself playing Matsumoto's weird dance back and forth as he popped in and out behind Eric and Laura in one of the warehouse scenes. It never did make any logical sense and still played havoc with editing continuity. Yet no one had made a note of it on the rating cards.

Marty didn't remember him as such a bizarre distraction during the sneak preview. If Marty ignored the players (easier with the soundtrack turned off), he could see Matsumoto nail together another re-assembly of the *Noh* stage in jump cuts. In one shot Matsumoto turns abruptly and eases himself over the back edge of the stage. He goes behind a free-standing *shoji* screen and emerges with a claw hammer. Then Matsumoto bends under the stage surface and yanks out double-head nails while the scene plays out in the foreground.

Tak came into the room and knew Marty's question without looking at the screen. "He's thinking, Build again. To know the past — repeat it exactly."

This was a foreign madness, Marty thought. Refined and civilized, and pretty near incomprehensible. Tak didn't seem to think so.

"Build what again?"

"There's a temple in the city of Ase, in Japan. One family there has re-built the temple on the same grounds for centuries. Every twenty years they tear it down and build it again. Exactly the same way, so you know that if you go inside you're going into the same temple that your ancestors would've experienced hundreds of years ago. Every generation rebuilds the temple so the knowledge of how to make one is never lost."

"So Matsumoto here, he's a genius? This is a deep ethnic cultural thing I'm supposed to get?"

"Well. . . . Maybe if you think of Japan as a . . . all of it, the whole nation as a theater. Every Japanese life is a kind of performance where the two faces — one for yourself and one for everybody else — each of them has its place."

"Like your dad, his own face, *honne*, his business face, *tatemae*. . . ."

"Like my dad. There's no confusion, no difference between a role and 'reality' because everyone understands why you do it — one face for them, one face for yourself. Nobody's crazy because nobody has to choose. Or at least everyone understands the choice. That way it's not destructive."

"So this Matsumoto, he's an okay guy."

"I think back in Utah . . . Matsumoto's . . . *kichigai*."

"You told me that one. 'Crazy.'"

"In Silver Cliff, Utah yes, he's a lunatic. Stuck with only one face. That's a problem."

"But Eric said both. When it worked, he was himself, *and* the character."

"Onstage, he was both faces? Mm. . . . Maybe that would be like having the mask face worn *over* the true face, then. Maybe it's . . . it's as if the actor here in the West doesn't choose and gets stuck in-between two faces at once. Or maybe no face at all. I don't know. But the way my father lived it, each face had its time and place. Never both." Tak retrieved Eric's *Noh* mask from a bookshelf. He hesitated with it, but Marty didn't need an explanation of why Tak had held on to it. "This one's named *Fukai*. From the *Kanze* and *Hosho* school. It shows the grief of a woman. She's deranged for a time, searching for a lost child. The story's called *Hyakuman* —"

Marty powered off the flatbed machine and swiveled his chair toward Tak. "So it's like re-building the temple, when a *Noh* actor imitates the past masters —"

"When he memorizes. Duplicates. Like re-building the temple, yes, I think so."

"If you just memorize the old dead guys, how do you ever go anywhere? How do you create anything?"

Tak pondered the question as he turned the mask in his hands. "'Create's' not quite the goal. It's like the tea ceremony. It's a theater of . . . it's not about 'action.' Not events. More like . . . meditation. They don't use props, you know, *things*." Tak swept his arm slowly across his body and opened his palm above his head. "A fan . . . is the moon. I mean, not me — when a real performer does it."

"And the people he plays —"

"No, there aren't 'people,' not like our 'characters.' The actor's not asking for your involvement or identification, it's impossible."

"So the mask?"

"Wear the mask, and you're beyond life. You're a ghost. An immortal god. A dead warrior, dead murderer, dead lover. . . ."

Marty's eyes went from Tak back to the Moviola screen and he turned the monitor back on. The old man's little image was still there as Marty continued listening. He didn't want to interrupt, to stop the flow of Tak's alien knowledge. Though clearly at a great age, Matsumoto had a wide, strong face; his once-high rounded cheekbones had sunk halfway to his jaw but the effect was to make him more solid, not less. Even while doing this stagehand work he was wrapped in the performer's embroidered kimono with a forward-leaning lacquered hat, his surface beauty intact no matter what the supposed inner state of the "character." It was a character Marty had no intuition for, not even one who would act out a lost-child theme.

He envied the strange man. This Japanese actor, even within his imposed role as an artist torn from his own people and ridiculed all his adult life as crazy, still knew where he'd come from. He needed no one's approval even if a fulfillment of Matsumoto's art could only exist in a context of a native audience's understanding where duplication of the past would be recognized and appreciated. A coded repetition, like myth and ritual. But if Matsumoto was only reproducing the exact steps and gestures of a master from six hundred years before, did his audience — if he had one — approve of the master, or of Matsumoto? Eric wouldn't have been able to live with the uncertainty. The painter holds up a canvas, but the actor holds up himself. It would be impossible not to care whether there was applause. Marty could guess Eric's response: that either way it's the presence of the actor, of the human that matters. But that was the stage, not a movie.

Marty's eyes drifted from Tak back to the editing screen. He turned a dial to make the reels spin forward: Matsumoto stands erect and goes unsteadily to the rear of the platform. Suddenly, like a snap to attention, he poses: he becomes a wooden statue, his feet are roots firmly growing into the polished stage floor. He has a great weight. Then he moves forward; his feet never lose contact with the floor, each one in turn skates past the other, his toes rising and falling with tiny slaps. Matsumoto has an uncanny density yet he's floating — a doubleness that slices the shiny surface. He pauses in the shot, gazing down, then spins on the soles of his feet and glides away.

Marty and his editors had included a few puzzled looks from their characters toward Matsumoto's presence to let the movie audience know that they found Matsumoto bewildering too. Yet neither the characters nor the filmmakers ever tried to explain him.

Tak stared too at the old man popping into the background of another shot and hammering relentlessly.

"Did you know the Utah warehouse was part of an internment camp?"

"Ah . . . no."

"It's the only part left standing. I suggested it to him — that he ought to take his wood and make a camp museum out of it. Like those pictures of his, on that wall of sheetrock there? He has hundreds of things like that packed away."

"Then what?"

"Put them up. Face them. Then forget. Move on. Matsumoto's stuck in that part of the past. Duplicating one part of the camp, I think, but without understanding it. Or cut off from it, or cut off from the rest of his life *by* it, completely." Tak frowned. "Other people get stuck in the past, you know, by ignoring it, or pretending it away, eh?"

That was aimed at Marty, of course. He watched Tak retreat to his office beyond the editors' workspace, then return with an armload of cardboard. He set it all on a table, then dropped another carton full of yellow film boxes at his feet.

"Here's your temple, Marty. I wish I could tell you what to do with it."

"What the hell is all this?"

"From Eric's wife. I opened one up. You know how they say a scene writes itself? But how would I know about making movies, I'm just a Producer. Nobody knows anything."

Tak touched the monitor image with his fingertip, watching the old man go out of the shot. "Right now, he's a figure of the dead. He meditates on the past. His audience meditates on *him*. You sense that everything around you is change. Attachment to life, to all its feelings, to passions, they're all gone. Attachment is the one real source of pain. What you're going for is to be done with living, even with the memory of it. Done with the chain of causation. When you're free of the binds, there's . . . peace."

"Yeah? And then what?"

Tak smiled and shrugged. "And then . . . you dance."

"C'mon —"

"That's the theory. Hey, I can't feel it much myself. But I've seen the alternative because now I've made a movie. I had attachments I didn't know ever existed. Such . . . stuff. I floated out there, right along with the actors. You did too, Marty. Take these boxes, go home, and dance."

62

*A*ll these years his brother had secreted away the recordings of Nyrop lives spent together.

The reels in their father's film boxes belonged to a traveler, a seer, a lens-pointer who took nameless location-families aloft in his fuselage while on the job but returned to aim his lens at his own family too. When Jim Nyrop finally went down into the earth, perhaps like a dutiful pilot their father had purposely left these films behind to be found and decoded. Their father's blackbox flight recorder (though yellow and labeled "Kodak") was an uncut movie of a failed life, but nevertheless had become a family bequest. It had now arrived after the love scene, like another family bequest that Craig-as-Eric had left Marty to finish.

Marty felt strangely old when he was unable to rent 16mm and 8mm projectors locally because the celluloid strips of his childhood images were recorded with obsolete technology. It was like the time-rift he felt trying to imagine his parents growing up without television.

Finally he bought two used projectors at a local pawn shop. They worked noisily but well enough, and the film reels left behind by his father, inherited through his brother, came alive, complete with a nostalgic warm tint when screened on one of the empty off-white walls where his paintings and photographs were to go someday, though Marty still hadn't painted or photographed anything. It seemed right that the first projector sounded like a single-engine plane trying to take off as he watched.

```
FADE IN:

EXT. LAKESIDE RESORT CABIN — DAY

A HAND-HELD CAMERA PANS across birch trees.
Catches the backlight on papery bark and
yellow-green leaves. CONTINUE MOVING from the
stand of trees, over a sand dune with cat-
whiskers of reedy grass bending in the summer
breeze.
```

PAN TO REVEAL

Lake Michigan lapping the Upper Peninsula shore
at Escanaba. The sun is brilliant, the sky is
clear and blue, the lake vast and ocean-like
but more gentle. Burnt pieces of driftwood and
their broken-off cubes of charcoal are
everywhere on the otherwise nearly white beach.

                                    CUT TO:

A sand castle. It's elaborate, quite well made
with a protective moat of foamy lake water.

PULL BACK to include two boys standing at
attention next to their buckets and pails. The
boys — MARTY and CRAIG NYROP — are eleven and
fourteen, wet and shivering slightly in their
baggy Hawaiian-print swimsuits.

They stare expectantly INTO CAMERA.

Everything about Craig seems fragile: his legs
are stork-like, his skin pale — a freckled
skeleton. His eyes are adult-sized, nearly
vibrating in their sweep across the camera
lens, searching us as we search him.

Marty, the younger, is shorter and sturdier,
with features similar to Craig's but blunter,
less pretty; his stare comes out of intense
annoyance.

WE HEAR their FATHER'S VOICE, a gruff, slightly
stammering drawl:

                         FATHER
                      (off-camera)
                  So this is what you've
                  been doing all morning.
                  Wh-who made this?

FATHER'S POV. THE CAMERA SWINGS back and forth
as the boys look at one another, not responding
to the voice.

                          FATHER (CONT'D)
                        (off-camera)
                    Who m-made the
                    castle? I expect a
                    goddamn answer.

                          MARTY
                    We both did.

                          FATHER
                    Uh-huh. For once you
                    boys didn't try to st-
                    st-stra, to throttle
                    one another? Let me see
                    this —

THE CAMERA PUSHES IN to a corner of the castle
as a wave reaches an outer wall and part of a
round drum tower crumbles muddily into the
sliding water. The Father's outstretched HAND
COMES INTO VIEW.

                          FATHER
                    What's this part
                    called? (A pause) Well?
                    What's this part of the
                    castle called? (Another
                    pause) Are either of
                    you gonna tell me
                    before the tide washes
                    out all your work?

                          MARTY
                        (Off-camera)
                    Lakes don't have tides.

                          FATHER
                    P-p-pardon me?

THE CAMERA SWINGS upward and finds sky, then
drops vertiginously only to rebound upward
again, finally arriving at Marty's face in SOFT
FOCUS. THE LENS MOVES IN AND OUT, looking for a
sharp-focus plane within Marty's hard-set
features.

                          FATHER (CONT'D)
                    What was that, young man?

                    MARTY
          Lakes don't have tides.

                    FATHER
          So your father's a f-fool?

                    MARTY
          I didn't say nothing like that.

                    CRAIG
               (To Marty)
          Shut up, dummy, just shut up —

                    MARTY
          You shut up, Bony Maronie —

THE CAMERA WANDERS from one boy's face to the
other's, resting on Craig's.

                    FATHER
          You stay out of it,
          Craig. Now — you know
          what that part of the
          castle's called?

                    CRAIG
          No.

                    FATHER
          It's a b-b- . . . it's
          a bar, a barbican.

A pause. Craig nods, averts his eyes. He holds
his elbow with the opposite hand crossed behind
his back, arching his spine like a bow,
becoming more child-like, even skinnier.

                    FATHER (CONT'D)
          You really helped build
          this?

                    CRAIG
          Yes.

                        FATHER
            You didn't let Marty do
            all of the work? (A
            pause) Answer me. Look
            at the camera and
            smile. Come on, it's a
            v-vacation, now isn't
            it? Look alive, goddamn
            it!

Craig looks up, INTO CAMERA, then down. Marty
pushes Craig out of the way, raising a wiggly
mass toward the lens.

                        MARTY
            Look what we caught this
            morning!

ON HIS OFFERING

It's a stringer of iridescently green perch,
their sides patterned with gray-brown
triangles, accented by brilliant yellow-orange
fins.

                        FATHER
            And who caught the most?

                        MARTY
            Craiggers did —

                        CRAIG
            Liar.

                        MARTY
            You did! Shut up!

CLOSEUP on the stringer of fish.

The camera dwells on the shiny skin, on the
eyes that still see, on gills that reveal red
suffocating flesh when they slowly flap open,
shut, open. A new VOICE IS HEARD:

>   MOTHER
>   (Off-camera)
>   For crying out loud,
>   Jim, haven't you shot
>   enough film? How much
>   is left in that thing?

>   FATHER
>   New reel.

>   MOTHER
>   Lord. Here, give me the
>   camera —

THE LAKESHORE VEERS up, down, sideways while
the Mother tries to take the camera from the
Father. Then his arm sweeps her back a little
roughly.

>   FATHER
>   Keep your fingers off
>   the lens! There's
>   a-a-acid in skin oil,
>   for godsakes. It'll
>   etch into the lens.
>   Would you want acid in
>   your own eyes?

ON THE MOTHER

as she recovers her composure. She is thin,
spare, but quite pretty, as pale as her oldest
son Craig. Her black swimsuit has pleated
skirting around her thin hips. She stands
rigidly for seconds in which nothing outward
happens, suspended blankly between emotions.
Then she smiles INTO CAMERA, her mouth making
the appropriate movement.

>   MOTHER
>   (Waving into camera)
>   Hi, everybody! Hi
>   from Escanaba!

THE CAMERA SWINGS BACK onto the boys, to find
only one left — Craig — with his head down, his
toes dug into the wet sand.

                        FATHER
            Okay. Have fun. Do
            something.

                        CRAIG
            Turn it off, please.

                        FATHER
            Just a little bit of
            film left. Do
            something.

                        MOTHER
            Craig, get it over with.
            Please! Sing "Robin Hood,"
            like you used to.

She smoothes his wet hair and lifts his chin,
pushing her own face against his in a 2-shot
closeup; she smiles into the lens, while his
eyes dart away.

                        MOTHER (CONT'D)
            Isn't he a handsome
            boy? Look Hon, this can
            be your castle — You
            know, in Nottingham.
            (Singing) "Robin Hood,
            Robin Hood, riding
            through the glen —"

                        FATHER
            For chrissakes Donna,
            he's fourteen years
            old. Now where's that
            little . . . where's
            M-Marty?

                        MOTHER
            Would you please stop
            sounding so . . .
            so. . . . You can <u>hear</u>
            it —

THE CAMERA SWINGS DOWN. Finds the stringer of
perch, ground into the smashed castle.
Blinkless eyes cloud. Gills strain at the dregs

of the moat water puddled around the collapsed
barbican and parapets.

                    FATHER
               That fucker
               Marty. . . . I'll give
               him something to think
               about this time —

                                        CUT TO:

THE CAMERA FINDS MARTY

in silhouette along the water's edge, dumping wet
sand cones out of his bucket, then stamping them
flat with his heels, stiff-legged and waving his
arms.

                         MARTY
               Godzilla! AAAIIEEE!

                         MOTHER
                    (Off-camera)
               Jim — the office called.

THE CAMERA SWINGS BACK onto her. She's annoyed
now too, waving her hand at the lens as if
swatting one of the lake's deer flies.

                         FATHER
               The office? What
               did they want?

                         MOTHER
               Please stop that
               camera, Jim. Pretty
               please? They need you
               back for the Cleveland-
               New York run. To co-
               pilot with George.

                         FATHER
               When?

                         MOTHER
               Tonight. Please.
               Turn that thing off.

She pushes her palm TOWARD THE LENS. Her hand
is shoved away. The CAMERA WANDERS, then finds
her again. She fixes a hairpin, finally frowns
and turns her back.

> MOTHER
> You can take the
> Cessna. I'll come back
> with the boys on
> Greyhound at the end of
> the week.

> FATHER
> Fine.

The CAMERA TILTS UP AND PANS across an approaching
bank of clouds.

> MOTHER
> (Off-camera)
> Is that thing off?

> CUT TO:

INT. CESSNA COCKPIT, ONE YEAR LATER — DAY

Jim Nyrop's POV of Craig in the passenger seat.
Craig nervously looks from the view of
countryside below back to his father.

> FATHER
> Want the controls?

> CRAIG
> No.

> FATHER
> Take the controls!

> CRAIG
> No! I don't know how —

> FATHER
> Figure it out.

> CRAIG
> No — !

The plane takes a sudden dip, then levels off.
Craig looks close to vomiting.

>   CRAIG
>   How come you never
>   stutter when you're
>   flying? Or swearing?

>   FATHER
>   That does it —

The ENGINE ROARS, the fuselage itself shakes.
They're going into a dive.

>   CRAIG
>   (Screaming)
>   Stop it! Stop it!

Craig pukes into his own lap.

>   FATHER
>   Take the goddamn
>   controls.

Craig cries.

>   FATHER (Cont'd)
>   You'll never be
>   worth a shit until
>   you show some balls,
>   little man!

Craig closes his eyes, wipes his chin on his
sleeve. The POV swings through the windshield.
They're falling like a rock toward a lake. The
camera goes black.

>   CUT TO:

INT./EXT. COCKPIT — DUSK

IN CLOSEUP a plane bucks a terrible storm, but
we're quickly aware that it's a plastic model of a
WWII fighter plane dangling on a string.

OFF-CAMERA Marty and Craig make vocal
EXPLOSIONS and engine SCREAMS.

                                              CUT TO:

EXTREME CU of a lit firecracker jammed into the
cockpit.

INSERT: AN EXPLOSION.

                                              CUT TO:

IN CU Craig sits on the Lake Michigan beach framed
by a roaring log campfire. He wears a bathing cap
and earmuffs, grips a driftwood stick, performing
as the pilot of the burning plane. He's SHOUTING
with his father's voice, capturing the quality of
Jim's vague drawl, a menacing Jimmy Stewart
stammer. The IMAGE IS WIGGLING as the cameraman
Marty LAUGHS convulsively off-camera.

                         CRAIG
              M-M-Mayday! Mayday!
              Lord above, hell and
              damnation, Donna! W—w—
              where's that stupid sh—
              sh—shit kid when you
              need him? Mayday, May —
              daaay, Goddamn it!
              D-D-D-Donna! I got skin
              acid! Sk-sk-skin acid
              in my eyes! I'm . . .
              I'm etched! Etched, I
              tell ya!

(EFX: A burning stick protrudes in the
foreground of the shot, Craig appears
engulfed.)

EXT. LANDSCAPE (AERIAL POV) — DAY

We FALL TOWARD the quilted earth again. Falling
forever, there's no hope of pulling out of this
plunge. The earth cranks 45° clockwise. Another
45°. Steadies. The ground becomes recognizable
— a CORNFIELD.

Closer, closer. We swoop down, tassel-high,
then miraculously back up, and find only the
sky, only blueness, only climbing.

The entire image flares, light-struck at the
end of a daylight changing reel. Dots flash —
it's the punched-out code at the end of the
reel blinking through.

The tail leader turns completely orange, then
red. Handwritten scratches skitter across the
white rectangle. Then only the flickering
reflection from the blank wall where
persistence of vision fills in and smoothes the
light beam that alternates on-and-off through
the projector's shutter.

                                        CUT TO:

. . . cut to nothing. Marty turned off the projector and curled
himself on the floor.

63

T he front door opened and closed softly. His heart leapt — Bibi still had her key. Was that good? She sat on the couch on the other side of the living room as he rearranged his bones on the floor, finally sitting against a wall. They watched one another, and he wondered if maybe each of them was thinking the other looked as if they'd been awake for days.

"Is the baby all right?"

"Sure."

He picked another spool of film at random and threaded it from the top arm, through the gate onto the takeup reel. The projector ground back to life. He felt Bibi's eyes on him as he watched the shadow-wall.

He saw himself hit a ball out of the frame at a Little League game. The camera follows him in his slow homerun trot, pumping both fists, taunting the opponents as he goes. While the projector clattered, the sounds of the silent footage come back to Marty alone — the cheers, the clop of his rubber cleats on the clay. Then the camera cuts him off, refusing to witness his two-footed leap onto home plate. His father has shown him, all right.

And that night at home the brutal slap across his left cheek had showed Marty too: no showboating, no hotdogging. And no one else's understanding or sharing of the triumph he'd felt going around those bases.

He turned off the projector and slid completely to the floor, lying parallel to the couch. He could hear Bibi shift her weight on the stuffed cushions, the fabric making a dry scraping sound. He reached out and turned the projector on again.

The Cessna is the star of the next show. Marty and Craig run from spot to spot with soapy sponges and sloshing buckets, pausing only to rub furiously at the plane's surface dirt, camping it up for the camera at how they are being driven like slaves. Marty does so only briefly, then withdraws into a sulk. Craig continues more readily, falling to his knees, raising his arms as if begging to be unchained. The camera swings back onto Marty, as he does nothing more to wash the plane. The frame holds him, waiting, then moving — a hand-held close-push, and as he glares at the lens he raises his bucket, then abruptly dumps his soapy water into the Cessna's open cabin door. The shot goes black, until a birthday party from months later appears, children smiling happy happy happy for the picture-taker.

He turned it off again.

"What happened? After the water?"

"The usual."

"What do you remember?"

"I got hit. Again. It's a wonder I'm not cross-eyed."

"I mean, what do you remember *feeling*?"

"Just. . . . Anger. Total anger. Like I was gonna murder his ass." But he understood: more than that, he'd felt a fury that had nowhere to go until eventually he learned that even fury wasn't allowed to be felt, either. He'd learned, too, that if he couldn't release white-hot anger and pain it was enough to give anger and pain to others and watch them squirm. He could, and did without compunction, become for a time the neighborhood bully. He thought he'd outgrown that, eventually becoming a willful and dynamic worker and thinker and organizer and imaginer, a member of a Guild of such people. But maybe it was all bullying, still. Naming, yes, but bullying. What vigilance would be called for now, with a child sleeping, waking, crying, all of it under his care, his boy someday running, leaping, reaching for his own grasp on life? Was the bullying like some virus, waiting like the pain of weeping shingles that would blister the skin, pain that lives in the spine of a father and never dies? Could it reappear at any moment?

Bibi came to the projector and turned it back on. The birthday party ends and another summer vacation comes on: Marty, mugging on a beach, footage he remembered his mother taking. This time he watched himself laugh while making muscles, breaking sticks, acting out "Zam-pa-no, boom boom boom" from a movie his mother had taken him to. His mother and Fellini. Who'd have thought? For the right person, he could be a performer in a home movie too, could act up, act out. . . .

"I was really a shitty kid."

"Any decent parent would've loved that kid, Marty. Looks like you never had much of a chance. With Big Jim, I mean."

"Sure I had a chance. At least I had parents for long enough. They weren't the best, but they hung out until I proved what a jerk I could be."

"You never let him cry, do you?"

"What — Tubs? Sure I do, just try and stop him. That was Laura, she was the one who didn't want —"

"No, stupid. *That* kid, that . . . little Marty —"

What was he supposed to do? Go kiss and hug and make it better for grainy images on a piece of film? "Where? You mean like, did I cut stuff out, like edit out the crying scenes in these movies?"

She came across the room and dropped to the floor and softly slapped him on the chest with both palms. "*Here.*"

He didn't know what Bibi meant except that it might be about something no one ever seemed to want — the boy he once was, with feelings too outsized, with wants that were too strong before they got buried. Bull-headed Marty who needed to be right, a kid whose notion of connecting was to impress, startle, awe. And he knew now that all of that burying of feelings had left a burning hole in him like a subterranean coal fire smoldering through black veins beneath the surface for years, until periodically it re-ignited and flared brightly and burst in the daylight's oxygen for everyone to see. His entire range of emotions had eventually become hit-or-fall-down-laughing. And the other kid in these reels? Maybe he and Craig just got different configurations of tunnels scorched through them and had tried to put the fires out in the best way that each of them knew how.

"It . . . it wasn't so bad. Being told what to do. That's all it was. Do this, do that. Kids don't know, they're stupid, they don't know anything."

"So what we just watched — now your Dad was a great guy? You're just a chip off the old block?"

"Shut up, Beebs —"

"Let him hurt, Marty."

His mind was bouncing and again he couldn't follow Bibi's meaning. Craig filled his thoughts — this was the home-movie-Craig who'd hurt plenty, Marty knew that now, but he'd blown his chance to let Craig come back to him, to re-discover family in Marty.

"Hurt — ? Craig's *dead*, what's the damn point of that?"

Bibi held her head in both hands. "Not your brother, idiot. . . ."

She patted him on the shoulder and it felt like acid, it was so sisterly. She took a half-dozen new baby outfits out of a shopping bag he hadn't even noticed before, looked in on Tubs, and went away.

64

D ays later Tak gestured for Marty to look down at the sidewalk along Hollywood Boulevard. Embedded in the polished synthetic stone were brass stars that marked the Walk of Fame. The three stars just east of Musso & Frank's front door were for William Demarest from *The Lady Eve*, then Harrison Ford, and TV Producer Quinn Martin. A "Martin," a "Ford," plus the actor Demarest who played the '30s character model for *User-Friendly's* "Dweeb."

Tak smiled. "Synchronicity? I guess a bit of a stretch, eh?"

Or maybe tonight it was "Destiny" on Marty's rusting Assistant Director radar, and not just wandering actors.

Tak chose the same booth at Musso's where their journey had begun. Marty liked that. Tak was developing a sense of how to arrange events, how to shape the tasks of daily life to give them a narrative. Dream & Factory, Marty thought. Film & Industry. Show and Business. Full circle.

It was Tak's purpose this evening to exhort MSC of Japan, Inc. to screw its courage to a sticking point, as Tak put it earlier, adding that it might be more like trying to glue a lead weight to a waterfall. "No," Marty suggested, "it's screw courage, and stick 'em on gross points."

Earlier in the day Marty had quizzed Tak on his ability to persuade MSC to follow its financial risk to the finish line and repair their distribution deal that was in danger of falling apart. But as Tak wisely pointed out, it wasn't MSC that needed persuading but two individual men far from home, Yamamoto and Kurumada breathing Hollywood air, such as the brown stuff was.

"So I told them, Marty: 'Think about it — approach it like your other research. The way the whole Industry works for anybody is — you have to take it personally. *Find* yourselves in a project, until you *need* to get it made, you *need* to see it in the theater. This is where the will comes from, the towering egos. You see? — this project can be very personal, even for employees of MSC.'"

"I like it."

"Then I said, 'Sure, it's a romantic comedy, but *User-Friendly* is a story about a little man with a great idea. Like the family business that goes up against the corporate giant. It's MSC against Matsushita or Sony. Haven't you gentlemen dreamed of bringing them down?' And I could tell, they were starting to *get* it. 'So you can identify with our script,' I said, 'where IBM or whoever tries to stop our "Albert" because of their corporate motivations. But this inventor — the little man, the Hero — cares only about his one problem. He has to invest these personal robots with whatever it is that makes us people, that singles us out from the masses. So our inventor's got to be a father to a mechanical child. Find his humanity, against corporate greed. That means he has to re-live his own childhood, re-create it. He's up against an oppressive, adult corporation, and he has to see all over again what it's like to grow up when you're clever, you're innocent, you're still open to wonder and awe —'"

"That was brilliant, *that* part, Tak. . . . 'Spielbergian,' the ads'll say. And it's all really there, on top of the romance."

Tak gently pumped his fist. "*Yes*. And this was the clincher, I think: I said, 'In Japan you've been raised to know that the nail that sticks up gets hammered down. But we've all wanted to stick up just once, haven't we?'"

"*Yes* —"

Tonight was the night, then, to make it clear to Yamamoto-*san* and Kurumada-*san* that having found their personal rooting interest in a story the two men wanted — needed —to tell, now it was time to intensify: go big. Corporate interests are corporate interests, theirs included.

As the two Japanese gentlemen joined them at their table the order of business then was to salvage the distribution deal that was currently in place. MSC had contracted to put *User-Friendly* into theaters across the country, but the distributors were trying to back out of an agreement or, sensing an opportunity with a neophyte producer, trying to increase their share of the take on a film that was going to be bigger than anyone had anticipated. They were making unreasonable demands over profit points, release patterns, and advertising budgets. It was too difficult for Tak to guess the entirety of the distributor's motivations without having a history with them, without knowing the structure of other deals. MSC therefore needed to make counter-demands — aggressive, Americanized, threatening demands upon the distributors. Tak told MSC that they simply had to draw the line: Keep our deal, in or out, yes or no. Negotiate by knowing what you absolutely must have, and be prepared to walk away if you don't get it. And by the way, he thought they should add, we might sue you for breach of contract if you say no, or maybe just for the hell of it and then we'll see how many other independents sign with you. Our lawyers — he borrowed one of Marty's pet phrases about swinging dicks and adjusted it for cultural nuance — have bigger *chimpo* than your lawyers. Yamamoto and Kurumada seemed to understand.

A waiter arrived. Something had caused all four of them to order open-faced roast beef sandwiches. Tak leaned into the meaty steam from his plate, then spoke:

"So you see — you have a chance here that cannot be missed. Every other entry into the business, every Japanese investment in Hollywood has been strictly financial. All the interested companies since Sony — each and every one of them, eh? — they say 'we will let Americans run the movie business. We are only their bank.' But you, gentlemen, MSC — really, *you* Kurumada-*san*, *you* Yamamoto-*san* — you have a chance to be hands-on Production Executives. To show the way." Tak laced his fingers together then clenched them into a two-handed fist. "MSC Pictures will be the studio of quality, making movies of mutual understanding, of reconciliation. You'll take part in the culture of movies to show the world that cultures don't exclude, they share. You'll make movies that last, that create a movie-made America and a movie-made Japan that understand one another. With world-class stars who will come to *you*, gentlemen. Let me connect, they will say. Eh? Let me connect with dignity, intelligence, taste, style. . . ." Tak allowed himself to chuckle. " . . . and a generous back-end deal, if you please. *Anata-wa* —you — Kurumada-*san*. You, Yamamoto-*san*. Make your stand for honesty and honor, truth and trust, and you can make this town yours."

Marty wanted to stand and cheer. He salted his roast beef.

Mr. Yamamoto nodded; he seemed to want to relax, release himself within the idea of mogulism, to become what one was not lucky enough to be born to — to be a wave at Hollywood's door. But he would not smile.

"These . . . distributors. Very, very rude."

"Then inform them that you'll break their financial legs and make your deal with the next distributor in line. *Totemo America no, ne?*" Tak turned to Marty: "Very American, right?"

Marty grinned. The four laughed together. Tak continued:

"If you agree, then we should release the Doberman Pinscher. We've kept him in a box for such purposes."

Yamamoto and Kurumada looked at one another and nodded. Marty knew that meant they would deploy their concealed weapon against the defenseless distributors — Paul Amato. It wasn't cruel, simply justified. The distributors had brought it upon themselves.

65

I n the final scene of *User-Friendly* "Albert" and "Ginger," restored to their original identities, re-unite — both with each other, and with their "true" personas. Ginger understands the intricacies derived from mistaken identity that have brought them to this point. Albert, still willfully naïve, is too unaware (or merely refuses) to know how this second chance came to be. But then his allergic reaction to her perfume recalls a scene with her earlier identity in which Albert's sneezing fit was brought on by the same scent. Animal essence reasserts itself in the present — an *achoo* as instinctive love, which should unmask her and prove to him that she's the same person he fell in love with, that she's been the right one for him all along. In the final shot of the movie "Dweeb," the doubter, falls out of a tree where he'd been spying on her, cast out of the Garden into the world of human love. From Albert's sneeze, Dweeb knows yes, it's the same woman and it's his urge to call her on it; but Dweeb lands helpless and speechless in the back seat of the Jeep that the impractical Albert has finally taught himself to operate, and the three of them drive into bliss. It's a happy ending.

What did the characters do to deserve that last drive into the sunset? Marty tried with all his might not to think about it being the drive that took his brother's life, the drive that had to be filmed months after principle photography had wrapped with stunt doubles at a discreet distance with the emphasis going completely toward a laugh over Dweeb's realization instead of jaunty closeups of the lovers. Marty tried to think only that it was the moment of reward for the Hero who had shed his pride and claimed his mate.

What was on the screen was comedy, but today this — what he was about to do — was . . . what?

He arrived at the address he'd tracked down through mutual, unsuspecting friends. He parked outside Bibi's new building and left Tubs in the car with a bottle where Marty could see him but Bibi would not; Tubs was not part of this equation, not yet. He picked up red lava rocks from the lawn edging and threw them at her balcony window. There was a sliding noise above his head. She peered over the stucco wall.

"Marty? What are you *doing*?"

"Hey, uh . . . hi."

"Where's the baby? What's wrong? I —"

"No, nothing, I mean he's right here, he's okay." He waved toward the unseen car and wanted a mandolin or maybe a dobro to serenade with, but knew that even *he* had to have limits on foolishness. "I want to . . . listen — for everything? Just . . . everything. Please, the Laura mistake. . . . Everything you can think of, all of it. Forgive me. I love you, and forgive me, Bibi."

He had done this with fear. He couldn't wait for a response because it might be the wrong one. He ducked his head and ran for the car. Marty drove and drove the rest of the night, back and forth across Los Angeles while Tubs slept. It felt as if his life depended on both the driving and the sleeping.

66

D ays later Marty slouched in his condo, still raw over the rush of childhood available to him in his father's old film cans and boxes that Tak had given him. He strained to hear if the sound of the Santa Monica beach could reach him through the walls, if the Pacific Ocean could overcome traffic noise. The phone rang. He dove at it, a new habit — he would strangle anything that might ruin Tubs's naps.

It was the child custody attorney he'd given his last savings withdrawal to. He had the sudden thought that if the insect realm had lawyers, they would be the termites. The attorney had bad news: Laura had not placed the child up for adoption, so the legal limbo of custody continued. There was hope, though, because courts were mysterious things and like some primitive cabal they might decide that blood counts. Marty was the only blood left besides Laura, so in her passivity it was his move.

When Marty ran with the baby through the Salt Lake airport he knew he'd given in at least in part to Bibi's moral judgment of him. It wasn't just that he'd been taken by surprise — bushwhacked, blindsided — by the sensation of unconditional, unearned protectiveness, of a need to nurture and love as a father might, a notion he had felt no right to claim as yet. But also it had been the first time in his life that he had felt inescapably responsible for another human being. Even as the gates to his recondite future were now sealed to him, leaving him only a small vestige of his former life after personal and professional ruin, in one way his world had become deeper, bigger; it was because of a child, and at least in part it was also because Bibi had made him look at his circumstances (and Tubs's too) and see what had to be done. With one hissed word — "decency" — she unknowingly supplied the push that got him out of a motel suite door with a child strapped to his chest and sent him down a highway and across the tarmac and into an airplane.

In its hugely successful release *User-Friendly* was giving Laura everything she wanted from the Nyrop brothers — the professional legitimacy, and the earned celebrity with wider career choices soon to follow. While he barricaded himself against even the vanishingly small possibility that Laura might come after her newborn, his abduction of Tubs was really only for clarity, for punctuation on his declaration that he, and not Laura, would raise the child. The most assertive act of his life had proven right. There was no pursuit, no inquiries were made, the chase scene was a dud. But now there was a limbo, neither moral nor emotional, only legal. Marty had to make sure that Tubs would remain his

He knew what his next call would be, the one he didn't want to make until now. He'd already used Bibi's giving nature for the sake of a movie, and now would try to use her again for the baby's sake. If the situation came before a judge he couldn't simply pretend to the court that Bibi was part of his case for custody. That kind of performance was beyond his powers. He somehow had to enlist her for such a scene. Not until he could demonstrate the reality of doing, cast Bibi to perform with him the authentic behavior of two parents even under imaginary circumstances, not until then could he ensure being put together — not with himself, not even with Bibi — but with this child. To act, then, in order to become decent.

Before he pressed Bibi's number the phone rang again.

"Hey, Marty Nyrop? The A.D.?"

"Uh. . . . Yeah, sort of."

"Marty, Joel Slayton. Producer, new outfit in town. Fire Creek Pictures. I hear that you're just what we're looking for —"

"And . . . what's that?"

"You about to move up to First?"

"I've got some, uh . . . unresolved issues there."

"Yeah, I heard some pretty fucked up shit. Look, we've got a feature going soon. We need a good First on board. Maybe you need a non-union picture, you know? Get one under your belt, maybe it'll help your troubles, and you'll get that experience. That fucking rare on-the-job experience, right? Be a big-time First on features. I want a Hitler running my set. Maybe you're that guy, huh?"

Marty sighed. Why not hang up? No, he wanted the diversion. "Right, at half the DGA minimum I bet."

"Aw, hell — that's always negotiable. Anyway, let's talk."

"I don't think there's much to talk about."

"No, no, wait a minute. Here's what I didn't tell you —"

"Really. Forget it. Besides, it ought to be the Director's call. You shouldn't be hiring a First and then force him on somebody."

"Yeah, that's what I'm saying. We got a hot, hot new guy. I want you to meet him. His first feature's about to come out, and *Jesus* I can't *tell* you the buzz on this thing."

"What thing?"

"It's called *User-Friendly*. And that's who we got — we got the director Martin Ford absolutely committed to this project! Whattya say? Him and you, the Marty Brothers!"

Hy Matlovsky would be impressed: Marty had just been put together with himself, actor and role, even as he hoped to do with himself and the baby, through Bibi. But he felt no completion, no invulnerability. He listened to the hearty laughter coming out of the phone. What was this guy's name? Taplin? Galen? Slateland? Probably more like Fred F. Asshole. "Listen, pal. . . . You're a liar, and a moron. You need therapy, but it won't be much help. You'll never make good movies. Ever. But you'll make many of them, and go far. Very far from where you came. So thank you, good luck, and goodbye." Marty hung up.

There were lives left unmade. The phone was still probably his best tool, so moments later to Bibi's patient "Hmmms" and silences he told her how Tubs might become legally his if he could show a court a solid home environment. That Marty was leaving town for good to do just that. Sacramento maybe. He avoided asking Bibi to give him *her* life too, in any precise way; but what did she think? "I mean, I just thought you'd want to know about it. About him. About, y'know, raising him."

"That poor child, Marty."

"Ow. C'mon, you don't really mean that."

"Don't tell me what to feel."

As he wondered how to go forward with Bibi he remembered how he had stood beneath her balcony and asked her for forgiveness but had run before she could answer. Did he have it, that state of absolution, that mercy?

"What . . . what I told Laura, in the note I left — You *would* be a better mother — Ah. I guess, or. . . ." This was a slip — fantasy had run right past him and taken the lead.

"A better *what*? What are you saying?"

"Would you think about it?"

"What . . . are . . . you *saying*? What *exactly* are you asking me?"

He didn't know. No, it was more that he absolutely did know and yet in the same instant he didn't know at all. There was an edge of anger to Bibi's tone, so the best solution to his Tubs situation no longer had a prayer. He wanted to hit or fall down laughing, retrieve something out of that plastic Box O'Behavior of his but there was no logical target to slug except himself. He laughed. "I'll . . . I'll do it if you'll do it."

"My god, Marty — This is a child's *life*. Would you get serious? We've got problems. And there's not even a 'we.' *You*'ve got a problem. At least one huge problem. Do you even have a job?"

"Job? No, but I . . . I think I am. Serious. I mean, I'm gonna get a teaching credential, I think. Y'know, if the cartooning doesn't work out. Maybe. Legally Laura's outta here, gone, it's like abandonment, and the lawyer says —" But how to ask her? Go simple, obvious. "Help me do this, Bibi. Please. Help me. . . ."

"Help you do what, Marty? You're going to have to say exactly what you want from me."

"I'm never gonna leave him. I will never leave him."

"And . . . ? What're you asking from *me*?"

"I'm begging you. It's not the right time to say 'I love you' again but —"

"Stop it. Don't — *Stop*."

"I'm on my knees."

"It's not *fair*, damn it." She hung up.

• • •

Twenty hours later Bibi was at his doorstep. She entered without speaking (as if she still lived there, he couldn't help thinking) and traced her fingertips over cartoon drawings on his drafting table, a spasm of new material for a hypothetical career change.

"It's something I'm trying out. . . . I've got an idea, for a comic strip? It's on the Industry, like the panels before, but it'd have a storyline. Syndicated, if I can sell it. That little guy there, he's 'Hollywood Harry' — some naïve kid from the Midwest who comes out to L.A. to write for the movies. Sort of Charlie Brown in

Babylon. Maybe that should be the title instead, y'know, screw copyright. . . ." It occurred to him that everything he'd worked on lately was about a naïve guy with self-awareness issues.

Bibi held up one of the strips, then another. She started to laugh at one where the kid is falsely arrested, and when the cops find out he's a would-be screenwriter everyone in the squad room starts asking him for help with story development on *their* scripts, which they all seem to keep at the ready in desk drawers. But Bibi's breathy laugh kept hitching until she sighed and closed her eyes tightly.

She turned away and went to the bedroom Marty had painted as a nursery. There were several dozen stuffed animals in big and little rocking chairs, and more stacked upon shelves. Tub O'Guts woke up and wailed with a rubber tomato face like the old-fashioned ketchup dispensers. Marty stepped past her and cradled the baby in his arms until Tubs cooed and rooted against the cloth diaper thrown over Marty's shoulder.

"You're all right with him so far. . . ? On your own?"

"Yeah. I think I can do this. I *will* do this."

Bibi pushed the heels of her palms into her cheeks, as if to drive any feelings back from where they had sprung. She took the baby's hand and kissed it, then briefly touched Marty's hand as they watched Tub O'Guts show his gummy grin and watch them back.

When Tubs was deeply wrapped in a vegetative slumber, Marty wheeled the crib near the closet and draped a spare blanket over one side to block light and sound. He went back to Bibi and lifted both her hands in his own, silently asking her assent to something undefined. At least the sensation of her palms and fingers on his was the answer to a question he'd asked himself in another time, long ago, at her Utah airport arrival — the Secret, the Meaning, yes, it was human touch after all. For the first time in more than a year the movie was out of mind, there was only the warmth of skin here and now until she gently pulled away. He started to apologize again for the scene with Exene in the motel room, but had the animal sense to stop himself before trying to rationalize the act with the excuse that Bibi and he weren't officially a couple when it happened. He hoped wildly that she understood what was unspoken and, for this one moment at least, that she accepted his flawed and wretched being. They embraced stiffly and briefly and at Bibi's suggestion they lay carefully apart from each other on the bed to nap as the baby napped.

In Marty's near-waking dream they cautiously made love, relieving themselves tirelessly in one another for hours until it ached as much as soothed. But the dreaming popped, disintegrated, when finally the baby stirred; Marty lifted him from the crib and lay him between Bibi and himself, and in the radiance of their heat the baby sank back into a motionless sleep. He and Bibi arranged themselves as they could around Tubs, and Marty wanted their lives to enter into a suspended animation, for this brief time to be endless. As he too grew sleepy again he reminded himself to think of names. He breathed in Bibi's scent, and the baby's, thinking, This angel, my Beebs, maybe she could give me, the fool, a second chance — maybe about a seventh chance, like she said once — and it's as if . . . as if. . . . And he murmured, "Daddy, daddy, daddy. . . ."

"Hmm? What's that, Marty?"

"I don't remember ever saying it. 'Daddy, daddy' —"

"Don't worry. You'll hear it, plenty —"

"Yeah. . . ." Thinking (or dreaming again) *and when that plane falls and they see me and I see them inside and I know my family needs me I'll run and hold out my arms that I know are strong enough and I'll catch the plane, catch the plane and set it gently on the ground and then I'll save them, save them all from everything Daddy Daddy —*

• • •

He would not see Bibi again for three years until she came to Sacramento for one day to assure Marty that he was doing all he could to get his baby — by then named C.T. — through the chicken pox. He had let himself imagine what it would feel like for the two of them to once again hover over C.T., and in the reality of her arrival it felt tearfully warm and good even as his poor child was temporarily miserable.

She made it clear that he was to show more faith in C.T.'s pediatrician, and as she drove home to L.A. and back to her completely new life as a nurse and in a relationship she had only sketched in for him, he watched helplessly as nothing in his own life as it was now — fatherhood, teaching, the forsaking of images except telling students how to make them — was enough to keep him any longer in her heart. Even if Marty were to take himself and his son back south, or anywhere else for that matter, she would always be 400 miles away.

And in this way the long road that had been his movie-constructed life finally ended.

Patrick Cosgrove

67

A quiet despondency has settled throughout the house since C.T. left for whatever it is that his mother has promised him. Lupe scarcely speaks. Had Bibi stayed, then with the baby boy's arrival it could've been the storybook version of how their lives should've turned out, a very pretty picture, however awkward and tentative. But instead the current family photo is a fake, a Photoshopped dupe with desaturated color, with the mismatched resolutions of image files that don't composite. The pediatrician who held Marty's hand through C.T.'s infancy and has more recently done much of the patchwork on C.T.'s self-inflicted skater wounds has agreed to accept Lupe and the new baby as patients. The boy is golden brown and hairy and beautiful and looks nothing like a Nyrop, and beyond that Marty has stifled every urge to hold him and smell him and hum to him and feel his skin. *That bonding shit. Not again, I will not have it.*

Even with Bibi back in L.A. they have a stable, if unsmiling routine. Lupe nurtures her child with a quiet and efficient privacy that has left her a wistful ghost whenever she ventures out of her room, which is rarely. She's become expert at finding things to mix with scrambled eggs. They've dropped any pretense that C.T. will return to walk the stage in June for his diploma.

The future is measured, it seems, in hours, even minutes.

Before his son bolted with Laura, Tak sent C.T. a DVD of *User-Friendly* to replace the hacked movie file he'd gotten from some torrent website. The DVD was certainly a more convenient way to watch the movie over and over, hopping around within its chapters with mouse clicks. Marty has known for a while that C.T. was repetitively watching the scenes between his birth parents — still all Marty can bring himself to call them — but today when Lupe's mood lifts just a bit and she volunteers to walk through the neighborhood for a few groceries, Marty goes into C.T.'s room and sees that *Use-Friendly* is not all that C.T. has been watching. Someone has also found and transferred all those yellow Kodak boxes of home movies to DVDs as well. Marty doesn't have any idea of what manner of conspiracy passed between C.T. and whoever did it, or what their purpose was, or why the hell they didn't ask Marty about it first, but here it is on his son's computer screen: the 8- and 16mm filmic history of the Nyrops, their home movies digitized. It quickly occurs to him that it must have been Tak. But why?

C.T. had been fiddling with these files of Kodacolor family history while he waited to see if Lupe and his newborn son would become part of him, and he part of them. It would be a forlorn exercise for any Nyrop to watch these home movies, but one that perhaps kept C.T. functional by way of distraction those last few days at home. Of course, Laura managed to put an end to all that.

Marty watches a few clips and tries to resist sinking into the funk he was in after seeing his childhood projected on the wall of his Santa Monica condo seventeen years ago. He guesses that Tak's intention was probably innocent enough; if you could give a kid movies of his secret dad as a boy and let him see the secret grandparents he never knew, why wouldn't you? Still, it seems odd that he went around Marty on this one. Not like him. Maybe C.T. did it himself, found the boxes somewhere in the attic. Marty will have to ask him but now, of course, when?

He clicks over to another desktop file to watch a few randomly selected shots out of *User-Friendly* and he's brought up short: C.T. hasn't been passively watching these old files; he's been editing them together, blending the home movie footage and *User-Friendly*. Marty cringes for perhaps the hundredth time as he thinks of the love scene.

By lifting a clip — anything from several frames of a closeup from the Nyrop reels to an entire scene in the original *User-Friendly* — C.T. is depositing his selected shots and scenes into a timeline of his own making, choosing for himself how the story of romance and robots should flow. But it's not just that. C.T.'s also using the layer-masking and compositing capability of his editing program to take snippets out of the Nyrop home movies and insert them *within* scenes involving the robot in a way that was once done with matte-shots, then blue screen, green screen, and now is more often done with computer-generated imagery — CGI — fabricated in a digital netherworld. Pieces of Nyrop history are getting pasted right into the middle of *User-Friendly* as if the filmmakers planned it that way long ago, as if they had shot the robot on a Utah green screen stage for the benefit of the CGI process that had yet to be invented.

Marty sucks in a quick breath when he recognizes Tak's implicit idea back when they were leaving Two Cedars. Tak must have given him these yellow boxes as an idea, one that he must've decided Marty had to recognize for himself: to use the home movies of Craig's and his own childhoods to rebuild a temple of sorts. To know the past, rebuild. And here those movies are, being used by C.T. within the *User-Friendly* storyline as raw material for robotic programming. C.T. is rebuilding the movie's timeline, not as Matsumoto would by repeating the past exactly but with his own inventiveness.

Marty had recognized the general possibility of C.T.'s idea — that to re-edit is to re-build — during the film's production, that "Albert" could give himself a re-made (but not confronted, not reborn) childhood by how he instructed a robot to imitate humans. Tak must've seen a sort of fit that the movie story of robots had with the lives recorded as Nyrop home movies, must've sensed the parallels even back then between feature film dailies and reels of skinny boys on an Escanaba beach. But nothing then had been connected; each of their lives in the movie company had been in disarray during a year of birth and death, and when it was over personal debris had littered every path out of Utah back to L.A..

Tak had said to take these boxes home and dance.

Here on a desktop monitor Marty's teenager is filling in the character gap, the absence of causation and drive in "Albert" that Tak and Marty had taken turns despairing over. There are already scenes in *User-Friendly* that show how common sense is extraordinarily difficult to explain to a machine, to bridge the gaps between the intuitive human mind and machine operating data. But when that visual analog model from footage of Craig Nyrop's home movie childhood can be scanned by a fictional graphics function within the robot's operating system and entered digitally, then "Albert Byrne" can in a sense give the robot his own childhood learning process, a childhood visually morphed into the robot's notion of how to rollerskate the world-map within its database. Even as Marty sees that C.T.'s contribution to solving this story problem is nothing but digital smoke and mirrors, he thrills at the results when Craig's and his own childhoods flow through the movie's editing software and into *User-Friendly's* robot brain.

In C.T.'s edits Craig and Marty become, each in turn, data for "Albert Byrne's" heuristic robot, the Byrne Personal Robot #1, or "Beeper" as he's quickly dubbed in the script. Little Marty and Craig and Dad and Mom each become pixels sent out by C.T.'s editing sleight of hand through Albert's instruction to a computer, as seen upon its anthropomorphic viewscreen. The audience sees what Beeper sees, therefore what it thinks, by watching the readout of the screen on its "face." The Nyrops emerge upon Beeper synchronized, visually inserted into the robot's head as pictures of human activity that a robot learning to walk and talk can scan, analyze, and mimic to create analogs for itself. "Morphing," in the effects-jargon of the day, becomes a process akin to character transformation, from human to robot, then from the robot-speak back into human behavior when Albert learns from his own creation what it means to grow up; not just in mechanical baby steps, but in what could be created later in the story as compassionate decision-making. Character growth from pole to pole and back again. Might a robot forgive? And teach a human how it is done? Might the Nyrops be edited as a loving family? It's yet unfinished, but Craig's Albert (through C.T.) is bending Craig's history into his own, and repairing it.

In C.T.'s *User-Friendly* re-make, the long-lost Nyrops are the role models as they become Albert's family, too. With a visual model of the Creator — Marty flashes back to Spielberg's *A.I.,* where even the most evolved robotic creatures want to know from whom they're descended, whom their Adam-once-touched-by-God is — Beeper can touch the face of its own God, in Albert. It fits. It would only have to appear somewhat plausible in story terms.

Marty smiles as his boy's edited improvisations play out. The vestigial Director still alive in him quickly sees that even if inserting the home movie footage weren't quite enough to fully complete Craig/Albert's character arc, C.T.'s re-make and any resulting clumsiness of continuity could easily be made seamless by filming the robot and a hand model on an effects stage in a one-day shoot. Hell, tomorrow. It would have good production value and keep the screen interesting when the stars weren't heating it up with jokes and "relationship."

Tak, by getting those yellow Kodak boxes digitized — how and when no longer matter — and handing them over to C.T., has led Marty back to whatever in the character's childhood they'd once found to be missing. Maybe Tak duped the film reels before he ever returned them to Marty in the first place, then hoarded the dupes until there was reason to convert them and send C.T. the DVD all these years later. It made Tak sound like a visionary, but perhaps only Marty failed to see that C.T.'s story, his boy's origins, would have to come out one day, and Tak had given Marty seventeen years to make it so. But it took C.T. to imagine how to bring it all together. *My kid did this.*

Then for a few moments Marty is paralyzed by the re-make possibilities of an entire, new chronology of his own, taking C.T.'s basic idea to a higher if more selfish level: since it's his childhood in these home movies too, he could take shots with Craig, Mom, Dad, and himself and fix things the way he needs them to be fixed. C.T. has already suggested how moviegoers would see what Albert the inventor would improve about himself when reinvention is available. Craig and Marty and their parents would all become movie stars teaching "life" to a robot, monsters redeemed by special effects and editing, and the hole in Albert's character would be filled in with the missing backstory of how Albert became driven by parallel needs that come from a hateful childhood, awful parents.

Marty could take it further: the audience could witness Craig Nyrop as Albert, editing his parents, as played by Jim and Donna. They could see how Craig/Eric-the-actor confabulates Albert's childhood the way he (and Marty) wish it had been; moviegoers would intuit how Albert has become a completed Self by the end of the story by getting from his digitally inserted parents what had always been left wanting. Providing, of course, Albert doesn't blow his chance with Ginger, doesn't make this new subtext and backstory overwhelm the spine of the romance. Given a little time, Marty could re-shape it all.

It wouldn't be so hard. Just a few shadowy outtakes would make the re-edit work, with some Kuleshov close-ups of Craig/Eric/Albert (as edited by Marty) watching his own past. The audience would read a Marty-directed emotion into Albert depending on whichever childhood moment his closeup was cut with. Bad parents could be used as negative role models by the robot, as well as by Albert; their parents' "Ones" could be taught to the robot as "Zeroes," and so Beeper would be shown by their examples what *not* to do until a moment of yes/no binary transcendence arrives on the screen, when the robot grows a moral dimension and makes its own decisions on whether to accept or reject the behavior of such people who play across its viewscreen face. Kuleshov collisions would work with a machine, too — shot A plus Shot B meet to create Emotion C. And thus Little Marty would have the last laugh because Big Marty used his mother and father as tools to fix himself in the eyes of the world. History could change.

He finally gets what directing might be.

But then as Marty runs *User-Friendly* back and forth and clicks on the reformatted copies of the family footage and he sees what might and might not be undone, something within himself is purged.

Enough. Marty won't claim in the present moment the things he never earned himself back then, unless it was a bag of gas in a diaper. He has a son; he has to live forward.

And what would he do with the thing, anyway? Some burst of ego, a pirate "Director's Cut" version out there on YouTube or Vimeo or wherever? Time has taught him at least that if *User-Friendly* ever worked as a successful story it was through the many, not the one: through Tak's production heroics, added to a decent screenplay written by a school friend; through the original Editor's precision and rhythmic sense; through Helmut's eye (though Marty had left Wolfer with only the one, not unlike himself); through the presence of the actors, even if they were only screen shadows.

And he realizes too as he stares at the screen that the biggest hole to fill turned out to be Craig Nyrop the human being, the brother, the way Craig's palpable life never found a shape and substance in Marty's life. This, he feels now in a deep visceral eddy, is why Craig came back to him like a stubborn anode, drawing out and sending energy from Marty back to himself; in the electrolysis of "family" they'd both been bathed, effervesced, and ultimately been scoured in, Marty was the only sustenance from family Craig had left.

So he passes on re-editing his life. Shots and shots of "You don't feel that way," "Don't be sad," "Do it right," "Do it *now, faster, better*," "You don't really mean that," and "How dare you, who the hell do you think you are?" are left intact where C.T. has cut them, used as Albert's source of need just as C.T. has imagined. If this ever proves worthy of re-doing, if somehow the world were ready for a re-released *User-Friendly*, then in all the re-cutting and re-shooting Marty would have to let only the truth of these home movies live, unchanged, or he would insist on editing out the family shots entirely. Even the DGA's fictional scapegoat "Alan Smithee" should have some director's rights.

Marty runs and re-runs the movie in C.T.'s room as his brother's digital surfaces start to spring back when pushed and probed, there's a substance to Craig beneath "my asshole brother" who stood before their father trembling and had already lost some terrible fight and been cast down from innocence before Marty knew there was a fight to be made. Skinny Craig only asked for what he had a right to ask for, had only needed as any child deserves to need, and when Marty became stronger by refusing to have those needs or to be anyone's child while still a boy, he didn't know his brother had given him that chance. "Cover me!" the cowboys shouted before running at danger on "The Lone Ranger" and "Hopalong Cassidy." Marty might've shouted it too, but the shouting had already been done for him, the fire drawn, the hateful words and blows absorbed, the danger already distracted enough that Marty could make it out of childhood without needing to be put back together with himself, only with others. And Marty's cover, his shell, his shield, was not his own creation. It was his brother.

Marty bows his head. *Oh Craiggers*

68

*M*arty is straining to focus on his classroom duties, using his kids to keep him functional while he decides whether to throw himself into a mosh pit of razor-wielding lawyers and go after Laura and her fortress of fame. But C.T. has made his own choice, and it was not to stay home.

Today Marty is trying to give students in the one Film Studies section of his teaching day a basic tool of storytelling. They're mostly quiet, many of them hunched low at their computer stations, the better to see their phone screens held between their knees as they text their friends. He long ago made peace with chronic messaging during his class; the video capabilities of smartphones make them classroom equipment often enough that he's not going to die on that hill, as his colleagues say, and spend his days policing the appropriateness of cell phone usage. The sheer rudeness of student inattention when he's trying to share learning belongs to their alien generation. Or maybe it's just a generation that would rather watch a movie, the greatest visual expression invented by mankind, on a 3-inch phone screen. It still baffles him that he should need so badly to improve his classroom management skills when he's teaching *movies* from personal experience. *I was there*, in the middle of it all, and so few of these kids give a rat's ass.

"So you won't find this in any textbook, I just made it up. But I call it a 'basic unit of information.' D.W. Griffith was one of the first — really, probably the first guy — to figure it out. Take any scene, if you have a character look at something or somebody, then you cut to what they see, then you cut back to how they react to what they've seen, that's your 'unit of information.' What've you got, whenever you do that? What's on the screen, what's in the viewer's head?"

There are no volunteers to offer a response, only a general shifting around, an aversion of glances to avoid being called on directly. Marty's too tired to work on them, to demand participation, to reflect upon whether he's asked a convergent or divergent question. It's sage-on-the-stage day: spray instruction and pray they get it.

"I'll tell you what you've got. Identification. You see the character look. You see what they see. You cut back to their reaction. What's happened? You know what's in *their* head, because you've seen what they've seen, just the way they've seen it from the same point-of-view. And when you see their reaction, you know how they feel about it and you know why because you've seen it too. You get their response. You identify — you feel what they feel, you understand them and there's an emotional connection between the character and you, the audience. So now what'll the character do? You've got a stake in finding out. That's anticipation, you're involved, you want to know what's gonna happen next because you're thinking and feeling right there along with them. Empathy."

He wants to tie this fundamental grammar of shot-making to earlier lessons of screen direction, reverse angles, matching action, the gears of continuity on the screen so the viewer doesn't drop out of the dream state of being absorbed into Story. But unlike his described imaginary character, the students aren't "right there" with Marty. Kids in one row of seats in particular have bunched themselves together behind one of the desktop computer screens at their table. There's little guile here, scant self-awareness as they addictively follow their viewing interests no matter how unseemly it is as classroom behavior.

Marty gives up trying to teach and goes to the end of the row where he silently watches them watch their chosen screen instead of him. Finally a student in the row at their backs hisses at them, *"Sssst — Guys!"* and they find Marty's eyes.

A mop-haired boy with complete trust that Marty likes him smiles brightly.

"Mr. Nyrop! Check it out — The Unit of Information!"

A few kids laugh nervously. Marty sighs and slides behind the chairs until he can see the screen they're watching: it's a YouTube clip promoting "Hollywood Birth Moms!" with a link to the show's new website.

"Isn't that C.T., Mr. Nyrop?"

It is. The word is out and going viral about Laura's new show. Its cable distributor has decided that the intrigue of the premiere episode is not whether Laura herself is a Hollywood Birth Mom —

clearly they are saying that she is — but whether there will be a happy ending to the discovery of her long-lost child. Apparently this simple question will carry the burden of audience retention as the mess of "reality" gets structured into a specific number of segments placed between a specific number of commercials. Simplify and delay: it's the great rule of the genre, and the kids are right — simplify and delay is its own unit of information.

The segment playing soundlessly onscreen is all reaction shots, cutaways, and inserts, all material that could be added in almost anywhere in a program. It's a reliance on the editing process alone to imply that all the shots in a sequence are related; just people in various emotional states cut with other people of various emotional states, while a voiceover narrator says whatever the show's Executive Producer wants him or her to say. Collision — and Lev Kuleshov lives another day.

Laura is knitting a story out of docu-fragments. It hurts when Marty watches C.T. on skates being followed by the camera along a sidewalk near 8th & O Street, the place Marty used to take him. Laura can turn this material into anything she wants and she wants to own C.T.'s childhood that she had nothing to do with.

Movement at the classroom door catches his eye: it's his Principal, gesturing for him to step into the hallway. Marty winces as he steps from his cave of a room, darkened for movie projection, into the glare of the tiled hall lit with too many fluorescent tubes. The Principal eyes him for a moment, trying to imagine a context for his bit of news.

"My office just received an email, Mr. Nyrop. There's an offer, a donation, and it sounds like it could be a very good thing for your students. Equipment, software. A *lot*."

"And it's from. . . ?"

"A cable production company in Los Angeles. I didn't recognize it. There's a request that you sign something that's attached to the email. I didn't mean to pry, but it seemed like more than a simple receipt. Some kind of release. What do you know about this?"

"Way, way too much."

Patrick Cosgrove

69

*A*s Marty pulls into his driveway a familiar satellite uplink truck barely fits its mouse-ears beneath the sycamore canopy that shades Marty's neighborhood from unseasonably intense heat. But columns made of dappled, peeling bark can't defend against the video crew who pour from vehicles that have dived into parking spaces along the curbs on either side of the street. Marty steps quickly into the house.

Through his living room window he recognizes the wise-ass Field Producer from the Juvie confrontation and watches her accompany C.T. toward the front door. C.T. is listening intently and nodding, not saying much as far as Marty can tell. Without a moat or drawbridge, Marty will have to go back outside and defend his home from the porch.

C.T. stops at the bottom of the stairs, hands jammed into his pockets, his pizza hat low on his forehead. Without skates he seems shackled. Marty steps to the edge of the top stair tread and waits C.T. out.

"She here? Baby okay?"

Marty nods.

"They just wanna get establishing shots. Some B-roll."

It's the sort of material his students had been watching earlier, shots that can be plugged almost anywhere to fix a flawed narrative. "From what I've seen online the whole show is gonna be B-roll, while she just makes crap up and cuts it together."

"She's . . . helping me out. It's cool. Giving me some stuff. She says I can maybe work on the show after a while."

"After you tell the world how you were abducted and raised in the forest by a troll."

"Ahh, it's not like that, Pops."

"And what's it like, exactly?"

C.T. stares at his feet. Marty looks up to see that the video crew has recorded every word, every expression. A phrase by a writer named Postman comes back to him, from his college days: we are entertaining ourselves to death. Or amusing, or whatever. And just what would a kid think these last seventeen years have been like, that he can treat them like dog shit to be scraped from his shoe? Does it mean nothing to a child that these years were relentless and thankless loops of cooking and cleaning, nursing and worrying, shopping and cleaning and laundering, bathing and dressing, of chasing vomit and diarrhea and tears, of hugs and stories and playdates, of homework done and not done, of driving and coaching and despair at losing one's self in sleepless servitude? *And would he know that I would do every fucking second of it all over again without a moment's thought?*

A parent, Marty realizes, looks at his kid and sees all of this history, this sacrifice, sees the child at all ages at once: C.T. is the baby Marty ran with and the video editor re-cutting all their lives; he's the crying boy on his first skates and the teen father of his own baby — all in this one moment, this "now." But so unlike an actor. C.T., he guesses, sees only the moment itself, sees Marty as standing in his way on a porch as the obstacle to some kind of dream-come-true life.

"Go on back, C.T.. Go live with her, live her kind of life. Tell the world that I'm not your Dad. You just have to do one thing for me. Look me in the eye and tell me that's what you want. That's all. Just tell me. Say it."

C.T. lifts his head slowly until he meets Marty's eyes, and holds the look. He then turns to survey the crew that is capturing this reality, this truth-telling. He clomps up the stairs onto the porch, past Marty, and into the house. Marty turns with him and closes the door behind the two of them.

● ● ●

A moment later C.T. is crying as he comes sock-sliding down the hardwood floor in the hallway.

"She's gone. *Fuck*. She's got the baby and she's gone. Motherfucking son-of-a-*bitch*.

Marty's gut flips. He's been at school all day, there is no way of knowing how long ago she left. Marty does to his son what he does to his students with attention problems. "Lift your head and look at me." There's no point in talking to him if C.T. won't meet his eyes. Finally his look flickers toward Marty, goes away, comes back as an unblinking stare. "C.T., what're you going to do?"

"How the fuck do I know?"

"What . . . are you going to do?"

Marty trusts that C.T. knows at least this one thing about him: that he's more bullheaded than even C.T. himself is. His kid understands that he won't win at anything by not answering.

"I don't *know.*"

Marty's first impulse is to call the police into this fine mess, to make them find Lupe and the child. But what if they did? Where would they take her, or send her and the baby?

"You'll find her."

"How am I supposed to do *that?*"

"I don't know either."

"How could she do this? He's my kid, too."

"Yeah. And nothing will ever change that. Being his Dad is not a choice. Lupe's the choice." C.T. stares at him, not at all sure of his meaning. "Pack a goddamn bag. Put a toothbrush in it."

In fifteen minutes they're heading south on the 5 to Los Angeles on a hunch.

• • •

They stop soon to fuel the car, hit In-N-Out, and after nearly five hours of manic lane-changing they press their way into the late afternoon quagmire of metal and rubber and concrete and brake lights and engine exhaust that is Los Angeles. This is not a chase scene. Marty has a strong feeling that wherever Lupe and the baby are going, they've already arrived there. Bibi has had no reason to hide her shifting addresses from Marty all these years, not once it became clear long ago that his pleas to her to share their lives together had failed. Since Bibi has left Sacramento only days before Lupe's disappearance, he thinks it's a reasonable bit of induction that their two exits are related. No obvious cause and effect, but he knows where Bibi's empathy lies. Lupe trusts her.

They break out of the freeway logjam and get onto surface streets near Westwood while there's still a last bit of sun above the horizon. This will be a test of some sort, and it'll test C.T., not Marty. If Marty is right, Bibi will be Lupe's protector, the anti-romantic, until she knows C.T.'s mind about this pursuit. C.T. doesn't *know* his mind about this pursuit. It'll be an interesting test and there is no point in calling ahead — Marty has never witnessed a movie romance climaxed by a cell phone call and that's his only reference point, and any scant element of surprise will work in their favor, not Lupe's or Bibi's.

After several wrong turns Marty finds Bibi's pretty little apartment building of glaring white stucco embedded with decorative ceramic tile flourishes from the '40s. They pass through an archway into a courtyard of grass and palms and birds-of-paradise plants and a jewel-bright turquoise pool. Bibi's door opens directly onto the courtyard; Marty knocks, waits only seconds, then pounds the thickly varnished wood.

A slat of black iron moves back from a judas hole in the door, then Bibi undoes several locks and chains and stands expectantly before them.

"You have her, don't you."

"Have who?" Marty is glaring at her, so she looks beyond him. "C.T., what's going on?"

C.T. walks away toward the pool.

Marty shifts to regain her look. "Lupe and the baby."

"No, they're not here. Of course not. When did they leave?"

"If I knew that, I'd probably know where the hell they went. C'mon, Beebs. Do you have them?"

She stares Marty down, and he has to remember that this is the woman who never once has told him anything untrue. But he has to be sure.

"Look, if you won't answer me, I'm coming in —"

"I did answer you."

He grips the door handle and makes the solid wood groan behind it.

"You're scary when you're this angry, Marty. None of this is about you, it's not your problem. It's not your fault. And you're so pissed you look like you're going to break something."

C.T. comes back; his look is anguished. "Pops, for fuck's sake —"

Marty gapes at Bibi, astonished. Seventeen years come rushing back at him. "Not . . . my fault? *Everything* . . . about this . . . is *my fault.* You know what's wrong with my whole life? It doesn't have *you.* Whose fault is that? My life is what it is because I haven't lived with *you.* And *I* did that, and. . . . Go ahead, hit me for being a jackass, go ahead, but I won't let that happen again, not to C.T.. He's gonna find her because I won't have him live the way I've lived, without *you,* Bibi. *God* —

His head feels like it's going to explode, and as he stares down at the concrete step to her apartment, whether through Bibi's deft unseen touch or because of the craftsmanship of a long-ago carpenter, the door slowly closes in his face until the doorknob lock clicks cleanly and irremediably.

70

The L.A. basin is a bowl of nothing tonight — nowhere to stay, no one to ask for shelter. Marty's not sure he can manage the drive back to Sacramento without a little sleep first. Or at least some road trip food. He wanders the Hollywood grid until he spots an Original Tommy's and pulls into the parking lot and remembers to call in for another sub to cover his classroom tomorrow. A sick-day indeed.

C.T. and Marty sit quietly in the car, stomachs gurgling, each hoping that the other comes up with some kind of plan. C.T. fools with the radio dial for a while at low volume but finds nothing.

"You know, that editing you did with the old home movies and *User-Friendly* — pretty impressive."

C.T.'s smile pulls off to one side of his face. "Ahh, it was just, y'know, some shit 'n stuff."

"Tak gave you that home movie footage on a DVD, didn't he?"

"Uhh . . . yeah. But he asked me, he said not to —"

"No, no, don't worry about it. Did he say anything about a temple? About a place in Japan called Ase?"

"Huh? No."

"Well . . . you made those changes, I saw 'em. Changes to what really happened. Sort of fixed things by having 'Albert' tweak a little bit of Nyrop history. Pretty effective."

"The inventor guy, he was just always like so fuckin' *stupid*, so I thought what the hell."

"So you saw your grandparents, you saw your father and me, the way we grew up. Nothing in those home movies was unusual. Stuff went on all the time. Until he was dead. Until we could breathe a little bit without him around."

"Huh. So when you had your chance back in Utah, maybe you wanted your own kid, and you could do it your own way."

"Well. . . . Sort of. Yeah, I guess — But not like he was. You have no idea how much I've worried about that, about being that kind of Dad."

"So it's, I don't know, you don't get it. That me and Lupe wanted something like that too."

"Because I'm like him? Big Jim, your grandfather?"

"Nah, because you wanted to get it right, get the kid right, and like steer everything around. Have a family, only better. You'd know that it was *your* kind of family. I mean, it turned out that you didn't *have* to be like him, 'cause you weren't. You're like the same, only different."

"And that's what you and Lupe are doing?"

"If I can fuckin' find her. You weren't ready either, were you?"

Marty had to think. C.T.'s abduction was so tangled up with trying to bring Bibi along. . . . And he sees now that when he left Hollywood for the sake of a child he never once asked her what she wanted or needed, that maybe he just expected Bibi to go along with it because, well, she was the angel Bibi. Or he'd gambled with the hope that she would go along. He never had the third act, the romantic climax: He ran with a kid and announced what he wanted but he never claimed *her*.

"Maybe nobody's ready. What a freaking weird thing, huh? To like, own somebody else. As a parent, you've got no idea what you're signing up for. But . . . you see why I did it, cut you off from all of that? From those two? Why I didn't want there to be anything of theirs, any chance of *them* showing up in you? I mean, I was wrong, wrong about so many things, but —"

"Yeah, yeah. I get it. But like if you're so worried about all that shit, how could you ask me and Lupe to let our own kid go? If there's just so much shit inside you from your own family, like you're worried about me and my real dad and shit, about how much the dad shows up in his kid — like if it's really goin' on, then how can you expect us to just. . .?" He flaps the fingers on his hand, a flying-away gesture. "And then the kid has to grow up and do it all over again because he doesn't *know*. I mean, like, don't you have to find out first? Give it a chance?"

Marty has no answer to that, here on this L.A. street. The sky is becoming magic, purple and orange over the circular Tommy's logo and the red tile roof, and he sees that he's failed everyone, especially his son.

"So what do you need, C.T.?"

"I just need to find my kid. And I need to find Lupe. Whatever it takes."

Marty nods and his head droops to the steering wheel. Then, for the first time since C.T. was a frightened toddler who had once wandered from Marty's grip and became for a short time lost in a forested park, and as awkward as it is now in the front seat of a car, C.T. wraps his arms around Marty's neck.

"It's okay, Pops." C.T. doesn't let go for several seconds. Marty is weakened — yet lightened, lifted — by C.T.'s touch, by an embrace that he's not felt in all these years, nor asked of anyone else, ever.

C.T. smirks and slouches back in the passenger seat and pulls his pizza cap low on his forehead

"So you're telling me, C.T., heart-of-hearts, this is what you wanna do now? Find her, live your life with her?"

"Yup."

Something has settled within Marty, become solid and resolute. "Then hold on to your nutsack, there, young man. We're climbing goddamn Mt. Olympus."

The tires squeal in protest as he pulls from the parking lot into traffic and weaves away from the aroma of burning ground beef toward the Hollywood Hills.

After turning northward in West Hollywood and winding their way up a slope, they park against a curb while Marty tries to get his bearings and figure out Tak's location from years-old memory. He doesn't have an address to punch into anything wireless and he's avoided L.A. for more than a decade. He still doesn't want to call ahead, to alert. An ADT-Bel Air Patrol car slithers alongside them and they get the long look from some hard-ass goon behind shades even in the dusky gloom. He shines a spotlight on them. They're a motley pair, C.T. and Marty, both of them in shabby t-shirts and in a car nobody who lived here would be caught dead in; but so far, anyway, they're doing nothing illegal on a public street. When the security-type is sure that they know that he knows they're here, he pulls slowly away.

"Final check: Do you love her? The question makes C.T. squirm. "I need to know. I know you love your son. It's unconditional, it just happens. In fact, if you don't feel it I'm gonna find the nearest full bathtub in this neighborhood and drown you right now as a public service. So c'mon. Lupe. Near's you can tell, far as you understand it — and I don't give a shit if you're seventeen or seventy-three or she's pissed you off or not — do you love her?"

C.T.'s jaw sets and he meets Marty's eyes this time without hesitation.

"Yes."

Marty fires up the engine again and moments later he recognizes an intersection and in another moment they're in the circular drive that curves between gigantic planters with an antique patina and a mix of tropical and Mediterranean vegetation. So Olympian.

• • •

Tak pushes a hand through his bangs, a gesture unchanged since Marty met him in 1989. There's just more gray to get the fingers through now. They're standing on Tak's lawn with a view that reaches the ocean on this rare, clear evening.

"So, you figured out I gave him the home movies. . . ."

"Yeah, but not why. Not right away. I had to make a trip back to Ase."

Tak frowns, then smiles with one of his knowing murmurs.

"Rebuild, you said. Remember, in the editing room? That a family in Ase has re-built the temple on the same grounds for centuries, every twenty years they tear it down and build it again. Exactly the same way, so you know that if you go inside you're going into the same temple that your ancestors would've gone into hundreds of years before. Every generation rebuilds, so the knowledge of how to make one is never lost. That's pretty much what you said, verbatim. I have this memory thing, even though it's usually about pictures, y'know, images. And then it *was* about some images — the Nyrop home movies. When you dumped those boxes in my lap and said, 'Here's your temple,' I didn't know you'd already made a copy."

"I remember. Rebuild."

"Yeah. Then dance. Only I didn't get it. For seventeen years I didn't get it. And then I'm sitting there at C.T.'s computer seeing how the Nyrops *were* getting rebuilt because someone dumped what'd been in those yellow boxes in C.T.'s lap too. Who else could it be? Who else would give enough of a crap to make the effort? And I'm pretty sure C.T. couldn't tell you exactly why or how he was doing it, but he was rebuilding the Nyrop temple, because maybe he could get some of it built right this time, no craziness, no *kichigai*. Teach a robot how it *should've* worked out with the creators who were anything but perfect. Parents who might even be forgiven by a machine. So, yeah. It wasn't hard to figure out it was you. You were messing with my mess, Tak."

"I thought ... hoped, anyway, that when I gave him the movies, maybe you and C.T. could find ... clarity, eh? Together, a certain clarity. I mean, I would've called, eventually."

"Well, yeah. . . . And now what?"

Tak stared off toward the distant ocean, gathering himself. "Look. I've got a Production office on the Universal lot. I've got a budget, I can do some hiring. He's just a kid, but that's how the business has always worked, eh? If you caught any of the credits on the Academy show this year? I mean, there was a *Disney*. . . ."

"Can't say I watched."

"The point is —I've seen C.T.'s videos. Maybe he's not a Cal Arts prodigy, but he's about as ready for an internship in editing as anyone else I've ever seen who got brought in at the entry level. He can live here, I've got money in places I don't even remember having places. I've got this *Night at the Museum* house except nobody ever came alive in it. I've had the same cook for fourteen years. A driver. Give me this, Marty. Please. I've got no family left. I've never had the greatest thing you've always had. Let me share it, feel it, take care of someone for once."

"You said you were moving, getting out of L.A."

"For this, I'd stay."

"*Give* . . . you?"

• • •

In the morning they wait sheepishly for Tak's chef to make them a steaming breakfast and they both down mugs of coffee for the trip home to Sacramento. The kitchen is half the size of Marty's entire house, stainless steel and marble and glass everywhere with countertop appliances that don't even have names. C.T. pushes his expertly basted eggs around his plate more than eats them.

Their L.A. trip has been a bust except to open a door that neither of them had ever thought of looking for. C.T. has scant stuff at home, but Marty thinks it'll help if his kid at least has his own funky clothes to wear. It feels like a graduation from something, but it also feels as if he has fought for seventeen years to keep his son to himself and he is now giving C.T. away. It's now Marty who is the refugee, with no place home.

"I've done everything I can for you and fucked up so many things maybe I *could* have done for you. But start your life, C.T., start this thing with Tak. You know, I'll just be up the street. Five hours up the street, but still. . . . Look, I know your mother could give you something in the business on a platter. But that's what it would be — giving it to you. You've earned a shot with Tak's company. It's yours. Work it. Give me time to find Lupe and the baby. I don't know how I'm gonna do it, but give me some time. If you're here, if you've got a job, a future — and if somehow we can make Lupe know about it, then — I don't know."

C.T. nods and they eat quietly, then head to the car, C.T. with his pizza hat squashed tightly against his skull. At least they'll be headed against most of the traffic this time.

71

T he return trip is less frantic, uneventful. In two days when they once again arrive at Tak's Mt. Olympus mansion no one answers the Art Deco doorknocker. Marty pushes a button that's probably a doorbell. Resonant chimes vibrate deep within the palace, but no one appears. He grabs a handful of the pea gravel used as mulch around some kind of twisted, exotic juniper near the door.

"Here, help me with this —"

Marty tosses some of the small pebbles against clerestory windows on the second floor, and gestures for C.T. to do the same a little farther along this front wing of the mansion. Nothing. They repeat moments later. Still nothing, so Marty throws a little bigger rock a little harder and manages to put that one through the doublepane. He can hear the tinkle of the glass falling inside onto a hard floor twelve feet below the window. A security alarm goes off. A hit-or-fall-down-laughing impulse he thought he'd left behind tugs at him. *Attaboy, Marty.*

The front door swings inward silently on machined hinges. It's Lupe who has wordlessly pulled it open, and when she sees them she tries to close the heavy slab but C.T. seizes the door's edge with one powerful hand, then drops to his knees at her feet and holds her sweatshirt with enough force that she can't leave but with her arms free to pummel him with clenched hands and she does, hitting him and hitting him and hitting him on the head and the shoulders and the arms until the force goes out of it and she falls to her knees too and they hold one another and kiss once and weep and do not let go.

An attentive uniformed nurse arrives at the door and doesn't know what to make of this, and so she and Marty watch these children who are parents and they watch each other and they wait. And finally Marty notices that behind him at the other end of the circular drive Bibi watches over all of them.

72

Days later Bibi comes into the house after helping Tak muck around in his backyard koi pond. The two of them find Marty and his little family in Tak's professional-grade home theater as they watch another image of a skater hurling himself off the top of fourteen steps and landing on the street below to the cheering profanities of his fellow aggressive skaters. But what Marty is really watching is his son, who has wrapped his arms around Lupe with their baby boy in her arms as she rests her head on C.T.'s chest and they are complete, and Marty's heart aches in the one way that won't break it. And he sees them kiss without words and he cannot go on thinking about it with his own words because in this moment all things and all time — all the past images of his life and the present moment — are vision and persistence at once, and are all together, inseparable.

Bibi steps behind him and slides her arm around his torso as she rubs her nose lightly on his right cheek. She fusses at a wetness there.

"Sorry. I'm leaking again."

"Liar. The bleb's in your other eye." Bibi kisses his ear. He thinks it's the most loving gesture he has known, and this time he can't even pretend that the flow down to his jawbone is from the bleb. The raw tattoo outline of a newborn's face seeps from his chest, staining his shirt. They should go, he thinks, he and Bibi. Because like a dog, they can, he could joke, but it's not the time for that. Only for gratitude.

And thinking, Him: *C.T.. Craig Takashi Nyrop. My son. My baby my child my baby —*

"Hey C.T. — you and Lupe got a decent carseat yet for Craiggers?"

"Yeah, Pops." He smiles. "No fuckin' car, but we got the carseat."

Marty has to cover his face with his scarred hands for a moment. He has such hope.

Patrick Cosgrove

Given the decades-long gestation of *Our Home Movies*, the story would never have reached a version that warranted publication if not for the donation of time, critical support, and finally enthusiasm given by a generous corps of readers. To them I offer my utter gratitude: Pamela Chateauneuf, Sherril Jaffe, Mira-Lisa Katz, and especially Joanne Marlowe for enduring multiple reads from the very beginning of this story, long ago, to its very end.

ABOUT THE AUTHOR

Patrick Cosgrove arrived in California as a graduate student in Film and Television Studies and was soon afterward accepted as a Trainee into the Directors Guild of America. For seven years he was an Assistant Director in the Hollywood studio system on such films as *Xanadu, Brainstorm, The Goonies* and *Top Gun*, and has been apologizing for *Howard the Duck* since 1986. After leaving the business to be the parent at home for his two sons, he became a public high school teacher and has taught American Literature, Studio Art, Photography, and Film Studies. He now lives in the Sacramento area.